The General and the Virgin

The powerful General Antonio de Santa Anna was beside himself with passion. Never in twenty years of lechery had he seen so perfect a face, so magnificent a body, such white skin, such hair, such eyes!

"I must have you . . . I should have taken you this morning when you were helpless," he groaned.

"I will only go to bed with the man that I marry," murmured Teresa, half-mesmerized by his intensity, knowing at any moment he could over-power her.

Santa Anna's fingers clawed savagely at her dress until it hung in shreds about her waist.

The virginal Teresa stood before him, her flawless round white breasts heaving with emotion.

Inflamed beyond endurance, the General moved in for the kill . . .

Teresa, the White Rose, and Emilia, the Yellow Rose, go from defilement and dishonor to passion and glory in this gigantic epic of love and adventure torn from the blazing pages of America's past.

Rose of Passion, Rose of Love

Jeanne Sommers

A Dell/James A. Bryans Book

Published by
Dell Publishing Co., Inc.
1 Dag Hammarskjold Plaza
New York, New York 10017

Dell ® TM 681510, Dell Publishing Co., Inc.

ISBN: 0-440-07515-7

Printed in the United States of America
First printing—June 1978

BOOK I

Bride of Santa Anna

1

WHEN TERESA MARIA de Alarcon Rosa went out into the patio that day and read Fernando's letter, she at once decided to visit his Saltillo home, with a regal disdain for half-measures. To her young mind, unhampered by petty conventions, her decision was obvious as soon as she read her soldier lover's passionate message. Other women might wait at home in tearful anxiety while their men were away fighting in the country's civil war, but not Teresa Maria de Alarcon Rosa! She had to go to Fernando, even if it meant following him over the rough Coahuilla countryside. To one man in the world she had said, "I love you," and to her that settled everything.

As she stood in the patio, the letter held in one small, slender white hand, she recalled it was here, in this very spot, under the old cottonwood tree, that Fernando had stood, so thin and so boyish in his new uniform. It had been only their second meeting, and she had hardly known what to expect.

"Teresa," he'd said, "I know this is very early, but . . ."

She had tried to help him, for he'd seemed tongue-tied. She'd stepped forward, stumbling slightly, to put her hand on his arm, he'd reached out to steady her and suddenly his arms were wrapped around her. She turned her face up to him, full lips half-parted and then, it had happened. His lips had joined hers and a small tingle of warmth had spread through her.

She'd pushed him away almost immediately, saying "Fernando, we must not!" But first, words had been whispered between them, and to her lips unbidden had come that final, binding phrase.

Later, when Fernando had gone off, she had stood in her room, full of strange, conflicting feelings—a sudden warmth suffusing her body. On impulse, she had removed her dress, her camisa, her underclothes, her stockings, until she stood naked. She stepped to the tall pier class to look at herself. She saw a creature with ivory white skin, full, wide, pink mouth, half-open, large melting brown eyes. The form was slender, but she watched her own hands go up to touch the round, high-thrusting white breasts with their rosy buds. Her hands swept down over gently curving white thighs and touched ever so lightly the rich triangle of fine auburn hair that matched the luxuriant cloud that half-fell over her eyes. As her hands continued to glide over the smooth, soft curves and planes, a rosy flush came over her, a sudden tremor shook her young body, and she wondered, *Is it a sin to love myself first* . . .

Her decision—and her obstinate refusal to change her mind—greatly distressed the de Alarcon household, especially her mother. Dona Helena had never been able to control the headstrong girl, even when her husband was alive. As in all such family matters, she turned the problem over to her late husband's mother. Dona Clara was more than a loving *abuela* to Teresa, she was the nineteen-year-old's idol and model for life.

The prospect of a long and perhaps dangerous journey did not distress the old woman; she was mindful only of its romantic aspect. Without considering the great physical strain involved, she decided she would accompany her grand-daughter to still the shrill harping of her daughter-in-law's acid tongue.

Yet, when they had left Dona Helena far behind, the carriage crawling slowly down the dusty Mexican roadways, the days between quick sunrise and sudden sunset soon began to seem interminable.

Outwardly, Teresa was cheerful companion, and daily held a kind of *salon* for her *abuela,* distracting the old woman from the intense heat and growing weariness of the four-hundred-mile trek.

But, when she was alone in the evening, trying to rest in the cramped, filthy room of a wayside inn, Teresa's dark brown brow would furrow with anxiety, and her hands clenched with the strain of all that she was going through. She slowly began to doubt herself and even her love for Fernando Martin Flores. And, when at last Saltillo showed on the horizon beyond the purple plain, with a sunset glow on its white adobe, she hardly dared to look, almost holding her breath in suspense, as the carriage steadily carried her closer to her lover.

Too excited and too tired to talk, they rode in silence past *haciendas,* between scarlet clustered vines, clinging with heavy fragrance to adobe walls, and the fringed spears of palms along cactus-lined roadsides.

On the outskirts of the town, they followed high monastery walls, until, around a sharp corner, they suddenly found themselves facing a squad of native soldiery with fixed bayonets.

With an exclamation of surprise, the coachman just managed to stop his horses in time. For a moment he leaned forward, examining the men blocking the way. Their clothes didn't help to identify which side they were on, but the coachman reasoned that no government troops would be guarding that road, because the revolt was said to be far south of Saltillo. He leaned over and took a chance.

"*Santa Anna y Libertad,*" he said loudly.

The sergeant in command saluted with a grave smile, and drew his men aside, so that the carriage could slowly roll forward again. The coachman lost no time in leaving the soldiers behind.

"Looks as though we are in the war," commented Dona Clara. "We'd better hurry to the Martin *hacienda.*"

A distant whistling noise became louder, and a sudden crash jarred the carriage. Glass broke somewhere, lots of it. Teresa uttered a low cry, but sat still and straight. Two more explosions came, one right after the other. Both were directly in front of the carriage and killed the horses. With a grinding of wood and metal, the carriage plunged into a crater hole. Through the windows, harsh noises echoed from the street: shouts and screams, and the rumble of falling adobe walls.

"*Abuela,* shall we run for cover?"

"Better sit still."

For once, Teresa obeyed.

A second later, the coachman yanked open the door and reached in to help them down. Teresa let the quaking Dona Clara go first. Then, when she was following, the coachman suddenly lurched forward, the weight of his heavy body pushing her to the carriage floor. His head fell against her bosom and then he crumpled lifelessly into the street.

The amount of blood on her clothes surprised her—big bright red stains; and she felt its warmth seep through to her skin. Dona Clara knelt beside the coachman, sponging his head with a sodden red handkerchief. Teresa's stomach churned. The old man had

caught part of the blast straight in his face. There was
a big red gap where his forehead had been, but his
fixed staring eyes were untouched. She realized that
her grandmother was crying. On trembling legs, she
stepped down into the street and gently pulled the old
woman away from the dead body.

Behind her, over the sound of crackling fires, heavy
boots pounded up the street, and she was brutally
grabbed by a meaty, unseen hand.

Teresa screamed, clawing frantically at the rough,
muscular arm now encircling her waist.

"Unhand her, you lout!" Dona Clara shrieked, wad-
dling forward to aid her grand-daughter. Two filthy
insurrectos caught the old woman's arms and held her
back.

One of the soldiers, a big young Mexican with a
square brown face marred by boils, walked around to
view Teresa from the front. He smiled with a peculiar,
unpleasant gentleness, as though at a child he disliked.
Without moving his eyes from Teresa, he ordered
Dona Clara taken away.

"No!" Teresa protested. "What is the meaning of
this?"

At once a sweaty palm was thrust over her mouth.
She knew instinctively what they planned but refused
to panic. Her mouth was still open, and she brought
her teeth together and chomped down hard on flesh.

The soldier growled his pain into her ear and
moved his hand to grip her throat. Her breath was cut
off so suddenly that her senses reeled and darkness de-
scended over her eyes. From far off, she heard a sharp
command not to do her harm.

Her faint was only momentary, but gave her captor
time to pin her arms securely behind her back and
lash them together with a length of rawhide. Before
her senses fully returned, Dona Clara's blood-sodden

handkerchief was forced into her mouth. She thought she was going to retch from the taste of the blood, but before her stomach could react, she was jolted by a different sensation. Like a sack of flour, she was lifted up and draped about the big soldier's neck, as someone else rubbed his hand carnally over her buttocks.

"*Caramba!*" someone chortled lewdly. "We got ourselves a real *ancho*, eh, Juan?"

As the big soldier changed positions, Teresa saw another thin, cruel face for the first time. She jerked her legs up and shot them out, catching the scrawny soldier full in the chest and knocking him over.

"Dirty bitch of a whore mother and bastard father!" he screeched, as he picked himself up. "I'll kill you for that!"

"Pedro!" barked the big young Mexican with boils, clutching Teresa's legs together in a tight grip. "Go about your business."

The scrawny man's eyes narrowed into dangerous slits. "She is my business, Juan."

The unpleasant smile that Juan had given Teresa was now directed at Pedro. "Only when the general determines she is your business," he said evenly.

Cursing soundly, Pedro kicked viciously at the dead coachman, and wandered off.

Teresa was glad to see him go. When allowed, she thought, she might be able to talk to this big soldier—Juan. But that hope soon faded. Time and again, as he strode forward, as though carrying no weight at all, he would move his head to the side and rub his hairless cheek over her full young breasts. The first time she struggled weakly, but she was no match for this giant.

Where an old market-place stood at the junction of the *Calle Cortez* with a lesser street, Juan suddenly stopped. From the center of the city came the staccato rattle of musketry. He feared for a moment he might be walking into a counter-attack. He listened carefully to the deadly sounds and then changed his course away from the battle.

At the next corner, he drew quickly into a doorway. A company of *insurrectos* swept by. They had been in action. Their faces streamed with sweat, and many were bleeding. A few men were being carried by their comrades. Juan recognized a captain he knew and shouted at him; but the captain shook his head wildly, and went on.

The revolt was obviously going badly. Juan thought about releasing Teresa and returning to his squad. He hated to give up such a prize, knowing what reward a beauty such as this would bring from the general. Still, he was a soldier and the course of the battle would determine if there were to be any rewards at all.

A block away, he spotted a group of soldiers guarding some prisoners in front of a crude café. As they drew near, Teresa recognized Colonel Morino, Fernando's commanding officer, among the prisoners. His face and bearing looked defeated, hopeless. The giant lowered Teresa from his shoulders, and pushed her to the café door.

"Are you holding women prisoners?" he demanded breathlessly of the nearest rebel.

"Too many," replied the soldier. Then seeing Teresa, he gave Juan a quick glance of appreciation. "But nothing to equal her."

"And see she stays that way."

The soldier shrugged.

Juan opened the café door and gave Teresa a gentle shove forward. Before she could turn, the door was slammed shut. It took a moment for her eyes to adjust to the inner gloom.

The sunset slanting in through the shuttered windows marked the earthern floor with bars of light and dark shadows. The air was rancid with the smell of stale food, spilt wine and the body odor of too many people packed too closely together.

Teresa's first thought was of her grandmother. But there were no aristocrats here; only common women of all ages, some even clutching their children close to their frightened breasts. They ignored Teresa as though she were not there, except for a woman who now stepped through a beaded curtain and faced her with curious eyes. Teresa's stare was just as curious in return. Never in her nineteen years had she ever beheld a woman like this one.

Tall and slender as a reed, except for breasts like ripe melons, the woman had glossy black hair pulled to the side and draped over the front of her right shoulder. The blouse she wore was cut low and barely covered the lower half of her breasts; and her skirt stopped just below the knees, exposing beautifully molded legs and ankles.

Her face was even more memorable, with thin black pencil lines for eyebrows and a touch of blue coloring upon each eyelid, making her dark eyes appear hard and cruel. She had an ageless manner, but she was still quite young. From her mouth dangled a thin brown cigar, its steady thread of smoke wafting upward with casual unconcern.

She gave a toss of her head to an older, fat woman behind the bar. *"Mamacita,* she's bound." Her voice was quick and rough, but there was fear in it, and a quiver ran through Teresa. Now she saw the fear in all of them, even three silent ancient ones dressed in widow's black. All the women there knew they would be at the mercy of the lustful victors.

The fat woman, who had been endlessly wiping imaginary glass rings from the bar top, nodded to the cigar-smoking younger woman and waddled around the open end of the bar toward Teresa, her face a stony mask. She grunted her disapproval at the mouth gag used by the rebels.

"Devils straight out of hell," she muttered tone- lessly, her pudgy fingers slowly unknotting the raw- hide.

Teresa attempted to wet her lips, but her dry tongue and mouth seemed stuck together; she could barely swallow and couldn't form words. The cigar-smoker noticed her problem and strode to the bar, her move- ments as fluid as a cat stalking a bird. Even pouring beer into a mug was done with a certain sensual grace.

"You're free," said the *mamacita*. "Come wet your throat."

Teresa hesitated, rubbing her wrists and hands back to life.

The cigar-smoker laughed raucously. "You'll pray for something stronger than beer before this night is out." She gave the fat woman a nervous look as if ex- pecting to be rebuked for her remark.

The fat woman's massive shoulders twitched with anger, but she took Teresa gently by the arm. "Do not mind my Anna-Maria, *bambino*. She does not fear the soldiers, just that they will take what they want and not pay her for it."

Anna-Maria gave her a startled, uncertain look, as surprised by this gentleness as Teresa was by the wom- an's admission of her daughter's profession. They moved to the bar, and though the fat woman's hand still rested under Teresa's arm, it was as though she needed support, her heavy frame drained by all that had happened that day.

The beer tasted bitter, flat and warm, but Teresa calmed her trembling stomach and drank enough to revive her shocked senses and bring back her self- confidence.

In spite of the blood stains, her clothes were the finest in the room. Anna-Maria eyed her curiously. "You're not from Saltillo?"

"No." Her voice sounded husky and strange. She sipped at the mug again before continuing. "San Antonio de Bexar in Tejas. I am Teresa Maria de Alarcon Rosa."

The mother, always ready to see where an extra *peso* might be earned, tightened her grip.

"And what are you doing in Saltillo, with a civil war breaking out?"

"I came to meet the family of my intended, *senora*. Fernando Martin Flores."

The mother and daughter exchanged quick, meaningful looks, and Anna-Maria averted her face to hide her mirth. They shared more than the name Maria, she thought. Then she felt a twinge of sympathy for Teresa. Fernando, at twenty-two, was built like a boy of fifteen, and he possessed as much passion as a bar rag sopping up spilled beer.

"And your years?"

"Nineteen."

The mother was surprised. "As much as that."

Her surprise was understandable. Teresa possessed an unusual face that could sometimes be as sweet and innocent as a twelve-year-old's, and at other times could be as mature and alluring as that of a woman in her prime. Her full, pink lips always seemed to be half-parted, as if in invitation to be kissed.

Teresa's age also took Anna-Maria by surprise. She was only just turned nineteen herself, but seemed much older than Teresa. For a moment she resented Teresa's beauty and youth and obvious wealth, all her advantages in life. Anna-Maria had been a *putana* for seven years. She had no memory of any childhood. Her memories mainly concerned men—a different one in her bed each night. It had started with her father, who had taught her how to survive in such a world. At one time she made up a game, the only one she'd ever played in her life, in which she kept track of all the men she bedded. After the total reached a hundred, she didn't know how to count higher and gave up the game.

The fat woman, who introduced herself as Carmen Morales, eyed the blood-stained dress. "But, *senorita,* surely your family did not let you travel alone. Where is your *dueña*?"

"It was my grandmother, Dona Clara. Two soldiers took her away and I don't know where she is."

A pudgy hand patted Teresa's cheek. "Don't fret, my child. My daughter and I shall try to protect you until this is over and you are returned to your grandmother."

"Thank you for helping me," Teresa said with genuine gratitude.

Anna-Maria mumbled contemptuously, using an obscene Saltillo expletive. "We will all be equal as women when they finish the battle. Even your grandmother may know again what it is to feel a man between her legs."

"Be still," said her mother severely, "and mind your tongue in front of the *senorita*."

She expected a retort from Anna-Maria and was amazed when none was forthcoming. There was sudden compassion in her heart for each of these young women. In her sixty years, she had seen too much war, too much bloodshed, too much rape. Men made war, men were responsible for the shedding of blood, and only men thought it their God-given right to rape those they were victorious over. It wasn't just her husband she loathed; she had come to loathe all men.

Carmen had been twelve when the soldiers marched

across her father's *peon* farm. Her father claimed that
they had come to liberate the peasants and bring land
reform. All they liberated was Carmen, taking her
away from her family. For six months she was passed
from soldier to soldier, until each man had gorged
himself on her youth.

The war ended abruptly, and then Carmen hoped
to escape from the trap she was in. One of the soldiers
who had not touched her, Franco Morales, invited her
to accompany him home to Saltillo, but then took advantage of her gratitude. While he sold drinks in the
front of his small café, he sold her, by then his wife, to
every patron who wanted her in the back of the café.

And when the children came, three girls and a boy,
he wasn't quite sure that they were really his, so, when
they were old enough, he sold his daughters as well.
Only the boy, when he grew old enough to know he
should be in bed with a woman and not a man, rebelled and ran away.

When Anna-Maria was fourteen, Franco took his
two older daughters to Mexico City, and Carmen
heard from him only when he needed money.

But as loathesome as Franco was to Carmen, she was
not above using people as he did. Teresa's beauty had
given her an idea. "My child," she said, again gently
patting Teresa's hand, "do not let my question embarrass you. Have you yet known a man?"

"No, *senora.* It is forbidden until I marry."

Anna-Maria cackled. She had known that Fernando
was too much of a weakling to have attempted anything with this innocent. "Don't admit it to these
whoremongers or they'll rub you raw in an hour," she
cautioned. "Nothing they'd like more than plant their
man-things in a *madonna.*"

"But," protested Teresa innocently, "won't their officers protect us from the rabble?"

Carmen bent her head gloomily. Despair engulfed her. Explanations—why didn't parents teach of the past horrors, why didn't anyone remember . . . ? Experience seemed futile.

"The officers are the worst, I guess," she said dully. "And the general—I spit upon and curse his womanizing ways."

"Who is he?"

"Santa Anna."

Teresa felt a great sense of relief. Santa Anna was well known in San Antonio as a gentleman and scholar.

"Then I am saved," she said with enthusiasm. "He is known to my family and will see to my protection."

Carmen Morales smiled sweetly. This was also good news for her. Her ransom demands for Teresa greatly increased in her mind. Now, all she had to do was figure out a way to keep the rabble of soldiers from seizing the delectable Teresa.

2

THE DEFEAT OF the federalists; their mad turning at bay for one last savage rally; their wavering and breaking; their disorganized stampede spurred on by a decimating fire and the bayonet's point: these were all stages toward victory that kept General Antonio Lopez de Santa Anna occupied until the streets at last were deserted and quiet. They were deserted except for the grotesque shapes that stretched in all the undignified awkwardness of violent death, with rivers of blood already drying between the cobblestones. They were silent except for the echoes of occasional stubborn fighting coming from the outlying *plazas* and *alamedas*, where pockets of government troops clung to their positions behind improvised barricades with the doggedness of men for whom surrender offers no hope of mercy.

It was near midnight when Juan Valdez, the big soldier with boils on his face, reported to Santa Anna concerning the beauty he had captured from the carriage. At first the general, a small, black-haired, immaculately turned-out man in his mid-thirties, ignored him. In Santa Anna's snobbish appraisal, the women of Coahuila were among the fattest and ugliest in all of Mexico. Juan must be exaggerating. Santa Anna constantly boasted that the fairest and most sensual

women in the country came from his home state of
Veracruz. But Juan was so insistent that the general
eventually decided to take a look.

"*Basta!* Find out which rooms they have set aside
for me and take her there. She had better be worth the
reward you are asking or my boot will find out how
far it can kick up your ass!"

As Juan rushed back to the café, he convinced himself he had nothing to worry about, even though Teresa had been over his shoulders all the time, and he
had concentrated on getting her to safety. At first all
he remembered was her large brown frightened eyes,
but he had no doubt she was beautiful, soft and seductive. But all women were beautiful, soft and seductive
to Juan—once he had them in bed.

A soldier stood guard at the café door and nodded
in recognition as Juan entered. Now the main room
was illuminated by candles in bowls on the tables and
along the bar, revealing that the walls were adorned
with colorful portraits of saints. From a small perch in
one corner, a yellow and green parrot squawked inces-
santly, releasing his tensions after the most frightening
day of his life—and waiting for more trouble to start.

The older and uglier women had long since been
sent back to their own homes. The soldier guards had
kept only the best for themselves and now sat at the
rough tables sipping drinks with them in quiet conversation. These were not Spaniards of lust, or French-
men of passion, who invaded the land and then departed after satisfying themselves with pillage and
rape. These were Mexican soldiers sitting with Mexican women. This was their land and their people, and
their general was to be the next president. They would
take care of their manly needs by wooing the women
instead of taking them by force.

Juan had scoffed at first when he heard Santa Anna's order to treat the women decently. In the case of Teresa, his hope that he would be rewarded with money by the general was an inducement, but animals do not need money when they have been away from women for two months—they need women. Even the general, famous for his many conquests, was becoming irritable and frustrated.

The quiet atmosphere of Carmen's café encouraged Juan. Saltillo was to be Santa Anna's big test of his army's self-control, and maybe they would control their frustrations successfully. They were feared in the land because of their blood-thirsty battles of the last two months. This had been losing the earlier support of the people, who were beginning instead to support the oppressive government of Bustamente. Saltillo was the largest city the rebels had attempted to capture— the capital of the state of Coahuila and Tejas. With its fall, Santa Anna would control all of the north-eastern and gulf states. Here he had to show the rest of the country that he came as a savior and not a defiler. The quiet atmosphere of the café promised well.

"Do you wish a drink?"

Juan's reflections were disturbed by the sharp inquiry from the large woman behind the bar.

"*Gracias, senora.*" Then he remembered his real mission and quickly scanned the faces at the tables. He didn't see the blood-stained clothing that he sought.

"Earlier this evening," he said casually, as he paid for his beer, "I left a *senorita* here for—ah—protection. She had been in a carriage accident."

Carmen had been expecting this confrontation for several hours. She suppressed her personal loathing for a man who could gag and bind an innocent girl like Teresa so cruelly.

"I'm aware of her," she said very softly, pretending to wipe the bar with a slow circular motion.

"Then she is still here. No one has taken her away?"

"*Si*. His orders." She sharply tilted her head and Juan's eyes followed.

Seated at a shadowy table was the scrawny Pedro, so filled with *tequila* that his watery eyes could hardly focus on the young woman who sat opposite him.

For a moment, Juan was more interested in the woman than his comrade. "Who is that with him?"

"My daughter. Anna-Maria."

Juan looked so astounded that Carmen smiled. But she had once been as pretty as her daughter—and more innocent. She had had to promise Anna-Maria half of what she expected to get for Teresa just to sit and get the ugly little man drunk, after he came crashing into the café and demanded Teresa be turned over to him.

"My congratulations, *senora*," Juan said, without taking his eyes from Anna-Maria. "She is *bonito*!"

Carmen examined him confidently. Now that she knew what attracted him, she felt herself a sure winner.

"One more drink and he will not know that she has left him for another. Do you wish to buy your friend a drink?"

Juan winked at her. With a salacious smile, he pushed some *pesos* across the bar. She signalled to Anna-Maria to pick up the tequila she poured out.

Juan's blood surged the moment she rose from the table. This was his kind of woman. With each step she took to the bar, his anticipation mounted. Her movements excited him. In his mind he could already feel the full, soft roundness of her beautiful breasts. Her mouth would be like new honey against his trembling lips; her skin would warm his hands and soothe his frustrated heart. And she would be much more of a woman than the fair one from the carriage; a woman he would not have to strain or struggle with, but who had the experience to satisfy his every desire.

"Anna-Maria," said Carmen, "the sergeant is the man who brought Senorita de Alarcon."

Anna-Maria leaned casually against the bar and turned her most alluring gaze on Juan.

"What do you want with such as she?" She slowly dropped her eyes as though to add: "When you could have me."

Juan was overcome. A blush darkened his brown skin.

"She is not for me," he stammered. "She is for my general."

The lift of her eyelids was so slow that his heart nearly stopped beating. "Then who shall be for the general's sergeant?" She spoke cautiously because she was still carrying out her agreement with her mother concerning Pedro, and yet here was a man—a customer—she could handle on her own terms. She didn't want to miss this one.

Juan, affected by the sexual implication of her question, hesitated, not knowing how to get her alone.

Anna-Maria knew her quarry. She shrugged and returned to the table with Pedro's drink, pretending indifference.

Carmen saw him struggling with the problem of how he could get Anna-Maria away from his comrade. She knew it was time to strike.

"Would you like to see this woman who is for your general?"

Juan nodded unwillingly, afraid that he might lose Anna-Maria. Looking back, trying to catch her eye, he followed her mother through the beaded curtains and down a dim hallway.

Teresa sat on a low stool next to the kitchen hearth with her head leaning against the adobe bricks, near

exhaustion. Her hair was disheveled and the blood
had dried dark brown on her dress. She was so tired
that her face had a wan, pinched expression.

Juan was appalled when he looked in through the
kitchen archway, and he quickly pulled back. He
would be a laughing stock if he presented this bedrag-
gled creature to Santa Anna.

"*Mamacita,*" he whispered. "I am in trouble. Can
she be cleaned up before I take her to my general?"

Carmen shrugged. "Possibly."

Juan read her correctly. "It could mean a great deal
of money for you."

Carmen averted her eyes. She was elated that her
plan was working so smoothly. But, still, she had to
play her role.

"He will not hurt her?"

Juan's jaw thrust out indignantly. "Has any woman
in Saltillo been hurt? It is his policy that such shall
not be."

Carmen had to admit that she had been amazed by
the behavior of the soldiers. She had been puzzled until this moment. Perhaps this general was different
from the invaders of the past. But different or not, she
had to forge ahead with her plan.

She pretended to hesitate. "*Si*, you speak truth. Go
help yourself at the bar and I'll see to this woman's
work."

"You'll not regret it," he cried, glad for the opportunity to return to the bar room and to Anna-Maria.

Carmen waited until she heard the beads clatter
with his exit. She entered the kitchen and took Teresa
gently by the arm. "Come, child," she said. "We'll find
you a change of clothing and a bed."

Teresa gladly complied, but as she trudged down
the dim hall, her heart was troubled. She had heard
the whispered conversation.

"Senora," she implored. "Will it be horrible?"

"What?"

"When I am with his general?"

"You heard?"

"Yes."

"In here, please," Carmen commanded.

Teresa stepped into the small bed chamber and stopped short. Seated upon the wood frame bed was a girl of near her age. The girl greeted her with a warm and friendly smile. She was slender with a freckled face and turned-up nose and save for her small, up-thrust breasts and pert little backside, could well have passed for a boy.

"This is my niece," said Carmen, carefully avoiding giving her name. "She will take your place, while you rest."

"My place? But why?"

"Dona Teresa," said Carmen, her voice rolling the title out with due respect. "I'm sure that your family will look upon me with gratitude for protecting you."

"But who will protect her?" Teresa protested.

"She has been carefully coached on exactly what to do and what to say. Put your mind at ease on that matter. Now, here is a bowl and pitcher to wash yourself. They're not fancy, but you'll find suitable night-clothes on the bed."

"Thank you," Teresa said very softly. She turned to the other girl. "Our dear Lord will reward you and look out for you."

The other girl, whose name was Luisa, smiled back, unable to suppress her feeling of excitement over the adventure ahead. She had been carefully coached by Carmen and Anna-Maria, but Luisa was a strong-minded girl who had wild ideas of her own.

"Come," said Carmen, "it's time to go."

Luisa rose, smiled again, and put on a floor-length cloak with a monk's hood that hid her face.

Pedro was fading fast by the time Carmen returned to the bar room, and Juan was upset about having to leave. Extracting a promise from Anna-Maria that she would wait for him and only him, he quickly took the cloaked figure away without once looking under the hood.

3

THERE IN THE dimly lit room, where the bedside candle sputtered in its bowl and a tattered shutter, three-
quarters torn from its bracket, rocked noisily in the
night air, Luisa seemed womanly among the shadows,
a delightfully writhing, churning feminine toy with a
single purpose—gratification.

She pulled the general's lean arms to her shoulders,
saying: "Am I not woman—?," and then whispering,
"Full woman . . . well trained. I know many plea-
sures." Santa Anna rested his battle-weary head against
her neck. "That's right, general, you let me soothe you.
You've been away from your home a long time and
you've got something that's longing to be tended to
as if it were at home . . . but I'll fix that."

Pitying him . . . she *was* pitying him . . . this little Coahuila creature . . . this peasant wench . . .
pitying Antonio Lopez de Santa Anna, a noble, a general, handsome, virile. A man for her to know for a
single night . . . and then forget.

She had been in his room when he returned from
headquarters. The sergeant, she insisted, had been
guarding her until just the moment before. Santa
Anna had been greatly disappointed. He cursed himself for accepting Juan's judgment of beauty. His

blood was already coursing richly from anticipation, and he suddenly didn't want to be alone.

Her voice was soft and melodious, tinged with the humming bird slur of the Aztec. She talked of her dull life in Saltillo while keeping his desire at fever pitch. She sat in the flowing cloak and beneath it, she was nude, he suspected, wanting to know.

Suddenly the general's head rocked with fatigue. Soft hands helped him to his bed, tenderly undressed him, prepared him for what he never dreamed was possible. Warm human flesh nestled close, and he was urged to use the rounded breasts, downy belly and taut thighs as a mattress. He had warned his man that there were to be no rapes in Saltillo. How they would laugh if they learned that he was himself victim of a sort of rape!

He rocked with the rhythm she created, building his manhood to a power long-forgotten. His hot breath panted, increasingly frantic, in her face. She worked hard to increase the excitement that slowly overcame his exhaustion, grinding her hips to gain full knowledge of his greatest pride—an abundant genital.

"Oh, you're good," she whimpered, and his beat took on an added power. Luisa was so engaging, so sexually experienced, that she charmed away the memory of his disappointment. He faltered, but with blithe banter and knowing encouragement, she revived his flagging power.

Quickly she worked on her own climax, building her biological surge to its own point of dispatch. Primitive, natural in all her emotions and reactions, she automatically put their actions into words, short blunt words. From someone else, the words would have seemed cold, peremptory, pornographic, but coming from Luisa, they were gusts of salacious delight.

The moist walls inside her gently gripped his erect

stiffness, the words boiled his blood, her hands kneaded his body to a screaming, panting, quivering, uncontrollable climax. He rolled away, his mouth agape, making the leather mattress squeal in protest.

Santa Anna lay exhausted, a wet cloth covering his deflated manhood, watching her nimbly don the clothing she had hidden under the bed before his arrival. To his weary, dilated eyes, she was transformed into something elfin . . . boyish . . . a will-o'-the-'wisp sprite. Her hair was short, deep black ringlets held tightly to her head by the sweat from her recent exertions. Her eyes were alive, flashing brown-black, allseeing, above a snub of a nose that almost wasn't. She had boyishly rounded cheeks, a small lively mouth, white even teeth, and a chin that was firm, determined. Her throat arched gracefully, and her small perfect-circle breasts and supple waist were those of a child-woman.

"Do you understand who I am to become?" he asked.

"Naturally. It is wise for every Mexican to know the star that guides Santa Anna."

This pleased his enormous ego. She was not afraid of him, and this pleased him, too.

"How old are you?"

"Eighteen."

"Did you know that I am twice that age?"

She giggled. "That's why it felt like you were twice the biggest man I've ever had before."

He sat sharply up in bed. She was like no one he had ever encountered before.

"It is my policy to reward those who do great service for me. What shall be your reward?"

"I've already had it," she said with a pleased laugh.

"No money?" He was incredulous.

"Don't insult me, general. My Tia will not allow me, to sleep around like her daughter."

"Your cousin is a prostitute?"

"The whole family," she answered indifferently.

Suddenly she was not making sense to Santa Anna. Valdez, who had brought her, knew that he never had anything to do with prostitutes—or their families. It left one too open to blackmail and scandal. His massive black eyebrows knit together.

"Who are you and what is your reason for being here?"

That same tone of voice would make soldiers cringe and shrink on the battlefield. It didn't phase Luisa in the least. She sat down on the edge of the bed and stared straight into his smoky black eyes.

"I'm an adventurer, like you. You are out to conquer a nation, I only want the conqueror."

"Me?"

She tossed her head and smiled. "Also, I want to see Mexico City and never see Saltillo again. Is that in the way of a reward?"

His heart turned over inside him. There was something powerfully sensual about this boyish child, but along with it, there was also something a little disturbing.

"Possibly," he said slowly. "But you puzzle me. You are not the girl who my sergeant took from a carriage, are you?"

"Supposed to be, but not."

Her candor was unbelievable to his ears. He was so used to being lied to, cheated and put upon that an honest person was refreshing.

"Do you wish to tell me the circumstances?" It was not a command; for the fierce Santa Anna it was uncommonly gentle.

"Oh, I fully intended to tell you before I left. I'll

need you now to protect me from my aunt's wrath when she learns I didn't do as instructed."

Santa Anna nodded, but was wise enough to keep quiet.

"The sergeant didn't know that I was under the cloak, believe me. My cousin made a pass at him so that he would hurry right back to her bed."

Santa Anna could fully believe that. He knew how Juan Valdez behaved when a woman was involved.

"I was to pretend to be the pretty one, and also pretend to be a virgin, which my aunt thinks I am, by the way. If you rewarded my virginity, like you did the girls in Tampico three years ago when the Spanish landed troops, then I was to take the reward to my *Tia*. If you raped me, which she was sure that you would do, what with your reputation, then she would come and demand payment for taking away my maidenhead."

Santa Anna examined her thoughtfully. "And you knew that you were in trouble because you really weren't a virgin?"

Her eyes widened charmingly. "Oh, but I really am, with a man. There was a half-try with one boy when I was fourteen, and the rest has been with an *escoba mango*."

"A broom handle!" Santa Anna doubled over in a fit of uncontrollable mirth. She delighted him as no one had in a long time. He could not remember the last time he had laughed so much.

"That's it," he chortled. "When I become president, I shall issue a broom handle to every woman in Mexico so that they can become as experienced as you."

"I pleased you, then?"

"Completely." Then he grew serious. "But your tale does not. What does your aunt intend to do with the senorita?"

"Gain a reward from the family for protecting her. She must be very wealthy, or so her clothes suggest. She was also travelling with a *dueña*, so she must be high-born."

"Travelling?" Santa Anna's interest was renewed. "Then she is not Saltillo?"

Luisa shook her head. "From a place I've never heard of before, San Antonio . . . something."

San Antonio de Bexar in Tejas, he mused. Santa Anna was a master at hiding his emotions, and he showed no sign of his excitement. Once, after he had helped Iturbide establish an imperial rule over Mexico, he had travelled north into Tejas. There he had found women as fair as those one would expect to see in Madrid or Barcelona. This was, indeed, exciting news. Perhaps the eye of Juan Valdez was improving after all.

"And the *senorita* is well?"

Luisa shrugged. "As far as I know. Her dress is all covered with blood, but I think it is from someone else. But they treated her badly." She noticed the sudden frown on Santa Anna's face and quickly continued, "Oh, not like we just did, but still badly. They had tied her hands and stuck a bloody old handkerchief in her mouth. I'd kick a man in the balls if he did that to me."

And Santa Anna was sure that she would.

"And her travelling companion?"

"I heard her tell my aunt that soldiers took her away. It was her grandmother."

Santa Anna's heart sank. If the old woman was from one of the rich and powerful Tejas families, it meant big trouble. He knew that Tejas wanted its independence from Mexico and that the United States wanted that area as a territory. To win his fight against Bustamente, he needed the support and soldiers that Tejas could offer. He already had some of their finest young officers in his corps, but he needed much more from Tejas. This one incident could ruin everything. He silently cursed Juan Valdez for ever having kidnapped the woman from her carriage. But then, without that, he would never have met this elfin child-woman.

"So," he said, rising and pulling britches up over his nakedness, "we seem to have all the news. Shall I send you home with an escort?"

"I was born here. I know all the streets and alleys. I'll be safe."

She rose quickly and came to his side. Without hesitation, she kissed him hard on the mouth.

"Wait!" But it was too late, she was gone. Gone as suddenly as the new fire she had aroused in his groin.

Santa Anna knew that he was no longer fatigued, yet everything in the past hour seemed to have made him forget his problems and responsibilities. She had come from another world, another existence, but had managed to snare him into intercourse. He cringed at what he had just done. It was all right for the other soldiers to take advantage of the prostitutes' meat, but never Santa Anna. Yet he was not a hypocrite, and it was this child and not his wife, nor his other aristocratic bedmates, who stayed in his memory. He thought about what they had done together and what she had told him. She had seduced him rather than blackmailing him.

"Jesus!" he growled. "Who in the hell is she? The little vixen never did give her name!"

4

YOUNG CARLOS JUAREZ knocked timidly on the door and entered. His heart was not in what he must do now.

"*Capitano,*" he called softly, holding his candle so that the sleeping officer would be able to recognize who called him. Once, another officer had almost put a pistol ball through Carlos' chest when he had disturbed him during the night.

"Jesus," came a weary voice from beneath the covers, "not dawn already, Carlos?"

"No, my captain," the youth answered apologetically, "it is the General. Someone has tweaked his ass and he's screaming bloody murder for you."

"What hour is it?"

"The third one after midnight, *senor.*"

The young officer groaned. Only the worst of news came at such an hour. With growing dejection, he swung his bare legs over the side of the bed and sat up. "Best light another candle, Carlos, so that I can see to dress."

Carlos' face beamed with delight. He was lighting candles practically before the words were out of the officer's mouth. He relished the moments he could be near this man and do his every bidding. Captain Felix Escovarro de Sanchez was his idol. And it always gave

him a delicious little thrill when he was allowed to
remain in the room and help *his* captain dress. And
even though the event had taken place well over a
hundred times in the two years he had worked for
Captain Escovarro, each time seemed like the first.

The twenty-three-year-old officer would rise, stretching his sinewy golden-haired arms to the ceiling,
thus emphasizing his unusual height—well over six
feet. Then he would shake his head, to bring himself
to full wakefulness, causing the mass of dark golden
curls to dance and bounce as though awakening, too.
He never wore clothing while sleeping, claiming his
whole body had to breathe to become refreshed and
rested.

This was what pleased Carlos the most, a chance to
study his idol in the full. It was not a sexual interest
on the sixteen-year-old boy's part, for he was not even
aware of homosexuality. It was just another chance for
him to find out what he might copy in his hero.

Carlos was even allowing his hair to grow on his upper lip so that some day he could have as an impressive a mustache as the captain had nurtured to lush
fullness in the virile style affected by stalwarts of
Santa Anna's officer corps.

But try as he might, Carlos would never be able to
match the captain's height, or his broad shoulders,
slim waist and lightness of skin. Carlos always grew
angry when the other officers taunted Captain Felix
about his light skin and suggested he must be *gringo*.
As far as Felix knew, there was no anglo blood in his
body. His ancestors had come from Old Spain to New
Spain a century before. All of his family were fair and
had faces more akin to Greece than Spain. His was a
face that an artist might select to recreate a young
Olympian god—with the smooth cheeks, the finely
modeled bone structure, eyes of milk chocolate brown

that were quick to laugh. Forehead, nose and jaws as squarely cut as an ancient Greek discus-thrower.

Fully clothed, he was even more sensual than in the raw. Loathing the chafing his neck always took from the stiff-collared uniform tunic, he was forever leaving it open so that a tuft of golden chest hair peeked out, suggesting the downy mass that covered the rest of his body. It was not by sexual design that he preferred to wear tight-fitting britches, thus revealing his man-hood, in repose, to be second to none. The tight fit gave him a closer feeling to his horse when he used his lean legs to command the animal in battle.

Captain Escovarro was a soldier first, a son of Tejas second, and a man last. Raised in a strict, formal, Catholic home he came very near to being a male vir-gin. Only twice in his life, and both times since com-ing to serve Santa Anna, had he felt the supple softness of a woman beneath him. Each time had left him with such a sense of guilt that he had immediately gone to confession.

Felix was very close to his religion. Once, while at military school in Spain, he went on a retreat to a monastery high in the mountains. He felt so close to God that he stayed for six weeks and almost decided to become a priest. A wise old friar saw deep into his heart and convinced him that one could still serve God by taking one's rightful place in the world. A year la-ter, after having been home for only a few weeks, he was on his way to serve another kind of god—Santa Anna.

Like the general, he learned he was a man who would be forced to accept a double standard of alle-giance. For Santa Anna, it was his great love for Vera-cruz and his fanatical desire to control the destiny of Mexico. Felix's family had always considered them-selves independent of Mexico City, no matter who

ruled in the capital, and long before the Americans
began their pioneer settlements. Tejas would never be
free as long as Bustamente ruled, and perhaps not
even after him. But he must fall before the next step
could be taken, and that course was in the hands of
Santa Anna.

On orders from his father, Felix had set out to win
his way into Santa Anna's confidence and secretly be
the eyes and ears of all who desired independence for
Tejas. In three years Felix had done well, becoming
one of the few men Santa Anna fully trusted. Even
more extraordinary was the fact that his word and reports were fully trusted by Stephen F. Austin and his
colonists. Austin, like Felix's family, was disturbed by
the talk of annexation to the United States.

Before Felix could finish dressing, Santa Anna came
storming into his room. Both captain and orderly
snapped to full attention.

"At ease!" Santa Anna barked, dismissing Carlos
with a toss of his head as he sat down and put his feet
on Felix's desk. Two heads shorter than Felix, Santa
Anna always preferred to sit when the two were together.

Felix's eyes swept over him appraisingly, surprised
that Santa Anna was in full uniform at such an un-
godly hour. The massive golden epaulets were not
mere swagger or show—the well-concealed padding
served to make him appear broad-shouldered and commanding. He was actually a small man built like a
slender wedge, with average shoulders, no hips, and a
shock of unruly black hair. His eyes, too, were dark,
and his smile slow and rare and infectious. On his
breast, above the golden embroidery, was the silver
badge proclaiming him the governor of the state of Veracruz. He seemed poised now between anger and humor, and looked at Felix as if he were some strange

specimen of prehistoric creature. "Did you receive any reports this evening on captured Saltillo women and where they were being held?"

"Many. But by nine o'clock they were all to have been released to return to their homes." Felix was puzzled. "Has something happened?"

"Something?" snapped Santa Anna. "Why in the hell do you think I am here?"

"That's what I'm also wondering, General," said Felix, relaxing and smiling at him. It couldn't be a military matter, Felix quickly determined, or else Santa Anna would have stormed through the door issuing immediate orders. Therefore, he decided, it was not all that serious a matter.

"Wondering!" Santa Anna exploded. "If you didn't have friends in high places in Tejas, whoever the hell they are, I'd send you packing right back."

Felix had heard this threat at least once a week for three years. It was always a prelude to something Santa Anna wished done and could not do himself.

"That's a fine idea, General," said Felix pleasantly. "I was hoping to get home for a while after this Saltillo campaign."

Santa Anna rambled on as though he hadn't heard him. "Sergeant Juan Valdez captured a couple of women this evening, and I have reason to believe that they are being held for some kind of ransom or blackmail attempt against me."

"That doesn't sound like Valdez," Felix stated.

"So far I've seen no evidence against him, Captain," said General Santa Anna. "That is for you to learn."

"Me?"

"It may well concern you," Santa Anna rapped out angrily. "The two women were from San Antonio de Bexar. From a rich family, so I am to gather. You, more than anyone, know how I need Tejas with me.

How the hell do you think I'm going to explain to
Senor Austin this incident?"

"Perhaps it isn't an incident, as yet."

Santa Anna smiled at him from behind the desk,
but it wasn't a friendly smile. He respected Felix because the young man was not afraid of him, but at
times Felix's optimism annoyed him. A true pessimist
by nature, he always looked for the worst in any situation. In short, terse phrases, he told Felix all that he
knew of the situation, careful to leave out his seduc-
tion by Luisa. Before dawn, he said, he wanted Felix
to unravel the entire affair.

Felix's first impulse on Santa Anna's departure was
to treat the whole episode as something that would unravel itself long before the coming of dawn, but then
he began to consider the implications more seriously.
Going over the reports of the evening before, he
learned that one Dona Clara de Alarcon had been *escorted* from her carriage to the *hacienda* of Senor Luis
Martin, a known loyalist and enemy of Santa Anna.
Felix had been present when the man's son, Lt. Fernando Martin Flores, had been captured and questioned in the middle of the battle. But it was the de
Alarcon name that worried Felix the most. It was a
name well known and respected in Tejas, although he
had never met any of the de Rosa or de Alarcon family. Any knowledge of the other captured woman was
harder for him to come by. Sergeant Valdez, eager for
Santa Anna's favor, had reported only to the general
and now the sergeant was nowhere to be found.

Close to dawn, Felix had a lucky break. Young Carlos, who always seemed to know what his captain was
after, spotted the scrawny Pedro drunkenly weaving
his way down the street, singing a sad lament about his
lot in life.

Faced with Captain Escovarro, Pedro sobered

quickly. In his whole life, Pedro had feared no man until he met Felix Escovarro de Sanchez. Sly, cunning, and a born cheat, Pedro was a master at winning any gambling game he played. Felix, shrewd about all gambling tricks, saw through Pedro at once. Schooled in the gentlemanly ways of the Spanish military, Felix gave Pedro only a quiet warning when he first caught him cheating. Pedro didn't take the warning seriously, but next time he was caught, he was severely punished. Pedro had never been caught in thirty years of cheating and came to look upon Felix as a golden devil who had been put on earth to haunt him. Thus it took very few questions from Felix to learn all about the carriage, the capture, and the detention of the captive at Carmen Morales' café.

As he had been instructed, Felix gave the information to Carlos to deliver to Santa Anna, and then he jubilantly returned to his bed.

5

A MAN'S SHOUT burst through the grey dawn, audible in every room of the café. Waking slowly from a bad dream, Teresa pushed herself up and frowned at the dim grey wall in front of her. For a moment she thought she was home, until the outlines of the narrow room brought her back to the present. She shivered. The dawn had brought a chill with it. The shouting started again, and Teresa stretched her hand out in the semi-darkness. "Grandmother, something's happening!"

She stopped; of course her grandmother was not there. A million hours before—the previous evening, in fact—they had been separated. Since then, Dona Clara had been a constant worry on her mind . . . where could the old woman be and what might have happened to her? Once more Teresa shuddered.

From somewhere near the front of the café, there came several more calls, the last one a loud snarl, and then she heard only the wind whining through the cracks in the adobe walls. Then silence . . . until suddenly there came a scraping noise, close at hand. Her blood chilling, Teresa jumped from the bed and looked for something to protect herself with.

"Oh, senorita!" Teresa sank back in relief; it was only the girl who had gone in her place the night be-

fore. When the girl stumbled into the room, Teresa
realized that she was even more frightened than herself.

"Senorita, the general's come. Nobody's safe!" Luisa
suddenly realized that her trick was failing. She burst
into tears.

"Hush," Teresa whispered soothingly, although she
needed comforting herself. "Are you just returning?"

Luisa shook her head. "Hours ago."

"Unharmed?"

Luisa's eyes, washed clear by her tears, opened and
stared innocently at Teresa's strained face, her self-
possession slowly returning. "Unharmed," she said,
then added: "And unsuccessful."

"What had you hoped to accomplish?" Teresa
asked.

Luisa said hesitantly, "Not what my aunt wished of
me, reward and all." Her look became troubled. "He
seemed a nice enough man and all I wanted was to get
away from here."

Teresa shook her head impatiently. "None of it is
your fault. I never should have let you go in my place.
I was taking the coward's way out."

"No, you were just plain worn out," Luisa said sympathetically.

After a moment, she added, "And I wanted to do it.
Oh, Dona, I would do anything to get away from this
miserable life with my aunt and cousin."

Teresa could well believe her. Teresa was still naive
in many ways but she was not stupid when it came to
judging people. She had been fully aware that Carmen
Morales was looking for a reward for protecting her
from Santa Anna, but at the time she had been too
exhausted to think of anything but sleep. She had suspected that Carmen was sending her niece into danger,

with the possibility of rape, but she had allowed the girl to go because she feared for her own virginity.

When she felt Luisa's eyes upon her, her thoughts came back to the present and she realized that it was getting light outside.

"Do you wish to get away so badly?"

"Oh, yes!"

"So be it! Last night you helped me and now I'll do everything in my power to help you."

Before Teresa could formulate a plan for helping Luisa, there was a sudden interruption. Two men appeared in the doorway. Beside the towering and still quite drunk Juan Valdez was a short and quite dapper officer with a shining forehead, a clean-shaven face, and a look of quick intelligence. "Senorita, this is General Santa Anna."

When Teresa nodded curtly, Santa Anna made a bow, hands stiffly at his sides, almost as if he stood before a queen on inspection. Here was a little rooster! she told herself and at once regretted her ungenerous thought.

Did the general sense the impression he had made, or was it only a natural defensiveness? In any case Santa Anna regarded her with awe. Juan Valdez was a genius when it came to selecting women! She was ideal, even several inches shorter than he—dainty and petite. And she was regal!

In spite of the fact Teresa stood before him only in a night dress, which clung to her womanliness in an enticing manner, she did not flinch or try to cover more of herself. She stood her ground and eyed him, face to face.

Suddenly, however, the flesh around his small dark eyes crinkled into a pleased look, and a voice, surprisingly deep, told her, "Senorita, I am at a loss to explain the unfortunate incident of your capture. What might I do to make amends?"

Recovering from her surprise, Teresa, with a serious look, addressed him sternly.

"First, please leave this chamber so that I can dress properly. Secondly, find my grandmother for me and assure me of her safety. And thirdly, as you seem to be the victor of yesterday's battle, inform the senora of this house that I wish to take her niece with me as a maid until I return to my own home."

At the door Santa Anna bowed, even more impressed. Teresa Maria de Alarcon Rosa was far more beautiful than he had anticipated. Not even the finest woman in Veracruz could match her. To him, her face was perfectly shaped, her body a sexual masterpiece he longed to possess. He vowed to have her bedded within the hour.

But in spite of his overwhelming desire for Teresa, he regarded Luisa with great respect. The little vixen, he thought admiringly, doesn't know failure. Sensing defeat and punishment at the hands of her aunt, she turned to Teresa for help like a courtier appealing to a queen. He admired quick-thinking spunk like that— and besides—didn't that make it easier for him to have both of them?

6

LUIS MARTIN'S DISMAY slowly turned to indignation and then burning anger. His home, built by his father, to be passed on to his son, Fernando . . . This madman couldn't take it away like that! He shook his fist in impotent fury. The thieves, the scheming corrupt rebels, had put him out bodily, so that their general would have a suitable nest for Senorita de Alarcon! Unless Santa Anna had evil designs on the girl and didn't want anyone to know, the treatment of him was unnecessary. Dona Clara had found her way to his house and had remained there as his guest. He would have welcomed Teresa the same way if she could have been found. Both women had come to Saltillo to stay with him, but the war had reached the town before them and separated them. But now they were reunited. Damn Santa Anna! He would not accept this treatment, the loss of his home. He would find a way to stop the Veracruz tyrant, he promised himself.

Teresa was unaware of what had happened to Fernando's father. She was enjoying the feeling of being safe at last. After a tearful reunion with her grandmother, she was resting in a chair by a bedroom window. Juan Valdez had rescued their luggage from the carriage, and Luisa had helped some of the Martin servants to prepare her a hot, soapy bath in a big tub. As yet she had not been presented to the Martin family, but she assumed they were just being kind and letting her rest after her ordeal.

Looking out on the overcast January day, Teresa saw about a dozen laborers working in the long drive to the *hacienda*. Suddenly they stopped to watch an approaching horseman, an impressive bemedaled figure, erect and soldierly, whose face was hidden in shadow beneath a military cap. Teresa recognized him at once.

Santa Anna lifted his cap, and a cheer rose from the peons. Teresa marvelled at the warmth of their admiration. The day before, they had been cursing the man who had brought them war. As she saw him more clearly, she grew uneasy. In the dim, narrow bedroom at Carmen's café, the general had scared her. On the trip to the Martin's *Casa de la Sol* in a commandeered burro cart, Luisa had chattered on and on about the man. Teresa had hardly listened, her mind still a swirl of emotions and fears. But now she could see that Luisa was not far from wrong: Santa Anna was a strikingly handsome man in his dark way. But there was something in his face she had seen once before, and as he rode closer she knew exactly what it was.

When she had been six years old, she had travelled to Spain with her father so that he might obtain further land grants from King Joseph. The King's brother, the Emperor Napoleon, was visiting the Spanish court, and little Teresa was presented to him. He had looked down at her with disdain, as he looked down at everybody who was below him. And Santa Anna also looked down at everyone with that same expression of arrogant disdain.

Now he stood before her, after being announced with awe by Luisa. "*Senorita . . .*" Santa Anna went to one knee before her chair and drew her soft hand formally to his lips. "Thank you for receiving me." His low voice was heavy with emotion yet he seemed exhausted.

Now, gently, he rose, and as his dark eyes went over her, she understood why Luisa was so obsessed with him. His gaze seemed to pierce right through her clothing and examine every pore of her skin. No man had ever looked at her in this manner before, and it gave her an uneasy and yet proud feeling.

Santa Anna's eyes lingered over her breasts. The soft silk dress clung to her nipples, and the general marvelled at the rise and fall of her bosom as she breathed. Like a ripe fruit, he thought. Ripe and ready for picking.

"Have you rested?"

"No. I've been waiting to be presented to Senor and Senora Martin."

"No need for that, they're gone. I've taken over the *hacienda* and shall have the room right next to yours."

Gone! Teresa was shocked. What did he mean—gone? Gone to heaven, or just gone away? They had not been *gone* when she had been told that her grandmother was safely with them.

Santa Anna watched her and waited, not maliciously but implacably.

"Where have they gone, *senor*?" she asked at last.

"It really matters little to me. I needed proper lodging for the two of us, and they tell me this is the best house in Saltillo."

His indifference annoyed Teresa.

"But it matters to me," she answered passionately, tossing her great cloud of reddish-brown hair. "They are the parents of my intended husband."

"Indeed? They mentioned nothing about a son."

"Well, of course they wouldn't. He was one of the federalist officers who was doubtless fighting you yesterday. Too bad he didn't win."

"Indeed?" Santa Anna said again, mildly astonished at the young woman's sudden vehemence. "Your intended? His whereabouts don't seem to be of great concern to you."

"I beg your pardon," Teresa replied icily. "We are hardly well enough acquainted for me to share with you the concerns of my heart."

"Ah, really?" said Santa Anna. "Still if he is one of my prisoners, that would concern me. For the proper payment, I *could* see to his release. You must certainly long for him in your bed to travel all this distance."

Teresa blushed hotly. "You're quite mistaken!" She paused and then began afresh, her voice charged with indignation:

"From what Luisa said, I expected you to be a gentleman; you're base and vulgar. I have known no man in my life and shall know no man until I am wedded to him under the canons of the church."

Santa Anna smiled. He was ready to take her to bed by force if he had to.

"Virginity is so temporary and useless," he said evenly.

Teresa looked at him steadily, almost insultingly, her soft brown eyes hardening with hatred, then laughed.

"Not to a lady, *senor*. It is her greatest possession and goes only to the highest bidder—her husband."

"A whore can also sell it to the highest bidder."

"If I were a man," she said coldly, "I'd bull-whip you."

"No man alive has ever dared to attempt it. There is none alive who could."

She looked at him bitterly and said, "Then it is a

shame that my father is dead. He would have thrashed you just for the way you've been speaking to me."

"It's obvious that you are not only a virgin, but very naive. Your father's Spanish blood probably ran hot over many more women than just your mother."

She was disgusted with him. She was used to the charm and sophistication of men like Fernando. This uncouth Mexican general was irritating, and she said something she knew would hurt his manly vanity: "You speak of women as if being an object of pleasure was their only purpose in life. What of love? Has any woman ever warmed your cold bed who was not forced there at the point of a bayonet?"

He flushed angrily. Only then did she see how dangerous a man he really was.

"Love is for fools and I find you to be the biggest fool I've ever met. There are ways of making you do my bidding, without this silly game of playing cat and mouse with your virginity."

"You beast!" she cried. "You can force me to your bed, even to bed with every soldier you command, but then you will have to kill me, because I will never yield to you alive."

"Foolish talk of a silly child! You will sleep in my bed tonight."

It was a threat—no, it was more like a promise, and she could not deceive herself that she was dealing with a man who could be talked out of rape. This was a forceful, domineering man! A man such as she had never met before.

They stared at each other like enemies, and he saw in her eyes hatred, bitterness and confusion. But as he continued to look at her, he ignored her expression and admired the new flush of beauty her anger brought to her face. That morning she had been a perplexed little girl in an ill-fitting night dress. In a few hours she'd grown up. Here was an exciting, provocative woman. There was a tilt to her head, the proud, assured poise of a defender of women's rights. And—that tiny waist! that amazing white skin! those liquid brown eyes! With a thousand women like her, he would not need an army, he could vanquish Mexico in a single night. He was becoming so obsessed with her that it was nearing madness.

She said quietly but firmly, "I shall not sleep with you tonight, or any night."

"Damn you, girl!" he roared. "You don't know who you're talking to!" Santa Anna rushed to her chair and yanked her to her feet. His voice was trembling with emotion, yet the tone was intended to convey irony, and was partly successful. But there was nothing ironic in the steely grip of his hands on her shoulders. Even if it cost her her life, she refused to cry out in pain or show her feelings on her face.

"I should have taken you this morning in that whore's room," he said. "It would have been the proper place to teach you humility." He gave a short harsh laugh, then his voice nearly broke as he went on wildly: "I've got to have you, Teresa. You are driving me crazy with passion. You will see that it is not so bad—after the first time—and as God is my witness, you know I've done you no wrong up to this time."

Teresa thought bitterly of the dead coachman, her frightened grandmother, and her own night of terror and fear.

From somewhere deep in her soul, she felt the strength of her father surge forth to give her courage. "I will only go to bed with the man that I marry."

His fingers clawed savagely at her dress and tore at it brutally until the silk hung in shreds about her waist.

"Enjoy your last rape," Teresa shouted, then stopped

breathless, and stood with her round ivory-white breasts rising and falling almost hysterically. She feared that he was out of control, completely irresponsible and therefore very dangerous.

Santa Anna could only stare at her body with wonder. Her breasts were high, perfectly round and uptilted, pointing upwards in a way that moved him greatly. They had been perfectly made for her beautiful womanly figure with its narrow waist and flaring hips. Not even in Veracruz had he seen such lovely breasts. He was mad with desire to touch them, savor their apparent softness, feel their touch against his cheeks and lips. He was used to women fighting to give him his full share of pleasure. Here was a creature that *he* wished to bring to fruition in every possible way. He was impatient to begin.

"Well," demanded Teresa, breathing heavily, "aren't you desirous to tear the rest of the gown away? Isn't that the way with you *common* soldiers?"

Santa Anna reacted as though he had been slapped in the face. He could only stare. Teresa felt heartened. Had she found the right way to hurt him? "You said I didn't know who I was talking to. In San Antonio, they say you *might* be the next president. Well, *Senor Presidente,* go right ahead and act like the mass of the people you are about to rule—uneducated *peons.*" Teresa began to feel more confident of turning the tables, of mastering him, despite the fact he could physically overpower her at any moment.

Never, since the age of fifteen, when he had taken his first woman while a military cadet in Spain, had Santa Anna ever been denied. This wasn't just a girl of eighteen standing bare-breasted before him, it was the strongest field general he had ever encountered. He could attack at once, for she had no apparent defenses. But would it be a prelude to defeat? No, an inner voice insisted, in thirty-six years he had never suffered any form of defeat. He didn't know how it felt and he never intended to.

He reached out and tore the remains of her clothes from her waist and legs. Then, to Teresa's utter amazement, he turned his back and did not look upon her completely nude body.

"You may believe me or not," he said softly, "but I did that only to show you that man is, and always will be, the master of woman. I have no wish to take you by force, no wish to rape you," he lied. "I shall wait for you to come to my bed tonight of your own free will."

He left without once turning back.

Teresa began to shiver from fear and tension and the chill in the air. Oddly enough when she controlled herself, she decided she was partially to blame. Had she dressed properly in a chemise and petticoats, he would never have been so successful in stripping her. She would never make that mistake again—at least not with him.

7

SANTA ANNA RETURNED to his headquarters in a rage such as his officers and men had never seen before. Everyone was at the mercy of his insults and fierce retorts. For an hour he closeted himself in his room poring over the lists of prisoners taken the day before. Even he was amazed to learn that over six hundred government officers and men had been captured. The majority of the men, he knew, would be quick to change their allegiance and serve him in his next battle. The officers? He weeded out their names until he came to the one he sought.

He sat for a moment enjoying the fantastic thought that had come to him as he rode away from the *Casa de la Sol*. He knew it was a daring, even dangerous gamble he was considering, but his cheeks still smarted from his last moments with Teresa. He was ashamed that he had not been strong enough as a man to turn and let himself look upon her full nakedness—and take advantage of it.

Now he must prove to her that he was a man who planned his own destiny. He got out some paper and a quill pen, and began to scrawl out his orders in open, flourishing handwriting.

Carmen Morales, still very disappointed at losing her reward, had gone to the old section of Saltillo that morning to arrange for a brewery to deliver more beer to the café. Most cafés and *cantinas* had had their kegs drained dry the night before and this coming night would be even worse, because the soldiers' drinking would start much earlier.

Just as she stepped out of the brewery, the street was filled with soldiers. Everyone within sight was herded together and forced down the street.

"What is all this?" Carmen demanded shrilly. "I have business to see to."

"You have business all right, old mama," a soldier grunted. "You are to be an official witness to the end of the *patrons* who take the *tortillas* and beans from our bellies and leave us to eat dirt."

"But I am not political," she protested.

"Who is?" he grunted and pushed her back into the crowd.

From the far end of the street, marching up to the high adobe wall at the back of the brewery, came a squad of soliders with a prisoner. He was a young officer, and he marched with fearless calm. It was not until he was pushed against the wall and a blindfold was placed over his eyes that Carmen took a careful look at his bold, handsome face, and then she gasped.

"*Senora,*" a frightened voice whispered at her side, "you know this one?"

"*Si,*" she whispered back, anguish filling her old heart, "he is one of our own." Before she could say another word, the orders were barked and seven rifles went off in the narrow street, shooting down the lone human target.

Carmen's eyes froze on the scene. It seemed to her that she stood forever and watched the body: jerking slightly backward, then the slow collapse of the knees, the head coming forward to hit the chest, the chest falling forward to touch the collapsing knees, and then the final fall onto the dusty street, sending up a spray of fine sand pebbles.

She stood until the street was deserted. She stood until the soldiers came back with a cart to carry away the body. She stood until her fat legs could stand still no longer and forced her to waddle away.

"*Adios,*" she whispered, "*Adios,* Fernando Martin Flores."

A few streets away, Antonio Lopez de Santa Anna began to smile as soon as he heard the rifle shots. He had taken advantage of his victory-given rights, the right of the conqueror. He calmly lay down on his bed and fell quickly asleep. Teresa was not with him yet, but he no longer had a rival.

8

OVER LUNCH, WITH her grandmother, Teresa did not mention the encounter with Santa Anna. Their conversation centered mainly on plans to locate the body of the coachman and see to a proper burial. Only once did they speculate on the whereabouts of the Martins, but Dona Clara was shrewd enough to drop the subject.

"If we are to get safely home to San Antonio," she advised Teresa, "then we must not be political. If, as the servants inform me, the general has taken over this house, then we must be careful to behave properly as guests."

Even if the host behaves improperly, Teresa thought bitterly, but did not say anything.

Teresa went to bed in the afternoon, forcing herself to sleep. She anticipated that her nerves would not let her rest that night with Santa Anna in the next bedroom.

Young Luisa endeared herself to Dona Clara by being resourceful and quick-witted. Using a small rig from the Martin livery, Luisa knew exactly where to go, whom to see, and what arrangements were necessary for the burial. By the end of the afternoon, the two women, with the help of an old parish priest, were putting the coachman to his final rest.

After sunset, Luisa came to Teresa's room with a taper and began to light the lamps. Teresa had been half awake, her nerves jumping, for over an hour. The sound of a horse rushing up the gravel drive had awakened her with a start. She had dressed quickly, not wishing to have Santa Anna catch her in bed or in her nightgown. A few moments later she heard his boots in the hall and the sound of a closing door. She went to the chair by the window and sank into it with a sigh of relief. She was growing drowsy there when Luisa entered.

"If you please, Dona Teresa, may I help you dress for dinner?"

"I am dressed, Luisa. If the general dines formally, he will have to excuse me."

"It is not the general, *senorita*. It is your grandmother who made the request."

Teresa cursed herself for not being honest with her grandmother. But how could she discuss such a lewd subject with the old woman? It would have been an embarrassment for them both. But then she realized that she was being naive. The general would have to act like a gentleman with her grandmother present.

Some perverse impulse made her select the frock she had intended to wear upon being presented to the Martins, although its low neckline and short sleeves might give Santa Anna the wrong impression. The brown moire was becoming to her hair and the skirts rustled when she walked. Four stiff petticoats underneath made them flare—and the extra layers of clothing gave her a sense of protection. Her only jewelry was the high tortoise-shell comb holding the tan cobweb of her *mantilla*. Never had she looked lovelier.

When she entered the hall, she stopped in surprise. Santa Anna was just leaving his bedroom. He wore a coat of white moire, breeches of white satin, and white silk stockings. His shoes, gleaming with diamond buckles, complemented the black of his hair, which shone with as many highlights as the gems. There was nothing on his court costume to suggest his rank.

"Will I do?" he asked, with a shy smile.

Teresa's first impulse was to be honest and tell him he was slightly overdressed for a private dinner for three. Her second impulse was to still the first and not set a sour tone for the evening. The second impulse won.

"Very charming," she answered softly.

Luisa stood riveted as though viewing the most handsome being she had ever seen. Santa Anna graciously offered Teresa his arm and motioned Luisa to lead the way with a heavy silver candelabra.

The adobe-walled corridor was as icy as Teresa's heart. A slight draft set the candle flames flickering wildly. It seemed an interminable time that Teresa had to let her hand rest lightly upon his arm. Fortunately her training as a lady carried her proudly through the ordeal.

Dona Clara was already in the brightly lit *sala*, seated regally before a roaring fire. A young boy, in a white jacket and dark trousers, had just served her a crystal glass of *madeira*. As they approached the old woman, Santa Anna bowed low from the waist.

"Grandmother," Teresa said with a twinkle, as she watched the imperious old lady's reaction on seeing Santa Anna for the first time, sensing her approval, "may I present the General Antonio Lopez de Santa Anna, who is our host? General, my grandmother."

For one long instant, they examined each other. There was a challenge in their eyes. The rotund *grande dame* eyed the man, and the man eyed her.

Each realized that the other was far from what they had expected.

Dona Clara, mindful of the fact that this man might soon be the president, extended her bejewelled hand for him to kiss. "De Santa Anna, you said, Teresa?" and then as Santa Anna stood back from her hand, "De Santa Anna family of Jalapa?"

"My grandmother is a walking *almanaque* of old Spanish families in Mexico, General," Teresa said with a laugh. "Her grandfather was once the governor of Coahuila and Tejas before he took his family north to settle San Antonio. Of course, it was known as Villa de Bexar then."

Santa Anna realized that Teresa's chatter was intended as a mask for her emotions. After their scene that morning, he was amazed, and yet pleased, that she was joining them for dinner. And he knew that she would be amazed to know that his attire was not for her benefit, but for that of Dona Clara. He wanted the old lady as an ally.

The casual talk had served a purpose, however, for Teresa was beginning to feel less ill-at-ease in the general's company.

"I was born in Jalapa," he said, accepting a glass of wine from the boy. "But my parents were both born in Spain."

"Ah, yes, I recall that." Dona Clara studied him a moment over the rim of her glass. "Forgive an old woman, *senor*, for a bit of puzzlement. Antonio Lopez de Santa Anna," she murmured, musing over the name. "If your father was Miguel Lopez, why do you affect the name of your mother's family?"

"You are well versed in family history," he said in amazement. "However, the fact remains that it was a marriage never sanctioned by my mother's people. When I was sent to Spain, at fifteen, to enter military school, only my grandfather was powerful enough to get me an appointment. He would only do that if I was entered as Antonio de Santa Anna."

Dona Clara nodded impishly at his explanation. "Well, every family seems to have one marriage that does not set well with either side. I can well remember the look on Don Roberto's face the day our son came home from Spain with Teresa's mother." She laughed, full of the memory. "As a boy in Spain, his worst enemy in school was Helena Rosa's father and to have her as a daughter-in-law was almost too much for him. 'Rosa!' he used to scoff. 'All roses have thorns, but the Rosa family have the most.' "

Santa Anna enjoyed the story immensely. Teresa was glad that her sensitive mother was not present. It was a story that still brought an angry flush to her face whenever Dona Clara told it—and it was told whenever Dona Clara wished to irritate her daughter-in-law.

Further family small talk got them through their wine, and it was now to Dona Clara that Santa Anna offered his arm when dinner was announced.

He acted as if Dona Clara were the hostess and he the guest. And the old woman responded. She kept the conversation light and non-political, eyed the servants to check that the serving was done properly, and generally held reign over the elegantly set table and excellent food.

Between courses, she reached over and patted Santa Anna's hand.

"That young servant girl of yours, Luisa, is a marvel. She will go far, if one can ever shut up her chatter. One look at you, senor, and I understand why Luisa is so entirely enamoured of you. Frankly, I cannot blame her, although she is far below your station. I am sure, if I were forty years younger, and you were not already married, I would see that you soon were."

At first Santa Anna had sat letting his ego enjoy her praise, but then his heart froze at her last remark. She was too knowledgeable or he might have considered denying his marriage. Still, what he was considering would not work until he convinced her he was free.

"Then, there still may be hope for you, *senora*. I have been a widower these past four years."

Dona Clara blinked. For a long moment, during which Santa Anna steeled himself in case she knew the truth, Dona Clara kept silent. Then she patted his hand once more. "Forgive me, General. I am a rude woman. I'll tell you the truth. I was not aware if you were married or not and was fishing for information. I pray you will find another love to replace the one you lost."

"I thank you for your prayers."

A silence fell as the dessert and coffee were served. Dona Clara pondered what topic she should now introduce. She turned the rings on her fingers, smoothed the *mantilla* over her comb, pleated the satin of her skirt, and opened and closed her fan. Finally she glanced up at Santa Anna. He was not looking at her but at Teresa. She didn't need to be told anything further, the prayer was already being answered. It had been a long time since she had seen a man with his heart in his eyes.

Without knowing it, Santa Anna had already won his ally. Dona Clara was already plotting in her devious mind the best possible way of getting Teresa out of her engagement to Fernando and turning her into the wife of a president. The old woman had been the daughter-in-law and wife of a governor, and had always planned for Teresa to be much more than that.

Unfortunately, she became so engrossed with the thought, that she did not notice that Teresa had said hardly a single word throughout the whole meal and had carefully avoided looking in Santa Anna's direction.

9

SANTA ANNA REMAINED below, over brandy and a cigar, when the ladies retired to their rooms. Dona Clara wished to stop for a moment in Teresa's room to speak well of the general, but Teresa said she was very tired and so Dona Clara left her. Teresa immediately shut her door and bolted it.

She returned to the chair by the window and slumped into it like an old woman, thankful that the dinner ordeal was over.

The wind pushed at the draperies and brushed her hot cheeks. It was a gusty night; little hurrying clouds ran across the sky. The moonlight flickered like a candle flame. Another storm was coming.

Tomorrow, she told herself, they must make arrangements to return to San Antonio. They were not prisoners of war, as she now suspected Fernando was. Santa Anna seemed to respect her grandmother, she thought. She would encourage Dona Clara into bullying him into letting them return home. And when Dona Clara wanted something, Teresa knew, she usually got it.

The wind rose, rattling the casements and blowing the mantilla about her face. It moaned in the *piñon* pines at the rear of the *hacienda*. But the sound was not loud enough to drown out a closer sound—a low tap at the bedroom door.

Soft as it was, the sound brought Teresa quietly to her feet. There was no question in her mind but that it would be Santa Anna. She knew the door was bolted; still, for a few seconds, she panicked. The knock came again, still soft and almost surreptitious as if no one else should hear. Teresa did not move. No power in heaven or hell was going to make her open the door or answer him! Then she saw something white slide under the door.

Some little time passed before she could steal herself to move forward and find out what it was. She picked up a note. The handwriting was small and elegant.

"We are in the servants' cabins behind the *hacienda*," it began, without greeting, "the last one on the row. Please see me tonight. Josephina Martin."

She read the note twice; at first she couldn't believe that it was not from Santa Anna and that the Martins were still so close to their former home. It was more than she dared expect. It had to mean that their servants were still loyal to them and could supply her and Dona Clara with transportation without Santa Anna learning of it.

She crept through the darkened house, mindful to stay clear of the still brightly lit *sala*, and let herself out through the dining room and kitchen. Moonlight lay on a wilderness of untrimmed rose vines. The light vanished when a mat of clouds obscured the moon. The darkness then was so complete that she had to wait until her eyes adjusted. She could make out shapes, no more. But soon the moonlight came back, and she made her way out of the vegetable garden onto the path behind the house.

She had anticipated that the note meant exactly what it said: that the cabins were right behind the house. The moonlight came, and vanished again. When it shone, it cast unearthly shadows, elongating and twisting the shapes of the livery stable, barn and root cellar she passed. It was no more than ten o'clock, but as she turned into the cabin row, there was not a lighted window down the entire lane.

She didn't hear any sound of footsteps in the howl of the wind. The instinct that warned her of their approach came from no physical sense, and it came almost too late. The cloud scudded away from the moon, just in time for her to see the sentry and before he saw her. She melted between two cabins, her heart thumping, and she prayed she wouldn't be noticed.

She had not expected soldiers would be on the property, but she understood why they were there. The Martins were prisoners and needed watching. They probably couldn't help her even if they wished to. Still, she had come this far and the last cabin was only four doors away. She waited until the moon again hid its face, and then she slipped from cabin to cabin until she was at the door.

It open immediately at her first light rap and she was pulled into a room illuminated only by the fire on the hearth.

"Thank you for coming, my child," said Dona Josephina, her voice high and sharp and strained. "Come to the fire, your hands are near frozen."

It was a single-roomed adobe structure, bare of furniture save for a double bed, wood table and two chairs. The woman was alone.

"Senor Martin?" Teresa asked.

"That is my second grief," said the woman, bringing the two chairs and setting them before the fire. "He has been like a madman ever since the soldiers put us out of our house, and I have not seen him since we learned that—" Her voice broke and she sank into a chair.

Teresa, puzzled and yet fearing the worst, sat beside the woman and took her hand. Many times, when he had been in San Antonio, Fernando had described to her the beauty and vitality of his mother. Teresa saw none of that. She held the hand of a forty-five-year-old woman who had aged an additional fifteen years in a single day. Her hair was matted and tangled, her face pinched and contorted into a permanent frown. She had become the symbol of all women who, since the dawn of creation, have borne the greatest burden of men's wars—the human anguish of families separated and destroyed. Teresa thought suddenly of the man for whom she had come to Saltillo and risked her life.

"You needn't tell me," she said dully, "I sense your news."

"*Madre de dios,*" the woman cried, "my boy . . . my *bambino* . . . my son. They put him before a firing squad and say that he is a spy. *Dios mio!* Who would he spy for? No one! No one! He was not even a good soldier. His *papa* even had to buy his commission for him. Why? Why did that *hijo puta* do this to my boy?"

Teresa mastered her grief; she must weep later. She felt fairly sure in her heart why the 'son of a whore' had Fernando put to death. It was perfectly clear to her now why Santa Anna had been such a *perfect* gentleman during the dinner party. He had eliminated the competition. Her fury was smoldering; she wouldn't weep for Fernando: she would avenge him.

"Senora," she said softly, "I must get back before I am missed. I am so sorry."

Even as she said the words, Teresa sensed how cold and uncaring they sounded—but Dona Josephina was no longer listening.

"Wait!" she said, sternly. "My son is gone, but my husband is still alive. What can I do?"

Teresa was perplexed. "What *can* I do?" she echoed, wanting to help.

The woman shook her head sadly. "*Si, si,* I understand. You do not know the *hacienda* and would not even know my husband if you stumbled across him in the dark. Still, I fear his state of mind. He wished from me many children, senorita. My ill health gave him only Fernando." For an instant Josephina Martin pulled herself erect with great dignity. "My husband bloomed anew when Fernando first returned from Tejas and spoke so glowingly of you. If not children, he thought, then many, many grandchildren. Don Luis was known to the de Rosa family in Spain and fully encouraged our son to pursue your hand." Then the queenly dignity sagged with grief. "Now there cannot even be grandchildren."

There was nothing Teresa could say. Long moments of silence stretched between the two women. The older woman did not even react when Teresa patted her hand and rose; she just sat staring into the flames, lost in her thoughts.

There was no goodbye, just as there had been no hello. As quietly as possible, Teresa slipped from the cottage and stood for a long time in the cold, gusting wind.

She felt dismal. She couldn't weep a lover's tears of sorrow, because she suddenly knew that she felt none. She could cry over Ferando as a lost friend, because he had been her favorite companion and a joy to be with. But love? His death made her realize what fear had haunted her on the long trip from San Antonio. She didn't even know what love was all about, let alone being in love with Fernando Martin. She felt, at that moment, a great sense of relief and then instantly was overcome with guilt.

She walked back to the *hacienda*, not caring if she was captured by the sentries or not. She realized now she could not count on the owners of this *hacienda* to help her make her escape. She could depend only on herself and must make her own plans.

The lights were still ablaze in the living-room and drew her like a moth. She was no longer afraid of him. She stood in the archway, glaring at him until he looked up from his cigar. He blanched when he saw her expression.

"Why would you want to execute him?" she cried. "He was innocent of your charges."

At such a sudden accusation, Santa Anna's iron control slipped for a moment. His hand trembled as he said nervously, "Of whom do you speak, senorita?"

She laughed contemptuously. "Fernando Martin Flores!"

"I thought as much," he said more calmly. "The moment his report came to my desk, I knew this scene would occur and you would make me the scapegoat because of my . . . ah . . . dastardly manner this morning."

She eyed him coldly and said not a word.

"Dastardly," he repeated, as if she had not heard. "But, in spite of all, *I am at war*!" He waved his hands as though to dismiss the whole subject. "Why do I waste my time? You are a woman and don't understand these things."

"Even a woman can understand death, senor."

"We are speaking of survival, senorita, not death! For several months," he lied, "I considered this man to be a trusted agent and spy for our side. His reports assured me we could march into Saltillo without the loss of a single life. *He lied to me!* He lied against our cause of freedom! Can you understand that?"

"I can understand that his mother weeps for a dead son and I for a husband who will never be."

Santa Anna scoffed. "Senora Martin then joins the mothers of my thirty-six lost men and the government's one hundred and six because of her son's stupidity. As for you, I cannot somehow picture you weeping over somebody you never loved in the first place." His hard eyes held her, as though to force her to accept each and every word.

Teresa had no answer. She was stunned by his knowledge of her. My God, she thought, he can see not only through my clothing at my naked body, but right into my heart and soul.

Santa Anna rose and carefully snuffed out his cigar. He took a few steps forward ready to depart. "Goodnight, *senorita*. I trust you will have a good night with your memories."

10

Luis Martin was tired. He had been tired before, but never like this. On other occasions he had always, after a period of rest, recovered from his defeats and turned them into victories. It was true that never before had he suffered such a loss. A business a man could rebuild. How did one go about replacing a dead son?

That morning he looked little different from the other *peons* working in the barn and livery. He was left to his own thoughts for the men didn't want to disturb him in his grief. Yet that was not all that troubled him. He was concerned about the mood he found himself in; it was as though someone else had climbed inside his body and now told it what to do.

He found himself admiring Santa Anna's fine stallion even though it belonged to the man he hated. It was an extraordinary horse, such as he had never seen before. From the other men, he learned that it was Arabian, for Santa Anna had boasted about it to them and given strict orders about its care. Luis could understand why a man would have such pride of ownership over such an animal, even a deep love.

"Why," he said, with mild surprise, "I can take something away from him that he loves." And suddenly he was overwhelmed by hatred.

He stayed close to the liveryman as the horse was prepared for the day. He had seen the general only from a distance, but he wanted him close at hand when he carried out his plan. He wanted to see Santa Anna suffer. He didn't have long to wait. Santa Anna strode from the *hacienda* and greeted the liveryman with uncommon friendliness. It was a cloudless, clear, crisp day, and the general's mood matched it. He swung easily into the saddle, ready for a brisk gallop.

Luis Martin stepped quickly to the stallion's side and pressed his pistol into its neck. The discharge into its flesh was deafening at such close range.

"*Caramba!*" Santa Anna bellowed. "What the devil!"

The horse faltered. Luis fired again, much closer to the heart, and the stallion screamed out its pain, its front legs buckling. Rage distorted Santa Anna's face as he was thrown from the dying stallion, and this so elated Luis that he momentarily went insane with revenge. He fired four times so fast that all of the shots missed the intended target, Santa Anna.

For a second, the two men eyed each other as the *peons* fled for cover. The heavy beat of the sentries' boots could be heard approaching. Santa Anna had injured his right arm when he fell and was having difficulty drawing his pistol. Luis fired again, more carefully this time, and Santa Anna suddenly found himself on the ground, the world spinning before his eyes. He could feel a hot burning in his arm and side, then a sticky wetness, then nothing.

Josephina Martin had heard the gunfire and came running from the row of cabins. She had feared this might happen.

"Luis! Luis! No!" she screamed hysterically, hurrying to her husband. He stood with a stupid grin of victory on his face. But not for long. A sentry's rifle spat, and Luis felt a sledgehammer blow in his left side. He was spun completely round before he hit the earth. Then the other sentries panicked, fearing their general had been assassinated, and they fired several times indiscriminately. Josephina was hit more than once and fell grotesquely across the body of her dead husband.

Then there was a long silence as the *peons* came out of hiding and stared with horror at the bodies. But the sentries were concerned with only one of them. They gathered over the general, and one soldier opened his clothing to find out if he was alive. They turned pale when they discovered where the bullet had entered— the round, bluish holes through his arm and side still bled. They seemed paralyzed then and unable to decide what to do next.

Teresa had sat by the window throughout the night, still in her dinner frock. She had watched Santa Anna's departure to go riding, and she had seen all that had happened, unable to do more than stare in horror. Watching the soldiers clustered over Santa Anna, she realized she couldn't let him die. His army would turn into a pack of savage beasts without him, and everyone on the *hacienda* would be blamed and slaughtered for his death. She had to do something. So she rushed out into the courtyard, clawing the billowing *mantilla* from her head, her lovely face whiter than the glossy hide of the dead stallion.

"Is he . . ." she whispered as she reached the soldiers, "dead . . . ?"

"Nearly," one of them said. "The shot went through his arm and into his side. It looks bad."

She stared down at the wound and swayed dizzily. For a moment, the soldiers thought she was going to fall. But she straightened up stoically, and when she spoke, her voice was quite steady.

"Get him to his room, senors," she said quietly.

The soldiers were impressed by her calmness.

Madre mia! one of them thought, his own knees still shaking. What a woman! The other one—the dead one—would still have been screaming her head off. But not this one.

Four of the men carried Santa Anna up to his bedroom with loving care, while others raced to find the army doctor. The sergeant of the squad remained in the courtyard. He was of *peon* stock himself and sensed how shocked and terrified the people of the *hacienda* must be. With gentle kindness, he ordered the grieving servants to take away the other bodies.

A numb, disbelieving Luisa came to the bedroom and gaped. For once her courage and even her voice deserted her. It was now Teresa who had to be her crutch.

"Help me undress him, Luisa," she said.

Luisa blinked, as though Teresa had suggested something unthinkable.

"Don't be an *asno!*" Teresa barked. "We've got to clean his wounds and stop the bleeding."

Together, they pulled off his clothes and dropped them in a sodden heap on the floor. Dona Clara, after one glimpse of the wounds, went to the kitchen to supervise the boiling of water and tearing of sheets for bandages. After they had made Santa Anna as comfortable as possible, Luisa kneeled beside the bed.

Santa Anna's eyes opened.

"Luisa," he muttered. *"Estrellita.* My little star, you look out for me." He fainted again, never seeing that Teresa was also in the room.

Luisa began to cry. Teresa came and took her hand.

"Don't cry," she murmured. "He wouldn't like it. And I'm sorry I called you a jackass."

Luisa came erect slowly, dabbing at her eyes.

"I was acting like one. He just can't die."

"No," Teresa said grimly, "he can't."

The doctor arrived at last and examined the unconscious Santa Anna.

"*Malo*," he muttered, "*muy malo*. Not so bad if he hadn't lost so much blood. What you have done so far has been to keep him from becoming a dead man." He addressed himself to Luisa, considering Teresa to be too aristocratic and beautiful to be of much practical use as a nurse.

"I'll need some men to help hold him when I probe for the bullet—it must be removed or else gangrene is going to set in. *Senorita*," he said to Teresa, "would you go for the men?" Then to Luisa: "I will need you to stay and help swab the wound as I probe."

Luisa blanched at the thought and nearly fainted.

"You go for the men," Teresa told her firmly. "I'll help the doctor."

"Which ever," the doctor said testily, "but you won't be helping me by fainting."

"Then I won't faint," Teresa said.

And she didn't all through the terrible time that the doctor's instruments probed in the wounds, and Santa Anna's rich Veracruz blood turned the sheets to scarlet. During the worst of it, when her forehead ran with perspiration and nearly blinded her, a cold cloth was gently applied to her face. She looked to her side and into the admiring eyes of her grandmother. That look buoyed her for the rest of the ordeal. Finally, the doctor straightened up triumphantly, the flattened slug of lead held in his forceps.

"Here it is, my worthy assistant!" he said. "Now let us dress the wounds." Teresa steeled herself for more.

When he had finished with Teresa's help, he looked at Dona Clara.

"Senora, you may direct your kitchen to start preparing hot soups and custards," he said. "When the general comes to, my able assistant can feed him. Only food can build back his blood. I'll be at the infirmary if you need me. If not, I'll look in this evening—early."

For an instant, he stared down at the patient. He had been with Santa Anna for fifteen years. In all of the battles they had come through together, he had never had to treat the general for as much as a scratch—until now. He sighed and left.

Teresa sat down trembling now that it was over, and Dona Clara sponged her face again. "I've got to get them started on the soup," the old woman muttered. She looked down at Teresa and added: "You are a real de Alarcon, Teresalita. You do me proud!" Then, before she burst into tears, she fled to the kitchen.

11

LUISA CAME TO sit with Santa Anna so that Teresa
could wash and change her clothing. Her dress was
ruined. That's two dresses the man owes me due to
blood stains, she told herself wryly.

Twice that morning, she dozed off in the chair beside Santa Anna's bed. Finally, Dona Clara sent her
away for a nap and left Luisa with the general.

In the early afternoon, he regained consciousness.
Teresa was back by then and succeeded in feeding
him. Gently, tenderly, she held his mouth open with
one hand and spooned the hot soup in with the other.
He eyed her with open curiosity, but said nothing.
After being fed, he drifted off to sleep, but was awake
again by four o'clock. This time it was Luisa who was
able to get him to take some hot broth and a few
spoonsful of rich yellow custard. He was asleep again
when the doctor came and remained so throughout the
night.

Keeping him alive had now become an obsession
with Teresa. It was all she thought about. Her life
seemed to depend on it. Her humiliating scene with
him now seemed centuries in the past. He was a human being who must live.

Near dawn, he again opened his eyes. Dona Clara
was sitting with him this time.

"Old woman," he whispered. "Are we both dead or alive?"

Dona Clara placed her pudgy fingers across his mouth.

"Hush, senor! You need your rest."

"I don't wish to rest. If I'm alive, I wish to live. I've got to live for the angel who has looked after me . . . do you see . . . ? But I'm married . . . unhappily . . . but still . . . Oh, I am so hot."

Dona Clara examined him closely. He was delirious.

"Say nothing more," she told him. "Sleep!" She thought he was living in his past.

"Sleep? I'll never sleep until I'm next to Teresa. But how?"

"Rest, senor. That will work out."

"Will it?" he worried, the fever troubling his mind. "Maria . . . Maria . . . why do you stand in my way? She is so beautiful . . . I want her so . . . even if you're still alive. Damn you! I'll make her my wife . . . in spite of you."

Dona Clara was on her feet now backing away from the bed. Her first instinct had been correct, he had lied to her at the dinner table. He sensed her departure, but, in his state of mind, thought she was his wife. "Don't leave, Maria! We must have this out! You've not been in my bed for four years . . . why do you hold onto me . . . why do you strangle me . . . ?"

Dona Clara had gone only as far as the hallway. She stood trembling. Her dreams seemed like shattered glass at her feet, and the despair of defeat gripped her heart. She had two choices open to her and each could result in a tragic mistake. She leaned against the door, her shoulders shaking with weeping.

Teresa found her there and put a loving arm around her.

"He isn't—oh, grandmama, he isn't—Oh, no!"

Dona Clara turned to her, controlling herself.

"He lives," she whispered. "He lives. Oh, I'm just letting my nerves get the better of me."

"Go rest now. I'll see to him."

Dona Clara shook her head. "No . . ." she tried to think of an excuse. Until she decided what to do, she didn't want Teresa to learn about Maria de Santa Anna. Help in distracting Teresa came from outside. The courtyard, even the very house itself, was filled with the thundering roll of a great many galloping horses.

"What in the world?" Dona Clara exclaimed. "Teresa, go see to that din. Make them understand that we have a very sick man in this house."

As Teresa hurried away down the hall, the old woman went back into the room. To her relief, Santa Anna was sleeping quietly. She felt his forehead. It was cool—the fever had broken. She bent her head to pray away her evil thoughts. She must not weaken now. She told herself, when you are quite well, senor, we must have a serious talk.

Teresa discovered that the noise came from a long colorful cavalcade that was passing through Saltillo on the way to the *Casa de la Sol*. The horses were caparisoned in bright silks; the straight-backed officers wore matching colors. This was the cavalry of General Martin Perfecto de Cos, who owed his position in the army to one simple fact: he was Santa Anna's brother-in-law. Santa Anna had once said of Cos: "The first mistake of my life was my marriage. The second was that the woman had a brother. I should have checked."

Cos was a constant embarrassment to Santa Anna— on and off the battlefield. His only daring was in the manner that he dressed himself and his cavalry. That they were all expert horsemen, no one could deny. Nor that they were all exceedingly handsome and virile.

But it was also true that they always seemed to be the last to arrive at a battle and the first to leave. Behind their backs, the common foot soliders jeered at them, making crude jokes and holding their hands over their groins for protection. Cos's men thought of themselves as *macho*; everyone else looked upon them as *maricon* or homosexual.

Cos himself was a little queer, but not in the sense of being a *maricon*. His capacity for love could cover no more than a single being—himself. A complete Narcissus, he had little interest in other people.

Cos was in high spirits now because he had heard that Santa Anna had been killed. He jumped from his horse and landed lightly on his feet at the bottom of the verandah steps just as Teresa was coming out of the house.

"Senor," she told him sternly, "please silence your men."

Cos blinked. He was not used to taking orders, especially from a woman. Only one woman had ever been able to intimidate him—his sister. He and Teresa stared at each other, wondering who the other might be, like two fighting cocks, hackles rising. It was just like Santa Anna, Cos thought, to have an exquisite creature around him when he died.

"Senor." It was almost a direct order now. "Silence them or move them out of the courtyard. Have you no decency?"

Cos smiled sarcastically with a flash of his white teeth. "Perhaps the beautiful senorita is the one lacking in decency." He removed his plumed cap and gave a cursory nod of his head. "She is addressing General Martin Perfecto de Cos, who has come to take command of the army and see to the removal of the general's body to his home state."

Teresa said sternly, "It would seem that you are too early on both counts, General. He lives."

"But it cannot be!" Cos gasped. "The courier said he was dead."

Teresa smiled pityingly, as if he were a foolish child.

"I'm afraid the courier was misinformed," she said. "Now will you see to my request? He needs as much rest and quiet as possible."

Cos, at that moment was beyond speech. He clamped his military cap on his head and stormed away to find a field nearby for his troops.

Only when he was back on his horse did Teresa realize how short he was compared to the other riders. Only the plume on his cap brought him up to their height. He was different in other ways. Where they were all as slender as young pines, fair of skin and nearly all golden of hair, Cos had a broad chest and heavy torso, with a dark olive complexion and hair as black as the night.

There was something about the man which disturbed Teresa. She wasn't sure what it was, but instinctively she knew that no one would be safe if Santa Anna died.

She returned to the sick room to report his arrival to Santa Anna, but he was now sleeping peacefully. So she told Dona Clara instead. Ah, de Cos, of course, the old woman thought. It was the name of a very well known old family in Veracruz. Now she knew exactly who was Santa Anna's wife and didn't have to be reminded of General Cos's relationship to Santa Anna. His presence presented her with a new problem.

"You stay with this general," she told Teresa, "and I will see to the other one."

Dona Clara soon found Cos and, for such a self-absorbed man, he was curiously respectful. A frequent visitor to San Antonio, and a secret, avid student of history, he was impressed by the de Alarcon name. He even boasted of the fact that he had been named after Martin de Alarcon, which may or may not have been the truth, for Cos was not above lying to make a greater impression.

He relaxed and hooked one short, but superbly turned leg over the cushioned arm of the *sala's* most comfortable chair. His face was wind-burnt from the recent long ride with his men. He loosened his saber belt and barely succeeded in stifling a yawn.

"Are you tired?" asked the old woman.

"A little."

"A cup of wine?"

"Thank you, no. That would surely put me right to sleep. And speaking of sleep, senora, how long do you think your patient will remain asleep?"

"The longer the better, General. The side wound left a terrible hole which will take a long time to heal."

"Then he still might die?" Cos asked hopefully.

Dona Clara looked at him. She, too, was disturbed by the man. It was not only the way he inquired about Santa Anna's health. It was something deeper. She suppressed a sharp reply and sat opposite him, as if she noticed nothing wrong.

"There is no question that he is still seriously ill," she said, "but I think the worst is over."

"What a waste of my time and backside," Cos said petulantly, "to say nothing of the strain it put on my horses and men."

A sudden idea came to Dona Clara. The man might give her some valuable imformation if she made him talk.

"Oh, my," she gasped, "what of the strain it must be putting on another? I pray the same mistake was not twice made. Oh, your poor sister."

"Of course, of course, Maria. How stupid of me not to have thought of it before!" Cos laughed. "If Maria heard about it, then last night probably saw the biggest celebration my sister has ever held."

Dona Clara pretended to be shocked.

"Forgive me, senora," he said, "I forgot that you would not be a party to what every citizen of Veracruz, regardless of their station, knows. My sister is a total bitch. She did not want Antonio as a husband, any more than he wanted her. To please both families, and lock the Cos and Santa Anna money together, they allowed the bishop to mumble a few words over them and went their separate ways."

"Perhaps they were too young. Youth always thinks of marriage as synonymous with love."

"Hardly young, senora. Antonio had just returned from serving with the Spanish army. He was twenty-six and my sister a year his junior."

Dona Clara was learning just what she wanted to know. "Hardly young," she agreed. "Are there children by this *unhappy* union?"

Cos laughed. "Senora, I do not mean to shock, but there must be union before there can be children."

Dona Clara pretended not to understand. "Are you suggesting that after ten years the marriage goes unconsummated?"

Cos shrugged indifferently. "Naturally, I don't have first-hand knowledge, but that has always been the rumor around Veracruz. Even when he was home all the time as the governor of Veracruz, they lived in two different mansions."

"Well, that can change," Dona Clara said casually. "She might come running to join him when he becomes president."

Cos laughed again, as if the old woman was very naive. "You don't know Maria, Dona Clara, and for your

sake I hope you never do. First, she loathes Mexico
City, the altitude makes her nose bleed constantly. Second, she is very liberal and a free spirit. She goes
about dressed like a Veracruz peasant and is far more
comfortable in the company of her women friends
than with men. She really should have been born a
man, she is so strong-willed and domineering. Our father always claimed that something must have gone
wrong at our birth."

"Your birth?"

"Oh, I failed to mention that we are twins, though
we are really separate children born seconds apart. We
never have been and never will be anything alike.
Really, we are not even good friends."

Dona Clara had heard enough, almost too much.
Cos reminded her too much of her own daughter-in-
law—a born gossip who was incapable of knowing
when to stop talking and which of the family stories to
keep secret.

She rose. "Perhaps I had better check on the general. Will you be staying here with us, senor?"

He shook his head. "I always stay with my men."

"As you wish. If General Santa Anna is awake, I'll
send my granddaughter for you."

As a true *caballero*, he rose gallantly. "I should have
guessed you two were related, Dona Clara, when I met
her. She is a ravishing creature and will make some
man very proud one day."

Dona Clara nodded her head in accepting the compliment, but smiled to herself as soon as she left the
room. Cos had supplied her with just enough information so that she could now predict who that man
might be. Two points in his gossip had greatly excited
her, for either could be used to help Teresa. Bishop
Beltran, in Tampico, was her cousin. If she told him
that the marriage was unconsummated, she was sure

that he could annul it. She was strongly against divorce
in any form, but she was just as strongly in favor of making Teresa a president's wife. If she had to, she would
give Bishop Beltran the second piece of gossip. Maria
de Santa Anna sounded perverted and thus not fit to
receive communion. The annulment could be Santa
Anna's for the mere asking. Now just keep him alive,
she thought.

The arrival of Cos irritated Santa Anna, but everything about Cos irritated Santa Anna—had irritated
him for ten long years. There were just too many
things about the man that were alien to Santa Anna's code. He had even suspected, strongly suspected,
after his marriage, that Cos would have been more
than willing to crawl into his bed in place of Maria.
Santa Anna had even considered letting him attempt
just such a move so that he could kill him and be rid
of him. When Santa Anna was bullied, more really by
the Cos family than by Maria herself, into making
Martin a general, all his suspicions returned. He
flooded Cos's troop with spies and was relieved to learn
that although Martin had many feminine tastes and
qualities, he was not a *maricon*. Even more surprising
was the discovery that his taste in women ran to the
older, stouter, more experienced prostitutes.

From that point of view, Cos's visit had some justi-
cation, Santa Anna thought with a chuckle as he lay in
bed. Saltillo was noted for its ample supply of old, fat,
ugly *putas*.

"A week! A week!" Santa Anna barked at him when
he was getting better. "You've been here a whole week
and have yet to come to me daily for orders."

"It's not my fault," Cos said sullenly. "Your officers
will not listen to me."

Santa Anna didn't blame them. "Because they know

foot soldiers better than you, Martin. What's this I hear about you making them all take a bath?"

Cos shrugged. "They needed it, Tony." Cos was the only officer who dared to be so informal with Santa Anna.

"*Merda!* They need to get back to war."

"Then let me take them back to war!"

Santa Anna smiled at him.

"You can't lead them from the rear," he said. "They'd smell a rat and desert on you."

Cos ignored the accusation as though it had never been made. "They would follow your officers, if your officers were told to follow me. Face up to it, Tony. You're going to be in that bed for a good month. A month! By that time, they will be so lazy and fat from just lying around that they will all look like a mattress tied in the middle with a cord."

Santa Anna had already thought of that and it worried him. His worries made him fret, and when he fretted he swore, and when he swore he was a very bad patient. In just one week, he had worn out the patience of nearly everyone. And he was always at his worst after a visit from Cos.

Dona Clara had learned, after the second visit, when to step in and call a halt to their screaming match.

"Enough for today, gentlemen," she said cheerily, sailing into the room like a ship on the open sea. "It's time for the general's nap."

"Nap be damned!" Santa Anna screeched. "I'm napping my way right out of the presidency!"

Dona Clara didn't know what to say.

"We'll take up this discussion at another time," Cos said cheerfully and left. He really didn't want to return to war or to Monterrey. He had found a woman in Saltillo who satisfied him—and Cos was not easily pleased. It was Carmen Morales.

A week later Santa Anna was in a more reasonable frame of mind. He had discovered it would take him a month longer to regain his strength, and the idleness of his army was costing him several thousand *pesos* a day. He had to decide what to do with his men in the meantime. He could send the army on, under Cos's command, to capture the garrison at Marzapi. It would not be a great victory or a fatal loss, either way. Still, he would protect himself to make sure that it was a victory. While he was making up his mind, he refused to see Cos for several days, which pleased the ladies at the *Casa de la Sol*. On those days he was a perfect patient.

Much of his good temper was due to Luisa. He no longer required round-the-clock nursing, but her habit of sitting by his bed from midnight to sunup persisted. At first, she was nothing more than a watchdog by his unconsicious body. She longed to touch him, to soothe him, to crawl into the bed with him, but feared she might cause his wound to open again. It had opened once, while he was in a rage at Martin Cos, and it took a few hours to stop the bleeding.

So she sat apart from him until she gained enough courage to rest her head on the bed and let her hand lie gently on his thigh. The next night, inch by aching inch, her fingers moved until they found the rod of his manhood beneath the sheet. He was so exhausted that her touch did not register in his brain and he remained lax, although her own desires were easily aroused by the mere feel of him. It was not until two nights later that life stirred in his groin beneath her hand. The soft caress of her fingers worked him up until his maleness was huge and hard.

"Take down the sheet," he whispered. "I'm awake now."

He knew he was still incapable of acting like a man.

It was impossible even for him to sit up without feeling faint. Rolling over and straddling her couldn't be
done—not yet. He was as unsure of how they might be
able to finish what she had started as she was. Of the
hundreds of women he had bedded in the past twenty-
odd years, they had all been taken quite simply without the slightest hint of anything perverse. Knowing
he was the first adult man in her life, Santa Anna expected little more than petting from his *escoba mango*
girl.

She left him that night totally exhausted and mentally confused. With her hands, cheeks, lips and
mouth, she reduced him to a state of weak confusion.
No person, ever before, had used his body in such a
way, and he had to admit he had enjoyed it.

Only with the coming of dawn did the guilt weigh
down on him and make him again a horrible patient.
But that night, when Luisa came to him again, he said
nothing of his guilt feelings. Even when she worked
him over again, he said nothing. He just lay there and
looked down at her—small, fragile, thin, hollow-
cheeked, wide of mouth, freckled—and could feel the
depth of pleasure that she sought to administer to
him. Her dark hair bobbed on her small head, and her
eyes reflected the mystery of what she was about. He
groaned inside himself, thinking: Why don't I accept
that it is Luisa between my legs? Why must I look
down at her face and see the face of another? Do I hate
Teresa and wish to debase her in this way? Or do I
love what Luisa is about and want it to be Teresa in
the same position? Why do I look at Teresa and melt,
when Luisa, who looks like a young boy, can make me
feel this way?

And that night, after Luisa had left him, he didn't
sleep. A jumble of people passed before his eyes—
Teresa, Dona Clara, Cos, Luisa, Colonel Montalbo,

Maria de Santa Anna, Juan Valdez, and Captain Felix Escovarro de Sanchez. In the hour nearest dawn, his thoughts centered most on the last name. He struggled from his bed, wincing with pain at each step, until he reached the desk and found some paper and a quill. His orders to Captain Escovarro had been so carefully thought out already that he wrote swiftly without a pause and was soon finished.

He was just crawling back into bed when Teresa came in with his breakfast tray. He stared at her as if he were seeing her for the first time.

Teresa put down the tray and stared at him in alarm.

"What is it, General?" she whispered. "Are you all right?"

"I just found out something," he muttered. "I just found out, because of your forbearance, that you are quite right. Never go to bed with a man unless you are married to him."

She eyed him suspiciously, as though he had again gone into a delirious state.

"That's right," he continued. "And that's exactly what I intend to do. No more of this black devil ranting and raging. When the time is right, I shall sit and have a long talk with your grandmother, in lieu of your dead father. Then we can plan from there."

Teresa looked at him, her eyes unbelieving, her wide, soft mouth trembling.

"How can you even think this way?" she whispered. "Have you forgotten that you had Fernando put to his death? You are insane with your personal wants."

He grabbed her swiftly and pulled her down into his arms. He kissed her until her hands ceased to beat upon his chest, until she sensed that this was not force but tenderness: tenderness and haunting sweetness, and the love that was not wanting in passion, but that went beyond animal passion, until he was filled up with it—with a warmth like a desert sunset, with a thrill that was like a choir singing in a cathedral, with great and rewarding peace.

He let go of her and she stood up.

"There will be no force," he said. "I only want you as a wife, if you accept me as a husband. Don't say anything now. Just go and think about it."

And Teresa went. He had anticipated that she would, it was all a part of his plan. He had carefully mapped it out as though it was a great military operation. Now he could see Cos that day without flying into a rage; could get his brother-in-law to hand-carry his orders to Captain Felix Escovarro, and then begin to enjoy his convalescence in a state of quiet anticipation.

He never once considered that Captain Escovarro might rebel at such unusual and unmilitary orders.

"My mustache!" Felix groaned. "He's actually ordered me to shave it off!"

"How else can you play the part he desires?" Colonel Montalbo shook his head sympathetically. "But consider that you have a far easier role to perform than I."

"Easy! Easy—"

"If Cos ever learns that I am giving orders on this march, he'll have me shot. You'll at least be safe with Santa Anna at the *Casa de la Sol.*"

"I'll trade you places in a minute. It'll be far easier fooling Cos than it is to bring this about. And why? Why not just a simple courier service, if that is his only intent? Besides, it's taken me five years to grow my mustache this long."

"It will take only five minutes to shave it off," Montalbo said cheerfully.

Escovarro fumed. "I curse the day I ever sat down and told that man the full truth about my background. His memory is far too good, and he sooner or later finds a way to use every scrap of information that crosses his view."

Montalbo only smiled.

Late that afternoon a brown-cloaked friar entered the courtyard of the *Casa de la Sol* leading a dusty little donkey. He carried his tall, muscular frame with a proud poise. His fair face was cleanly shaven, and the dark golden curls of his head looked as though someone had recently placed a soup bowl down on his head and shorn away the excess locks.

The *peons*, working in the courtyard, reverently crossed themselves as he passed, and with simple grace he blessed them in return. Because the *hacienda* housed a sick man, they never once thought to question his arrival.

It was Dona Clara who answered his ring at the front door, and her face beamed with pleasure upon spotting a priest.

"Senora, God be with you. I am Father Felix and have come from the Bishop of Tampico."

"From Bepo?" Dona Clara exclaimed excitedly, clapping her hands together. "How marvelous! He's answering my prayers already!"

Captain Escovarro inwardly gasped. He had almost stumbled into his first error on this mission. Luckily he was a personal friend of the bishop and recognized his nickname.

"Do you realize how silly I feel?" Felix asked grimly, after the fluttering Dona Clara had left him alone with Santa Anna.

Santa Anna gave him a look of mock surprise. "Why, Father, whatever do you mean? Am I mistaken or didn't you once wish for a religious vocation?"

"I knew it!" Felix fumed. "You never forget a thing. But, frankly, I'm at a loss to see the need for such a masquerade."

From beneath the covers, Santa Anna brought out a heavy sheaf of papers and passed them over to the young officer.

Felix looked at him with a puzzled expression. Then silently he began to read. When he was finished, he looked up again.

"The plan seems reasonable enough—if Cos can carry it out."

"That's the whole point, Felix. He might just try to fail so he can blame it on our officer corps. I'm going to make him a great and glorious hero. Once his vanity has tasted victory, I can send him and his kewpie doll horsemen far into Chihuahua and be rid of him."

"And you couldn't accomplish that with a normal courier service?"

"That's what Cos anticipates." Then softly, merrily, he began to laugh. "When Doctor Gonzalez was here today, he dropped a couple of very interesting pearls. No sooner had Cos returned from getting his orders from me than a strange illness befell some of his officers. Gonzalez has them in the infirmary, although he can't quite determine the cause of their aches and pains."

"Is it a yellow illness crawling down their backsides?"

"Hell, no!" Santa Anna exploded. "It's Martin's fear that I'll try to run the battle from this sick bed—which, of course, I fully intend doing. No, you watch. Daily, as the need arises to get information to Cos, these men will get better and return to their outfit. They will have kept a close watch to see who has been running back and forth between headquarters and the *Casa de la Sol*."

"And no one shall have."

"Only a simple country friar and his jackass!"

Felix studied the man with unconcealed amazement.

"There's just a couple of things wrong with that," he said at last. "I can't march into headquarters in this outfit without their recognizing me. And how is the information going to get back from Mazapi?"

"You always see the problems, don't you? That's why I wanted you. But I have already seen to both matters. Doctor Gonzalez's medical orderlies will be the couriers between Montalbo and headquarters. Now you have an orderly—Carlos, isn't it? The two of you, as I recall, attend early morning mass several times a week. The practice shall be continued, except that it will not appear unusual for you as a priest to slip into the confessional closet for a bit of private conversation with Carlos."

"It seems like a lot of drama to make your brother-in-law look good," Felix said drily. "Mazapi isn't really that important."

"Cutting through to the core again, Felix?" Santa Anna had not intended to put all of his cards on the table that early in the game, but he knew Felix Escovarro too well to leave the young officer with only half the reason for his masquerade. "Well, to fully bring you into the picture, I'm going to get married."

"But you are already married!"

"You know that. I know that. Cos knows it—the lady in question does not. Hence, the need to get Cos quickly to Chihuahua after his victory."

"What priest is going to marry you when you are already married?"

Santa Anna smirked. "The one that I created."

Felix's Adam's apple jerked in his muscular throat.

Slowly he put up his hands as though to ward off an unwelcome thought.

"But that wouldn't be a legal marriage, General," he choked.

"Exactly!" Santa Anna said gaily. "However, it's the only way I can get her into this bed."

Felix stiffened, as though he had been struck.

No, he thought, this is wrong. This was against all his sensibilities, his code, his religion. A decent man couldn't help another man to turn a young lady into a—a whore.

"General," he said gently, "I don't think I can do this . . ."

"What the devil!" Santa Anna began.

But Felix went right on.

"It would be a shame, an insult to the church."

"The devil with the church! It will have nothing to do with the church."

"No? The girl and her family might think otherwise. They will believe that . . ." His voice trailed off as another realization hit him. "Oh, no!" he gasped. "It's the de Alarcon girl, isn't it?"

"I thought that would have been obvious," Santa Anna answered icily.

"Then be reasonable, General, please. You were the one who wanted to keep them from harm so there would be no trouble in Tejas. Can't you see the harm it will cause when they learn the truth?"

Santa Anna was smug. "Perhaps they need never learn. Perhaps I shall keep her as my wife. Once I am President, I can make it all legal with a stroke of a pen."

Felix's head came up slowly, and his eyes were bleak and miserable. "Then wait until you are President to marry her."

"I will say this only once, *Capitan*," Santa Anna said

darkly. "As soon as I am able to get out of this bed and stand, a ceremony will be performed. In the meantime we shall see to the Mazapi campaign. You are dismissed!"

Felix started to salute and then realized how foolish that would look. He turned and fled.

All that Dona Clara had learned in escorting Father Felix to Santa Anna's room was that the General was a very close friend of Bishop Beltran, and that the Bishop had sent a priest to see to Santa Anna's comfort and spiritual needs during his illness. She saw it as an answer to her prayers and prepared a comfortable room for him. Then she went to the kitchen to discuss with the cook what manner of dinner they might set before a young priest to loosen his tongue.

All that Dona Clara told Teresa was that a priest had come to stay and talk with Santa Anna. With a thankful prayer to God, Teresa sighed with relief. Never in her whole life had she felt the need for spiritual guidance as she did now. She had been thinking about Santa Anna, and the more she thought the more confused she became. She wasn't ready as yet to discuss the matter with her grandmother. It was apparent to her, with each passing day, that Dona Clara was growing to admire the man more and more, and might advise her according to what she felt in her own heart and not what might be best for Teresa. The priest would be a more detached adviser.

Coming into the *sala* that evening, she introduced herself to him without hesitation. "Good evening, *Padre*. Welcome, even though this is not our home."

As Felix turned from the fire, into which he had been gloomily staring, he noticed her poise seemed to vanish, and for an instant, there was a frightened look in her eyes. Then she recovered, and she addressed him easily and with confidence. "Forgive me if I stared for a moment. Somehow I pictured you in my mind as being slightly older."

She looked at him, awaiting his greeting and blessing. Eyes, like crushed velvet, seemed to melt under the whiteness of her skin—a skin so smooth and white that it was difficult to distinguish between it and the creamy white of her lace *mantilla.* This night a single diamond necklace sparkled at her throat and seemed to accent her swelling round breasts.

She extended her hand to Felix, and he brushed it with his lips. Felix realized that, for the sake of convention, he must speak, but he knew that any words he uttered would be inane and meaningless. He could not think; his mind had suddenly become an immense vacuum, which seemed to be filling with a torrid flood of surging blood, which raced from his temples down to his bare feet. No woman alive had so affected him. The warmth of her flesh still lingered on his lips. He realized that he was still loutishly holding her hand and he quickly dropped it.

"You, senorita, are Dona Teresa, I am sure. The resemblance to your grandmother is unmistakable." He mumbled the words, feeling at once they were not the words a real priest would have used.

Apparently she did not notice his confusion, perhaps because she was still confused herself. "You are correct," she replied, opening her fan. Her eyes were staring again, and she hid them for a moment behind the cobweb of lace and ivory. *Que hombre!* she thought. How did a man such as this give himself to God? All the priests she had ever known were old and fat and grumpy. His face could never be grumpy, although she recalled it had been very sad when she entered. And so tall! She barely came up to his shoulder.

If priests needed to be strong to fight Satan, she mused, then the devil had met his match here.

"And you, Father. How are you addressed?"

Felix stammered and then saw no reason to confuse things with a false name. "Father Escovarro," he mumbled and knew how stiff it sounded. Then he regained his aplomb. "However, my parish is small and I am known as Father Felix."

She laughed. To Felix, it sounded like a breeze rustling autumn leaves. "Your parish is even smaller now, *Padre*. May we, then, too, call you Father Felix?"

Before he could reply, Dona Clara came sweeping into the *sala*. She was queenly and ready again to play the part of the perfect hostess, even for a country priest.

"Here you two are," she said cheerily, "and well met. Now, Father Escovarro, may I offer you a bit of supper?"

He nodded and stood momentarily confused. "I seem to be but one and can think of only this solution." He extended both of his arms. "I will escort you both."

Charming manners, Dona Clara thought, placing her hand on his arm. He just had to come from good breeding, she reasoned. Moreover, if he was under Bepo's charge, he served a true gentleman.

Felix glanced under his lashes without turning his head, and he could see the diamond sparkle at Teresa's soft white throat half hidden by the lace of the *mantilla*. Suddenly he knew that he had never wanted anything in his life so much as to press his lips against that cool whiteness and slowly move his lips up to hers. *Por dios!* He had to stop it and start acting like a priest.

His first test came with the saying of grace. His excellent memory served him well and he repeated, almost word for word, the prayer the Bishop had used the month before in Tampico, when he and Santa Anna had been the Bishop's guests.

"Why," Dona Clara exclaimed, "you sounded just like Bepo."

Felix laughed. He had started to relax into his role. "I'm afraid, Senora, I would get a stern lecture if I addressed His Grace thus."

"Grandmama can get away with it because they are cousins."

Felix was thankful for that gem of information. "I was not aware of that," he said, smiling at Dona Clara. He offered in return a boast he had heard the Bishop make to Santa Anna. "Then you must be aware that we have high hopes of his soon donning the red cap as a Prince of the Church."

"No!" Dona Clara puffed up until her snow white head seemed a radiant crown. "A cardinal! A cardinal in the family! How terribly exciting! You must tell us more."

He shrugged. "It is still mostly speculation, you understand. As the Bishop tells it," and he repeated what the Bishop had told Santa Anna, "when Pope Gregory was elected last year, he was miffed that no New World Cardinal even attempted to reach Rome. Of course, they would have arrived too late to ballot. With the death of the Cardinal from Cuba—and Spain having lost Cuba as a colony—the anticipation is that the red cap will be moved to Mexico."

His account of the Bishop's dinner conversation, the gossip and anecdotes, saw Felix safely through the many courses Dona Clara had prepared.

Never once did he have to resort to lying, even when he complimented Dona Clara on serving a grander meal than her cousin. As he recalled, the penny-pinching curmudgeon provided a very sparse and tasteless meal.

For the first time, Dona Clara frowned with displeasure, and Felix concluded he had gone too far.

"Are we being hypocrites, Father?" she said sharply. "Here we sit in another man's house, eating another man's food, and trying to block from our minds his family's horrible end. This is an ungracious way to end such a pleasant meal!"

Felix's mind raced. "Ungracious?" he said. "Hardly that, senora. The house and food are material things. The former owners no longer have need of them. They are not being used wrongly by you—or the general upstairs. He needs shelter and time to heal his wounds. You should be blessed for caring for him."

The old woman sighed with relief. She had been troubled even before the Martins were gunned down, when they had been evicted from their own home. The friar had convinced her none of it was her fault.

Teresa was glad to be alone with the young friar. She had said very little during the meal, but had hardly taken her eyes off him. Not until the end, when he put her grandmother's mind at rest, did she realize that in spite of his handsome face and virile body, she could look on him as a priest.

"Father," she said softly, her eyes looking down, "I am in need of confession."

Felix froze. The joy of the evening vanished. Since his days in Spain, he had respected the priest's function. Just as he could never perform a fraudulent marriage, so he could not enter the confessional with her and pretend to play the priest's part.

"I am sorry," Felix said carefully. "But I, too, have need of a confessor tonight." Words came from the past to help him. "The sacerdotal soul is a secret place and must be free before it can do God's work." He remembered how Friar Boz had looked in saying that . . . there had been a gentle, understanding smile as if he had realized his words would keep Felix from entering the priesthood for life.

"I understand," Teresa said, although she really didn't. "Can . . . can we at least talk? I am so confused."

He could sympathize with her there. He didn't know what Santa Anna might have said already, or attempted, but he could well imagine. What was it Santa Anna had told him: "She doesn't know I'm married . . ."? He had seen Santa Anna seducing an innocent girl like this before. Of course she was confused. The general was a master at manipulating people. Wasn't he himself a prime example as he sat there in the bulky wool cassock? Suddenly Felix loathed the man he admired. He wanted to help Teresa to escape from Santa Anna, but first of all he needed to know much more about their relationship. He rose and smiled.

"Talk seems to come more easily over a cup of coffee." He offered her his arm. "We can then call it conversation and not confession."

"Here's your dinner," said Dona Clara, coming into Santa Anna's room. Then she added sharply, "General, lie down!," for Santa Anna was half out of bed. "What's got into you?"

She pushed him down on the pillows and tucked in the covers, then set the dinner tray on his lap, and surveyed him with disapproval mixed with admiration. He was not a lie-a-bed, that was for sure. But if he didn't stop taking risks and opening the wound, he might never heal.

"Senora," said Santa Anna, "there is something I must know. What happened after I was shot? Did the sentries capture the man? Who was he?"

Her face clouded. The moment of truth had come too soon. She walked to the *guardaropa* and mechanically straightened the wash bowl and pitcher. When she felt ready for him, she turned and faced him. "Is it worrying you, General?"

"Yes, I've got to know," Santa Anna cried. "The man actually attacked my horse, you know. Was he *loco*?"

She moved back to the bedside and looked down at him. "In his way, yes, he was mad. He was just taking something you loved away from you."

"But why, Senora?"

"The doctor forbade me to tell you," said the old woman. "But I can't lie to you. Since you've asked, it shows your concern. The man was Senor Martin, the owner of this *hacienda*."

Santa Anna gave a sharp sigh, but he waited, as if he knew she hadn't finished.

"A sentry shot him," Dona Clara slowly went on. "His wife got in the way of the fire and was also killed. We saw to their quiet burial the next day."

"Senora—" whispered Santa Anna.

"I know what you seek," said Dona Clara. "Wherein lies your guilt for their deaths? It was, of course, the talk of Saltillo that you ordered their son shot. If it was a military matter, then I cannot sit in judgment on your decision. I don't wish to be political. If you had any other motive, then that is between you and God. What happened in the courtyard was something else. Soldiers, they tell me, are trained animals. These were well trained. They saw their leader fall at the hands of another and were quick to retaliate. And now you know what happened."

Santa Anna's stiff body relaxed and he sank back on the pillows. "It has made it a mite uncomfortable staying on here," said Dona Clara drily. "The servants are in a quandary as to who is still a guest and who is the new landlord. Oh, they've seen to our every need, but the coming and goings rattle them."

"Yes," Santa Anna said softly, wondering how much the woman knew, "the quicker we put their minds at ease the better. Are there any surviving relatives?"

"Only in Spain."

"I'll see that they are contacted and offered a reasonable price for the property."

"Why do you want the place?"

"Don't take my words wrong, senora, but I've long admired it. It is between Mexico City, Veracruz and San Antonio, where all interests seem to be."

"Interesting," observed Dona Clara, "if you are a circus juggler. Mexico City, for your presidency, I can understand. But the reference to San Antonio baffles me."

He was quick to pick up her obvious omission of Veracruz. He was playing with a more crafty cat than he had realized. But he was too good a general to avoid her ploy and give her a chance to get the upper hand.

"You failed to mention Veracruz," he said carefully. "But my interests there are obvious, aren't they?"

"Perhaps," she said, carefully thinking out the words that could not be taken back once they were said, "except you'll have no need for the governorship once you are president."

"Exactly," he murmured. Was that all, or had he been given rope to hang himself? "And then there is my family."

"Oh, yes, I forgot that your mother is still alive. But General Cos isn't in Veracruz, is he?"

He stared at her blankly. "I don't understand. I never said anything—"

"Then I'll make it clear to you," Dona Clara interrupted, in a cold hard voice. "General Santa Anna, although your brother-in-law is a formidable gossip, it was your own babbling which proved you a liar. With my gift for following ancestry trivia, it was quite easy to discover the place of Maria de Santa Anna in your life—and that she is still alive."

There was a shocked silence, and then Santa Anna rushed into an explanation before he lost his courage in front of this formidable old woman.

"The loss of a wife does not always mean that she is buried, senora. It was an unfortunate marriage from the first, and remains so to this day."

"Then start fresh."

Her remark was so unexpected that he turned his head and stared at her, and she caught her breath, for his eyes were as cold and remote as the winter sea. He gave her a bitter laugh. "What do you propose, senora—that I kill her?"

"In a way, yes," she said calmly. "From the information that I have obtained from General Cos, it seems quite possible to have Bishop Baltran annul the union or grant you a divorce without the stigma of Excommunication."

"Well," he stammered, "Martin really did babble and you picked up all the pieces. Still, what is in all of this for you?"

"Isn't that obvious, General Santa Anna? I wish my granddaughter to be the wife of a president."

"What you wish, and your granddaughter wishes, might be two different things, senora."

"That," she said with firm determination, "will be my problem, General. Your problem is to prepare the necessary papers for me to dispatch to Bepo— Bishop Baltran."

Having finally revealed her plan for his approval, she left him to consider it.

Santa Anna lay back still holding the tray of food on his lap. "*Que mujer!* What a woman!," he whispered. "Damn, if only she were forty years younger, I'd turn this into an empire for her."

He picked at the cold food, his hunger already forgotten in the relief at finding the old woman was far more astute than he had thought and could be a useful ally. They both desired the same thing, but for different reasons. Still, he wouldn't be rushed. Either course—annulment or divorce—that she suggested could have serious after-effects in Veracruz. The cumbersome financial entanglement of his family and his wife's, their shared property and holdings, were the very backbone of his revolution. Would the de Alarcon family be as obliging about the use of their money? No, he would have to think this out very, very carefully.

12

"ARE YOU AWARE of what has been going on around here?" Teresa asked, as she poured the rich black coffee into the Martins' best china cups.

"I think so," Felix answered, settling into a chair next to the fire. He added, hating the necessity to lie: "I was already in Saltillo when the Bishop's letter reached me about the General."

She brought his coffee and stood for a moment before the fire. "There was an execution in town, did you know?"

He knew. He had questioned Fernando the night before. He had found him a frightened young man sent to war too soon. The execution order had baffled him at the time, but he had forgotten it in the rush of events since then.

"I'm aware of it," he told her softly.

"Well, *Padre,* that is the cause of my confusion. He was my *novio.*"

The cup and saucer rattled in Felix's hand, and he made haste to put them down on a side table. That the man had been her betrothed shocked him and raised an ugly suspicion about Santa Anna's motive that he preferred not to think about. He tried to remain calm.

"I am sorry," he said in a neutral tone.

She said, her face troubled, "I must sound very un-caring to you." He had thought that he was the one who must sound uncaring. "You see, *Padre*, we had only seen each other twice in our lives. Oh, he was nice enough, and a perfect gentleman, but . . . but . . ." She turned away to stare at the fire.

Felix wondered how he could help her. He wished he knew more about women. "But you began to doubt, is that what you wanted to say?"

She nodded without looking back at him.

"Did these doubts come before or after his death?"

Teresa sank down on the low stool by the fire. "I don't know. I think both. The closer I got to Saltillo, the less I wanted to be here. Marriage would take me away from my home, my family, and it frightened me that they might not like me."

"That all sounds very natural."

"Up to that point, yes. But after his death?" Her head jerked up. "Father, I felt nothing! Nothing at all! I have yet to cry my first tear for him."

Felix knew how she felt then. He had not been able to cry when his brother was killed in a riding accident. It was days before the full realization of death sank in.

"That is not unusual," he said compassionately. "Grief doesn't have a set hour to strike."

"Grief," she said dully. "It is not my grief, or lack of it, that made me ask for confession. It was the feeling of utter relief I felt when I heard that Fernando was dead. Oh, Father, I didn't wish him dead, believe me. But his death freed me from a marriage that I began to dread. That's why I'm confused. Have I sinned?"

"To this point, it sounds as though you have only been human, which is something we all must live with." He stopped then. Why must he play Santa An-na's devil's advocate, when it went against his nature? Or was *he* now sinning? Was it for his own interest and advantage that he wished to know her true feelings? "Perhaps," he added coldly, "you no longer wanted him because you already loved another."

Teresa faced him then. Now she trusted him. For the first time, he sounded like a priest to her, penetrating to the heart of the matter without pretense. Their eyes locked, and she felt the power of his very being enter her soul and give her courage.

"I'm not sure now that I know what love is, Father Felix. That's also part of my confusion."

"That's understandable, Teresa. There are almost as many different kinds of love as there are stars in the sky. We have our love for God and still hold a different, special feeling in our hearts for Mary, the Blessed Mother. Nor is that the same love that we cherish for our parents and grandparents and brothers and sisters. We can love nature, the earth, our homes and even the little personal things we hold dear. I gather that your love for Fernando was more akin to that which we bestow upon good friends and boon companions. But the love of man for woman, and woman for man, is the most difficult of all loves to define. It develops deep in the soul and is felt strongly in the heart if it is true love."

It was even then developing deep in his soul and being felt so strongly in his heart that he knew life would never be the same for him again. In that short evening, she had crawled beneath his skin and taken over every fiber of his being. He had not just fallen in love with her beauty, although he marvelled at it. Her presence gave him comfort, a sense of pleasure and warmth. He longed to touch her, to hold her, to love her tenderly. But he knew it would never happen.

"Thank you, Father Felix," she said softly. "You've helped me to see that I was a hypocrite when I said 'I love you' to Fernando." She averted her eyes and blushed. "I said it after he kissed me . . . my very first time. It was the only time he kissed me."

"And it did not stir your soul?"

She shook her head slowly. "That one didn't, no. But a later one . . . with someone else . . ."

Felix, watching her with growing love, was seized with revulsion. Why did he have to probe into her feelings any more? He thought he knew who this "someone else" was.

"It was," said Teresa after a moment, "it was something I began by detesting." A tremor ran through her body. "Still, I didn't hear bells or see comets in the sky. There was tenderness, though. Yes, I guess that is what amazed me the most. Where before there had been nothing from this person but demands and cruelty, there was now tenderness and compassion."

Felix waited, listening anxiously, afraid she was about to announce her love for Santa Anna. He gave the devil his due for knowing when to change his tactics to win such a prize.

"But," whispered Teresa, "I am not sure that it means love."

"And you must be sure," he whispered fervently. "Very sure." His spirits rose. His earlier fear and forebodings now seemed ridiculous. Teresa was too intelligent to marry Santa Anna without loving him. Santa Anna's wishes, as base as they were, did not matter. Felix, playing Father Felix, had a better chance to plant thoughts in her mind than did Santa Anna.

From the outside, to the *peons* and the soldiers, the *Casa de la Sol* seemed to settle into a quiet routine, but to those living inside, it was hardly the *House of the Sun.* With returning health, Santa Anna grew more arrogant and more demanding: the patient once more became the domineering general. Dona Clara's daily request for his agreement to a divorce got nowhere and they had hostile exchanges. Felix's refusal to stage a false marriage caused trouble between the two men. General Cos's delay in attacking the Mazapi garrison kept Felix running to the church with angry messages that even brought a blush to the face of young Carlos. Luisa's nightly demand for Santa Anna's manhood was draining him, and he knew that he had to get rid of the girl or have an angry confrontation with her he might not win.

Teresa was the only one saved from his grim moods. Like a love-sick young *caballero*, he courted her with sweet words and smiles, and made no further attempts to kiss her. She read to him, and he told her long, amusing stories about his days in Spain and Veracruz. When he wished, Santa Anna could be the most modest and charming of companions—and he now wished.

And to Felix's bitter disappointment, Teresa began to respond to Santa Anna's charm. They ate lunch together in his room, and her light, bell-like laughter could be heard through the upper hall. In spite of her own problems with Santa Anna, Teresa's changed attitude pleased Dona Clara. It made it easier for her to arrange a marriage between them.

One afternoon, Dona Clara was caught unawares while sewing in the windowed alcove off what had been Senor Martin's second floor study. Santa Anna came in to find some writing paper. A bookshelf hid the alcove, so he couldn't see Dona Clara. Instead of returning to his room, he sat at the desk and began to write. He worked for a long time. Dona Clara decided not to disturb him and sat waiting for him to finish. At last he was done and he read through all that he had written. A muffled sigh escaped him. He put his hands to his eyes and rubbed them, as if his head were aching.

Dona Clara didn't wonder at his attitude, concluding that he was at last preparing the divorce papers for Bishop Baltran. She was tempted to emerge and discuss them with him when there was a knock at the door and Luisa entered.

Dona Clara shrank back in her chair. If Santa Anna caught her coquettishly playing hide-and-seek . . . so, she would wait now until both of them left. If would be better to wait until he brought the papers to her.

Luisa approached the general with her usual bounce, swinging her hips in what she thought was a seductive manner, and smiling.

"*Buenos dias,* General," she said, kissing him on the cheek.

Santa Anna did not return the greeting or the kiss.

"Sit," he said curtly, indicating a chair on the other side of the desk.

Luisa sat down and crossed her legs, pulling up her dress to expose her ankle and calf.

"You once said that your reward would be to leave Saltillo," said the general. Then he added, in a voice that chilled Dona Clara's blood, "In exchange for using my *bicho* as your *escoba mango.*"

"Only if you go with me."

"Don't be foolish! You know I am unable to travel yet."

"Then why speak of my leaving?"

"Because I have something I want you to do for me."

Luisa bit her lip. "Where?"

"Tampico."

"*Muy bueno!* That far! I would be too afraid, senor!"

The general's voice was icy. "You would not be alone. Two soldiers would escort you."

Luisa's eyes widened. "That frightens me even more. They will both want to use me."

Santa Anna's hand smacked the desk with a resounding crash. Luisa flinched. "They will have their orders and will carry them out!" Orders, he thought, to make sure she was kept in Tampico for several weeks, no matter what they wished to do with her. He smiled to make his words seem more friendly. "Besides, you will not be gone that long and you are the only one I can trust with this mission."

Luisa slid to the floor and crawled to nestle next to Santa Anna's leg. She pushed his robe away and rested her cheek on his bare knee. Dona Clara frowned disapprovingly.

"My General, I shall miss you so . . . miss every part of you. But Luisa will do as you say."

"Good! You will take these papers to Sergeant Juan Valdez. Do you know him?"

"*Si*," she said sadly. "He is the big one with boils on his face."

"That's right. Now, listen carefully. I do not want you going directly to him at my headquarters. Wait for him and catch him on the streets."

"No need. He is nightly with my cousin at the café."

"That's good. He will know what to do, you don't have to worry. I've made his instructions plain about the delivery of these documents to the right man in Tampico."

Luisa pouted. "If he is to do everything, then why must I go?"

There was silence for a moment; a silence charged with deep feelings. Then Santa Anna said, in a voice so thick with rage as to be almost inaudible, "Because I order it!"

Luisa's courage returned. She rose with an impudent attitude. "I am not one of your soldiers that you can order about. Give me the reason for my going to Tampico."

"Reason be damned!" He grabbed her wrist and twisted until she was down on her knees. "Who in the hell do you think you are?"

"I am your lover—," she choked.

The expression on Santa Anna's face as he glared down at her terrified Dona Clara. "Lover," he sneered. "You are nothing more than the little slut that I let suck my manhood! And if you ever want to see it again, you will do as I say."

The words didn't hurt Luisa as much as they offended Dona Clara. Such vulgarity! He wasn't the gentleman she had thought him to be.

"You just want to get rid of me so you can laugh more with *her*."

"We will do more than laugh!" Looking down at Luisa's jeering face turned up to his, Santa Anna added, "As soon as I get a certain report from Tampico, I'll marry her."

It was a hit, a palpable hit. Luisa was stunned.

"And what of me?" she gasped.

Santa Anna sat looking at her. At last he said flatly, "Your fate is in your own hands. If you still desire what rises between my legs, you will not fail me in Tampico. Need I say more?"

Luisa hung her head and sadly shook it. She would always desire him, no matter how many other women came in and out of his life. He was the only man for her and she would do his bidding.

"Fine." Santa Anna got up. There was triumph in his eyes, and some other emotion that was less pleasant. "Now help me back to room and I might let you play with the *bicho* one more time before you leave."

Dona Clara listened to them go out. She was beginning to see Santa Anna as spiteful and small-minded.

She had got her wish that he approach the bishop, but she didn't feel victorious. Her heart was heavy and she suddenly felt very old. For the first time she wondered if Maria de Santa Anna had stayed out of his bed because he was an animal with peasant tastes and morals. Now she began to doubt that she wanted the same for Teresa.

13

For the next few days, Dona Clara avoided the general. She was in an ugly mood. She stormed about the *hacienda,* berating the servants, quarreling with Father Felix, and reducing Teresa to tears on two occasions by her caustic comments about the amount of time she was spending with Santa Anna—which was increasing daily. Teresa had never seen her grandmother behave so badly. Usually the old woman's foul moods made her as cold as ice or bitterly sardonic. Teresa couldn't imagine what had upset her so much. Now, when Teresa tried to talk to her about the possibility of marrying Santa Anna, it was her grandmother who was unresponsive.

Before long, the old woman's mood affected everyone at the *hacienda.* The women servants were so nervous that they started and shrieked if anyone surprised them. The men servants did their chores quickly and disappeared into the cabin row. Only Santa Anna seemed unaffected, but then he never saw Dona Clara.

But the general did have a visitor. Sergeant Juan Valdez rode into the courtyard—alone—with good and bad news for him. The good news delighted Santa Anna. The forger he had entrusted with producing the documents he required was a fine craftsman. Santa Anna now held title to the *Casa de la Sol* and all other

Martin possessions. But that wasn't all. Beautifully penned on creamy parchment, with the bishop's own seal stamped into the red candle wax, the forger's masterpiece freed Santa Anna from his first marriage. Then there was what appeared to be a personal letter from Bishop Baltran himself, granting Santa Anna the right to marry immediately and wishing his great cousin a happy union, together with a personal note of greeting to Dona Clara. Even the near-sighted bishop would have had trouble disclaiming that it was his signature.

The bad news Santa Anna ignored, as if it didn't interest him. The scrawny soldier, Pedro, had been stabbed to death in a waterfront brawl as he was attempting to sell Luisa to a group of sailors. Luisa had escaped, and Juan Valdez had been unable to find her.

As soon as Juan had gone, Santa Anna sent for Dona Clara. The old woman was in the yard and took her time coming into the house. She had not been eating or sleeping properly, and it showed. She had lost so much weight her clothes no longer fitted her properly.

A tremor ran through her when she saw what Santa Anna held in his hands. She straightened and stood tall. The shawl slipped from her head. A magnificent head still, with loosely bound white hair. Her cheeks were no longer round, but in the planes and hollows of her remarkably unlined face, an ageless beauty still showed.

When Santa Anna welcomed her, Dona Clara's huge dark eyes focused on him. All her strength and determination seemed to have returned.

"Senora, pray let me present to you all the documents you have been harping on for so long. You will find everything quite in order."

True breeding, they say, tells in the end. Dona Clara marched forward without the slightest change of expression, took the papers from his hands and carefully examined them. "How did you obtain them so rapidly?" she said with complete aplomb.

Santa Anna chuckled. "The Church knows how to butter its bread, Senora. Oh, rest assured, the Bishop will be just as quick with requests once I am president. Now, the way is open for us to make the final plans."

"When you write, thank Bepo for his speed," she said calmly. "We are leaving soon for San Antonio, or else I would write him myself."

Santa Anna stopped stroking the documents and stared at her. "Don't you mean that *you* will be returning to San Antonio, Dona Clara? Teresa will be staying here with me." Already he was behaving as if the documents alone gave him title to Teresa.

"*We* are leaving, senor," she said firmly. "The liveryman is seeing to the purchase of a carriage and coachman for me."

"Teresa did not mention this to me," he said quietly.

"She was not consulted."

Nor was he. He said nothing. He continued to watch her. She began to feel the way she had when he first arrived—a prisoner. Then he said, "Of course you realize that the country is at war. You'll need a military pass to return to Tejas."

It was unnerving to her to realize how easily he read her and played on her fear. Obviously her attempt to get away was doomed, but her determination didn't weaken.

"That changes nothing," she told him. "I can no longer sanction this marriage."

"Why not?"

"For reasons of my own which I find good and sufficient," she said curtly.

"Reasons be damned!" he roared. "Who are you to deny me?"

"Who are you to demand?" she said, in a voice that shook despite her efforts to control it.

"Oh, God, if you weren't a lady I would—would—"

"Would handle me like you did poor little Luisa," cried Dona Clara, and Santa Anna heard her laugh. He couldn't believe it and listened again. No, he had been right the first time. She was laughing at him.

Santa Anna turned his back on the old woman so she couldn't see his face—his impotent rage. If only she were a man! He heard her depart and then his rage erupted. He snatched the inkwell from the bedside table, hurtling it at the mirror on the opposite wall. The crash showered the room with broken fragments and blotches of black ink.

He sat there brooding—plotting. There had to be a way to overcome the old woman through Teresa. Turn her against her grandmother! He waited all afternoon for Teresa to come to him. He didn't know that the old fox had taken the chicken out of the coop for protection. Just after her conversation with Santa Anna, Dona Clara had sent Teresa into Saltillo with the cook and liveryman to buy supplies. On their return close to sunset, Dona Clara told her granddaughter that the general was sleeping and shouldn't be disturbed.

Teresa's non-arrival only increased his wrath. By the time a young Mexican girl came to his room with his dinner tray, he was so worked up that he slapped the tray from her hands and began throwing the crockery at her fleeing figure. Teresa heard the noise and decided it would be best for her to put off seeing him until he'd calmed down next day.

That evening everyone was unusually quiet at the dinner table, locked into their own thoughts. Dona

Clara, never one to beg, decided she would beg the next day if Santa Anna would not let them go. But she would not stoop so low as to beg anything from Santa Anna; she would beg Father Felix not to perform the marriage ceremony without her agreement. Felix's thoughts were equally depressed. He had seen Juan Valdez leaving the *hacienda* and had talked with him. Juan had been very open about his mission, because Felix was a captain. He was also proud that Santa Anna was so pleased with the documents he had brought back. But he did not tell Felix that the documents were forged. He assumed Felix would know that. The result was Felix felt he had lost the battle. Now Santa Anna could get a real priest to perform the ceremony.

Teresa's worries had nothing to do with documents, marriage, or Santa Anna. That evening she examined her grandmother's face carefully and it troubled her: Dona Clara did not look at all well.

There was no coffee in the *sala* that night. They all mumbled their excuses and retired to their rooms earlier than usual, glad to be alone.

By midnight Antonio de Santa Anna was drunk—meanly, savagely drunk. He was very quiet about leaving his room, no one in the *hacienda* was aware of what he was doing. *Tequila*, which usually put him into instant good humor, tonight curdled sourly in him. Even on those occasions when he had wrecked whorehouses, he had not felt like this. Then even the shrieking women had been joyous—a challenge to his wanton prowess to see how many he could possibly possess in a single night.

But this silent, brooding, drunkenness was quite different. He felt deserted, deceived, degraded. The desire inside him now was beastly and brutal, mingled with his growing anger. He wanted to bring the old woman down from her high perch. He wanted to force her into granting her permission.

She thinks herself so regal, he told himself drunkenly. She thinks her granddaughter is too good to become my wife . . . Nobody's that good. Who does she think she is? Who does she think I am? God damn her to hell. What does she think I'm made of? This is flesh and blood—as good as Teresa's flesh and blood!

His groin ached with desire. It had been because of Teresa that he had sent Luisa away, and now his need for her left him frustrated. He cried, drunken memory allowing him to recall all the sweetness and pleasure Luisa had given him. Now his sodden tears were for the girl herself, wondering where she was, if she was scared and lonely, if she was thinking of him.

The bottle was empty, so he stumbled back to Senor Martin's liquor *guardaropa* and grabbed another corked bottle of *tequila*. With a vicious jerk, he yanked the cork loose with his teeth and took a long swallow. The liquid burned his throat like acid. He coughed, choked and fell back into the *sala* chair. The room, with its fine furniture and attractive decorations, moved before his drunken eyes. He grinned, then chuckled, ending on almost a devilish cackle. With mocking disdain, he eyed the liquor cabinet again.

"*Adios,* Senor Martin," he whispered sarcastically, as though a ghost had been hovering in the room and he was preparing to exorcize it. "*Adios, Casa de la Sol!* *Buenas noches, Casa de Santa Anna!* You are now mine and forever." He raised his eyes to the ceiling, in the direction of Teresa's room. "And you shall be mine and forever. No one can tell General don Antonio Lopez de Santa Anna what he may or may not do in his own *hacienda*. No one! Do you hear that, old woman?"

He stood up suddenly, no longer wanting his words to be wasted on the silent furniture. He wanted them to be heard by the one person they would have the most impact upon. He stumbled, then straightened up, swearing. But drunk as he was, he traveled straight as an arrow up the stairs and down the dark, silent corridor.

Dona Clara had been unable to sleep. For hours she had sat huddled in her bed, watching the candles burn low and then lighting new ones to take their place. Ever since her talk with Santa Anna, she had had a horrible premonition they had to leave the *hacienda* tomorrow or else she would never leave it alive.

Santa Anna stood in silence outside her door.

If I knock, he mused, I wonder if she'll let me in? He shrugged. He'd get in one way or the other even if he had to break down the door. He rapped gently, then stood back and waited. He heard, after a moment, the swift scurry of bare feet.

Dona Clara slid back the bolt and opened the door a crack. Santa Anna thrust a foot forward, stopping her from closing it again.

"Oh, no!" she whispered. "No!"

Then he was forcing his way inside, grinning evilly at her.

"Dona Clara—" he began.

She leaned forward suddenly, sniffing his breath, then drew back.

"You're drunk, senor!" she hissed. "Leave me!"

"As you were going to leave me? No! They say only drunken men say what is really on their minds. Do you believe that?"

"I have never had to put up with a drunken man, so I would hardly know."

He made a sour face. "What a dull life you must have lived!"

"That is hardly your concern."

"In a way it is my concern," he declared, wagging his head foolishly. "I'm going to make sure that Teresa's life does not end up as dull."

"Senor," she said firmly, "I will not reopen that subject at this hour or in this place. Please go!"

"Go?" he snarled. "I'll tell you where I'll go if we don't settle this matter right here and now. I'll go right down the hall to Teresa's room and do what was my right to do in the first place."

Dona Clara backed away from him now, terror in her eyes. Her white hair hung loose to the middle of her back, soft-curling, and her eyes were big with fright.

"No," she murmured, "Do not ruin her."

His laugh was evil. "Why do *ladies* always feel they will be ruined using what is there for only one purpose? Probably because they've never had a real man put it to good use. Is that your problem, senora? You never really had it?"

The old woman braced herself, her dark eyes flashing. Her arm snapped to her side and then forward. The flat of her palm slapped him so hard that his head jerked back. But he was only momentarily stunned. It was then that she knew she had made a mistake in striking him. It was the excuse he was looking for. His eyes blazed with hatred. The swift thrust of his hands she anticipated, but she was unable to escape. His strong hands, clawing her shoulders, were like fingers of steel. He shook her so forcefully that she could hear her eyeballs rattle in their sockets.

She didn't scream; he didn't curse. Their struggle went on in silence. She was finally able to get her hands up, reaching for his eyes, but he twisted aside,

and her nails dug long furrows down his dressing
gown until they reached the bare skin of his arms. But
he merely tightened his grip and shook her more.
Vainly she scratched his arms and then beat on his
chest with her fists. Slowly, inexorably, she was being
pummelled to near-exhaustion. The air was shaken
from her lungs, but she continued to fight, using her
nails, her hands, even her teeth, until Santa Anna muttered:

"*Ay de mi!* What a fiery *puta* you would have
made!"

"*Hijo de puta!*" she gasped, her strength gone. "The
son of a whore should know such a thing."

Suddenly, he wanted to degrade her completely,
make her common, make her stand in shame. No
man—or woman—dared call his mother a whore. With
lightning speed, his hands closed over the collar of the
flannel nightdress. She heard the sound of tearing
cloth and felt the night air cool upon her skin. Her
first instinct was to cover her nakedness with her
arms; then to match him at his own dreadful game.

She left her arms at her side and drew herself tall
until her back was straight; her head rose to a proud,
regal angle. But she was not Teresa. Santa Anna did
not turn his eyes away.

It wasn't awe that made him stare, it was total
amazement. Her breasts were still full and firm. Her
skin was not ancient and wrinkled, as he had supposed, but had retained its youthful smoothness. A
small woman, devoid of excess fat, but rounded like a
Botticelli model.

For the second time, she saw her error. Her nakedness had not sent him fleeing in shame. There was a
dreadful drunken lusting in his eyes that terrorized
her. Her body deflated into a quaking hulk.

"No!" she whimpered. "Please . . ."

Her plea came dully into his sodden brain. For a moment he had forgotten who she was, what she was. His carnal self had taken over and he had stood gazing at her body with no other interest in mind than savoring its worth. With each passing second it grew more enticing to his drunken, frustrated mind. He lost all connection with time and place, as though the growth being born beneath his dressing gown was no longer controlled by his mind, but was straining to become the master.

He was aware of her turning to flee; partially aware of the speed with which he moved to thwart her, numbly aware of roughly lifting her off the floor and crashing her body down upon the bed. There was that instant when he saw the mouth open and heard the first note of the scream. His hand came down hard on her mouth, forcing the sound back into her throat; and then he was descending, blotting out her body beneath him . . .

With his concentration so intent upon building his own desires to their fullest, he was steadily working himself sober. With each savage stroke, he came nearer and nearer to the full knowledge of what he was doing. Her face was purple so that he was forced to take his hand away before she choked.

Dona Clara was almost incoherent. She gasped for breath. A moment before, when the world was fading fast, she thought she was dying. Now that she could breathe again, she prayed that she would die. But the prayer was in her mind, her lips could only moan. Her whole body was racked with grief and pain. Santa Anna could see her throat quiver with wild, unceasing sobbing, her head thrashing, her white hair sweat-soaked, the sides of her face smacking despairingly against the pillow. But instead of bringing compassion to his heart, her anguish tended only to encourage him. He was the master, the lord, the *macho*. Now she could deny him nothing.

"Stop," she murmured at last, the single word shuddering up from her sobbing throat. When he slowed his rhythmic thrust, she screamed at him: "Stop!"

Santa Anna stop? Not since he was fifteen had he been forced to stop once he had begun. Still, he didn't want her screaming out again. There was nothing else to do. Slowly, without missing a stroke, he brought the pillow over her head and kept it there with his forearms.

Dona Clara tried to struggle, but she was choking under the pillow. And her moans and squirms were an enticement to Santa Anna, helping to build him higher and higher. She was no longer a sixty-year-old woman—someone to be debased—but the sum total of every woman he had ever possessed. He was mad with the all-consuming fire that was exploding in his groin.

When she went limp beneath him, he chuckled, sensing her fire had been quenched before his.

"Fight me," he mumbled. "Fight me to my own finish!"

When she didn't answer him, he hesitated, taking the pillow away. She stared at him with a hatred that would last forever.

"Fight me!" he snarled. She didn't answer, only stared.

He boxed her cheeks back and forth to rekindle her anger. Then he stopped. Her head hung loosely to one side, her eyes staring upward into nothingness.

"Don't play possum, old woman!" He grabbed at her chin and brought her head forward again. The pressure of his fingers caused the lips to part and a horrible gurgle of air escaped from her lungs.

"Dirty bitch!" he cried. "You can't die! You can't do this to me!"

Already the flesh was turning cold beneath him. "Live," he whimpered, "live!" But it was too late.

The burning candles in the *sala* had at first frightened Luisa and she skirted the house to come in by the kitchen portal. No sound came from the room as she inched from shadow to shadow toward it. Instinct told her that the room was empty and at last she went in, noticing the *tequila* bottles and the candles down to their last inch. She extinguished the candles and went noiselessly up the stairs to the second floor.

An hour before, hiding the horse she had stolen in the woods, she had intended to kill Santa Anna. Now, with each step nearer his bedroom, she began to falter and doubt her ability—and wish—to do so.

Her idea had been born out of fear and misery. She had been amazed that neither Juan nor Pedro had attempted a single sexual move toward her during their fast-paced three-day ride to Tampico. Not even when the three of them had shared a grubby room in the coastal city was there even as much as an off-color joke. It had stunned her, but then they had taken her to a waterfront bar and attempted to sell her as a *puta*. She had screamed and fought and clawed until she caused the brawl that cost Pedro his life. Only when he lay dying did she learn that he was only carrying out Santa Anna's orders. In total panic she fled from Juan and went into hiding.

That night she slept under a pew in a church. At dawn, she found her way to the stables and waited for Juan Valdez to come and claim his horse. After his departure, she stole a horse and followed him back. Only on the last day did she lose Juan and take a wrong turning. But then it didn't matter. She was near enough to Saltillo to find her own way back to the *Casa de la Sol.*

The door to the general's room creaked slightly as she carefully opened it and slithered inside. After the darkness of the corridor, she blinked at the candle-light. A new puzzle confronted her—the room was empty. Here, too, the candles had burned down to their last inch. The empty *tequila* bottles downstairs came back to her and she suddenly knew exactly what had been happening there that night.

"I'll cut out his gizzard!" she fumed, flouncing back into the corridor and heading directly to Teresa's room next door. Intending to surprise them, she twisted the knob with great force, but the door was bolted and did not move.

She considered, for a moment, pounding upon it and cursing until they were forced to open it to quiet her.

"Little Senorita Simper-face wouldn't like that, would she?" she said to herself maliciously. "Oh, no! Mustn't let her *dueña* know that she was learning the use of a *bicho*."

Her boyish face crinkled into a devilish grin at a sudden idea. "Why not? Who better to find them strapped together than the *abuela* herself?"

She hurried around the corner into the corridor of the next wing. She had anticipated having to rouse the old woman and stopped short upon seeing a light beneath her door.

Tapping lightly with one hand, she tried the latch with the other. The door gave under her pressure and she was again stepping into candlelight from darkness.

At first Luisa was not quite sure what it was she was viewing. Santa Anna still stood rooted to the floor in numbed bewilderment, his dressing gown still open. That he had just finished having intercourse was ob-vious to her. Her mind wasn't alert enough at that mo-

ment to guess who his partner might have been. All
that she saw was the stricken look on his face.

"General," she whispered cautiously, "what is the
matter?"

Santa Anna turned, slowly, almost as if in pain. He
blinked, trying to bring her face into focus. "Luisa,"
he stammered, "what . . . what are you doing here?"

Her anger for a moment made her forget everything
else. "Not playing *puta* to some sailors, as you ordered," she said violently.

"Oh . . ." That was all he said. He spoke so weakly
that it worried her far more than if he had cursed at
her. She had never seen him like this before and he
frightened her. Sensing that the room held danger, she
quietly pushed the door closed and then looked round.
She saw at last the naked body on the bed.

Her mind told her that it was Dona Clara's room,
but she was not prepared yet to accept it was her body.

"Teresa?" Her question was hardly audible.

He didn't answer, only stared.

With trembling hands, Luisa lifted the pillow and
gasped. The dead eyes were so accusing that her worst
fears were realized. She hated him thoroughly at that
moment, even more so than she had in Tampico.

She closed her eyes and turned her head from side to
side, trying to decide what to do. Was it murder? A
heart-attack? An accident? Her reason screamed at her
what it was. For even her illiterate mind could not
suggest anything else except rape.

She had always known that soldiers found great
pleasure in it. One could not grow up around prostitutes without knowing that. She had even been prepared for Santa Anna to rape her at their first meeting. But she had not been prepared for the
unutterably intense bodily rapture that she had expe-

rienced from him—that exquisite mingling of pain and ecstasy—and that she still longed to feel again.

If he had sinned mortally, then hadn't she as well? There was no doubt about it. They were birds of a feather, craving the same ultimate peak of sexual union. No, he might try to desert her, but her very presence on the scene proved that she was incapable of deserting him.

As though leading a blind man, she took him back to his room and left him sitting in a chair. Returning to Dona Clara's room, she ticked off in her mind what she must deal with. The torn night dress on the floor had to be taken away and a new one found in the *guardaropa* chest. The woman had to be re-gowned, the bed made tidy, her hair smoothed out and the eyes gently closed. The covers had to be pulled up under her arms and her hands left to lie as though in sleep. All had to look natural. Luisa pondered her final problem—the candles. Had they been lit or not when Santa Anna had come to the room? She didn't want to waste time going to question him, reasoning that his drunken mind might not even be able to remember. She decided to leave them burning until they sputtered out, just as it might have happened if the old woman had passed on in her sleep.

Santa Anna was pitiable upon her return. He had been sick all over himself and the room reeked of it. Still playing his nurse, she cleaned him up and prepared him for bed. Then, rekindling the long-dead fire, she carefully burned the night dress and his soiled dressing gown.

Her next errand took her back to the *sala*. She put the *tequila* bottles back in the cabinet, as though they had never been removed; wiped the table dry of any stains; and removed the remains of the candles. She would make it appear that Santa Anna had never left

his room that night, and she would be his alibi until
her dying day—if need be.

"Can you speak?"

The voice was Luisa's, Santa Anna realized. His
head was splitting and he didn't feel like speaking to
anyone.

She had sat beside his snoring figure throughout the
rest of the night and now a pearl-grey dawn was
breaking in the east, and it was time to prepare him.
She had been in the house long enough to know its
timetable. The cook, she knew, would already have a
kettle on the stove, anticipating the arrival of Dona
Clara into her domain. Long before anyone else was
astir in the *hacienda*, the two women, over coffee,
would have planned the three menus for the day. The
old Mexican woman's mixture of superstition and common sense would have her pounding on the Dona's
door in less than a half-hour. Luisa didn't have much
time.

"Can you speak?" she repeated.

"Leave me alone," he grumbled. "I don't feel well."

"You felt well enough last night," she said snidely.

There was an unpleasant silence. He tried to sort
out what was truth, what was nightmare, and then attempted to avoid it all.

"What are you doing here?"

"I told you last night, although you were too far
gone to understand. They were unsuccessful in selling
me as a whore. Your orders failed. I stole a horse and
came back."

"Orders? I issued no such orders. I swear it."

"What good is your oath? You're outside of God's
reach now."

"And what is that supposed to mean?" he said violently.

She couldn't tell him, but he read the answer in her

face. He grimaced, as though reliving the entire nightmare in a single flash of recollection.

"Oh, God!" he cried, sweat broke out across his brow. "What kind of animal have I become?"

Luisa didn't answer. Only he, and he alone, could answer that. She sat looking at him, her pixie face as cold and still as death.

"I suppose she's . . .," he mumbled.

"Yes. The pillow . . . although what came before probably helped," she added coolly.

Santa Anna sank back on the bed, his face ashen, his mouth working, shaping words that never came out.

"I'm ruined!" he finally bellowed, then his voice broke. "They will hang me, Luisa," he mumbled.

She looked at him, and smiled with grim mockery.

"Something like being sold to sailors as a whore, isn't it, General? How does it feel to be in a situation your soldiers can't save you from?"

"Dear God, Luisa! Help me . . ."

Luisa bent forward, her thin lips smiling.

"For a reward, General?"

"Anything!"

He lay very still and waited.

"I've seen to everything," she said softly, but firmly. "It will appear as though she died in her sleep. There is no trace that you drank yourself into a stupor—or did a stupid thing thereafter. I'm ready to say that I returned after dark and spent the entire night in this room."

"So," Santa Anna said heavily, "we come to the price tag."

"Yes, General," Luisa said, "we do. But I am not ready, as yet, to name it."

He feared the worst. She was going to demand a marriage proposal.

"Luisa," he whispered, "I can't offer marriage."

"Did I ask for that—not even a false ceremony!" Luisa said cruelly. He blanched. "Oh, yes, General, it was easy for even little Luisa to learn what Juan was after in Tampico." Then she got up from the chair and walked toward the door. In the doorway she turned. "Marry her," she said. "Marry her today, General—and then make sure your bed is left vacant for me. You will never get rid of me again."

14

Casa de la Sol WAS SHROUDED in grief. The forceful
presence of Dona Clara was much missed. But her
death went unquestioned because of her apparent ill
health the week before. In death she was still able to
affect those whose lives she had touched.

In private Teresa was inconsolable, having lost not
only a grandmother, but her idol and truest friend.
But in public, her breeding and training stiffened her
spirit with a tearless strength. During the funeral mass,
she was the regal lady that Dona Clara would have
wished her to be. Her steadfast courage set an example
for the others.

Felix Escovarro had come to love the old woman as
though she were his own flesh and blood. She had also
been his strongest hope of preventing Teresa's marriage to Santa Anna. He made arrangements for the
parish priest to preform the services, with himself acting as little more than the altar boy.

Santa Anna could feel the anguish inside himelf
now. Never before had he felt his soul to be in such
peril. He had acted like a pagan, brutal and savage. He
vowed never to again let drink and lust combine so as
to overcome his reasoning powers. His grief was not
for Dona Clara, but for himself. An animal quality in

his make-up had been exposed and it sickened him. If he wished to become president, the incident must never be unearthed and he knew that he had to erase it from his mind. Of course Luisa was a threat to him now. She was just the type of pawn who was capable of squirming her way across the chessboard to become a queen. He would have to be very careful of her.

For days, a steady, cold drizzle had been falling. The clouds were slate-gray and ugly, and the gusts that blew over the plains were bitter cold.

Felix sprawled on the couch, his big frame loose-muscled and relaxed, but his face was frowning.

"I want to end it," he said, without looking at Santa Anna.

The general ignored him. Felix had just returned from his morning visit to the church and the news he had received from Carlos was not to Santa Anna's liking. The reports before the general were as bleak as the January weather. He rose and started to pace about the second floor study that had become his retreat since Dona Clara's death. Because his own bedroom was connected in his mind with that horrible night, he now avoided it except for sleeping.

"I want to end it," Felix repeated. "I want to go back to being a solider."

"You said that before. The job isn't finished."

"We will all be finished if we have another day like yesterday," Felix said quietly. "Did you see the desertion figures? What Cos isn't killing with these little battles, fear is. If you don't go back soon, you won't have an army to go back to. Your plan isn't working, General. Cos is beating you at your own game. Let me go back and take command in your name."

Santa Anna looked at him.

"Have you forgotten your other function?" Santa Anna snapped. "Is it my fault that the old woman had to die and cause a mourning period that postponed the marriage? As for the deserters, put a few *pesos* here and there and they will come running back."

"You think that everybody's got his price, don't you?" Felix said.

"Think? I know it!"

Felix looked out of the rain-streaked window, at the drizzle that was changing to sleet, the trees trailing fantastic icicles.

"For soldiers, yes," he said. "For others it isn't always money."

Santa Anna snorted, conveying his contempt.

"In this case you are putting yourself with the others. Well, Felix, you will not have long to wait now. The question has been put to Teresa and I only await her reply."

Santa Anna had amazed Felix since Dona Clara's death. He had been calm, even-tempered, solicitous of everyone's feelings. He'd taken to dining with Felix and Teresa so as to escape Luisa, and he was always kindly and amusing. Felix began to think Santa Anna was really in love, especially when he showed him the documents from the bishop.

"Then why must I wait any longer?" Felix asked. "You have your documents. There is no need for fakery. The parish priest will perform the ceremony when the time is right."

Santa Anna shrugged. "It's not for me to say, Captain. Teresa has taken a great liking to you and will want you present."

"But not to conduct the ceremony."

Santa Anna looked at Felix in mock shock. "When it can now be legal?" He smiled and thought to himself: loyalty was Felix Escovarro's price-tag.

Teresa sat very still in her favorite window chair. She had been thinking for days, but her thoughts went round and round in endless circles. The general told her he must get back to his army, but he wished to marry her first. She knew she didn't love him; not as she now believed love should be. But she tried to reason out which came first, love or marriage. De Alarcon marriages were usually arranged, although her parents' hadn't been. There was no doubt in her mind that her grandparents had been blissfully happy together; she could not say the same for her parents. Even before her father's death, she had sensed the cold indifference between them. So, which form of marriage was really the best?

She was lonely. She was homesick now that her grandmother was gone. The *hacienda* was too empty, with too many bad memories.

"Can I grow to love him?" she whispered, her dark eyes narrowing. She stood up slowly and walked toward the clothes press. "Can I grow to love him?" she repeated as she drew out a dress that Santa Anna was very fond of. She put it on slowly, like a sleepwalker, then made up her mind and went to the study.

Santa Anna and Felix watched her enter, both tense. Teresa looked at the two men for some time before she spoke.

"I'll marry you," she said quietly.

"You'll marry me?" Santa Anna echoed blankly.

"Whenever you say."

"Say?" Santa Anna was suddenly excited, as happy as if he had won a great battle. "I say now, the sooner the better."

"As you wish. Father Felix, it's all right. I don't want a church service anyway."

Felix was stunned. This was happening too fast for

him to follow. "I'll go into town and get the priest."

Teresa laughed. "Whatever for? You are the only priest that I wish to marry me."

"She's right," Santa Anna said. "You're the man for the job."

Felix looked at Santa Anna. He was trying to think of something to say, words to express a disgust that was bottomless. But in the presence of Teresa, he was unable to say anything or do anything.

Santa Anna silently congratulated himself on the wisdom of his plan. He had baited the trap with the bride-to-be and the false priest would be unable to worm free.

Felix, hating himself, begged off joining them that evening for their wedding dinner. "I would be a third cog in the wheel," he told Teresa, vainly trying to smile pleasantly. Santa Anna had pretended to protest, but he was angry with Felix, though he wouldn't show it in front of Teresa. The simple service had been a disaster from start to finish. Felix had mumbled and stumbled over the words, as though to underscore the fact that it was all a mockery against one of the most sacred services of the church. Teresa didn't notice, as she, too, mumbled her replies. She was still unsure that she was doing the right thing, but as soon as the vows were uttered, she knew there was no turning back.

It wasn't until the dinner was half over that she began to relax. Santa Anna was a remarkably different man when in the company of a beautiful woman. He was warm, charming, debonair and gracious. His wit was so stimulating that he heard Teresa laughing freely before dessert. He put her at ease and she grew comfortable in his presence.

He had refused to drink during the dinner, had not attempted to rush things to the only conclusion he had in mind, and gave Teresa the freedom to return to her room alone and quietly prepare herself for her wedding night. Santa Anna had won, there was no need for rushing.

Just as he was climbing the stairs to his own room, the sound of a rapidly approaching horse turned him back. He was on the front porch before the courier was even off his horse.

"General," the soldier gasped, giving Santa Anna a weary salute, "I've ridden direct from Colonel Montalbo. While we have been playing, the government has quietly moved fresh troops up from Mexico City. We'll be overrun by morning."

"Where are General Cos and the horse soldiers?"

The young man, his face streaked with rain and dirt, grinned knowingly. "They haven't been seen since the rain started, General."

"Dirty bastard!" Santa Anna growled. The curse was an excuse to let him quickly sort out his thoughts. He could be a bridegroom and loser, or a general and a winner. The choice was really not his to make, he also had his price. "All right," he barked, "go to the livery in the rear and wake them. Get yourself a fresh horse and have them saddle one for me. Don't wait for me, but go directly back to Montalbo. He's to attack that garrison the moment after you get back. Do you understand?"

"Yes, sir!" he shouted cheerfully, no longer feeling leaderless.

"One more thing," Santa Anna ordered. "As you go back through Saltillo, tell them at headquarters that I'll expect a squad mounted and ready to ride with me within the half hour."

Tired as he was, the soldier would return to the battle with a singing heart. *Viva Santa Anna!*

Santa Anna pounded on Felix's door as he passed

and was already dressing when the young captain entered his room. He quickly told him the news while putting on his uniform.

"I'll go back to town at once," Felix exclaimed, "and get ready to go with you."

"No, you will not," Santa Anna said gruffly. "You will stay right here!"

"Here?"

"Here!" Santa Anna repeated savagely. "Do you think I'm going to leave her alone? If we have to break and run at Mazapi, Bustamente's troops could march on Saltillo by sundown tomorrow. She's a virgin, Felix. The first real virgin that I've ever been able to say was mine. Only a *priest* can protect her and keep her in that state."

"But I am not a true priest."

Santa Anna regarded him with wide-eyed admiration.

"No," he said, "but you are one smart man. You are a respecter of women, and thus trusted by your General. Let me find out differently and I'll track you to the ends of the earth."

Felix nodded.

"You will need to be kept informed," Santa Anna said, returning to business. "I'll take your boy Carlos with me, he can continue to act as our secret courier. You do trust him?"

"With my life."

"Good. Now I must tell her."

Felix was almost smiling as Santa Anna left him alone. She would not be Santa Anna's illegal bride that night. She would be safe. She would remain a virgin. Every time Felix thought about it, his relief grew. This might be his chance to save her. By the time he heard Santa Anna ride away, he was actually grinning.

At first Teresa wasn't quite sure of her emotions.

When Santa Anna entered, she was propped up among her pillows, her hair spread out over her shoulders. Santa Anna stood in the shadows, making no move to come to her.

"I'm not afraid," she whispered.

He went over to her then and she was puzzled by his military uniform, but when he was close she put up her arms and he came into them. She kissed him as he had once kissed her; soft, clinging, full of tenderness.

It was maddening for Santa Anna. She had aroused him at first sight in the bed. Now the soft kisses were driving him to the brink of casting everything aside just to stay with her. A chill stole down his spine, almost like an unwanted ghost in the room. What he had desired in life he had always been able to get—either by guile or force. Now he wanted her so desperately that he quaked. But there was a barrier holding them apart—a barrier stronger than his need to return to the battle. He was being laughed at, mocked and challenged. He had taken something that was not his to take and fate stood by for payment in kind. For once he was going to be denied the chance to sate himself whenever and however he pleased.

As he kissed her, he opened his eyes and saw that she was staring back at him. He shuddered. She possessed the eyes of Dona Clara. Suddenly, convulsively, Santa Anna brought his hands up and broke her grip.

"I'm late!" he said hoarsely. "Tonight I must be with my army!"

Then he turned his back and walked away from her. At the door he did not even pause, but went on down the stairs and out into the wet, cold night. He did not feel the cold, because his heart was already pure ice. By cunning he had gained Teresa; by his own despicable action he might have lost her. The ghost that stood between them was housed in her eyes and he couldn't erase that stare from his memory.

Teresa sat there among the pillows, and stared at the door that Santa Anna had closed behind him.

My wedding night, she thought dully, My wedding night! How long had she been warned by her mother of the dread it would hold? Would it have been a dreadful thing with Fernando? Funny, she mused, his face was no more than a blur in her memory; his image was fading as fast as his life had faded. And would it have been dreadful with Santa Anna? Any more dreadful than his taking her by force weeks before?

Santa Anna? General? How queer, she thought. We are now husband and wife and he is still not Antonio to me. Fernando was Fernando. Father Escovarro is Father Felix. But my husband is still the General. Then suddenly, softly, she began to laugh over this oddity. She laughed very quietly, but her slim body was shaking. It went on and on and she could not stop. It was not until she lifted her hand to her face and found it wet that she discovered that the sounds she was making were no longer laughter. Tears. At last the tears were coming. The pent-up grief was being released to cleanse her mind and spirit. No one was there to see or hear her final farewell to her grandmother. No one was there to see or hear her relief at being spared a wedding night. But the emotions of sorrow and gladness were mingled in her tears.

The attack on the garrison during the stormy night took the enemy by surprise. With the arrival of Santa Anna near dawn, his soldiers rushed beyond the garrison without orders, and drove the government soldiers into a hasty retreat.

Relishing his return to battle after so long, Santa Anna capitalized on the quick victory. With resistance growing less and less, he stormed the state of Zacatecas, won the support of the state of San Luis Potosio with a single battle, and continued his march south. City after city fell as his dream came nearer. It took two months, and four hundred miles, to bring him within sight of Mexico City. His army of supporters was now a legion. The government gave in.

Within the month, he was elected president. He had now been away from his bride for three months, although Luisa had been constantly by his side. He was again poised and confident—and arrogant. Whatever ghost had haunted him, he felt sure it had been exorcised by battle. Leaving Cos to serve as his vice-president, he prepared to travel back to Teresa as His Excellency General Antonio Lopez de Santa Anna, the President of the Republic of Mexico.

BOOK II

Enter the Yellow Rose

15

THE RED ROAN's low-throated snort was the first indication to Sam Houston that there was anything wrong along the lonesome trail.

"What is it, Boy? What ya hear?" Sam asked softly, his hand touching his mount's smooth neck in a soothing gesture.

A whimpered whinny answered. Sam Houston's blue eyes narrowed and his lips tightened, causing the cleft in his chin to pucker. With a flick of the reins, he turned his horse's head and started him through the manzanitas, ducking the whipping branches.

Sam Houston's hand was on the butt of his gun as he cleared the bushes. There was no sound, no warning crackle of underbrush. The red roan's ears pointed stiffly dead ahead. An intermittent flash of the heat lightning that had been playing over the landscape since the approach of sundown momentarily lit up the shadowed terrain.

"God!" Houston spat out and sent his mount crashing through the underbrush.

A pinto pony, trembling with weariness, almost ready to drop, but faithful, stood guard over a fallen rider. A woman, alive—or dead. She lay in the soft turf behind a pine seedling. She was on her back, arms outstretched, with one leg flat on the ground, the other

drawn up with her *alpargatas* heel almost in contact
with the firm golden-brown flesh of her buttock. Her
gray skirt was drawn up, and Houston noted the absence of any undergraments. Houston took her to be a
young girl.

He saw behind her, dangling from the limb of a cottonwood, a scalped human being, a man, the sightless
eyes open and staring with a macabre intentness. His
horse neighed and stamped its feet.

Sam's own eyes were somber as he swung down.
Such sights and tragedies were familiar to him. For
three years, in his teens, he had lived with a Cherokee
tribe; in the War of 1812, he had fought the Creek
Indians. After his wife deserted him in 1829, he again
returned to Indian Territory to live with the Cherokee. He had seen this all before, too many times. But
never had Sam Houston been able to look upon such
horrors without being swept with bitter feelings of revenge. His eyes hardening with resentment he turned
from the sight of the dangling body and examined the
girl again. Her head was hidden in the shadows of the
trees, but he knew what he would find. He steeled
himself to go over to her, but another low whinny
from Boy stopped him. He now heard from down-
wind the sounds the horse had noted.

From somewhere back on the out-of-the-way trail
from which he had come, horsemen were approaching
and in a hurry.

Houston pressed an ear to the hard, cold earth. The
horses were shod. It was not the Indians returning, but
whoever it was, they must not find him with a dead
man and a girl. He was a stranger. He would have no
chance with men who might act first and ask questions afterward.

He also had other reasons for not wanting to be involved in any trouble with the Indians. He had spent

months, traveling thousands of miles, to learn first-hand for President Jackson if the Indians of that territory would help to take Texas away from Mexico.

The Indians, too, might already be listening, so he began to lead his horse farther into the underbrush. As he reached the girl, she suddenly moaned and tried to rise. He was shocked to discover she was still alive. With little time to waste he squatted down beside her. Her scalp was untouched, but there was a line of dried blood from her temple to her chin.

"Are ya alright?" he whispered.

She looked at him dully, her eyes still glazed, and then she fainted again.

Slinging her over the faithful pony's saddle and tying its trailing rope to his own, he was off before the pounding hoofs on the trail behind had come close enough for him to tell how many riders there were.

He made his way through the canyon-head hurriedly, but cautiously. Once beyond it, he did not move ahead on the trail that led straight to Nacogdoches, but swung upward on a wooded, winding, almost obliterated pathway that led behind the rim of the canyon. It twisted backward to join the curving main trail from the blistering prairie. He was unlikely to meet up with any rider along there, and he wanted to think about the puzzle he had found. There were no Indians he knew of who would hang a man after scalping him . . . and then leave a live witness. Well, maybe she could help him solve it.

Not far from the top of the winding pathway, Houston swung down, took the still unconscious girl from the pony and found her a resting place beneath an out-cropping. Only then did he realize that she was a fully mature, deep-bosomed woman, tall, only five inches shorter than he was. Her breathing was uneven, and he lightly touched her high forehead, but there was no fever.

He studied her face for clues as to who she was. The high forehead and cheek bones suggested Indian blood. The raven black hair, however, was not coarse but soft and silky, more like a Mexican woman's. There was also suggestion of Mexican in some of her features, but her nose and chin were almost European. Her skin coloring left him guessing. Not red, or brown or creamy, it was a light golden—yellow—like pure honey scooped fresh from the comb, glinting with innumerable little lights.

Houston stood up, a slight evening breeze making the fringe of his buckskins dance. He took off his coon-skin cap and wiped his brow with its fur, his eyes sweeping the horizon and coming back to rest on the abode town of Nacogdoches, hunkering snugly in the midst of low-lying foothills.

This had been the start of his journey—*La Villa de Nuestra Senora del Pilar de Nacogdoches*—the Village of Our Lady of the Pillar of Nacogdoches. It was the beginning of Tejas and the *el Camino Real*—the King's High Way, the link between the Tejas east and far away southwest. For three generations, the sleepy little town had been all Mexican, a gateway for American settlers. When that gateway to immigration was closed in 1830 by the Mexican government, the face of the village began to change and it became a smuggling center for those who did not have Mexican passports.

Sam Houston did not possess one. His only passport was to "the Tribes of Indians, whether in amity with the United States, or as yet not allied to them by Treaties, to permit safely and freely to pass through their respective territories, General Samuel Houston, a citizen of the United States, thirty-eight years of age, six feet, two inches in stature, brown hair and light complexion; and in case of need to give him all lawful aid and protection."

' It didn't mention Texas and that was why he had to be doubly careful in not running across any Mexican patrols.

"Senor, que esta usted?"

Houston hadn't noticed her eyes open. He looked gently down at her not wanting to scare her after her nightmare experience. But the black Aztec eyes weren't scared. The woman obviously liked what he said— a big muscular man with a deeply tanned face.

"I don't speak no Spanish, miss," he said softly.

A wisp of a smile crossed her sensuous lips. "I am with a little English, Senor," she said. She touched her forehead and winced. "Ouch. The horse, she really threw me."

"Is that what happened?"

She frowned. "All that happened to Emilia, *si*." She shrugged. "Emilia, she was too late to stop the other thing. You saw?"

He nodded. "Indians?"

She laughed. It was rich and throaty. "No Indian, but still savage. This man I do not even know and still they do this to him because of Emilia."

"But why?"

She looked at him as though she couldn't believe he had asked such a foolish question. "Because Emilia go with that one and not with them. I spit on them. Emilia go with no man she not pick herself."

Houston began to understand. But why scalp and hang a man because he won out over you with a whore?

"There must be more to the story than that."

She eyed him carefully, her dark glare sizing him up.

"You no GTT man, right?"

"I don't think so. What is it?"

"Gone-To-Texas man. GTT. The worst. Scum and murderers and thieves. *Gringos* who are wanted men in America and think they are outside the law in Nacogdoches. No, Emilia see you no GTT. But who?"

"Name's Sam Houston, miss. I'm just visitin' hereabouts."

She smiled. "Sam is nice name. Me? Emilia Rosa Hoffman Morillo."

Houston laughed. "Well, Emilia Rosa Hoffman Morillo, now that we have established that, are you all right?"

She looked at herself. "Let me see: two feet, two legs, two hands, two arms, two ears, two eyes." Then she chuckled. "Two breasts and all else is but one. Emilia all here."

Houston gave a deep laugh. "I should say it is all there." More breasts than he had ever viewed before. "And all in working order."

Emilia had not understood. "Yes, I am working. I'm dancer at the *Cantina del Monte*."

This delighted Houston even more. "They didn't scalp that guy just because you wouldn't dance with him, miss. Are you a lady of the night?"

Emilia's eyes twinkled. "Not all times. But when I do it in the day, I must charge more because I am tired."

Houston could not control his mirth. "You are really something, Emilia Morillo."

She looked at him with the sympathy of a school teacher eyeing a backward student. "No, senor is wrong. Morillo is name of my mother. Hoffman is name of my father, but I did not know of him."

"Is he dead?"

She shrugged. "Who is to know? He came, he knew my mother, he left. I was his only present."

"Hoffman," Houston mused. "Sounds German."

She puffed up proudly. "It is! My own people are old Aztec and later Mexican. My father all German. You see him in me? That is why in the Cantina they call me *Amarillo Rosa*—the Yellow Rose. Is not fitting?"

It certainly was. Houston looked at her approvingly. Aside from her quick wit, she was extremely beautiful. Her eyes were lively and her golden skin glowed with an inner warmth. She was assured and radiant and clearly no man was her master. Houston liked independence in a man or a woman.

In spite of himself, he found he was comparing her with the other women who had crossed his life—and especially Eliza and Tiania. Cool, snobbish, indifferent Eliza—but a woman he could never close out of his heart. And Tiania, a warm love to soothe the chill from Eliza—quiet, demure, a princess of her people. He chuckled to himself, wondering what they would think about being compared with a whore. At times he had looked upon them no differently than he now looked upon Emilia. They, too, were whores in his mind, giving or holding back their womanly favors when it suited them. Each time they went to bed with him, he wound up paying for it in one way or another. At least, he thought, Emilia was honest about it.

"I'm curious," he said. "Why did you ride out after the man if you didn't know him?"

"I was not alone, senor. My bravery is not that great. No, I was with the *vigilantes*, but we got lost from each other."

"*Vigilantes*? Why not the soldiers?"

"You are a stranger. The soldiers are lazy and too easily bribed. Thanks to our *alcalde*, we have law in spite of them. Don Adolfo Sterne tries hard, but there is still much mistrust between his people and mine."

"Sterne? Adolphus Sterne? A Jew?"

"*Si, senor*, he is."

Houston was annoyed with himself. He couldn't
have missed Sterne. Perhaps he had been too careful
and should have mixed more when he first came this
way. Sterne, a rosy little Rhineland Jew and a great
wanderer, had been in Nashville, Tennessee, at the
same time as Houston. He might be very useful now
he was mayor of Nacogdoches.

"It's going to get real dark soon," he said. "Do you
feel it's safe to go into town?"

"It's always safe for the Yellow Rose, senor," she
said with a grin. "No man in his right mind would
wish to kill me. Look what he would miss in so
doing."

"You don't even fear the men who scalped him, do
you?"

She eyed him seriously. "*Si*, I fear them, *senor*. Why
do you think I want the *vigilantes* to capture them?"
Then she smiled. "But how can Emilia fear when she
is with a strong one such as you?" She eyed him again,
as she had done several times. "You are brave, I can
tell. You remind Emilia of the quiet strength of the
raven."

Houston was momentarily stunned. It was the name
his foster-father, Oo-loo-te-ka, Chief of the Cherokee,
had given him—The Raven.

16

Night brought to Nacogdoches the cooling breezes
that accompanied the lightning in the foothills. It was
late when Houston and Emilia rode in, but their arrival didn't go unnoticed. Huddled on the steps of a
dark doorway beside the plaza near the *Cantina del
Monte*, Pablo Herra, sergeant of the local army garrison, followed them with his small, lizard-like eyes. He
knew *Amarillo Rosa*, but not the man she was with.
He noted Houston's deep tan, his strong lithe body,
the way he sat on his horse—and wondered.

By the time Houston was tying up his weary horse
beside the plaza, Herra was already hurrying away.
There was someone who must be informed about this
newcomer, someone who was interested in every
stranger who came to Nacogdoches these days, but particularly one of Houston's caliber.

Stopping only long enough at the *Cantina* to accept
the drink Emilia offered him, Houston untied Boy
again and led the weary horse down the street to the
livery stable. After making sure Boy was comfortable
for the night, he sauntered back up the street to
Brown's Tavern.

"Room," he told the spindle-shanked clerk who
slouched behind the desk. "One with a bowl and
pitcher of water. Got to clean up."

"Travelin' far?" the clerk asked jauntily, as he switched about the battered register.

"Far enough," Houston said, casually signing his name.

"You wantin' a three or four person room to share?"

"No single?"

"Ain't had one in three years. Town's always *purty* full."

"Smallest possible," Houston said, then added quickly: "I could use some hot water, too, if you can rassle it up. Been plumb needin' a good shave two-three days." He reached for the key the clerk was taking from the rack. "Gimmie . . . Reckon I can locate it without you shaggin' up the steps."

He knew the clerk was eyeing him curiously as he moved across the splintery floor and climbed the steps. The same ferret eyes might have widened had they been able, a short time later, to see him at his preparations for meeting the mayor of Nacogdoches.

As no one else was staying in the room yet, he locked the door and took carefully rolled clothes out of one of his bulky saddle bags. One by one, he unfurled them and drapped them about the room to air and lose some of their wrinkles. A half hour later, he examined his face in the cracked wavy mirror with satisfaction, rubbing his hand across his closely shaven lantern jaw. He would do—at least for the time being, and for all he had in mind.

Washing and shaving over, he slipped into a pair of green trousers and a ruffled shirt. Standing before the cracked mirror, he carefully tied his stock, which was so ornately patterned that not even the most flamboyant of eastern dudes would have sported it. After a desultory brushing of a reddish coat, he donned it and went downstairs.

The clerk's small eyes nearly popped from their

sockets. Even the Spanish patricians didn't dress in this rainbow style. It needed a big effort for him to give Houston directions to the Sterne house without laughing.

Some people outside did laugh and make rude comments, but Houston ignored them as though they were not even there. After a five minute walk through cramped streets of rich red adobe huts, he came to a plaza and several wood frame houses. One house, aglow with lights, reminded him of Virginia. It was the only one with a coat of paint. The others, of sound enough construction, were weathered to the same reddish-brown as the earth they stood upon. As instructed by the clerk, Houston counted off the houses from the largest and approached the Sterne house.

A handsome black girl, in spotless white apron and cap, opened the door with a broad smile.

"*Bonsoir, monsieur*," she said.

It surprised Houston to hear French spoken this far west of New Orleans. Before he could work out a reply with the few words of French he knew, a red-faced little man came out to greet him.

"Governor! Governor Houston!" The little man chirped. "I couldn't believe my ears, but it is really you. Welcome!"

Short of neck and wide of shoulders, his shock of white hair beginning to grizzle a bit, Adolfo Sterne looked every inch the man he was—one who got whatever he set out to get. And damn the odds or the method!

Houston beamed. "Well, I understand it's now Mayor Sterne. My congratulations."

With a twinkle in his soft brown eyes, Sterne shrugged his shoulders modestly. "This is now home, so why not help run it?" He winked. "Just like a young man I once knew in Tennessee who went off to

Washington City as a Congressman and made it turn him into a Governor. But enough of my chatter in the hall, come and meet my guests and join us for dinner."

"No, Adolphus," Houston said. "I didn't know you had guests. I'll come back some other time."

"You'll do nothing of the sort," said Sterne firmly. "These are people you should meet and they will be delighted to meet you, Governor."

"My friend," Houston said softly. "I haven't been the governor since 1829."

Sterne frowned. "But how can that be? You were re-elected that year. We even heard about it way out here in the Redlands."

Houston knew that he would have to talk about it, even though it was a part of his life he was trying to forget. "I resigned, old friend. My bride of three months returned to her father and took my interest in that way of life with her."

Adolfo Sterne was a very accomplished man in many respects, but few recognized his greatest gift—knowing when to let a subject drop until later.

"Bosh!" he snorted. "Tonight we'll rejoice at your presence with us, *Governor*. Tomorrow there may be time for the past. Come!"

The living room was a blaze of lights and color. Houston had forgotten that it was so near to the Christmas season—a celebration he had totally ignored for four years. Over the thick china punch bowl, filled with a hot spiced German wine, Houston reacquainted himself with the Sterne family and was introduced to the other guests.

Frau Sterne, "a merry dumpling of a woman" in Houston's eyes, would always remain Frau Sterne to him. Her husband might be able to transform himself into Don Adolfo Sterne and master Spanish, but she clung to her Rhineland dress and manner and speech, although, with close friends like Houston she would use her passable English. Her teenage daughters still looked as if they belonged in the old country. Houston was glad to meet them all again, and then gave his attention to the guests.

Colonel Henry Raguet, a Pennsylvanian of Swiss descent, was a man well past middle age, but of commanding presence. Over six feet, with a square, ruthless face and deep-set eyes beneath craggy, graying brows, he surveyed Houston with a sneer at the corners of his thick lips. Here, Houston knew, was a merchant of great wealth, a man who had set himself up as a czar of the fertile Redlands. Houston was amused to think how upset Raguet would be if he knew his real reason for being in Texas.

The second guest was a few years younger than Houston, but just as tall, and was the epitome of a Spanish patrician. His handsome face, arrogantly aloof and fair for a Spaniard, seldom smiled. Once a flamboyant chaser of senoritas, he had turned quite serious when the death of his eldest brother brought family responsibility.

"Governor," Sterne said, "may I present Don Miguel Escovarro de Sanchez."

Houston smiled gently as he shook hands. "It is my honor, senor," he said. "I had the pleasure of meeting part of your family a month back. You have one of the nicest *rancheros* I've ever laid eyes on."

"Thank you, Governor," Miguel said in halting English, but full of pride. "May God always keep it so."

"Oh," Houston mused, "you mean the war. Well, that shouldn't affect you too much unless Bustamente wins. You have a brother with Santa Anna, don't you?"

"Yes, sir! Felix is a Captain!" Now Escovarro's face

glowed with pride. "Families from all over Tejas have sent sons to help since the capture of Saltillo." Then he frowned. "Except from Nacogdoches."

At these words, Houston saw Raguet's shaggy eyebrows lift to his forehead, as though to warn the young Don that such matters were not conversation for the parlor.

Houston then turned his full attention to the third guest, Raguet's seventeen-year-old daughter—Anna. Her father guarded her jealously and made sure she dressed plainly. This, however, only enhanced beauty. Her clear blue eyes sparkled with fun and her liveliness kept a rosy blush constantly on her cheeks. Her light brown tresses framed a heart-shaped face and a mouth that Houston had once heard described on another girl as a "cupid's bow." That "bow" came slightly open in astonishment at the sight of Sam Houston in his rainbow costume. Before this peacock, Anna felt like a drab hen. Now, with a sweeping gesture, Sam took her hand.

"Miss Raguet, the fairest young lady I've spied west of the Sabine, to be sure!"

Her lips quivered in amusement. She could be grateful for a compliment, but not one so inflated as that. Frau Sterne's eyes grew round in surprise, and Colonel Raguet nervously drew his host's attention to the time.

Houston saw Sterne bristle and sensed that the little Jew tolerated Raguet only because he was the most important citizen in the town. Sterne didn't wait for his servants to announce dinner, but marched his guests into the dining room. It didn't appear to Houston that his sudden arrival had caused any trouble in setting an extra place. He learned later that the place he sat at had been set for Mrs. Raguet, who had sent an excuse for not coming. Her absence did not affect Sterne, but miffed his wife, who took it as an insult. Throughout the meal, she favored Houston with her attention, for he had helped to turn what might have been an uncomfortable dinner party into a success.

Over cigars and coffee, the men discussed everything but the war, Texas, and what should happen to that vast land. No one delved into Houston's reasons for being there, for which he was glad.

When the grandfather clock struck nine, Colonel Raguet rose, as though on cue, and informed his daughter it was time to leave. His parting words were formal and without sincerity, but Houston hoped that Miss Raguet was sincere when she asked him to call.

As often happens, the first guest to leave broke up the party, and soon everyone got up to go. As Senor Escovarro was also staying at Brown's Tavern, he suggested that he and Houston should walk back together. Sterne looked a little hurt at Houston's departure, but made him promise to return for a long chat the next day.

"Men such as he," Escovarro said as they walked across the plaza, "are an asset to this land."

"But not Raguet?" Houston said.

"You can see that in so short a time, senor?"

"I know a little about the man, but I've seen his kind too many times in life."

"Yes," Escovarro answered sadly, "They take up their space on earth and give nothing in return. He is not like Senor Austin, that is for sure. Did you meet him on this journey?"

Houston shook his head. "Nope. Stopped in San Felipe, but he was up-country. Did run into one old friend, though—Jim Bowie."

"Is he well, senor?"

Houston frowned. "Well enough for a man who lost his wife and young'uns. Hittin' the bottle a little too much, though."

"One can hardly blame him," Escovarro said sympathetically. "Speaking of the bottle, senor, may I offer you a drink from one and show you the only marvel this *villa* holds for me?"

"Sounds like a fair offer, senor. That spicy wine did nothing more for me than make me want to pee."

Escovarro laughed. It was the first time Houston had seen him laugh. "That bush looks like it's thirsty, Governor."

Miguel Escovarro was the kind of proud, honest man Houston liked. They had several drinks together in the *Cantina del Monte,* and had a frank talk about war and the future of the land. Escovarro explained how Colonel Raguet continually frustrated his attempts to get help for Santa Anna from the part of the state.

"The man is an imbecile and will ruin—" Escovarro stopped abruptly as an ancient Castilian in soiled linen sat down on the inside of the ring of tables. "Enough of war," Escovarro said excitedly. "Now you will see the only thing that makes my stay in the Redlands a pleasure."

The aged Castilian tucked a battered violin beneath his chin and divided his attention between the music he brought from it and a long cigar. This overture was intended to silence the noisy Mexicans there. Once the Mexicans were silent, they helped to silence everybody else. If any Americans sauntered over from Brown's Tavern and made a lot of noise, the Mexicans glared at them until they quieted down. The entertainment could then begin.

The cantina was the only one in town that offered entertainment nightly and a fandango once a week. It would never have been admitted in the homes of the mayor or Colonel Raguet, but the dancing girls were selected for more than their dancing ability. But once a night the real talent performed—the *creme de la creme. Amarillo Rosa!*

Houston was astonished to find this was the woman he had rescued on the trail. Such was her fame that, when she was about to appear, everyone came pouring out of the smoke-blackened, airless chamber next to the ballroom. For the next fifteen minutes, the beak-nosed crone serving drinks had no customers and didn't touch her own pot of black coffee. A hundred watching men had thought of nothing but the raven-haired Venus, whose act made them deeply excited—and deeply frustrated.

Her partner, a pasty-faced professional dancing man, enhanced her fresh beauty by his very mediocrity. She had a sensual style, and she held a smoke-grey *mantilla* around her shoulders until she was ready to let it swirl outward. Those who had not seen her perform before gasped as she spun round and round, showing off her body. Houston was among the gaspers as her full breasts were revealed. Jugs, he thought, using a Tennessee term. Real, humdinger jugs.

Amarillo Rosa now had her male audience where she wanted it. She waited until there was complete silence in the ballroom before she let her first heel click sound. Then gradually she let click follow click until she developed a strong, rhythmic beat that she matched with her legs and hips. Gracefully her arms swung out and back as the castinets on her fingertips caught up with the beat of heels. Then, to make sure every eye was riveted on her, she allowed her massive breasts to move to the beat.

At that moment the ballroom crowd responded with a roar—"*Oles!*" from the Mexicans, and a mixture of shouts and whistles from the Americans. And as she turned and swayed and swirled and dipped and tapped, the roar in the ballroom increased until it seemed as if

the crowd had reached its loudest level. But her final
leap onto her partner's shoulder, and then her slow,
tantalizing slide down his body, as if seducing him before their very eyes, won an even louder response. She
lay at her partner's feet for several seconds, letting the
noise thunder over her. Then she slowly rose and
stood tall and regal. At that moment, there was not a
man present who would not have given all the wealth
he ever hoped to possess to spend a single night with
her—including Sam Houston.

And as if to show her audience what it was missing,
she took three low, provocative bows to each side of
the ballroom. Her dancing costume was cut so low that
Miguel Cortenoz, the proprietor, rubbed his hands in
glee. The dry throats caused by seeing that much of
her ample breasts would keep the beak-nosed crone
serving drinks for a long time.

Now the noise was unbelievable. Everyone was on
his feet, clapping, shouting and stomping. She now
weaved her way through the throng like a queen
among her subjects. Who would she favor that night
by allowing them to buy her a drink? She was the
thought in each of their minds. The noise abated only
when she paused by the table of Miguel Escovarro and
Sam Houston.

Escovarro was still very excited, Houston mildly
amused. Escovarro had been attempting all week to
get her to notice him, and now it never occurred to
him that the only reason the twenty-four-year-old
beauty had noticed him tonight was because he was
with Sam Houston.

But her selection of Houston and Escovarro was not
pleasing to either faction of the ballroom crowd. The
Mexicans sneered that the "patricians" always got the
best of everything—including *Amarillo Rosa.* The
Americans, mostly roughshod cowboys and men out-

side the law, grumbled and swore at the Yellow Rose for wasting her time with such a duded-up dandy as Houston when there were real men of the world available like thmeselves.

"*Senorita!*" Escovarro gasped, jumping to his feet. "May I please present myself and friend? I am Miguel Escovarro de Sanchez and my good friend is the Governor of Tennessee, Sam Houston."

Her eyes flashed as she looked at Houston. Then, with a seductive smile, she said to Escovarro, "The *senora* will have a drink ready for me, would you be kind enough to fetch it for me?"

Escovarro, his face blushing like a boy's, was off in a flash. With the same grace as if she was still dancing, she took Escovarro's chair and stared mischievously across the table at Houston.

"Governor," she said, with a coy lilt to her voice that sounded as if she were accusing him of some wrongdoing, "I was not aware that I had been rescued by such a dignitary."

He laughed softly, worried about being overheard. "Here I am not a governor, just plain Sam Houston."

She gave him a smile that was radiant, and made every man watching know that his luck had run out for that night—as far as the Yellow Rose was concerned. "There is nothing plain about you, Sam Houston," she said seductively. "And you pose me a real puzzle."

He looked at her, wondering what she meant.

"Don't look so stern," she scolded good naturedly. "Emilia was just trying to figure out if you seemed more of a man to her in buckskins or in your present finery."

The drinks with Escovarro and her performance had put Houston in a reckless mood. "Don't decide," he advised, "until you see the whole product in the raw."

Emilia eyed him for a moment, judging to what extent liquor was doing the talking. Deftly, without anyone seeing, she took a key from beneath her garter and slipped it into his hand. "One invitation deserves another."

Houston murmured, "What about Miguel Escovarro?"

Emilia grinned. "Are you speaking for yourself or for me?"

Houston said gently, "You must know how smitten he is with you?"

"Which one isn't?" she said. "Which one? They wear their purses on their arms so Emilia can see who desires to pay the most for her. *Pesos?* I have more *pesos* than time to spend them." She gave him a self-assured look. "Once, when I was very young, I would dream of this day. Now it is here and I feel nothing. Do you know such a feeling?"

He knew it too well. "Yes," he said, without elaborating.

"Then we are *simpatico*," she said. "I felt it from the very beginning."

"But have done nothing about it until now."

She shrugged and said softly, "You are an easy man to read, *senor*. The women you have probably known are countless . . . still, not a single one have you ever paid for. *Correcto?*"

She had read him well. He not only never had, but had never needed to. During his present journey, he had put women out of his mind, something he would have been unable to do ten years earlier. Emilia was the type of woman you couldn't forget once you got involved with her. Was she trying now very subtly to find out what he was willing to pay? He didn't want to mislead her. He was almost broke. The government owed him nearly thirty-five hundred dollars for his travels in Texas so far.

"You are quite correct," he said slowly, "and way off base. Best you look to Miguel, *senorita*. His purse is much fatter than mine."

"Interesting," she said without emotion, "But it was not to Senor Escovarro I gave a key. Well, here he is back, so we will just have to wait to learn what Governor Houston intends to do with his key."

As if to teach Houston a lesson, she now turned her full attention to Escovarro, smiling radiantly at him and ignoring Houston. When he had finished his drink, Houston rose to leave and the other two didn't press him to stay. Escovarro expressed his regrets, but was obviously pleased. Emilia only smiled.

Houston was in a bad mood by the time he reached Brown's Tavern, had another drink, and retired to his room—or part of a room. The single bed and half of the double bed were already occupied by snoring, drunken cowboys, still fully clothed and booted. Houston was not about to share a bed with one of them in his finery and changed back to the buckskins. Even then he couldn't sleep; the key he had was too tempting.

Near midnight he rose and went back to the cantina, telling himself he needed another drink. He cursed his weakness, knowing a drink was the last thing in the world he wanted. The noise from the ballroom kept him from entering, and he walked round the building to find the back stairway. On the second floor, he wondered how anyone could stay the night there: the din from below was unbearable.

Again he cursed himself, fearing he would barge in and find her with Escovarro. But her door was open and Emilia stood near the window, her hips thrust out as if ready to spring into a dance.

" 'Spectin' someone?" he asked sheepishly.

She took a dangling cigarette from her lips and said very seriously, "One key a night is my motto."

Then he was inside, grinning at her, the key thrust forward in his open palm. With the same lithe movement she had used on the dance floor, she came across the room to snatch the key and close the door.

"One thing, though," he said grimly, "I ain't got—"

She didn't let him finish. She went up on tiptoe, her dark eyes closing. Her arms crept around his neck, and her lips touched his, warm and tender. Her passion for the man was building. There was something about his combination of male hardness and gentleness that had aroused her interest from their first meeting. She had feared she had lost him earlier that evening, feared she wasn't good enough for him. Now that he was there, she thought, I can manage him. She brought her hands down and cradled his face between them, lingering over the caress.

Houston was slower to respond. As a woman she thrilled him, but she was also a whore. He felt passion in his loins, but in his heart—like one of her customers.

He was unsure of his feelings. "Well?" she said, removing herself from his embrace.

"Yes?"

"I'll get undressed now," she said, taking the *mantilla* from the crown of her hair. "Is that all right?"

Houston blushed. "Do you—do you—?"

"Want to be alone?" She laughed. "It's not necessary, unless it will embarass you."

He turned away, feeling stupid. His mind seethed at his own fumbling ways. He had been with a woman before, many women. Why, he wondered, couldn't he just make love to her as he had to the others?

Emilia watched him as she quickly let down her hair and stepped out of her one-piece dancing costume. So that her body could move freely during the performance, she wore nothing under the gown. With a flick of each foot, the scarlet dance shoes went flying. Their twin thuds against the wall made Houston turn round.

With her hair cascading over her shoulders, her lips slightly curling, she was an entirely different woman. This was not the carefree person he had rescued on the trail, nor the seductive, snake-like performer on the dance floor. She was a different, more private creature now, standing proud and tall—and ready.

She climbed into bed, extinguished the lamp and waited. She had known shy men before and had always been indifferent. But Sam Houston was a man she looked forward to enjoying to the fullest and thus gave him time to overcome his shyness.

Houston slowly undressed, telling himself that, in the dark, it could be just like any other time. He crept in beside her and her silky warmth made him quiver. As if she were his first woman, he was clumsy and awkward as he moved on top of her. He closed his mind to all but what was happening between them.

Emilia was alone in working up any passion. She tried to overlook the fact that he was little more than an emotionless log crashing hard against her breasts. When she tried to kiss him, he ducked and held his head against the side of hers. With no response, her own passion began to fade.

It was all over almost before it began. Houston had been away from a woman for too many months. Suddenly, he knew what the strange churning in his stomach was all about: he felt dirty, cheap and damned. Silently he rose and dressed. He prayed that she wouldn't light the lamp, for he could not bear to face her. The room was suddenly full of the ghosts of other men who had possessed her and it sickened him.

"Aah!" he snorted in self-disgust and left without saying anything more to her.

It was not the first time a man had treated Emilia that way. Passion without love was an essential element of her trade. But with this man, she had hoped it might be different. There was something about him that could make her love him and keep herself for him alone. But he had crushed any such hope. She had seen the look in his eye when she undressed, and she should have put him out then. It had never hurt before to be looked on as a whore, not even when the "good" women sneered at her on the street. Her pride had always protected her. And there would be no outward change in her tomorrow—nothing to reveal how much Sam Houston had wounded her pride.

She lay unable to sleep on the narrow little bed. The smell of him was all around her like a living thing—around her and within, filling up the emptiness of her heart. Am I doomed, she wondered, to never know love . . . ?

Houston jumped at the chance next day to become a house guest of Mayor Sterne's. It removed him from the plaza area and any risk of running into Emilia. He suffered a moment of embarrassment on learning that Miguel Escovarro was joining him and Sterne for lunch, but Escovarro was a true patrician and never made any reference to their adventure of the night before.

That afternoon, after Frau Sterne's maid had cleaned and pressed his peacock costume, he made a social call at the Raguet residence.

Colonel Raguet was in a different mood from the night before and welcomed him warmly. Raguet was no fool. He saw Houston as a powerful man who would make a better ally than an enemy.

Anna was in an anteroom off the parlor, tutoring

two handsome young bachelors in Spanish. Houston envied the young bucks for being so near to her. She was even lovelier in sunlight then she had been in candlelight, he decided. Her brown hair was so light as to be almost gold, yet her lips were not the shell-pink usually found in fair women, but deep rose, and her eyes were sea-blue, soft and velvety. She was slender rather than thin, high of bosom, soft-curving, and she made her simple clothing look worthy of a princess. Oh, to possess a girl like that . . . Houston was doing his best to forget the encounter with Emilia. If anyone could help him to do that, it was Anna.

"She will be finished shortly, Governor," Raguet said, offering Houston a seat. "My daughter, I'm proud to say, is quite a linguist and thus an asset to me. These two young men are clerks that I have hired and it is essential that they speak Spanish."

"I can see where knowing the language would be important, Colonel." Houston laughed nervously. "Perhaps she wouldn't mind taking on an older student."

"Have you a real need for it, Governor?"

"Perhaps," Houston said with a grin. "This land holds many opportunities, I do believe."

Raguet pursed his lips. "But, Governor, what of your interests in Tennessee?"

"Colonel, let's be honest with each other. I haven't been governor in four years, so the title is unnecessary."

"Oh, I'm well aware of that," Raguet said slyly. "There are not too many people who come into this area that I let escape my notice. Especially, when they are a former congressman and resigned governor." He stared challengingly at Houston.

"That's all in the past," Houston said calmly. "Tennessee was exciting when I was a young soldier and a young lawyer. Now that the state has one of its own in the White House, it's growing too fast."

"Could it be that the man in the White House also has his eye on this territory?"

"Oh, I wouldn't know about that," Houston lied. "But it would make a great new state, wouldn't it?"

Raguet regarded him coldly. "If a man is really shrewd about his own future, he should be able to see the folly in such thought. As an independent republic, it would hold out many more advantages."

"Will Mexico ever allow that?"

"Sooner than they might allow Jackson to get his hands on it." The colonel studied him. "Think on it, Governor. Austin would have us stay with Mexico; Jackson would turn us into another Tennessee. Aaron Burr's dream of a western kingdom is hardly dead . . . Ah, Anna is finished, sir. Shall we join her?"

Houston thought carefully about this conversation. The colonel was not the type to make idle chatter about such an important political matter: he was trying to persuade Houston to make a choice.

The next day he left to spend Christmas with Jim Bowie and to get his chance to meet Stephen Austin. He saw himself suddenly as a man in the middle, knowing what the President wanted and what Raguet wanted and soon to learn what Austin wanted. He had to decide which one to jump in with.

Raguet, however, held an extra ace that the others didn't have—a daughter ripe for marraige.

17

THE NIGHT HOUSTON left town, Emilia prepared for her performance with extra care. She was determined to shake off the lethargy she had experienced since he had walked out. She told herself it didn't matter, but in her heart she knew she was wrong. Although she tried not to show it, the town gossips realized something had happened to her, and, although they didn't know what it was, they spread the news.

Miguel Cortenoz was furious with her, along with every male patron who had attended her indifferent performance the night after she had put on such a dazzling display for Houston and Escovarro. It was not her lacklustre dance which infuriated them, but her sudden refusal at the end to join the audience and favor any man for the night. Like a sulking child, she had stormed from the ballroom and locked herself in her room. She didn't cry; she had forgotten how. She just wanted to be left alone and refused to answer the repeated knocks at her door. By morning, her actions had become a subject for speculation in the Mexican part of town—with many vicious tongues ready to give their own interpretation of her behavior.

"*Stupido*!" she told herself many times the next day. "Are you growing sentimental like your mother? Bah! Do that and you will end up with no *pesos* after your body has been used up, because you were too generous. Be like your father, Emilia. Cold and strong and heartless."

By nightfall, she had resolved to dance until they were hoarse from shouting, and then when she made her selection, to state a price that would stifle the shouts in their throats. For ten years she had given her body without real thought of the financial return. Now men would have to be able to afford her. She would make herself rich enough to buy love for herself.

The door opened behind her just as she finished dressing. It had been happening all evening and was beginning to irritate her. "Not again, Estella," she snapped. "Tell your father I am almost ready and will dance."

But it was not Senor Cortenoz' teenage daughter this time. A harsh laugh made her turn round and she blanched at the sight of the two men in the doorway.

"Now ain't she suppun, Harv?" the taller of the two sneered.

"Jes lak frog's fur," he cackled, punching his partner in the ribs.

"What do you want?" she demanded, trying to keep the fear out of her voice.

"Want? Hear that, little brother?" The rangy cowboy sauntered into the room. "The Mex ain't got much of a memory. First she makes it so we an' our money don't look good enough for her. Then she gets her sneakin' little brown brothers to chase the shit out of us. Want? You tell her our wants, Harv."

The bow-legged little man leered at her. "Most everything," he said with a chuckle. "Most anything we decide to make you do to us."

"Get out of here!" she snarled. "Get out before I—"

The tall cowboy moved with surprising speed. One

rough paw grasped the front of the costume, the other slapped her hard. "Dirty little Mex bitch," he growled. "You screwed us up around here."

Emilia didn't scream. She had been beaten before by much rougher men and knew a scream only worked them up.

"Some bitch," Harv Henderson chortled. "She's a cool one, Warren."

"Shut up!" he screamed, giving Emilia such a vicious backhand to the jaw that it sent her sprawling onto the bed. He pounced down on her and began to press himself against her. Emilia was street-wise. She steeled herself and tried not to struggle, just to relax. He could force himself as much as he wanted, but she would remain detached.

Warren Henderson grew angry. At first, he took his spite out on his brother, rather than Emilia. "What in the shit you just standin' there for, fool? Search the damn room! She's gotta have more loot on her than that creep we took away from her an' killed."

"And whose stinkin' idea was it to nab the old fart as he came up the back stairs?" Harv fumed. "Who was it said she'd have more money than the old fart?"

Warren jumped from the bed and glowered at his shorter brother. "I'm goin' fart all over you, if you don't get hoppin' and—"

The door came flying open and Estella Cortenoz stood for a moment in total bafflement, looking from Emilia to the two men. A blood-chilling scream filled the room, even as she turned to flee.

"Get her!" each brother shouted to the other charging to get out of the door first.

"No!" Emilia shrieked, jumping off the bed, "she's done nothing."

By the time she got to the hall, she could see them

at the outside door, vainly trying to pull Estella back inside. Other doors were cautiously opening along the corridor, and she screamed at one of the dance hall girls to go down the front staircase and warn Cortenoz.

She scampered back inside her room, her jaw and brain beginning to shriek with pain. From the dresser table drawer, she took the Colt revolver she had never used before. She heard Estella's final scream followed by a tremendous crashing and thumping down the stairs. She dashed back into the hall, her heart cold with hatred. Frightened faces peered out at her and she screamed at them with contempt as she ran past. There was gunfire outside and flashes of orange lightning illuminated the main doorway. The gunfire could be heard down the narrow alleys and across the flats to the distant rangelands and the darkness of the foothills.

Then the shots ceased as suddenly as they had begun. Emilia rushed outside on the landing, gun in hand. Below her, the brothers stood on the outside stairs. The burly, frog-built one stumbled as Emilia watched, then pitched over the railing, crashing on his face, shirt and vest dyed with blood. The other brother merely grinned sardonically, then Emilia realized he had been shot, too. He coughed, and blood boiled from his grinning lips. He sat down on the stairs as though he was very weary, his head tilting forward on his chest. Then he suddenly lost his balance and rolled down to the bottom.

There was a brief silence, broken at last by the sobbing cry of a man as he raced from the shadows to a lone figure—a woman—sprawled nearby on the ground. It was Estella's father.

As though his lament had signalled them, the citizens of Nacogdoches slowly gathered in the street. Emilia tucked her gun into the folds of her skirt, just as she knew other people below were hiding their weapons before the soldiers began investigating. She went down then to see if she could help Estella, whose bloodstained head was cradled in the arms of her father. She knew at once by the father's grief there was nothing to be done. He was crying silently in that manner beyond despair that is worse than any frenzied hysteria, his arms holding Estella's body as if he would never let her go.

Emilia turned away, more heartsick than she ever remembered. The corridor was very quiet as she went back to her room. She sat very still on her bed, feeling that in some way she was responsible for Estella's death.

Meanwhile, Miguel Cortenoz picked up his daughter's limp body and carried her down the alley and around the corner to the front door of the cantina. Two of the patrons hauled one of the long wooden tables to the center of the ballroom, and he carefully put his daughter down on it and faced the silent gathering.

"*Mi amigos*," he said, his voice firm, "this night there will be no gambling in the back room and the dance-hall girls will not dance. Please, now, give me a little time with *la chiquita*, and later you will come back, yes, and have a few drinks of remembrance with us."

They left him alone with his grief. But within an hour, the doors of the *Cantina del Monte* were flung open again. With the help of the beak-nosed bar woman, Cortenoz had bathed his daughter and dressed her in a gown of white lace. Her *mantilla* made a natural covering for the table, and one of the dancing girls wove a garland of white carnations through her black hair. Candles were placed at her head and feet.

A scrawny little old woman, her wrinkled face ravaged by grief, stepped hesitantly into the cantina. Cortenoz recognized her as the housekeeper for the parish priest.

"Senor," she wheezed, "my sympathy. She was a good girl and a regular churchgoer."

Cortenoz nodded his head in thanks.

"But," she added quietly so only he could hear, "that is not my only reason for coming to this place." She gestured scornfully toward the bar and the dancing girls. "I thought you should be told that the *padre* is up-country and will not be back for days."

The news displeased Cortenoz. The manner of a funeral was a matter of prestige with his people. Their lives were arbitrary, they were forced to live as best they could, but death made them the central figure of a ritual as elaborate as their families could provide. The priest was almost as important as the dead person in the drama.

He said thoughtfully, "What will be, will be, old mama. We shall just have to rely upon our good friends to make up for the missing *padre*. Will you tell them so?"

The old woman blinked her watery eyes. It was the first time she had even had a peek inside the "din of iniquity." Deep in her heart was a secret desire to see why it was such an evil place, but she couldn't tell anyone that, and in any case her duty came first.

"For the child," she mumbled, "I will see what I can do."

At first, it was just the men of the Spanish-speaking part of the town who strolled into the cantina, paid their respects, and then went to the dark back room for a drink. But, by early evening the women and children were coming from their mud and adobe homes to help Senor Cortenoz mourn through the night. Only here and there in the tightly packed ballroom did an American face stand out.

Emilia changed into a simple wool dress, and went down the inner stairway to the ballroom. She knew she was taking a risk. Already some of the dancing girls were openly blaming her for Estella's death. But she had to go. This much she owed Estella—this much she owed that sweet, pure girl who had never harmed a soul in her few years of life.

Cortenoz was near the door when she came down. He stood still, looking at her. The other dancing girls were still in their costumes, their make-up running down their faces in streaks from weeping. Cortenoz had been angry because people might think their attire didn't show the proper respect. Actually, the men thought nothing of it, and the women were secretly thrilled because they had never seen the *"putas"* in their bright costumes. And they all hoped to see *Amarillo Rosa* in her full regalia.

If they were disappointed by Emilia's simple dress, Cortenoz was not. He was greatly moved by the respect she was showing to him and his child. He whispered to her:

"Come. Together, we go see her. She is so beautiful."

Emilia walked quietly into the big ballroom, ignoring the undercurrent of whispers, and Senor Cortenoz escorted her to the long table. Everyone drew back, leaving them as much alone as possible with the dead.

Emilia looked down at Estella, tightly controlling the wild grief inside her.

"Cry!" Cortenoz said suddenly, harshly. "She would have cried for you!"

Emilia raised her eyes to stare at Cortenoz.

"Would that we could change places, senor," she whispered.

"I know, I know," Cortenoz murmured more gently. "Don't blame yourself too much, Emilia."

"Don't blame myself?" Emilia whispered. "Because of these men, I have now caused two deaths."

"Say rather that we both were responsible. You and I—and perhaps even Colonel Henry Raguet."

Emily stared at him blankly.

"*Si*," he said sadly. "He would do anything to get my business run out of Nacogdoches. Those two have given me trouble before this, and I am sure they are in his pay." He shrugged. "And who knows which of the *gringos* here tonight are his new spies and troublemakers?"

"I didn't know."

He patted her arm gently. "Because I did not wish you to know. Worries would keep *Amarillo Rosa* from dancing her best. *Si*? Now we have paid our respects for all to see. Will you stay downstairs with us for awhile?"

She could feel hundreds of eyes watching her every move. "Senor," she sighed, "if it is all the same, may I go back to my room now and come back later?"

He was a compassionate man and understood her. He gave her a warm smile and held out his arm. "I shall see you back to the stairway, senorita."

When she went back to her room, the aroma of cigar smoke met her as soon as she opened the door. For a moment she was scared. She pushed the door wide to see who was there.

Don Adolfo Sterne rose quickly to his feet, blushing with embarrassment.

"Forgive the intrusion, Senorita Hoffman," he stammered, waving the cigar smoke away, "and also the stench of tobacco. I took the liberty of lighting a cigar because I didn't know how long I would have to wait for you."

Emilia said the first thing that came into her head. "I allow men to smoke in my presence, Mayor Sterne."

"Thank you." He looked sheepishly at the open door. "Could we possibly have a little more privacy?"

"But of course," she replied with a grin, closing the door. "However, you should know that the *Monte* is closed for the night to all forms of business."

Don Sterne looked even more embarrassed.

"Senorita," he gasped, "I am a happily married man."

She smiled warmly. "And I would do nothing to change that, even if I could, senor. When I know a man is married, I wish nothing to do with him."

"Good!" Sterne said grimly. "Then I don't have to apologize for not coming here to seek your favor."

This only increased her curiosity. "Why did you come?" she asked bluntly.

He motioned for her to take a seat on the bed. "There may not be much time, so please listen carefully, senorita. The two men who were killed were employees of Colonel Raguet." If he expected to surprise her, he was disappointed. He said abruptly, "Do you own a pistol?"

She nodded and took the revolver from beneath her pillow. He put the barrel to his nose. "This piece has not been fired, for a very long time."

"That is true," she said. "I hope you didn't think I killed them."

"That is what the rumor-mongers would have one believe."

"But why?" she cried. "I have no enemies."

Sterne eyed her compassionately. "The enemies one is not aware of are oft time the most dangerous. This gun might say to me that you are innocent, but others will believe what they are told to believe. For your own safety, Senorita Hoffman, I advise you to leave Nacogdoches."

She laughed. "Just like that . . . leave. Even though I'm innocent?"

"I ask it because you are innocent. The colonel has sent for the provost marshal to come up from San Augustine. He and his squad could arrive as early as dawn. Believe me, on the colonel's orders, they will not find you innocent. Your name is well known in the *Villa* and thus Raguet can use you against Cortenoz."

She wanted to scream at him that it wasn't fair, but she remained calm.

"That may be well and good," she said, "but how am I to flee?"

"That," Sterne said gruffly, "we will leave in the hands of your friend, Senor Escovarro." It had greatly surprised him earlier to learn Escovarro considered himself a personal friend of hers. "He is due to leave for Santo Antonio tomorrow and will take you along."

"But I hardly know the man."

Sterne shrugged—who was he to believe? "I'm hardly interested in your private affairs, senorita. The Senor has made his offer and I now make mine. Take as few things with you as possible and come now to stay the night in my home."

Emilia was astounded. "But you live right under the Colonel's nose."

Sterne chuckled. "And therefore it is the last place in town that he would think to look when you are found to be missing."

"But what of Senor Cortenoz and the burial? I must tell him of course."

Sterne made an impatient gesture. "I shall tell Senor Cortenoz in good time. Until then, what he doesn't know, they can't force out of him."

Emilia glanced round the room and sighed. It had

been home to her for three years. She had arrived penniless, and Senor Cortenoz had befriended her and introduced her to her dancing partner, Pablo. For a moment, she thought of Pablo and all that he had taught her. It would be unfair to leave without saying goodbye, but she would do as the Mayor told her. At first she hadn't taken his news too seriously, but when he offered to let her stay in his home, she began to appreciate the seriousness of the situation. There was a slight quiver to her knees as she rose and walked to the closet. Into a straw shopping bag she rammed a couple of dresses, a pair of shoes, a shawl and her favorite *mantilla*. From the dresser top, she scooped all her jewelry, *mantilla* combs, and make-up. Next, she went to the bed, hesitated and then laughed. It suddenly didn't matter who in the world knew where she hid her money. She threw back the covers and slit the side of the loosely sewn mattress with her hands. Sterne discreetly turned his head as she extracted three bags of silver and gold coins.

Without a backward glance, she marched to the door and out. Don Sterne could not help admiring her courage. She hadn't whimpered or debated over what to take, as his poor wife had done when they were suddenly uprooted. He hadn't been keen to come, fearing Raguet himself. Escovarro had persuaded him that he—a Jew who had suffered himself—couldn't let an innocent suffer. It was an unbeatable argument. He and his people were the innocent who had suffered time after time as Emilia was doing now; he had to help her. Now the pride he had been feeling for Emilia was turned inward. He would remember this night as one of the proudest of his life.

18

At dawn, the Sterne family began to prepare Emilia for her journey. After a sleepless night, she was weary so she felt the disguise they provided was fitting—the clothes and make-up of an old woman. She had been unable to sleep when Frau Sterne told her the last guest to use the room they gave her was Sam Houston. She was annoyed with herself for being so foolish, but every time she closed her eyes, she saw his face—not as he had looked when he was in her room, seeing her as a whore, but the warm, tender, compassionate face she had awakened to on the trail. It was that laughing giant she had fallen in love with, not the bear she had gone to bed with. How stupid, she told herself, to think for a moment that he might return your love!

Before noon, they were on their way, with Escovarro in the lead on a grey mare.

Because of his high position in the town, the army provided him with an escort of two mounted soldiers. They showed no interest in the hunched up little old lady astride a docile jackass. Emilia kept her head tucked well back into the shadow of her heavy shawl, and encouraged the soldiers' idea that she was in deep mourning.

But as they slowly crossed the velvety rangeland, with the noon sun making purple shadows on the

foothills and conjuring up mirages on the open plains
ahead, Emilia had plenty of time to think about her
departure and to realize she was leaving all her problems behind. She began to relax.

One consolation surely was that she would never
have to meet Sam Houston again. It seemed absurd
now to have missed a night's sleep on this account. A
woman in her business had no right to think of love at
all. As she rode along, she tried to dismiss him as he
had dismissed her. She had to think of the future now
and all she had to do to establish herself in San Antonio.

Emilia had been so lost in her own thoughts that she
hadn't noticed the growing nervousness of the two soldiers. Escovarro stopped and let Emilia's jackass catch
up to his mare.

"Don't look around," he said softly, his lips hardly
moving. "But there is a dust cloud on the plateau,
which has been keeping a steady pace with us for over
an hour."

Her heart beat faster, and she asked nervously, "The
army?"

He shook his head. "The soldiers wouldn't be worried if they thought it was their own army. More than
likely it's a Comanche raiding party."

Her dread of the army was nothing to her fear of
the Indians. "Can this beast run?" she asked.

Escovarro frowned. "I've been wondering the same,
senorita. We shall just have to see if anything happens." Then he smiled warmly. "Don't worry, you'll
not be left behind."

Emilia warmed toward him. "Senor," she whispered,
so the soldiers wouldn't hear, "I—I've treated you
badly."

"Please," he said, "no words are necessary."

"My mind tells me differently. Why did you put yourself in danger by taking me?"

He laughed to stop himself from expressing his feelings. "I treasure beautiful things," he said gallantly, "and I hate to see them destroyed."

"And you, too, think they would have killed me."

Escovarro stared at her face half-hidden in the shadow of the shawl hood. "Can you think of anything that would frighten our people more? Raguet would have made sure that it all looked quite legal, and just as legally he would have started buying up the land of the Mexicans who fled an hour after he had seen you hung."

The thought made Emilia shiver. "I wonder what it was like before the Americans started coming to our land?"

"Beautiful," he said simply. "My father says it was like old Spain, but without the constant wars."

Escovarro tried to hold her attention because he didn't want her to notice that the other riders were gaining on them. "It is my fondest hope," he said cheerily, "that someday I might be able to show you our family *ranchero*."

Emilia scoffed. "Me? Your family would die a thousands times over if you brought home a *puta*."

Escovarro's handsome face frowned with annoyance. "You do not have to be so harsh on yourself, senorita."

Emilia laughed softly. "It's the truth."

"Not to me," he said hotly. "And I'd whip any man who dared call you that."

Emilia had heard that sentiment many times from men who were trying to deceive themselves that they weren't with a whore.

"Thank you," she said, but her voice didn't sound convinced. "If you had once been with me, you might not be such a *caballero*."

Miguel Escovarro could no longer hold back what was in his heart. "Senorita, I've been saying prayers to the Blessed Virgin because you turned me down that night. Your eyes told me that your thoughts were with Senor Houston. I cannot blame you, he is far more man than I shall ever be."

Emilia responded with a choice epithet that made him blanch. "I don't see him taking a chance on my safety . . ."

"Senor!" one of the soldiers shouted, "they've begun to gallop!" It was possible now to see their pursuers *were* Indians.

"Move out!" Escovarro shouted back, slapping the docile jackass on the rump. The beast brayed and reared, but Emilia held on. Then the animal turned stubborn. Escovarro slapped it, Emilia kicked it in the sides with her heels, but it just dug its hoofs deeper into the dusty trail and refused to move.

The Indians had dipped down on the far side of the plateau to ride around to the front and trap them in the valley. The two soldiers were now frantic, screaming and cursing at the immovable jackass. Then, as one, their fear took them over. They spurred their horses around and headed back toward the *Villa*.

Escovarro shouted at them, but they ignored him and galloped on. Soon they disappeared in a dust cloud. Escovarro quickly surveyed the terrain and felt desperate: there were few places to hide. Now he could hear the thunder of the Indian ponies, but as yet he couldn't see them at the head of the valley.

"Off," he shouted to Emilia, taking his Winchester out from its boot under his left leg, and sliding from his mare. He gave the horse a resounding smack to drive it away and turned to catch Emilia as she came tumbling down from the jackass. The jackass suddenly became smart and followed the riderless mare at a wild gallop. Escovarro and Emilia were now left alone to face the Indians.

He didn't speak, but grasped Emilia by the arm and pulled her quickly to the nearest rocks. Just before lying down next to her, he saw the mare and jackass disappearing in a dust cloud. At least *they* would escape, he thought gloomily.

Not until the ground began to rumble beneath them did he realize how scared Emilia was. She was trembling. He rolled on his side and pulled her gently to him. Her head nestled against his shoulder, and he pressed his cheek to her hair. This had been his dream for so long that it now seemed unreal. But the touch and smell of her hair wasn't a dream, nor the tremulous rise and fall of her breasts pressed closer and closer against him as the earth shook beneath them.

Then the pounding hooves slowed and stopped close by, and they heard excited shouts and guttural voices. Escovarro could picture the Indians examining the deep ruts the stubborn jackass had made. His only fear was that they might inspect the area more closely and see some footprints. He slipped out his six-shooter and held it ready. At any second Emilia expected to be clawed away from his embrace by brutal hands. But suddenly there were loud howls and the pounding of the hooves began again. The Indians were pursuing the jackass.

He said with great relief, "They took the bait. I thought that jackass might fool them."

She stared at him. "But for how long?"

The sexuality in her frightened glance unnerved him. "I don't know," he stammered.

Her eyes were shining and enormous. "I didn't know what a coward I was," she said, nestling back into his embrace and kissing him several times. "Oh, God, without you I would have been screaming my head off." She thrust her hands in his hair and caressed his face. "I think it was your face that saved me. I kept peeking and it never altered. Thank you." Holding his chin in her hands, she gave him a final tender kiss and sat up.

Escovarro marvelled at his good luck. He was far too much in love with her to realize that the kisses meant little to her: they were a release for her tension and a simple expression of thanks. But he assumed they meant much more.

. She jumped up and shielded her eyes. "They're almost to the horizon. What now?"

Yes, he thought, we've spent enough precious time on our feelings. He put his six-shooter back into the holster and picked up his Winchester.

"Best we get to the other side of the plateau and try to find safe shelter for the night. As soon as they see the horse and jackass are riderless, they'll start backtracking."

"The jackass!" she cried, her eyes blazing. "Every last thing I had in the world was on that beast."

"Except your life," he said simply, taking her by the arm. "Let's start moving."

"Oh, that's easy for you to say! Have you ever had to work for a *peso* in your life? I suppose you think Cortenoz paid me well for being *Amarillo Rosa*? In a pig's eye! All I got was first choice of the richest patron each night. My clothes, my shoes, my food, all came out of Emilia's earnings."

Escovarro wondered, as they trudged along, whether Emilia's non-stop talk was merely a nervous reaction or whether she was trying to tell him something the kisses hadn't. She was gesturing broadly, talking breathlessly, and her eyes were wild. "And to lose everything is not as bad as the next problems we face, you know. The biggest."

"What's that?"

She stared at him. "What could we have possibly done today—forty or less miles? And with animals! It will take weeks to get to San Antonio on foot."

He suddenly realized what she was hinting at and he didn't like it. A return to Mayor Sterne's house for new horses could prove to be more dangerous than attempting to cover the remaining three hundred miles on foot.

"Whatever we do," he said firmly, "we will not turn back. I still have my money belt, and there is a Waco village a day to the south."

She scoffed: "They are still Indians."

"I've stayed with them before. They'll trade for horses."

"And ride out after us the next day for scalps, the money belt and the horses?"

Her negative attitude was beginning to irritate him. "Do you have a better suggestion?"

Emilia kept silent. She wasn't being fair and she knew it. Nothing that had happened was his fault. She merely needed someone to rant and rave at. But, deep inside her, she was also worried that they were getting too close. His kisses were far more sensual than she had wanted them to be, although she was the one who had started it. But she hadn't time to think any more about it.

"Look!" he cried. "What's that?"

A quarter of a mile beyond the plateau was a low cluster of rocks on the plain.

"There's no reason for a pile of rocks to be out there," he added. "It has to be a building of some sort, and if so, defensible."

Emilia was determined to keep silent, not to encourage him any more. He glanced strangely at her, as if wondering why she was being so sullen now, and when she turned her face away, he scrambled down off the plateau and strode angrily forward. Emilia had to hurry to keep up with him. Her shawl and long wool dress were heavy and cumbersome. She had to hitch the dress up above her ankles so she didn't trip. And with each step, they grew angrier and angrier with each other.

Escavarro had been right: it was a building of sorts. At one time, many years before, it had probably been part of a Waco Indian village, but he saw no signs of recent habitation. With a mocking half-bow, he presented the door-less entrance to Emilia, who had arrived panting behind him.

It was so dim inside she could see nothing at first. There was a smell of decaying hides that had dried to turgid leather, and smoke from a hundred fires had blackened the ceiling. The floor was littered with broken pottery, and Emilia was so puzzled she forgot she wasn't speaking to him.

"What happened here?" she asked.

Escovarro was relieved she'd broken her silence, and he studied a piece of broken pottery to show how seriously he took her question. "The Wacos are a very frugal people," he finally answered. "There must have been an attack on them. See the tomahawk marks on the pottery. The Comanches must have driven them south a long time ago."

"But," she protested, "they are all Indians. Why do they fight and kill each other?"

Escovarro laughed as he stood up. "Didn't you know they were not civilized?" he said, with a mocking innocent look. "No more civilized than we are and look what we are doing right now in *Mejico*. Territory is power to them as surely as it is power to Santa Anna and his army."

"But not with this much destruction."

"I pray you never have to see the destruction of that mad horde," he said with a chuckle. "Well, enough of that. Let's clear away a couple of those far corners for the night."

Emilia looked around. "There's no wood."

"Even if there were," he said, "we couldn't afford a fire. The smoke would give us away. Are you tired?"

She shrugged. "My legs, mainly." She gave a short, soft laugh. "That's funny for a dancer to say, isn't it? Perhaps I should have danced along after you instead of walking, and snapped my fingers like castanets."

It was her way of thawing the chill between them. She snapped her fingers and high-stepped over the pottery to a windowless corner. By the time she had cleaned an area big enough for her to lay down, she felt as if she had no strength left.

"Rest awhile," he said gently. "I'll find a spot to keep a look-out." He started to leave and turned back, taking the six-shooter from its holster. "You'd better have this, just in case." He grinned. "The army and Raguet seem to think you know how to use one of these, but do you?"

It was the first time she had smiled freely all day. "You had better have more trust in your ability with the rifle than my ability with this."

"In a little while, we may not have to show off our ability, senorita. The sun will be down and they will give up the chase."

"Senor," she said, hanging her head, "for travelling companions, we remain quite formal. We left *Amarillo Rosa* at the *Cantina del Monte*. Here is only Emilia Hoffman."

"I am your servant, Emilia, if I may also be Miguel to you."

She grinned. "I'll sleep on it."

The first echoing report woke her instantly. It took no more than a second for her to identify the noise and her surroundings. All in a single motion, she sat up and faced the gaping entrance. Yet everything was so still that she soon had to convince herself she had really heard a rifle shot and not dreamt it.

She didn't know how long she'd been asleep. It had been almost sundown when Escovarro went outside. Now, through the entrance, the world was washed in silvery moonlight. The distant plateau was etched in blacks and greys, and seemed near enough to touch. The moon was high enough in the sky for its beams to come pouring down the smoke-hole in the ceiling and spotlight the entire center of the room. The moonlight and silence combined to give Emilia an eerie feeling as if time had stopped.

A second rifle shot broke the spell; it was followed by a scream of someone in pain. A man. She wondered if the Indians also had rifles. Could that have been Miguel's scream? If not, where was he?

The more she thought about it, the more certain she was. They had killed Miguel and now they were coming for her. This room had already seen one horror and now it was about to see another. She riveted her eyes on the entrance and grasped the butt of the revolver so tightly that her knuckles turned white.

Suddenly she saw something.

A shadow appeared outside. It couldn't be Miguel. He would have called to her and come walking right in. He wouldn't have been so furtive. Then she saw what her senses already anticipated. Someone was moving cautiously along the outside wall preparing to take her by surprise, not realizing the shadow had given the game away.

Emilia sat frozen with terror. She heard a shuffling

sound and hoarse, asthmatic breathing. Her worst fears were then realized: The breathing wasn't Miguel's.

A face thrust forward into the yellow-white circle of moonlight. So grotesquely did the moonlight shadow the features that Emilia gasped. It was an Indian, and he displayed a row of brown, broken teeth, as he told her: "Squaw of the jackass, stand and come!"

Emilia did not understand the guttural Comanche voice, but guessed his meaning at once. She pressed her back firmly against the wall and tried not to show her fear.

Now he stepped fully into the circle of the smoke-hole. He was tall and powerfully built. A deep scar from the corner of his right eye to the ear lobe gave that side of his face a twisted, fierce look. But Emilia's eyes were not on his face. As soon as she saw the rest of him, a wild fury shot up in her and brought her raging to her feet.

"Those are my money pouches around your waist," she cried. "Give them back at once!"

He leered. "*Español?* Some I speak." Then he gave a series of croaking grunts, which she took to be laughter.

"Good, then give them back!" she told him.

"*Mio!*"

In spite of the danger, she wouldn't be cowed. "They are not yours, they are mine." she said hotly.

The Spanish words were spat out too fast for him to understand, so he continued to grunt out his laughter.

Emilia decided she was not meant to die, not yet, for he could easily have taken the knife from his waist band and thrown it at her. He wanted her alive, at least for the moment. But she feared being taken back to the Comanche village more than she feared death. She pretended to move to see what he would do. His head followed her, like that of an old turtle. With a speed that caught her off-guard, he lunged forward and his big yellow claw shot out and clutched her hand.

"Mine," he repeated. "*Mio oro, mio mujer*!"

Emilia couldn't move her hand. The steely fingers were clamped like a vise. But her other hand was free. She was damn sure that he wasn't going to keep her gold, and double damn sure that she was not going to be his woman. The revolver, concealed by the folds of the wool dress, was ready if she had the guts to use it. Her mind rebelled at what she must do, even as she was doing it. She drew the six-shooter up to her side and thrust it forward until it touched the muscle wall of his stomach. Later she would not be able to recall squeezing the trigger, her finger had been frozen around it for so long. Her only recollection was the fierce noise and a horrible stinging sensation in her fingers.

The Indian's grip relaxed. He blinked at her, as if startled. Then his mouth contorted into a hideous oval and with a great howl, he grasped at his belly. Fearing that he was going for his knife, she tried to re-cock the revolver and aim it, but she was too nervous. It didn't matter.

The man wasn't thinking about his knife; he was desperately attempting to hold his intestines from spewing out on the hard floor. With both hands, she held the gun steady, aiming for his heart, and the Comanche stood upright as if he was giving her a better target so she could end his pain. But she didn't need to fire. Over his face came a look of calm surprise. His eyes were still open, inquiring, as he started to fall. From the entrance came a fierce moan. A Comanche, half the age of the fallen one, stood appalled at the sight of the body. With a shriek of "My father!," he raised his tomahawk high over his head and charged.

A rifle cracked behind the young Indian, and the closeness of the discharge lifted him into the air and spun him about. He came down a short distance from his father. He died instantly, but a spark of life remained in the older Indian, and he moaned over his son before dying.

It was a terrible sound. It pierced Emilia's heart. Then, with that protective switch a mind will make after being under a terrible strain, she saw only her money pouches. She went to retrieve them on limbs that felt wooden and weak, but before she could do so, Escovarro appeared and brushed her away with a brusque, "This is no work for a lady, Emilia. I'll drag them out!" But as he dragged the Indian youth outside, she quickly snatched her money pouches from the older Indian's waist. He didn't look dead; he looked asleep and peaceful.

"Good God," Escovarro cried, "are you still standing over him?"

"I killed him," she said stupidly.

"And I've got to find a place to hide him and the others."

"Others?"

"There were four," he said in a satisfied tone. "Didn't you hear the first rifle shots? I saw them hide their horses up in the plateau-rocks just a little before sundown. Before the full moon rose, they started creeping across the plain on foot. I thought I had spotted them all, but this one got away from me. I'm sorry if he scared you."

Emilia blinked. Suddenly the whole room was unsteady; the floor swung to and fro under her feet. It all came flooding back at once. Only then did her hand begin to hurt, and she looked down at it foolishly. It was black with gun-powder burns. For a moment, she tried to recall how she had gotten back the money pouches, and still retained the six-shooter in her right fist.

"I'll take the gun," Escovarro said gently and at the same time helped her back to the cleared corner. "Why don't you sit down for a while? I'll take care of him and then . . . then I had better go for the horses. After that, we'll try to find something for your hand and your dress."

She looked down and saw that her bodice was not only covered with black soot, but was spotted with little dark brown patches of drying blood. Her head grew light and her knees began to buckle.

She thought her senses had become hazy for just a few seconds, but when she was in control again, she didn't know where she was. The place was warm and dark and sheltered. Her dress was gone; she was wrapped in a coarse woolen poncho that itched against her bare skin. Escovarro's arms were around her, and his face was against her hair.

For a time she lay still against his shoulder, preparing to accept all that had happened as little more than a bad dream. Her eyes were beginning to adjust to the darkness; she saw a hint of rough stone walls and a ceiling. There was light somewhere—a dull red glow, like a tiny fire. She turned her head to find out where she was.

Escovarro lifted his head. He laughed softly and whispered, "It's a small cave on the plateau. I found it when I came back for the horses, and decided to bring you here instead. From here, I can watch on the other place in case any of their friends come looking for them."

"They haven't so far?"

"No, and it's only a couple of hours until sunrise. That's why the moon has already set."

The air was chilly, and she pulled the poncho tighter

around her. "My dress? Did you take it off?" In the darkness, she couldn't see him blush. "Yes," he stammered.

Emilia giggled. "I am usually the one who has to undress my customers."

Escovarro burst out laughing, and that made her laugh crazily, too. She nestled against him, still laughing so uproariously that she could hardly manage to keep her head still.

And then, as though on cue, they ceased laughing at the same instant. In the darkness, without fumbling, he found her mouth with his lips. With urgent desire, he pressed her close and tasted again the sweet, honey-scent of her mouth.

Gently, he lifted her heavy hair to one side and put his lips softly on the side of her neck, and when his arms finally encircled her, he gripped her so tightly that she wanted to cry out, but her throat felt constricted and no sound came. She needed passion, needed it desperately to cleanse her mind of the past few days. She told herself that she wouldn't be foolish this time like she had been with Sam Houston. Whether in the *Monte* or a cave, she was determined to look upon Miguel Escovarro as just another customer of the night—payment or not.

It was only when he had slipped his hand under the poncho and she felt the palms of his hands against her nipples that she could whisper, "Love me."

They were not the words she had intended, but it was too late to alter them or call them back. Her whisper had released him to pursue his fondest dream and he was now unstoppable, and no matter how or where he touched her with his lips, they became like a velvet caress that she had never before experienced.

Aroused to a near-fever peak, she gave way to womanly desire rather than trained instinct. Gently, she rubbed the palm of her hand down over his chest and belly and to his crotch. She soon found him and paused. Beneath her hand lay a pulsing giant that astonished her. Suddenly, she was the novice unsure of her next move.

Escovarro muttered something against her throat and fondled her bare breasts. He was fully aroused, trembling with anticipation. Again he muttered something to her, and then let his mouth go down to close around a swollen nipple. His hand snaked over her belly and fondled what he sought until her breathing was heavy.

She spread her legs tremblingly, as though fearful of his first advance. He was not overeager and allowed the forepleasure of the moment to go on. Her passion soared, and she began to feel impatient, wanting him to begin. "Oh!" she murmured, feeling the full weight of his body on top of her, squeezing her heaving breasts. His first thrust was painful, and she wanted to scream out against the agony that his massiveness was causing her . . . until the agony slowly turned into overwhelming ecstasy.

She moaned with pleasure as his thrusting rhythm seemed to take over her whole body. For once she wasn't playing the part of the *puta*, but of a real woman. There was no money involved, nor thought of money. His desire for her was not crude, carnal, but deeply sensual and loving. Out of mutual need, they melted into an unspoken union of equal giving. Miguel Escovarro shuddered as they reached the climax together. His body stiffened, and the climb of her own desire reached a swift, nerve-shattering peak of sensation. She felt the full flood of his maleness as stormy waves of fire surged through her loins, complete, intense, fulfilling. . . . .

BOOK III

The Conquest of Teresa

19

TERESA HADN'T LOOKED forward to Santa Anna's return from Mexico City, but when at last he arrived in
triumph, she tried to play the role he wanted. And the
President, feeling she was serious about establishing a
husband-wife relationship, stayed away from Luisa.

Santa Anna had had mixed feelings about returning
to Saltillo. His vanity made him homesick for the
semi-tropics of Veracruz and the adulation of the people of his home state. He wanted to flaunt his new
laurels where he was sure of a warm reception. Saltillo
and the *Casa de la Sol* seemed colder in every way,
even though spring was on its way. And the house was
a constant reminder of Dona Clara, whom he had
tried to forget. His memory of the old woman had
much to do with his changing attitude toward Teresa.

On their first night together—their delayed wedding
night—Teresa wrapped herself in a thin robe and sat
nervously brushing her hair. She was bewildered by
Santa Anna's attitude. Five hours before, he—her husband—had returned to the *hacienda* after a long absence and greeted her with no more than a peck on the
cheek. At the dinner table, she was all but excluded
from the conversation, and as she listened, she was appalled by what was said.

"The man is a fool," Santa Anna said, addressing

Felix Escovarro exclusively. "It took him eleven weeks
to travel from San Antonio to Mexico City. Only a
fool would travel when he was that ill.

"Or a desperate man," Felix answered cautiously.
"Senor Austin is a man with a vision."

Santa Anna scoffed. "Too big a vision. Imagine the
impudence of the man coming to ask me to give up
Tejas." He laughed as if it were a great joke.

"That is the hope of many in Tejas, *Senor Presidente.*"

The stuffiness of the title made Santa Anna laugh
even more. "We need not be formal with each other,
my young friend." he winked. "You didn't hear me
calling you *padre* with each breath, do you?"

For the first time in three months, Felix felt uncomfortable in his role. When he and Teresa had been
alone together in the *hacienda*, he had relaxed so well
that it had almost become his real self.

"But," Santa Anna said quickly, noticing the young
officer's discomfort, "the man will have a long wait
for his dream."

"He doesn't give up easily."

Santa Anna smiled slyly. "Unless another man of
reason makes him see the folly of his mission."

"That should be an interesting meeting. You are
both bull-headed, stubborn men."

"No," Santa Anna said slowly, "I won't do it myself.
The power is mine, of course, but I detest the irksome
details of negotiation. The job shall be yours, Felix.
You are both men of Tejas, except that you were born
to the land and Austin wasn't."

Felix didn't want the job, but saw no way of refusing it. How could he talk Stephen Austin out of something that he, himself, also wanted for his family and
people?

"How do I know the man will even talk with me?

With you away from the capital, he may already have returned to San Felipe."

"Hardly," he snickered. "I have him in prison."

Felix was aghast. Now he had no choice but to go to Mexico City and see what he could do for the old friend of his father.

It hurt Teresa deeply that Father Felix made his goodbye to her at the end of the meal. It was far too cool and ungallant a farewell from someone who had been her constant companion and friend for so long. She trusted and respected him almost as much as she had Dona Clara.

It was Felix who was on her mind, as she sat brushing her hair that night, and not her husband. The conversation had revealed to her how little she really knew about Felix. She was surprised to learn he was also from Tejas. More surprising, however, was the way in which he allowed her husband to order him about—almost as if he belonged to Santa Anna and not to the church.

A knock at the door brought her mind back to her husband. At her call, he opened the door and came in.

"Good evening," she whispered.

Santa Anna leaned back against the closed door, and his eyes grew heavy as he looked at her.

"You are so lovely," he said.

Teresa thanked him with a smile into the mirror. When he said no more but went on staring at her, she rose and walked stiffly to the bed. A maid had already turned back the sheets and plumped the pillows.

"Wait!" he said, as she began to lie down. "Would you disrobe for me first?"

The request amused Teresa more than it surprised her. "There was a time," she said with a light laugh, "when you took that matter into your own hands."

Santa Anna wasn't amused. It brought the ghost of Dona Clara back to him.

Teresa told herself that the man was to be her husband for life and so he had the right to ask her. As she began to slip her robe off her shoulders, she heard him bolt the door, but still he didn't approach her. He leaned against the door, his arms hanging loosely, with a slight tremble in his hands. Only the soft quickening of his breath suggested how excited he was becoming. Teresa stood nude before him, and as his eyes travelled over her, she watched him.

I am now his master, she thought with surprise. Her fear of him had gone. She realized she could dominate him now with her body.

To demonstrate her power over him, she didn't wait for him to say anything but did what she thought was next expected of her. She got into the bed and pulled the sheet up to her chin. Nestling back into the pillow, she stared at him, her eyes inviting.

He did not see the invitation, only the mocking reminder of another's eyes.

"I—I—," he gasped. "Forgive me . . . not tonight."

He quickly unbolted the door and left as quietly as he had come.

Teresa was shocked. She didn't understand him. This was the second time he had rejected her. It was a blow to her vanity. Her tears came quickly, and she sobbed herself to sleep.

Days passed, and Teresa waited nervously each night for Santa Anna, but he didn't come back and didn't explain. It was almost as though he were two different people, a warm and thoughtful husband during the day and a cold and unapproachable stranger as soon as it was dark. Teresa was unsure how to handle him. She knew so little about men that she began to wonder if they had a monthly problem similar to women. There was no one she could ask so she suggested one afternoon very timidly that she should visit her mother. She expected him to refuse his permission, but he jumped at the suggestion, as long as it was reversed: he would send an escort to San Antonio to bring Dona Helena to visit Teresa. That suited Teresa just as well, and she accepted his offer graciously.

That night he came to her room after she was in bed and all the lamps were out. She had anticipated that he would return eventually, and so she went to bed nude each night. Now she heard him grope across the darkened room and take off his clothes, and then she felt his touch. As long as he couldn't see her, Santa Anna felt safe. No ghost would haunt him. With a great sigh he fell on her and struggled and fought his way into her, and Teresa, crying out, felt her blood wash between them. But at the end, it was Santa Anna who couldn't control his emotions. Try as he did, he couldn't hold back his bitter tears, the expression of his troubled mind. Teresa cradled his head against her breasts and listened to him sob, and even with the pain that burned between her legs, she puzzled over this strange man.

The act had not brought a sense of love, only of pain. Had it pained him as well? she wondered. Again she chided herself for knowing so little about men.

Santa Anna, whose tears were from shame—shame that he couldn't love her as fully as he wished—soon got up and returned to his own room. He couldn't stay all night with Teresa. He knew Luisa would be waiting for him, but he didn't want to sleep with her. He realized then that he didn't want to sleep in that house another night with anybody. It had been foolish to come back to Saltillo at all.

Before he entered his room, he tried to look eager

and friendly so that Luisa wouldn't read his true feelings.

"Good, you waited for me," he exclaimed enthusiastically, never for a moment doubting that she would be there. But then to stop her from trying to get him in bed, he asked her, "Are you as bored with this dusty little town as I am, my dear?"

Luisa's boyish face brightened. "More so," she replied. "I saw more of you in Mexico City than I have here."

"Tomorrow we shall change all that."

"We're going back?" she cried.

He smiled. "Oh, Luisa, much better than that. I'm going to show you a land much more enchanting than the capital. Rich and green and fertile and warm. A paradise." No longer did he have to pretend false enthusiasm. He was talking of something he dearly loved and it showed in his face. "Do you recall when I gave you your first banana in Mexico City?"

"How can I forget? I fell in love with them."

And that was one reason why he couldn't help loving her. She thrilled so to each new experience he gave her that it made him feel powerful and god-like.

"How would you like to walk out into a patio and pick a fresh banana right off the tree?"

She giggled. "Is that how they grow?"

"By the acre."

"I'd love it. Where is this place?"

He said the words as though he were describing heaven. "In my home state. A few years ago, I began to build a country estate near Jalapa. It is long past the time for us to go and see to its completion."

A single word had spoiled the mood. "*Us,*" she sneered. "Did she finally break down and perform her wifely duties?"

Santa Anna had given Luisa the impression Teresa

was to blame, that she had rejected him. He was sorry now that he had mentioned it to her.

"That has nothing to do with it," he snapped.

Luisa began to laugh in a ribald way. "That's the difference between being a man and a husband, a winner and a loser."

He glared. "And what does that mean?" As much as he loved her for her sexual companionship, he also feared her, for she knew too much.

"Mean?" she said demurely. "It means that I kept my ears open while in Mexico City. It means that I know you've been a naughty boy with *older* women before—"

He cut her short. "That was different! I was only twenty-eight and fighting a war."

She sniffed. "Some war. In the morning you were a Spanish captain and were promoted to lieutenant colonel for beating the rebels by noon. After lunch, you changed sides and got the rank of full colonel."

In spite of himself, he argued back. "Because I could see that Augustin Iturbi was going to win all of Mexico."

"Which he did," she said softly, "and became an emperor. And only when a young colonel became the dashing suitor for the Emperor's 60-year-old sister did he become a brigadier general."

"Damn you!" he cried. "What have you become, a walking record of my past history?"

Luisa had learned fast how to survive in the world of Santa Anna. "The past doesn't interest me as much as the future," she said, letting each word strike home. "Now, who is this *us* that are going travelling?"

As though he were suddenly a deflated balloon, Santa Anna relaxed. He was still the master of Luisa Morales, in spite of all of her knowledge. He had never once considered taking Teresa to Veracruz, but he wouldn't give Luisa the satisfaction of knowing that.

"If you were not such a little hot-head," he said gruffly, "then you would have realized that it meant only you and I. Now I am tired, and it will be a long journey. Pack and be ready to go by mid-morning."

He handled Teresa quite differently the next morning over breakfast.

"It's family business in Veracruz," he said apologetically. "Until the country is stable, I don't want to put your life in jeopardy. Besides," he added reassuringly, "I sent an escort for your mother yesterday. You have to wait for her arrival."

The anger Teresa felt in learning that he was leaving her again didn't last. She was soon relieved to see him go. She realized that she still feared him. He had dominated her in bed. There had been no love in it—on either side. He was too distant, a stranger. And she wanted love. Perhaps her mother could help her to understand. She had become used to her long separation from her family and the genteel people of San Antonio, but now she was impatient for her mother to arrive and share all her secrets about men and the true nature of love. Santa Anna hadn't taught her anything about love; her feeling for him was closer to hatred. But how could you hate someone you didn't know? It was strange, but for a moment she almost wished that the understanding priest was her husband. Felix was the kind of man who could really make her love. She shuddered at the sacrilegious thought and said a prayer to chase it away.

Teresa had raised no problems for Santa Anna, but he didn't escape from Saltillo without one angry confrontation.

"Is a president above the law?" Carmen Morales shouted, throwing her huge frame in front of Santa Anna's caravan as he was riding through the city.

Luisa, riding at his side, started to shout at her aunt, but Santa Anna waved her to silence. The scene was already embrassing enough without her turning it into a cat fight. He thought he could subdue the woman.

"I am the law," he growled, as though to dismiss her.

Carmen eyed him coldly. "You are a cheat! Not only did I get no money for protecting the woman you took as your bride, but you stole my niece away as well."

Santa Anna fumed. "I do not conduct business on the street, senora."

Carmen plunked herself down in a sitting position and grinned up at him. "Then ride right over me, *El Presidente*!"

"Damn!" he snarled at Luisa. "I curse the day you were born to these mad people."

Her aunt's behavior didn't worry Luisa in the least, for the simple reason that she had helped to plan it. She leaned over and whispered to Santa Anna. "She is a harridan, but right. Pay her for my virginity and she'll forget about your wife."

Santa Anna was furious. He snatched out a pouch of coins and threw it down on the street so hard that the leather split and the coins rolled free. At the same moment, he spurred his horse forward and Carmen rolled away from its hoofs just in time.

By the time the full dragoon escort had caught up with their general and president, the street was full of frantic figures clawing and fighting over the loose coins.

Carmen Morales didn't even attempt to retrieve a single coin. She stood, glaring after the departing horses, her fists clenched.

"Ashes!" she snarled. "From this day, even to your last, each victory you seek shall end as ashes in your mouth!"

20

THE NEXT FEW months passed rapidly for Teresa because, in Santa Anna's absence, she had to manage the *Casa de la Sol*. It was a hard struggle to keep the Martin *hacienda* and farmlands in working order. She wrote asking for Santa Anna's advice on the management of the estate, and received back only glowing reports on his own progress, with a dutiful post-script about how much he missed her. Teresa grew to admire and even love the *hacienda peons*, treating them as her father had treated his servants in San Antonio; she was soon accepted and looked up to as a protector.

Her mother had been of little help to her. Dona Helena had come hurrying down to Saltillo, hoping to be received by the President himself, for after all she was his mother-in-law. She was very disappointed when he wasn't there, but after waiting for three months for him to return, she began to take her frustration out on her daughter, who was always talking romantic nonsense about love.

"Love," said Dona Helena coldly, "has nothing to do with it. He is a man who has achieved much and has a great future. That is all that matters."

"But, Mama," Teresa protested, "I'm aware of all that. What I need to know is how to make him a husband."

"By being with him," she told her daughter severely.

But Dona Helena knew that wasn't the answer Teresa needed, and she wished she could have said something more helpful. Whenever she had needed someone to confide in herself, she had always gone to Dona Clara, no matter how much she disliked her old mother-in-law. But now that Teresa needed the same kind of help, there was no Dona Clara to rely on, and she certainly couldn't take her place.

"Oh, Mama, do you really think I should be with him?" asked Teresa, almost in tears. "I've been so unhappy worrying about our relationship. How did you and Papa grow to love each other?"

Senora de Alarcon wanted to be truthful with her daughter, but could not. She had known love before marriage, and then disappointment, bitterness and frustration was all she had been left with. She had almost rejoiced when her husband died, to save her from their horrible feuding.

"It just took time," she said and stood up. "And I think it is now time for me to head back home. I feel I'm missing too much. I'm dying to find out how the scandal ended."

Her mother loved gossip and scandal. "What scandal is that, Mama?" Teresa asked politely.

Dona Helena decided that now her daughter was married, she was mature enough to hear the scandalous details. "Well," she enthused, "one of the most prominent bachelors in all Tejas brought no less than a prostitute to his aunt's house in San Antonio and tried to pawn her off as a *real* lady. Senor Escovarro sent the little tramp packing and boxed her nephew's ears very soundly."

"Escovarro?" Teresa asked. "Are there many families of that name in Tejas?"

"Only one of importance, my girl. You wouldn't remember the boys, of course, they are much older than you. Miguel is the one I speak of, now a disgrace to the family name."

Teresa was curious. "You said boys. He has brothers?"

"Two, as I recall. One was killed a few years ago on their *ranchero* and I don't at this moment recall his name. The other was a strange lad who went off to Spain to become a soldier or priest or something. Let me see . . . Oh, yes. Felix. Felix Escovarro de Sanchez. Probably didn't amount to a thing in this world."

No, Teresa thought, only the most beautiful man I've ever seen. The mere mention of his name sent a secret thrill through her body. Father Felix was the one she should be talking with, not her mother. But did she really want to talk to the priest about her husband or just because he was so warm and reassuring?

The next day a message arrived from Santa Anna. The message said little, but the messenger was special—Carlos Juarez. During the months that Carlos had acted as the courier between Santa Anna and Father Felix, she had made friends with the boy and admired his firm devotion to the priest. Now she was anxious to have first hand news of Father Felix.

"I haven't been with him recently," Carlos said. "For the past month, my cap . . . my *padre* has been with the President."

"Is he well : . . the *padre*?"

Carlos suppressed a smile. He knew Felix was playing a role, and that meant Teresa's marriage was a fake. But he considered it a military matter far above his powers of reasoning, and he had dismissed it all from his mind.

But he couldn't dismiss Teresa from his mind. She was a madonna—a goddess—in his eyes. He felt weak

and foolish in her presence, and a fool for not finding
an excuse to stay longer with her after Felix had left
him behind. She had the same power over him as did
Captain Escovarro—they each made him forget his
peasant past and feel he was an important person to
them.

It did not fluster him then when Teresa asked him
to delay his departure and be her escort to Santa Anna's country estate.

Carlos proved to be a great companion and made
the journey seem adventurous and enjoyable. Teresa
had never seen land like it before. On the third day,
the path began to rise, gently at first, and then fairly
steeply, as the river beside it grew rockier and full of
rapids which became wilder as the valley narrowed
into a small gorge. The path changed to a roughly-
trodden way above a green rush of water, where no sun
came. Trees closed in overhead; ferns dripped; the
horses' hoofs echoed on rock. But for all its apparent
seclusion, the little gorge was a highway for men and
animals: the ground was beaten flat with footprints,
and there was ample evidence that mules, donkeys and
horses came that way daily.

They came up a steepish ramp through the mangrove trees, and emerged at once from the shade of the
gorge onto an open plateau perhaps two miles wide
and a mile deep, like a wide ledge on the mountainside.

The fields of Santa Anna's estate were here, sheltered on three sides by banana trees. Eastward, towards the Gulf of Campeche, the land fell away in
deep ravines and gorges tightly clogged with vegeta-
tion. Behind the fertile ground, to the west, soared the
mountainside, blue-green even in the brilliant sunlight,
because of its dense semi-tropical foliage.

There was nobody about. They passed vegetable
fields, climbed through vine-rows that terraced the ris-

ing ground, and enjoyed the shade as the path wound through a grove of heavily laden citrus trees.

"Oh my!" Teresa exclaimed as they rode out of the grove. "It is absolutely unbelievable."

Carlos was delighted with her reaction. "This is why I tell you nothing of the *hacienda*, Dona Teresa. Is it not glorious? I will ride ahead now, to tell of your coming."

Teresa slowed her horse, enjoying being alone as Carlos rode up the sloping carpet of green grass. There was a cool breeze from the gulf that wafted before it the scent of citrus and warm earth. Teresa slid down from the horse to stretch her legs as she looked at the enormous building that seemed to rise right out of the green hill it stood upon.

Santa Anna had told her of the house in his letters, but had never really described it. To Teresa, it was like a white mountain of piled squares that soared upward for four stories. From that distance, she couldn't see that it was many buildings linked together by numerous patios and inner courtyards. Even the four-storey central unit was a square, constructed around a massive patio with dancing water fountains and fish ponds.

The path suddenly widened into a crushed stone driveway that swept up to the entrance. Half-way up the drive, a grinning little Mexican boy came running to take Teresa's horse from her. As she had done several times on the journey, Teresa began to go over in her mind the words she would use in greeting her husband. She tried to forget that it was really Father Felix she had come to see.

A white-aproned, giggling girl met her at the huge oaken doors and led her through a cool hallway and into the sun-drenched patio. Still giggling, she scurried up the wide tiled stairs to the second floor. Teresa, awed by the beauty of the patio, turned round and round in admiration. When she faced the stairs again, she saw a figure standing above her, in the shadow of the over-hang, watching her every move. She didn't know who it was.

"Good afternoon," Teresa said. "I am Senora de Santa Anna."

There was a long pause, then the figure stepped into the sunlight and stood on the top step. Teresa marvelled over the gorgeous fabric of the woman's gown and lace *mantilla*. Then she saw her face. She gasped.

"Luisa! You look lovely!"

The regal clothing made the boyish Luisa seem much more mature. She eyed Teresa suspiciously as she moved slowly and majestically down the stairs, but still she didn't speak or greet her.

"Is someone calling my husband?" Teresa asked at last.

"It is *siesta* time," Luisa answered coolly.

"I should have realized that when I saw no one about. Well, it's just as well. It will give me a chance to get rid of some travel dust before he's awake."

"He isn't here," Luisa said then.

Teresa caught her breath.

Luisa added quickly, "Look, you've come at a bad time. The President was called away to Veracruz because of a death in his family. The *hacienda* is over-crowded with guests already. You might have told someone of your plans to pay a visit."

Teresa was growing angry. "I don't see that that matters now, Luisa. Just show me to my husband's room."

"That is my room."

It was like a slap in the face. Teresa controlled her anger with difficulty. The servant girl came scurrying back down the steps and started giggling again as she passed Teresa. It only added to the insult from Luisa.

Teresa's hand flicked out, stopping the girl. She said coldly, "I am Senora de Santa Anna. Please go and inform Father Escovarro that I am here."

The girl looked at her as though she had lost her mind, and then turned to Luisa for instructions. "Senora?"

"*Senora?*" Teresa exploded. "Have you taken over my title as well as my husband's bed?"

"Hush!" Luisa cautioned, glancing at the servant girl.

Teresa scoffed at Luisa. "Well, the little baggage is suddenly quite proper under her fine clothing! You're even playing the charade for the servants."

Luisa glowered. "Damn the servants! It's the President's guests I'm worried about. They are here for a *tertulia.*"

Teresa forced a smile she was far from feeling. "At the moment I am not concerned about the guests or a ball." She released her grasp on the frightened servant girl. "Now tell this girl to go get Father Felix."

Luisa looked even more uncomfortable. How could she tell Teresa there was no Father Felix at the *hacienda,* only the handsomely uniformed Captain Escovarro?

"Go back to your duties," Luisa told the servant girl. "I will take care of this."

The girl was gone like a shot. Luisa came down and stood facing Teresa.

"He is not here, either."

"And where is he?"

Luisa shrugged. "Possibly with the President."

"All right," Teresa said grimly, "I'll give you five minutes to find me a room. I will wait for their return, ball or no ball."

Luisa wasn't afraid of Teresa, only of how she might upset the household. She had come to enjoy being the mistress of that fine estate. When one of the first guests had mistakenly called her "Senora de Santa Anna," the President hadn't corrected him and she had slowly begun to act the role. Santa Anna had even encouraged it by buying her expensive French gowns, and laces and shoes from Spain and Portugal. There were some who snickered at first behind their fans at Luisa's untrained ways, but Santa Anna saw to that as well. He provided Luisa with a tutor, an aging French princess who had long been exiled from her own land. In a few months, she had taken the niece of a prostitute and turned her into a president's lady. Luisa would now fight to the death to keep from losing all she had gained.

She eyed Teresa coldly. "You may wait for them at the *Casa de la Sol,* where you belong."

Teresa's jaw dropped in astonishment. "Are you actually refusing me a room in my own home?"

"This is not your home," she said. "This is *my* home!"

Teresa reddened with anger. "We shall see how long it remains that way after I have spoken to my husband. Enjoy it while you may."

Before the tears came, she turned and fled, almost colliding with Carlos as she ran.

He hung his head sheepishly and nodded to where the Mexican boy stood holding their horses.

"I'm sorry, Senora. I did not wish you this embarrassment."

Teresa blinked. "How did you know?"

He grinned. "Maria is telling everyone in the kitchen and stable of you."

Teresa put her head in her hands and laughed helplessly. "Oh, Carlos!"

"Senora, what's the matter? Are you all right?"

Teresa raised her head. "Yes, I'm all right. I just feel so foolish."

"If I'd known they would not be here, I'd never have brought you."

"Of course you couldn't have known. Don't blame yourself."

"What now?"

"We made it from Jalapa in half a day, so we'll make it back to the same inn we stayed at last night."

"You do not wish to go south to Veracruz?"

Teresa held her breath. "Would that be wise?"

Carlos smiled helplessly. "I don't know, senora."

"Let's sleep on it."

Luisa's first impulse was to treat Teresa's visit as if it had never happened, but later in the afternoon she considered its possible consequences more seriously. It was a long road back to Saltillo and a short road to Veracruz. She had to get to Santa Anna before Teresa did and convince him she'd acted wisely. While her guests were sipping on chilled drinks in the formal courtyard, Luisa slipped away to the quarters of the dragoon permanently assigned to guard the President's estate. She carefully gave the captain in charge the orders she wanted carried out.

Teresa spoke very little on the way down from the *hacienda*. She kept a short way ahead of Carlos, riding cautiously around the steep corners, but most of the time allowing her horse to go as fast as the roughness of the path would allow. They met nobody, and came in good time through the tangle of the mangrove forest and back up onto the dusty road to Jalapa.

It was late afternoon, and the humid part of a tropical day. The breeze had dropped, and even the roadside grass drooped lifelessly. Teresa felt hot and sticky and irritable.

Carlos called to her, "There's a troop of horsemen coming fast, *senora.*"

"Horsemen?" said Teresa, almost as if it were a foreign word she had never heard before.

"Be prepared to ride fast if they are bandits."

Teresa laughed. "They would probably be more gracious than where we have just come from."

They continued to ride, with Carlos constantly looking over his shoulder. At last he sighed. "It is only a military patrol. Shall we join them for the rest of the ride into Jalapa?"

"We shall see."

She soon learned they had no choice.

"We are to see you safely back to Saltillo, Senorita de Alarcon," the sergeant of the six-man guard said gruffly. He was annoyed at being sent away from the easy life at the *hacienda.*

Teresa started to correct him and decided it would be futile. She realized Luisa was behind it. "Thanks," she said a little hollowly. He had, at least, taken one decision out of her hands. In the morning, she wouldn't have to debate between Veracruz and Saltillo. She couldn't help smiling inwardly at Luisa's daring.

"And you," the sergeant barked at Carlos, "are to report back to the *hacienda.*"

Teresa saw the angry flush rise in the boy's face.

"It's all right, Carlos," she said sweetly. "You have been a good guardian on our travels and I thank you." She stared until she had his full attention. "Besides, you have been too long away from your duties and the *padre.*"

Carlos understood then and smiled. "*Adios* for now," said Carlos amiably. He turned his horse and rode gracefully away at a full gallop. Two miles down the road, and out of their sight, he reined the horse off the track and across country. An hour later he was on the road for Veracruz.

After spending the night in Jalapa, her guards hurried Teresa home to Saltillo at a pace that exhausted her, and on arrival, she went to bed for several days.

When at last she went downstairs again, she was surprised to find the sergeant and his five men still at the *Casa de la Sol*. The sergeant, whose name was Perez, was still fuming, but no longer at Teresa.

"Senora," he said, when he came to present her with the messages that had accumulated during her days of rest, "my first words are of apology. I was unaware of your station."

His eyes told her much more. He was confused at finding Teresa was the real Senora de Santa Anna and not the one he knew at the *hacienda* in the tropics.

"And," he continued, "may I present my orders and a letter from the President?"

Teresa wasn't quite sure why he was presenting his orders to her, but accepted both of the letters he held out. Even after she read that he and his men were permanently assigned to guard the President's property in Saltillo, she didn't understand. It was only when she read the acid note from Santa Anna that it all became clear.

"Senora," Santa Anna wrote, "you nearly created for me an undesirable embarrassment and scandal. You will confine yourself to the *Casa de la Sol* until further word from the undersigned."

"Confine myself?" she cried. "What am I, Sergeant, a prisoner?"

Sergeant Perez hung his head in embarrassment. He had grown to admire her on the trip north, for she was not a woman who complained.

"There were verbal orders as well," he said sheep-ishly. "We are to escort you everywhere you go off this property, Senora de Santa Anna."

She laughed bitterly. "Except for this unfortunate little trip, I have been no farther than Saltillo in nearly a year and a half. I fail to see the need for re-straint on my travels."

"I'm sorry, Senora de Santa Anna. I am only a sol-dier taught to follow my orders."

"Don't ever call me that again!" Teresa cried. "Guard me, make me your prisoner, watch me night and day, but don't utter that name in my presence. It's beginning to sicken me that I am forced to carry it to my grave."

Perez backed out of the room as though he had been soundly reprimanded by the fiercest officer in the en-tire army. He vowed to make her imprisonment as easy for her as possible.

Again the months rolled by, and this time there were no letters from Santa Anna at all. No letters meant no funds. No funds meant that she was forced to see that the lands of the *casa* provided for her and the peasants who tilled and planted and harvested the fields. To forget the bitterness of her unhappy mar-riage, she devoted herself entirely to the people and the land.

"Escape?" she told Sergeant Perez, as she came in from the fields one day in mid-September, after set-tling a squabble over harvesting rights. "It is your President who has escaped from his responsibilities and left me a prisoner of the land. He has done nothing for the people who supported him and had faith in him."

The sergeant shrugged uneasily. "It takes time, Dona Teresa."

"The Egyptians built pyramids faster than he meets the needs of this country."

Perez hid his snicker behind a ham-like hand, then he scowled.

"Is there something you wanted?" she asked.

Perez had come to look upon Teresa as more his commanding officer than his charge. He admired and respected her more with each passing day. He felt he could trust her above all else.

"It is a personal matter," he said, scuffing the toe of his boot into the courtyard dirt.

"A woman?" she asked, amazing even herself at the effortless way the question came out.

"A lady!" he quickly corrected her and then he blushed. "Oh, Dona Teresa, it is not that . . . if that is what you were thinking it was. I mean . . ."

"All right, Sergeant, no need to go into details. Who is the lady and what is the personal problem?"

Perez glowed. "The lady is the dream of my life and the problem is her mother. She will not allow me to marry Anna-Maria."

"Why?"

His square brown face pouted like a child being scolded for something he didn't do. "I do not know. I—I was hoping you might be able to help me by talking with Anna-Maria or her mother. Frankly, the mother scares me."

Teresa didn't feel capable of handling affairs of the heart when her own were in such a mess, but she relented.

That evening, after dinner, Sergeant Perez brought Anna-Maria to the *sala* and left the two women alone.

Teresa kept quiet until the soldier had departed. A different Anna-Maria faced her. The painted face was gone, so was the low-cut blouse, but Anna-Maria was still a seductive figure even in a simple dress and with an up-swept hair-do. Teresa could not help but compare her with Luisa, and the transformation that had taken place in both of them in the past few months.

"Well," Teresa said, "this is a surprise."

"Thank you for not giving me away in front of him. That was my biggest worry."

"Why should I hurt Sergeant Perez? He is a decent man."

"I know." Anna-Maria came closer to her, and there was something in her walk that reminded Teresa of Luisa's march down the *hacienda* stairway. "I hoped you might be able to help."

"Me?" Teresa was incredulous.

"Believe me," Anna-Maria pleaded, "I love him and want to marry him. But my mother thinks I'm too good to marry a common soldier."

Teresa tried not to smile at that. "I see," she said quietly.

Anna-Maria's eyes flashed. "Oh, things have changed, senora. Mama has sold the cantina, and I've not been with a man since Luisa started sending regular amounts of money from Veracruz."

Teresa, with perfect self-control, didn't reveal even a hint of her feelings.

"Then the problem escapes me," she said calmly. It would have been so easy to be cruel, but she couldn't lower herself to their level.

"No, you understand," Anna-Maria said honestly, "but you can't bring yourself to talk about it. Mama's afraid of the day when the money from Luisa will stop, and I'll have to go back supporting her. If I'm married, that day may never come."

"Do you really want to marry him?"

"More than anything in the world."

Teresa eyed her closely and realized she was sincere. Teresa then had the choice of being vindictive or gracious.

"Are you aware of who I have become?" she asked quietly.

Anna-Maria gulped. "I didn't until he told me."

"Is your mother aware that I am Senora de Santa Anna?"

"No." Her answer was barely audible.

Teresa's voice was strong and firm. "But she is aware that Luisa is passing herself off as the wife of the President of Mexico!"

"Yes," she murmured.

Teresa smiled coldly. "Then I shall forget we have had this conversation, Anna-Maria."

The girl blinked, not understanding. "I don't follow you, senora."

"Your mother once tried to ransom me back to my family, but Santa Anna got me instead. The shoe is on the other foot. Either you marry Sergeant Perez, or I let Santa Anna know that the money that should have been coming to me and the *Casa de la Sol* has been going to your mother instead."

"Thank you, senora, thank you."

"Don't thank me until you see if your mother bites at the bait."

"She will have to, senora."

"Oh? And why is that?"

"Because she respects you and your word as a lady."

Teresa had never felt less a lady in her whole life. She was playing the game as Santa Anna might have played it, and she was disgusted.

21

CARMEN MORALES SAW the wisdom of agreeing to Anna-Maria's marriage. Luisa, with her hold on the President, was her main interest now. Her greedy eyes were already looking far into the future.

It upset Teresa to attend the wedding. If Sergeant Perez hadn't put it on such a personal basis, she would have declined.

"Senora," he said, "you have made love possible in my heart, and it has changed me. I am an orphan and orphans do not know love. You would do me the greatest honor by being my family when I stand to take my vows."

How strange, Teresa thought, that I am able to make love possible for others and not myself! Judging from what she had learned from Sergeant Perez about life at the country estate, Luisa was blissfully happy in her new life. Carmen Morales glowed in her new role as an independent woman, who no longer had to rely upon selling flesh and beer for her daily survival. Anna-Maria was a radiant bride, although a few old Saltillo hags sniffed at her daring to walk the aisle of the church in virginal white.

Teresa was also making love possible for the *peons* and farmers of the old Martin land. It had not taken her long to fathom the reason for Luis Martin's wealth and power—he had cheated his own people. For the first time in their lives, they were now getting a fair share back from their labors.

Three months had now passed since Carlos had left her on the Jalapa road. She hadn't heard from him or from Father Felix. It made her feel increasingly lonely.

The autumn sun cast long shadows over the yard as Teresa wearily pushed her chair back from the desk she'd had placed next to the weighing scales in a corner of the main barn. The farm records used to be left to Luis Martin with nothing written down, but Teresa had started a more businesslike system, thus becoming a slave to the paper work of her own invention.

Through the wide, heavy hinged door, which opened onto the courtyard of the cabin row, she could see little Arnaldo's shadow as the boy raked up oak leaves. She waited for the bullet-headed shadow to materialize into Arnaldo himself, then called to him, "Arnaldo, find your father for me, please."

She closed her tired eyes, praying it would take the always slow Arnaldo longer than usual to find his burly farmer-father. Someone approached, and she nearly cursed the boy aloud for being zealous in his duty for the first time.

"Am I disturbing you?" It was a voice she had been praying to hear and thought never to hear again.

"Oh *padre*!" she gasped, jumping from the chair so quickly that she toppled it. The sunlight was behind him, and all she could see was his tall figure. In two steps she was close to him, locked into what he tried to keep as a fatherly embrace.

"Oh, Father Felix," she cried and then she couldn't stop her tears.

"Here, here," he said with careful politeness. "I am

not used to having beautiful women cry over me." He held her close and patted her head as though she were a child. At that moment, he longed to kiss away her tears instead.

"I . . . It's been so long." Her voice was taut with strain. "Oh, what a goose I'm making of myself. I'm just so happy to have you here."

"I would prefer that no one else learns of it for a few days."

"How I wish it were that simple! I am . . ." She withdrew from his arms and bit her lower lip in confusion. "Father . . . what is this? I hardly know you out of your robes . . . and . . . That's it! You've let your hair grow back in." Then she laughed. "And a mustache!"

She had always sensed that, under the billowing brown priestly skirts was hidden a muscular body, but even in her wildest dreams she had not come close to conjuring up an image of his true virility. The buckskin shirt and trousers molded to his frame like a second skin, making the golden tuft of hair at the shirt seen more like an extension of the light tan leather garb than of his own skin. His handsome face was weathered to a golden hue from being almost constantly in the summer and autumn sun. Many of his travels, for reasons he couldn't discuss, had been made on foot and had hardened his leg muscles to the point that they were nearly bursting out of his trouser legs. The massive bulge at his crotch also made his trousers seem too small for him. He looked wonderfully fit.

And then he laughed. "My changed appearance's one of the reasons why I want to remain incognito for a few days. I'm waiting for news from Carlos. He's the only one who knows I'm here."

Teresa frowned. "It may be a hard secret to keep I'm under guard, you know."

He didn't know and it surprised him. "Who? For how long?"

"A troop of six, under Sergeant Perez. They've been here since they escorted me back from Jalapa."

Felix Escovarro pondered the news for a moment and smiled. "No one saw me arrive as I came by foot over the back fields. Besides, Perez is a good man. Would it harm your reputation to house a strange man for a few days?"

"Oh, Father, be serious. It will be my pleasure to have you here as a guest."

"Good. Can we go inside then, before someone does see me?"

Teresa consulted the clutter of papers on her desk. "You go on in, Father. You know the way to your room. I have one small bit of business to attend to and then I'll join you."

Felix carried a picture of her in his mind as he picked up his knapsack and walked easily to the *hacienda.* It was not the same picture he had carried in his mind for the past eighteen months. Her transformation was provocative. He remembered her as a fair and dainty young girl—a combination of ribbons and lace and scented finery. Softness had come to her face since she had allowed her chestnut tresses to fall loosely about her shoulders. He noted the new fullness of her breasts, unencumbered by flattening straps, allowed to move freely under the clinging lines of her simple cotton work dress . . .

"You want me?" a voice asked Teresa. This time it was Arnaldo's father.

"Why else would I send for you?" Teresa's voice was petulant, like a little girl's. The man presented her with a problem that embarrassed her. A year before she wouldn't have been able to deal with it

"Sit down, Manuel." Teresa pointed to a chair. "We must talk."

Without moving toward the chair, he shifted his lazy fat frame from one flat foot to the other. "Don't have nothing to talk about."

"I order you to sit!"

The heavily built man caused the chair to disappear beneath his bulk.

Teresa had been debating all day on how best to talk to Manuel. Now, with Father Felix in the house, she wanted to finish with him as quickly as possible.

"You are probably aware that the Gonzalez girl almost died this morning giving birth to her child. In her pain, she finally admitted who had fathered the baby. The mid-wife informs me that you are responsible for three or four other children by our young girls."

"Senor Martin always said it made more field hands faster."

Teresa's eyes flashed. "Senor Martin is dead and so are his ways. This is not a reproductive farm for human beings. Isn't it enough that you have already given your own wife twelve children?"

"Can I help it if the young girls like to play around with my big one?"

The words came from Teresa's mouth even before she realized what she was saying. "Play around one more time, Manuel, and I'll give orders for it to be cut off!"

Manuel stared straight ahead. Only a slight quiver of his wide nostrils betrayed his rage. "Your problem, senora, is that you don't have one just like it to keep you comfort at night. Maybe Manuel would leave the young'uns alone if he had something worthwhile to replace them with."

"Get out!" Teresa snapped, and she looked so angry that the Mexican toppled the chair in fleeing.

For a moment, she forgot Father Felix was waiting. The Mexican had touched a nerve and made her see, for the first time, that she might be a topic of gossip and speculation among the farm people. They didn't mention it to her face, but no doubt they wondered why she wasn't with her husband. The thought of Santa Anna made her think of Father Felix. She had someone to discuss her problems with at last.

She gave the kitchen girls the rest of the day off, and made some coffee and piled a plate high with cookies.

She knocked on Felix's door. The second floor study had become her favorite room in the whole house. It was where she and Felix had talked for hours while Santa Anna was becoming president. Those days now seemed very distant. She feared that it might take too long to rekindle their old friendship, and things would remain unsaid that had to be said.

Felix didn't help her. He had changed into a pair of soft white cotton trousers and shirt. Had it not been for his mass of curly golden locks, he would have looked like a peasant. He was so much a man that she had trouble remembering that he was also a priest.

Over coffee, he talked about his travels and the jobs he had done for Santa Anna. Just small talk, nothing personal.

"Then that explains your disguise," she said. "Was it difficult getting Mr. Austin back to San Felipe?"

"Not really. He's quite a man. In a few days, I'll know exactly how much of a man he really is. That's the news I'm waiting for from Carlos."

"Carlos is in the north?"

"Yes, with Austin. We just wait for his decision as to whether we're going to fight or not."

"Fight? You don't sound like a priest."

He was tempted to tell her the truth. "I don't feel like a priest," he hedged. He added quietly, "The treatment of Mr. Austin was terrible. He almost gave up his will to live before Santa Anna had him released from prison. I can't help it, Dona Teresa, my allegiance is with Tejas."

"And what of your allegiance to the church?"

He looked away, not wanting to face her. "It is no less, or no more. But I can no longer continue to serve Santa Anna."

"I can see why you might say that," she admitted. "You never should have been forced to do other than church work. Am I wrong, Father, in saying that he uses people for his own purposes and then discards them like an old shoe?"

"That is near the truth."

"I feel so wasted. I'm not a wife to him, Luisa is. Still I feel like the one who is sinning. Even if he were here, I wouldn't be able to bring myself to love him as a wife—or as a woman."

"Perhaps you will feel differently some day."

"I thought so once, but not now. The only way I'll be free of him is if I become a widow," she said without emotion.

He looked down at her as she sat beside him, and he thought: And I'll be there to try and claim you.

Her brown eyes, fixed so urgently on him, read his thoughts, and they softened, they filled with tears. She turned aside, and he saw her profile, delicate and chill, inexpressibly shaken. She wanted him to be nothing more than just a plain man.

"Father," she whispered, and after a pause, added: "Felix." The pulse in her white throat trembled above her brown dress collar.

"Teresa," he said, his hand reaching out and holding hers.

She struggled to regain her self-control, reminding herself he was a priest. But the tears of need were so pressing in her eyes that she couldn't hold them in. She swallowed. After a moment she spoke again, tonelessly: "For a moment I forgot *who* you were."

She did not look at him. Her eyes were fixed on the coffee cup on the low table. But she felt the grip on her hand loosen, fall away.

Then Felix spoke, and his voice seemed to come from a great distance: "And I can't forget *what* you are."

Then Teresa laughed aloud, with a bitter undertone that sounded despairing to Felix. He recognized its harshness, desolate and infinitely derisive. She had suffered too much, he thought.

"What am I, really?" she murmured. "Luisa thinks nothing of climbing into my husband's bed as many times as his stamina will allow, but I must hide my desires behind rigid rules of moralistic church law. I wish I was daring. I wish that we were both free from our separate vows for just a single hour."

He looked at her desperate face. Her lips were tight with bitterness; the exquisite distended nostrils seemed carved from marble. It was a mouth that needed kissing to softness; a nose that must smell the scent of love.

He caught her in his arms and pressed his mouth hard upon hers. She melted against him. He felt the excited, tumultuous beating of her heart against his chest. A wild rapture swept over him. His large hands caressed her demanding body, hot and seeking, and her firm flesh softened and yielded.

They were aware of nothing but their coming together, satisfying their desperate hunger for each other.

Then he felt her draw back, away from him.

"No," she said firmly. "We can't . . . not now."

"I turned priest again," he said gloomily.

"It has nothing to do with us. I've always found you . . . desirable." Then striving for her old detachment, and succeeding only in making her voice uneven and breathless, she said: "I'm afraid that once we start there will be no ending. I can't be responsible for dooming you to hell. My thoughts have already doomed me."

"Teresa, you may hate me, but there is something I must say."

"No," she cried, jumping up. "Any more words and I'll be right back in your arms."

"That is my intention, if you will just listen."

She covered her ears with her hands and fled from the room. Their relationship had already gone too far.

Felix cursed himself for not telling her the truth earlier. He had been so close, but the fear of losing her was too great. She was going to have every right in the world to hate him forever, and he had to make sure that didn't happen. The time of truth had to be postponed.

Teresa's fierce resolution to blot the scene from her memory was a hard one to keep. The first few days weren't so hard. Every instinct of her upbringing kept her going through the day. It was at night when her resolve would slip. The memory of his arms around her, crushing her with cruel force, his hot lips on hers in mad, unchecked kisses brought her blood surging into her cheeks. She walked up and down in angry frustration, and dropped at last exhausted.

"Why does he have to be so much of a man?"

Why did she feel drawn to a priest? Why—why—why? The very question cut her. She had a sneaking desire to bring him down to the level of all men as a punish-

ment for having married her to Santa Anna. There
was something perverse in her somehow, she thought.
She could see it now. It must be so or the sensuality in
Felix's character would not have drawn her as a mag-
net from the first. She hadn't a doubt now that Luisa
or Anna-Maria would have crawled quickly into his
bed, priest or no. But was she any better?

When four days passed without a further move on
Felix's part, the first skirmish between love and pride
began. Tears of vexation came in spite of her determined effort to maintain her resolve. She had to face
the plain truth. She was in love. It wasn't a whim or a
fancy that would go away after he left. He was the
man she wanted forever: virile, manly, masterful. Her
love might doom them both, but she knew she had to
admit it to him sooner or later. She accepted the fact
at last in a burst of bitter tears.

And then Carlos returned. It was a different Carlos
who now sat with Teresa and Felix. He was jubilant
over the news he brought.

"Oh, what a fight," he exulted. "Suddenly the fog
lifted and there the two sides were, gaping at each
other in surprise. Castaneda wanted the Texans' cannon and they yelled back 'Come and take it.' I don't
know who first fired, but a rattle of muskets came from
everywhere. Then they gave them the cannon, right
in their faces. Wow! What a roar and shower of nails
and old horseshoes. That was it. Castaneda's troops
broke and ran for the road back to San Antonio."

"What does Austin say?"

"War is the only recourse after the battle at Gonzales."

"Where is General Cos?"

"In San Antonio. He has it under military occupa-
tion and is confiscating weapons, searching houses, and
arresting people all over the place."

"Oh, no," Teresa gasped. "Will the war be fought right in San Antonio? Will my mother be safe?"

Felix tried to reassure her. "I doubt that Cos will want to fight, he never has before. Besides, if the Texans move quickly, they can cut off his supply trains from the south."

Carlos grinned. "They are not only doing that, but Mr. Austin is leading an army of 500 to throw General Cos out of San Antonio and out of Texas. That's why he says you're to break your ties with Santa Anna and come right back. You're needed at home, Captain."

"Captain?" Teresa said. "Are you going to take a military rank, Father?"

Carlos blushed at his blunder. It was the only thing he held against Captain Escovarro. His respect for Teresa was so great that he felt she deserved to know the truth.

Felix ignored the remark. "I am going to do what I must do, that is all. Now, it is late and we must get an early start in the morning. I'm sure Santa Anna has had this news for days and is not sitting on it. Dona Teresa, may I impose upon your stable by buying a horse? My legs got me here slowly for a reason. I'll need four fast ones to get me back."

"Take your pick, Father," she said.

"Thank you. Oh, don't disturb yourself in the morning, we'll be leaving quite early. I'll come and wake you in the servants' quarters, Carlos. Good night."

"Good night, sir. Good-bye, Dona Teresa."

"Good-bye Carlos," she said. "Safe journey."

When Felix said good-bye to her, Teresa gave him a curt nod and turned away. When she turned back, he was gone, and she stood fuming.

He's going to leave me again, she thought. Just like that! Poof! In and out of her life almost as quickly as

Santa Anna. With a toss of her head, she stalked back
to her bedroom and began her nightly pacing to ease
her frustrations.

She was so lost in her thoughts, and unaware of the
passage of time, that sudden shouts in the yard
brought her back with a violent jolt. She ran to the
window and stared down in disbelief. She had heard
nothing, but the courtyard was packed solid with soldiers on horseback. One rough-looking man was haul-
ing Carlos, kicking and cursing, across the yard.

She threw up the sash and bellowed: "Unhand him!
What is the meaning of this?"

"Who's there?" someone called out at the dark
house.

"Senora de Santa Anna," she called back. "What are
you doing?"

"Excuse our intrusion, senora," a smooth voice
floated up to her. "I am Colonel Fazio on special orders from the President. As we suspected, we have
caught the first of the two spies we seek"

"Nonsense," she scoffed. "I will be right down as
soon as I dress."

Teresa had not yet undressed, but she knew they
could not see her in the dark window. She needed the
time to warn Felix. He was awake at the first touch of
her hand.

"Don't say anything," she whispered. "Just go to my
window and look out. I'm going on down. Stay in my
room, they won't search there."

She went directly to the burly soldier who was holding Carlos with his arms behind his back. "He is only
a boy," she said impatiently and removed the man's
hands. She didn't feel fear, just blind rage.

"More than a mere boy," Colonel Fazio told her,
smiling down at her sweetly from his horse, his Span-

ish thickened by his native Italian accent. "We know that he is a courier recently returned from San Antonio. We have watched his travels for days."

Teresa laughed and hoped that it sounded relaxed. "If that is his only crime, Colonel, then I am the guilty party. San Antonio de Bexar is my home, and he brought me news of my mother."

The Italian soldier of fortune eyed her narrowly. "Your husband thinks differently, senora. He suspects that this was to be the boy's rendezvous point with Felix Escovarro de Sanchez."

"Father Felix, a spy," she said with mock shock. "The thought is utterly preposterous."

Colonel Fazio smiled. Escovarro's charade as a priest was well known to many of his fellow officers, and they had chuckled over it when it served their purpose. It sounded to him as though Escovarro had fooled this woman as well, and to make it easier to capture the man, he decided it might be best to let her continue to think along those lines.

"Perhaps," he said gently. "But the fact remains that he disappeared from Mexico City when a man by the name of Stephen Austin was sent back to Tejas. Some who know Escovarro spotted him in San Felipe, and then he disappeared again. He will show up here, I am sure."

"And then?"

Fazio was matter of fact. "He will be shot. He may have already told the Texans too much, but he will not be allowed to tell them anything more."

Teresa eyed him coldly. "Then you are looking in the wrong place. That priest has not been here for over a year, and Carlos was not carrying messages for the church."

"I have no reason to doubt your word on either

point, senora. I will still have to keep the *hacienda* under guard until we can be sure he is not coming here."

"Under guard," she scoffed. "Colonel, this house has been under guard for several months."

Out of the corner of her eye, Teresa had seen Sergeant Perez come scurrying into the yard, pulling on his clothes as he ran. After the wedding, she had given him permission to take one of the better cabins and fix it up for his bride. She prayed that the sergeant would back her up no matter what she said. Perez knew that Felix was there, because he had seen them talking one day.

Fazio wasn't easily fooled. "Then how did the boy get in if it is so guarded?"

Perez had heard enough of the conversation to determine what the situation was and which side profitted him most. He jumped forward and gave the Colonel a snappy salute. "Sir, Sergeant Perez, in charge of the *Casa de la Sol* guard dragoons. The answer, sir, if I may, is that the lad was known to us as a courier for the Senora de Santa Anna and allowed to enter without challenge."

Teresa sighed thankfully.

"And what of this priest, Escovarro?"

Perez didn't have to lie. "I have not seen a priest on this property since my arrival, Colonel."

Fazio was snide. "That means nothing, Sergeant. No one saw or heard my dragoons ride on to the property, either."

Perez gulped, but was not intimidated. He considered himself a professional soldier and resented the large number of foreign officers that Santa Anna had recruited rather than let true Mexicans rise in the ranks. He shrugged. "This is Saltillo, my Colonel, where nothing moves after sundown. I established the same guard hours as was our custom at the President's estate."

"All right," Fazio barked, seeing that he was getting nowhere. "Do you have some place to lock up the boy, just in case . . .?"

Teresa stepped forward. "He will now stay in the main *hacienda* with me, senor." She took Carlos by the arm and marched him into the *hacienda* without looking back.

Colonel Luigi Fazio smiled to himself. He considered Antonio de Santa Anna to be a fool on many accounts, but he had just viewed his most foolish mistake. His mistress was pap and his wife whole wheat. He could understand Santa Anna's desire to have her guarded from other men, but what a waste of womanhood! He motioned for Sergeant Perez to follow them and check that they were secure for the night.

"I'm sorry," Teresa said shakily, as the sergeant joined them in the foyer. "I got you in deeper than I intended."

"Senora, you didn't put the words into my mouth."

"What are we going to do?" Carlos asked briskly.

This thought had been worrying Teresa, too, but she wasn't going to admit it. "There's not much we can do until morning. Carlos, you go on up and stay in Father Felix's room. It's all right, he's over in my room watching the soldiers from the window. He'll be safer there, and I'll just stay up and try to think of something."

Carlos looked troubled, but obeyed.

Perez was also looking uneasy. "Look, senora, you heard them. They will shoot Escovarro without asking questions. If they catch him with you, they will shoot you as well."

"*I'm* quite safe," she said firmly. "Are they going to shoot the wife of their President?"

"As a matter of fact," said Perez frankly, "it is very possible. Your enemy is quite strong."

"Enemy?"

Perez dropped his eyes. "Senora, it was Senorita Luisa who sent us that day. We . . . we were told that if an accident should befall you, that we would not be held to account."

Surprisingly, it did not shock Teresa. "You mean that you were given license to murder me?"

"But we could not," he quickly protested. "And now after all that you have done for me . . . well."

She smiled, warmly and sincerely. "Don't worry about me, Sergeant Perez. If I can just get the two of them safely away from here, I'll take my chances with Luisa and President Santa Anna."

"Such selflessness is the truest mark of pure love, senora."

"What?" She said it blankly, her hand unconsciously touching her breast.

"What has been in your heart and eyes these past few days hasn't been hidden. I will somehow help you get him to safety."

Perez assumed she knew that Escovarro was an officer and not a priest. As she had helped him with his love affair, so he would help her with hers.

"Thank you," she whispered, "we will talk again in the morning."

"Good night, senora."

Anna-Maria was wide awake when he crawled back beside her on the straw pallet. She, like almost everyone from the cabin row, had crept into the night, clinging to the shadows and eavesdropping.

"What does it mean?" she asked, her voice quivering.

He pulled her into the crook of his arm and comforted her. For a long moment he didn't answer, his mind racing. After leaving Teresa, he had reported back to Colonel Fazio and then made a leisurely round of the *hacienda* yard, casually talking with the sentries that the colonel had ordered posted. It didn't take long for him to gain all the news and gossip out of Tejas and the President's headquaters on his estate. What he had learned was bad news.

"There is to be war," he finally said, with a long sigh.

"Will you go?" He sensed rather than heard the fear in her voice.

"I am a soldier."

"But we are hardly over the last war," she protested.

"I know, my sweetheart, I know."

He was silent again for so long that Anna-Maria thought that he had fallen back to sleep. His sigh came right out of the depths of his soul. "With that war I did not fear, because I had nothing to lose. Now I am filled with the fear of losing you. You are the only good thing I have ever had in life."

"Oh, Pedro," she cried. "Can't the senora help us?"

He laughed. "She is looking to me for help, Mari-aleta."

"Why?"

"You heard the colonel. They want Captain Escovarro."

"But you told him that he was not here. Even the women I was standing among knew you spoke the truth. Let them go look for him elsewhere and leave us alone."

"Anna-Maria," he said slowly, "is this true of everyone at the *hacienda*? I mean, do they all believe that he is not here?"

She slapped his shoulder playfully. "Don't talk foolish. If he was here, they would be talking of nothing else."

Perez suddenly recalled how cautious Escovarro had been in approaching him and how he had thought at the time how odd the conversation had gone. An idea suddenly came to him.

"Darling," he whispered, "don't raise your voice when you answer me. These past four or five days, has anything been different around here?"

In the darkness, Anna-Maria shrugged. "I don't think so, except for the senora's unusual temper."

"Temper?"

"She hasn't let any of the house servants do their work and has been doing her own cooking. They're lazy anyway and haven't minded."

"*Caramba!*" he wheezed. "She has really kept him hidden."

Anna-Maria shivered. "He *is* here!"

He hugged her close in answer and she began to cry softly.

"Hush, my sweet, hush!"

"They will shoot you," she sobbed. "They will shoot you all when they learn you have lied."

"Ah, but they will not learn." He tilted up her chin and kissed her. "You wish me not to go to war, *si?*"

"*Si.*"

"Tomorrow Pedro Perez thinks he starts to keep that promise." He reached over and gently fondled her breasts. "But for the moment, are you tired?"

"Never for you."

And later, when he had rolled away from her exhausted, and the rhythm of his snoring had taken on a steady beat, she lay awake, but unafraid. With any other man in her life, she would have been demanding how he meant to keep his promise. With Pedro, she did not have to hound or beg or plead or threaten. She felt comfortable and secure with her man and knew that whatever he said was the right thing to do, would be the right thing for her. She kissed him tenderly on the shoulder, snuggled next to his warmth and was almost instantly asleep.

Teresa didn't know the time. She had drunk so many cups of coffee that her stomach was acid sour. Sometime during the night, when her bone marrow had turned chilled from the cold, she wrapped a shawl around her shoulders and took the big iron coffee pot and tin cups out to the yard to share the hot liquid with the soldiers who kept parading past the windows.

Their gratitude was so gentle that her fear they would storm the house at any moment and begin searching evaporated. Bone-weary, she did what she thought would now look natural to them, and went back to her own bedroom.

The room was bitter cold, and she went to close the window sash. Felix sat huddled in her favorite chair, a comforter wrapped about his shoulders. He had dashed to her room after the warning and had remained there, taking his cue from the conversation he heard from the yard below. It was not concern for his own life which had kept him from returning to his room and dressing, but the fear that he might endanger Teresa.

She leaned her head against the window, staring down into the yard. "I asked Sergeant Perez to help get you away." Her fear for his safety was genuine.

"Don't be idiotic! He's been put in enough danger already."

She shivered from the cold, weariness and worry.

He rose and wrapped part of the comforter about her, unmindful that he was clad only in a pair of woolen long-johns. She welcomed his arm and the comforter about her shoulders. They were both a part of the warmth and support that she sorely needed.

"And I don't want you getting involved, either," he said. "You've gone about as far as you can go."

She sighed. "I'm not a child, but there are some things I haven't come up against. This feeling I have for you is one of them and it's a little frightening. I want you to go away yet I fear that I'll never see you again. I want to be near you and I want to run away from you. I dream of you and try to forget my dreams. I . . ."

This time the kiss turned her dream into reality. Teresa accepted the soothing comfort of strong male arms without reservation. She closed her eyes and ears to the sights and sounds of trouble, nestling close to his chest. Arms that had longed to hold her passionate body now encircled her protectively. She shuddered and crept closer to the reassuring strength of his masculinity until her trembling conveyed a new fear. His kiss and embrace were protective and nothing more. She had been the one to check their first encounter and now Felix was letting this second opportunity quickly slip away.

Teresa was not going to walk out her frustrations that night—the last night she might ever see him again. She thrust her hands into the tight curls of his hair, she touched his eyes, nose, cheeks, and lips with her lips. With an instinct that was new to her, she dared to rub against him in sensual delight, like a purring cat. The gray wool long-johns were scratchy to her hands. An intense, delicious capriciousness overcame her as she deftly popped open the under-wear buttons from neck to crotch. The comforter fell away, but she no longer needed its warmth.

With great tenderness, her hands enjoyed a warmth unknown to her. She marveled at the furry softness of his chest and stomach hair; and the fiery heat that emanated from his muscular torso. But it was the heat burning up her pelvis that surprised her. Santa Anna's body had been cold, even the skin of his manhood. But pressing against the wool of dress and long-johns was a flaming rod that threatened to burn right through the double layer of cloth.

Felix Escovarro was shaking with passion and wonder. This was only his third woman in twenty-five years, and he was benumbed by excitement. He, too, had found the other bodies cold and professional. With Teresa, he thought he was going to expire from the fever she had aroused in every inch of his long body. They were children playing at a game without knowledge of its rules, with Teresa the more astute learner of the two. When his fingers became all thumbs, fumbling at the removal of her dress, she quietly stepped back from the embrace and let the garment fall to the floor. In wide-eyed surprise, his jaw slowly dropped as she deftly extracted a petticoat and undergarments and revealed her curving womanly body to his hot gaze. As if he were a child needing guidance, she took him by the hand and led him to the bed, pulling the underwear from his shoulders before crawling between the cold linen sheets.

His mind was too befuddled to recall sliding in beside her. He tasted again the love on her mouth, sensed her feverish hunger, and gave himself up to her demand for uncontrolled passion. Teresa stiffened at first under the massiveness of his manly assault, clenched her fists at the joyous joining until her hands were wet, then turned the union into a frantic, savage meshing of bodies that left them both so weak and limp that they drifted into a fairyland sleep without disengaging . . .

22

TERESA DIDN'T GET out of bed right away. Sometime during the night, Felix had put his long-johns back on and now lay asleep on the floor, rolled up in the comforter. After seeing where he was, she couldn't look in his direction again. She lay on her back, staring at the rough beamed ceiling and reproaching herself for having given in the demands of her flesh. It would be the first and last time, she reasoned. An experience, nothing more.

She got out of bed and dressed hurriedly. She wanted him away from there that day so she could restore her life to its normal routine. She needed love and needed it badly, but the evil in what she had done overwhelmed her. It was bad enough just realizing that she had become an adultress, without wondering what words she would use in making her full confession.

Coming into the kitchen, she was surprised to find it already busy. Stacks of steaming *tortillas* rested in the warming oven, and two iron skillets on the stove wafted out the sweet aroma of re-fried beans. But the biggest surprise was in finding that Anna-Maria was hard at work.

Anna-Maria smiled at Teresa, but her eyes warned her to keep quiet.

"Leah," Anna-Maria said to the young kitchen girl who had been frying the *tortillas*, "those will only be half enough to feed all the soldiers. You'd better go grind more corn-meal."

"By hand?" Teresa asked, suddenly remembering that all the chores had been postponed after Carlos' arrival. "Manuel and I were to have taken the wagon of corn to the mill yesterday. Tell some of the other girls that I said to help you."

"*Si*, senora," she said, smiling slyly at Anna-Maria,

"We will also need ham and eggs for the Italian colonel's breakfast," Anna-Maria said to Teresa. "Dolores didn't want to go to the smokehouse or chicken coop until you approved."

"Do it," she said to the second girl in the kitchen, seeing that Anna-Maria wanted them to be alone.

As soon as the kitchen door closed, Anna-Maria took two bundles out from the underneath the preparation table.

"This is the plan of my husband," she said proudly. "Here is an old uniform of my husband that should fit the senor, and this holds some of my clothing for the boy."

Teresa blinked in astonishment. "And how is this plan supposed to work?"

Anna-Maria smiled broadly. "I will give you my husband's words. You must have breakfast with the colonel as a proper hostess and to keep his mind occupied. When his soldiers come to eat at the servant's tables, the senor will slip among them, eat his breakfast and then go to meet my Pedro in the stables. Later they will ride out as though on regular patrol."

"And Carlos?"

She giggled. "He may not like it, senora, but it was all we could think of to save him. Since dawn, I've had girls coming and going from the kitchen so that the soldiers would stop paying attention to them. When he is dressed in my things, he, too, can slip from the kitchen and across the yard. Pedro will have horses ready for the boy and I, and you are to send us to town on an errand. Does it not happen like that here everyday?"

"Yes," she agreed weakly, "but without the danger. You will both be in trouble the moment you return without them."

"Senora," she whispered, "we shall not return. We shall take our love away from this coming war."

Teresa sat down wearily at the table. Her dizzy glow of having just experienced love evaporated in comparison with this true love put to such a test.

"Anna-Maria," she said, "I will do all you say. I admire your courage and wish . . . wish . . ." She couldn't say it, but oh, how she wished she could also walk away so easily!

She didn't have to finish for Anna-Maria to see into her heart. "If you wish to leave, do so. Pedro can work out a plan."

"No. The colonel would not let his most prized prisoner leave so easily."

"Don't you mean your husband?" she said coolly.

"I am more the prisoner of your cousin than of Santa Anna."

"The little tramp," Anna-Maria scoffed. "But how long can that charade continue?"

"As long as she has him and I do not," she said.

"Do you love him?" Anna-Maria asked curiously.

"Not in the way that I see you love Sergeant Perez." Teresa didn't want to answer any more questions. "I'd better get this clothing to them before the girls return."

Teresa dropped the bundle off with Carlos first, with every intention of having the boy take the uni-

form on to Felix. But Felix had returned to his own
room and was already dressed in his buckskins. They
couldn't look at each other, and her words had an edge
to them as she outlined the sergeant's plan. Felix only
nodded his silent acceptance of it.

As Anna-Maria had anticipated, Carlos was adamantly against dressing as a girl.

"I'm no *maricon*," he shrieked.

"*Mire*," Felix stormed, "it is only to save your life,
muchacho! Do I have to make it an order?"

Carlos hung his head and fought back bitter tears. It
was the first time his hero had ever raised his voice to
him and that hurt more than the thought of having to
parade around as a girl.

Felix hated himself the moment his temper flared.
He knew it was not right taking his anger out on Carlos, when it was Teresa he wanted to scream and rant
at. How could moonlight bliss turn into such a sour
dawn? He wanted to shake her and shout the truth
into her ears and then love her as she had loved him.
Time, and the presence of Carlos, were against him
doing anything.

Then he softened, but only towards Carlos. "I'm
sorry, my little courier, I didn't have a very good
night. We must now make some plans of our own."

Carlos accepted the apology with a broad grin. He
took the bundle from Teresa and didn't understand,
as their hands touched for a bare second, why hers were
so icy cold.

Felix didn't realize that his words to soften Carlos
would be heard quite differently by Teresa and
harden her heart and body to frigid ice. She was so
stunned that she could only stand and listen as they
made their plans.

"Did you stop at the Esparza ranch on the way back
from Tejas?"

"No, senor, my horse was fresh and able to make these last ten miles."

"Good! Then Fazio won't know that they are friendly to me. You go to Senor Esparza and wait for me. If I am not there by sundown, you go on to my father's *ranchero* without me."

"I will wait."

"Only till sundown," he said sternly.

Carlos grinned. He would wait for the man until his dying day.

Anna-Maria came and told them the soldiers were eating and Escovarro should join them quickly. In five minutes, she would have the girl leave the kitchen so that Teresa could bring Carlos down, and then she should join the Colonel.

Felix started to say good-bye to Teresa, but the cold fury in her eyes made him flee before he cursed at her. He stormed back to Teresa's room to change into Pedro's uniform.

Anna-Maria had seen both of their reactions and had been amazed. *Caramba,* she thought, she is in love with the priest who would be a soldier. It was not hard for Anna-Maria to see how that was possible. In the months that he had spent in Saltillo, going to church each day in his brown skirts, she had often seen him on the street and cursed the church for taking such a man out of the brothels. And having now seen him in the tight-fitting buckskins, she realized that he was more of a man than she had ever dreamed. If she had been Teresa, she would spurned Santa Anna for the likes of Felix Escovarro any day of the week.

As Teresa and Carlos passed Dona Clara's old room, she suddenly stopped. "Wait a moment," she said, and then added petulantly, "Carlos, stop fidgeting. I know it's a little uncomfortable with your own clothes on under the skirt and blouse, but you've got to keep the shawl from falling off your head." Then she grinned. "You do have a pretty face, so don't let any of the soldiers get near enough to pinch you."

He stood blushing and scowling as she went into her grandmother's room and reached far back into the desk drawer. Her fingers closed around the leather pouch, and she clutched its weight to her breast as she rejoined Carlos in the hall.

"*Mi amigo*," she said, her voice full of warmth for the first time that day, "this was my grandmother's 'emergency gold.' This, I suppose, is an emergency. If it is needed, use it. If not, the senor will know how to get it to my mother, who may have need of it if war comes."

Carlos gasped at its weight. "Senora," he protected, "this much fills me with fright. What if I meet bandits?"

"Then give it to them," she said with a laugh. "For such a purse, they will spare your life."

"I—I—" Without warning he leaned forward and kissed her on the cheek. "I love you!" He picked up the skirts and ran so quickly away that his rolled up pant legs began to fall down.

It took the starch right out of Teresa. She sat down on the top stair before she fell down and rested her cheek against the cool plaster of the wall. In spite of the tenderness of the words, they worried her like unbidden ghosts. They were words of love, and in all the passion of the night before, they had been uttered a single time.

"Senora," a bark came from the foot of the stairs. "How long am I supposed to wait for my breakfast?"

She glowered down at the pompous man and was tempted to tell him to go straight to hell. She did just as well in her own words. "The servants will see to your needs whenever you are ready, Colonel. I do not sit with strange men unless my husband is present."

With a fiery flush rising all the way over his bald pate, he marched into the dining room and snapped out his demands to an amused Anna-Maria.

My, my, Teresa thought. I seem to have the ability today to make all the men in the world turn surly. She rose and walked calmly down the stairs and into the dining room. Without once glancing at the man, she addressed Anna-Maria.

"When you are finished serving the guest," she said, as though she gave orders to Anna-Maria daily, "you will take Carlita and the list I left in the kitchen to do the marketing."

"No one is to leave the *hacienda* grounds today," the colonel said harshly.

Teresa said quietly: "Colonel, you overstep yourself. Much to the amazement and pleasure of my husband, I've managed to turn this piece of property into a money-making venture. I daresay it probably helps pay for the lavish salary you must demand. There are daily routines that I will not allow you to tamper with."

He scowled at Anna-Maria. "Go do your shopping." Then he sprang back at Teresa. "Where is the boy?"

She laughed insolently. "Why, I let him escape during the night."

"Bah!" he fumed, and attacked his plate of food viciously.

As soon as she was through the kitchen door she leaned against its jamb as though exhausted. Then she whispered: "Go quickly, Anna-Maria. God's speed to you all."

Anna-Maria took one of Teresa hands in both of hers. "When I first saw you in the cantina, I thought you were spoiled and vain and never wanted to become like you. Today I would admire being just like you."

"Go," Teresa said weakly, wanting her gone before the words brought about another emotional outpouring.

Anna-Maria understood. With all of her heart she understood, and left quickly.

Neither Felix nor Carlos had any trouble in crossing the yard and making it to the stable. Pedro already had the horses saddled in their stalls and was making idle chit-chat with some of Fazio's soldiers in the courtyard. Not wishing to be seen together, Felix went into the darkest reaches of the stables and left Carlos near the heavily laden corn wagon.

Felix felt the presence of someone else even before the person loomed up out of the darkness.

"Who is it?" he demanded. "Who is there?"

A lucifer was struck, blinding him for a moment in its flare. When it died to single flame on its wooden base, Felix began to relax, his fist unclenching. It was only Manuel, one of the field foremen.

"Oh, Manuel," he sighed. "You gave me a fright."

The Mexican, who was still annoyed at the way Teresa had reprimanded him on the day of Felix's arrival, calmly touched the match to a candle bowl he had brought with him and set it carefully down on a bale of hay.

"Do not worry, senor," he said smoothly. "Its glow cannot be seen in the front of the stable."

"I don't see the need for it," Felix said reasonably.

"Manuel does." He grinned until the gold cap on his front tooth glittered. "Manuel sees much, now. How does one address you? *Padre*? *Capitano*? Oh, no Manual sees that you have been reduced to a lowly sergeant. Too bad!"

Felix threw up both hands in a gesture of rage. He

knew what the wily Mexican was up to. But the quick movement of his fist was too late. Manual, on guard, jumped back, drawing an ancient pistol from beneath his blouse.

"Don't move," he snarled. "I'm not afraid to kill you."

"But I am afraid to die," Felix said calmly. "Why are you holding me at gun-point?"

"For the money," he said, in a voice he might have used to a dog. "The thousand *peso* reward to anyone who can prove you are at this *hacienda.*"

Felix's glare was cold and calculating. Time and the man's ignorance were his only protection. "Can you trust Colonel Fazio to pay you? He is not one of us."

A slight grin of triumph cracked Manuel's mouth. "That is only the reward for information, senor. I shall demand much more for the body—dead or alive."

"Are we beginning to bargain?" Felix said stupidly, but on purpose.

"Has the senor something to bargain with?" Manuel asked. "At what price do you value your life and freedom?"

The answer came from behind Felix. "As high as I am able to bargain for it, senor."

Felix looked back and gasped out, "Oh, Carlos! Why didn't you stay in the front of the stable? Get on back!"

To Felix's surprise, Carlos ignored him and eyed Manuel levelly. "Well, " he barked, "are we talking terms or not?"

Manuel stood blinking, and then he began to chuckle. "I would answer if I knew if I was dealing with a girl, a boy or a *maricon.*"

"Shut up, *blackmailer*!" Carlos sneered, snatching the pouch of gold coins from beneath the skirts and waving it in Manuel's face. "If you want any portion on this, you'd better speak quickly."

Manuel eyed the heavy pouch with unconcealed greed. "A portion?" he leered. "I have the gun and can take it all."

"Not really," Carlos remarked so resignedly that Felix stared at him in wonder. "The soldiers will question your need to kill us when we are unarmed. They will search you and find the gold, and then will hang you for a bandit."

Carlos' warning and his calm manner momentarily upset Manuel and took away his advantage. "*Basta!*" he snarled. "It has to be five times the thousand they would pay me for information." He faced Felix, who again turned his wondering gaze on Carlos, still unsure what was the boy's plan. He knew Carlos was penniless, the pouch a trick of some sort. He imagined Carlos was trying to lure Manuel far enough forward so he could spring at him and disarm him. He assumed that Carlos would quickly agree to Manuel's demand to get closer.

"What?" Carlos barked. Then he laughed. "You are a piglet with no sow to suckle upon. You can have just twice their reward or nothing!"

Manuel scowled. "Your mouth has been cracked by taking too large a *bicho, muchacho!* Four times the amount!"

This time the laugh was sardonic. "I have been under the impression that your mother gave birth to children. I was mistaken! Thrice and no more!"

Manuel's face twisted into a bitter rage. "All," he shrieked, raising the gun and pointing it at Felix's head.

"Then, nothing!" Carlos screamed back.

Sweat streaked down Felix's face and ran down his throat, soaking the uniform. He could do nothing but look down the dark barrel of the gun, then he sensed that they were not alone. Manuel suddenly jerked back, and then forward, all in one movement, dropping the gun and tearing at his back with both hands. Over his face came a look of pained surprise. His eyes wer still open, inquiring, as he started to fall.

Before he had collapsed on the stable floor, Sergeant Perez was yanking the pitchfork out of his back and tossing it aside.

"Quickly," he rasped, "help me hide him."

The words brought Felix back to his senses. "Don't be idiotic," he snapped. "Once we are gone, they will find him and put Teresa in danger."

"I've also got my wife to think of," Perez flared. "She's in the front of the stable ready to leave right now."

"I am here," Anna-Maria said, stepping out of the shadows. "And he is right."

"Oh, Anna-Maria," he pleaded, "please go back."

"No," she said adamantly, "we have got to reason this out and come up with a different plan."

"We don't have the time."

Her voice was so commanding that they couldn't help but listen to her. "Time? She is the wife of the President and could have turned us in to Fazio at any time without harm to herself. I am not leaving here until I know she will be safe or is with us."

"Yes," Felix said, as though the original thought was his, "she is going with us."

"How?" Perez demanded.

"I have already thought of that," Anna-Maria said trumphantly. "She was to go to the grain mill yesterday and didn't. Today she will go."

"Without Manuel as a driver?"

"And who will talk her into it?"

"It will still leave the body."

"Colonel Fazio won't buy it and will send soldiers after us."

They had all been talking at once, voicing their fears, until someone had to assume command. "Enough," Felix said softly, but firmly. "Anna-Maria's thought has merit. Leave Perez and me here to work out the details, and you two set off before you become suspect."

"No," she protested, "not as before. I will take the boy to town and no farther. Pedro, I will wait for you at my mother's old cantina."

"All right," he agreed, knowing better than to argue.

"That's fine," Felix concurred. "Carlos knows his orders."

The two men gave them a half-hour start before they put the next phase of their plan into operation.

"Leave?" Teresa was incredulous. "Sergeant, you are becoming as impetuous as your wife. I can't leave. Give me one good reason."

Quietly, he told her of Manuel's death and she paled.

The noise of their voices brought Colonel Fazio from the *sala*, where he had taken up residence after breakfast as though it were his own home.

"Is something the matter?" he asked.

"No, my colonel," Pedro answered. "I was just discussing the food situation with Senor de Santa Anna. The corn meal and flour are all gone."

"Didn't two of the servants already go into town to shop?"

"That is beside the point," Teresa said smoothly. "We were discussing the need to get a full wagon of corn into the grinding mill. The few pounds that the girls could bring back on horses wouldn't last half a meal."

Fazio was a suspicious man by nature. He was also a Roman and had no knowledge of farm life.

"Is this flour so necessary?"

Teresa laughed. "Not if you're not a Mexican. It is needed for the men's *tortillas* as much as it is needed for your *pasta*."

"Take me to the wagon, Sergeant, while I consider the problem."

After they had gone, Teresa had to decide what she was going to do. If she refused to go with the wagon, she was all but dooming them to failure. And once she had left the *hacienda*, there could be no returning. Trying to put Felix out of her mind, she told herself that she would have to do it for Pedro's sake. She didn't want him charged with the murder of Manuel, and the wagon of corn was needed to get his body away. With a heavy heart, she went to her room and began preparing for the journey. She suddenly had a premonition that if she didn't escape now, she would never have another opportunity. If war came, she would be looked on as an enemy. Santa Anna would never be able to acknowledge openly that his wife was an enemy. She would be even more of a prisoner than she and Dona Clara had been during their first few days at the *hacienda*.

The squeak of wagon wheels on the hard gravel made her stop brooding. She went to the window and shook her head in dismay. The soldiers were dumping the corn out of the wagon onto the gravel.

Her instant fury turned to disbelief as she came storming into the courtyard, for Felix Escovarro was one of the hardest working soldiers removing the corn.

She said uncertainly, "I trust you have a good reason for this, Colonel."

"The best." The curtness of his tone had a way of making everything he said sound like a command. "I want to make sure that no one is hiding under the corn."

"I'm sure the men will appreciate your zeal for duty when their teeth grit on the dirt in the meal."

He ignored her as though she were not there. "Did you find anything, Sergeant Perez?"

"Nothing, sir."

"Then have the men reload," he commanded. "After that, you will pick two of my men to escort the wagon to the mill. *All* of your men will stay on the *hacienda* grounds."

Teresa heard the order. Everything seemed to be going wrong. She searched Perez's eyes for a clue to his thinking. He purposely kept them expressionless so Colonel Fazio wouldn't see his concern. He was just thankful that Felix had not already loaded Manuel's body under the corn. Felix was also relieved that he had not already dressed himself in the clothing he had stripped from Manuel's body in the stable stall. But both men were now weighing the same problem: How to get the body into the wagon in the open courtyard?

Dona Clara had always told Teresa that trouble breeds upon itself. Without knowing it, Colonel Fazio kept her belief alive.

As the soldiers worked reloading, Fazio turned his attention back to Teresa. Her attire seemed highly inappropriate for the wife of Santa Anna. He sniffed as though a foul odor had suddenly come into the air. "Does your management of this farm include working in the fields, senora?"

She had no recourse but to humor him. "Have you ever been in a grist mill, Colonel Fazio?"

"Hardly, senora."

She laughed. "Had you ever been, you would know that my costume is quite appropriate. It is dirty and filled with meal dust. This old dress and straw hat fit its decor far better than silk and a lace *mantilla*."

His eyebrows arched. "Surely, you're not considering going with the wagon?"

"I never considered not going with it. Isn't that why you told Sergeant Perez to send soldiers along?"

"Hardly," he repeated. "I was thinking mainly of the woods between here and town, and how easy it would be for a man to slip into the wagon as it rolled along."

Humor hadn't worked, so she reverted to sternness. "You are determined to upset the routine around here, aren't you? Have I ever once tried to tell you how to go about catching your unseen spy? No! And I'll not tolerate you telling me how to run my business."

Fazio, his face immobile, his body rigid, blinked once and gave Teresa a quiet solemn reply. "I follow my orders to the letter of the law, senora. At no time were you to be allowed to leave the *Casa de la Sol* or make contact with Felix Escovarro."

It was said so simply, so matter-of-factly, without malice or anger, that Teresa was caught completely off guard. She couldn't understand why Santa Anna was so worried about her seeing Father Felix.

"Very well," she said softly, "I place all the problems of the farm and the feeding of the soldiers in your hands. As a prisoner, I have no other obligation than to go and sit in my room. Good morning."

"Wait!" he barked, before she could turn away. He hated these dirty, smelly people. He hated the arrogance of their well-bred women, like the one before him. Why, he thundered in his mind, couldn't they be like Italian women, content to do nothing more than have babies and feed their husbands well? He wasn't quite sure how he was going to handle this woman.

"I'm waiting," she said insolently.

"Senora, I am not as a rule a hard man, but I find myself a puzzled one. You seemed very determined to make this trip, and it makes me wonder why."

"Because you are not Mexican," she said coldly. She eyed him, her face a mask of glacial calm. "And neither am I. Give these people the least little excuse and they will cheat and steal you blind. Why don't you go to the mill in my place, Colonel? The wagon is almost reloaded. But make sure they put the right weights on the scale, they have some which are double weighted for a double charge. And follow my corn through the entire mill; they have been known to hide the good corn and replace it with cattle fodder. Then they will weasel and cry and try to raise the grinding charge on you."

Fazio sighed. He wouldn't be caught dead doing what she suggested, it was too menial. "How long will it take you?"

"What with this senseless delay, it will be late afternoon before they will have it all ground."

"All right."

Teresa fought to keep any triumph she felt from showing on her face and turned to go back to the house.

"Where are you going?"

"I beg your pardon." She eyed him as though he were the dumbest fool walking the earth. "They don't grind the corn for nothing, you know. I've got to get the money to pay for it."

Fazio's angular face lit up with a sudden inspiration. "Very well, senora. Oh, by the way, as long as you have to go into the house, will you be knid enough to bring the boy Carlos back out with you. I will keep him with my soldiers until you return."

She moved mechanically across the yard and back into the *hacienda*. She was still too dazed by his last command to comprehend that it meant total defeat. With a sinking heart, she really began to feel like a prisoner.

Because it had been her intention to get the money from the safe, her feet automatically carried her to the second floor study. As she passed the open bedroom door, a wry thought came to her. For people attempting to cover-up Escovarro's presence, they were certainly dullards. The man's buckskins lay over the back of the chair by the window.

They weren't dullards, she thought a moment later, as she passed the second bedroom. They were damn fools. Not only were Carlos' saddle-bags lying in plain view, but Felix's knapsack and clothing lay in the bed ready for repacking. She paid scant attention to the captain's uniform, concentrating bitterly on the brown wool of the priest's robe.

"It all should be destroyed," she said to herself and walked on to the study.

After opening the safe and mentally calculating the amount that would be required to pay the miller, she told herself: Damn fool! You're not going anywhere without a Carlos to turn over to Fazio.

Now she was thankful she had given Carlos the gold. She prayed that he would use it to start a new life for himself. Anna-Maria? Teresa now looked upon her as a very cunning and enterprising young woman. In time, she would sense their dilemma and find a way to return without arousing Fazio's suspicion. In time, she also reasoned, Felix Escovarro would find his own means of escape. He had so far gone undetected as one of the common soldiers and might get away in that disguise.

Fazio was their only problem. Looking at the stacks of coins, which had accumulated from the harvest sales, she wondered if the safe held enough money to

bribe the Italian. She scoffed at the idea. There was
no doubt in her mind that the man would destroy her
before he would go against Santa-Anna's orders.

Destroy. Her mind locked onto the word, and suddenly she was racing back down the corridor. Snatching the buckskins from the chair, she allowed herself
one quick peek out of the window. The reloading was
finished and the soldiers were standing idly about. She
didn't see Perez or Father Felix among them.

Once in the other bedroom, her hands worked fast.
All of their belongings were dumped onto the bed,
and she added kindling and wood from the fireplace
scuttle.

"Stay and die, or destroy it and lie," she said aloud,
as the first tiny orange flames began to leap up-
through the dry wood and clothing. She then calmly
returned to the study and casually began counting
gold and silver coins into a leather pouch.

The smoke began to irritate her eyes and nostrils.
Too soon, she told herself, beginning to panic, and she
slowed down counting of the coins. Only when the hall
became a wall of grey fog and the study was quickly filling with smoke did she begin to hurry. Now there was
no doubt in her mind that the bedroom would be an
unapproachable inferno.

The alcove windows of the study had been opened
so few times that they had warped and swollen. She
struggled with them and cursed at them. The smoke
burned her eyes and went into her lungs and made her
cough. Near blind from her own tears, she fumbled
about on the floor until she found the footstool and
began frantically to beat the alcove windows with it.
An eternity seemed to stretch on and on before she
heard the first shatter of glass and the squealing whine
of splintering wood. She went on smashing only long

enough to make room for her head and shoulders to stick out into the fresh air.

Already the men in the courtyard could see the smoke coming from the escape hole she had made.

"The boy's gone!" she shouted down to them. There was no need to fake a note of panic in her voice. "He's set the house afire! Help!"

In spite of the danger she had put herself in by waiting too long to sound the alarm, she couldn't help smiling at the confused orders that began to come from Colonel Fazio. Carlos was to be found at once! The fire was to be put out at once! The senora was to be rescued at once! No one was quite sure who was to do what, and Teresa purposely added to the confusion by screaming and crying for help.

Perez and Felix were in the stable when they heard her shouts. They, too, had long since determined that their original plan was a wash-out and had been arguing on what to attempt next.

"My God!" Felix cried. "I've got to save her!"

Perez was able to catch him by the arm before he could lunge away. "Wait! Didn't you hear her? She said the boy's gone. The senora knows the boy has gone and is attempting something. If it works, we've got to be ready. Go ahead and get dressed in Manuel's clothes. The fire seems to be in the back of the house, so I'll clear out the courtyard and give you a chance to get the body on the wagon."

Felix didn't have a chance to argue. Perez ran into the yard and immediately took command from the bewildered Colonel Fazio. He sensed that the fire could not do a great deal of damage to the thick-walled adobe structure, but still sent the majority of the soldiers to the rear of the *hacienda* to form a bucket brigade.

Perez ordered his own five soldiers to mount and go in search of Carlos.

"Why only your men?" Fazio screamed shrilly.

"They know the boy on sight," he shouted back over the noise. "Your men would be picking up every farm lad of that age for miles around."

Fazio didn't trust the sergeant or his men. He had sensed from the first that they were too sympathtic to the senora.

"I'm going with them to command," Fazio said petulantly.

Perez didn't even bother to answer, he was busy with yet another problem. Seeing the smoke, the farm laborers began streaming into the yard. Many he sent to help in the bucket brigade, and others to begin retrieving things from the *hacienda*.

Suddenly he realized Dona Teresa hadn't yet emerged from the smoking building, and the fire might not have been a ruse on her part. His fear rising, he called for two soldiers to follow him and raced into the building up to the second floor.

The bedroom was an inferno, worse than he had anticipated. The beams of the ceiling were ablaze and dropping fiery cinders on the wood floor. The three men tried to look for Teresa, but were driven back. Perez made for the study where Teresa had been last seen.

After raising the alarm, Teresa had attempted to get out. The broken window had created a flue, and the hall smoke came billowing into the study to find the air vent. It became so heavy and oppressive that she was forced to crawl along the floor. She found the air there less acrid, but already her lungs had taken in too much smoke. She had only a moment of lightheadedness before the blackness came. Ironically, she collapsed right in front of the open safe.

Perez didn't even ask Fazio's men for help. He scooped her up into his arms and staggered back along the corridor. Fazio's men were mesmerized by the money. Like children attacking their presents on Christmas morning, they loaded themselves with all the coins they could carry before the smoke drove them out.

Felix waited his chance and then hefted the meal-sack-wrapped body onto his shoulder. He was almost to the wagon when the farmers and their wives began to emerge with furniture, pictures and tableware. They were in such a quandry that they paid little attention to him, but he was going to take no chance. He kept the burden on his shoulder, walking slowly across the yard and around the corner to the kitchen entrance. From the kitchen window, he could see that the fire was centered on the back wing of the house and might not spread any farther.

Once he was in the dining room, he mingled with the other peasants grabbing at what they could and then scurring out. No one had time to question what he was attempting to save.

Smoke was now pouring down the main stairway, and he took a firmer grip on his cargo and tried to take the stairs two at a time. On the landing Perez and Felix met, staring at each other's burden with worried eyes.

"The back bedroom," Perez said, coughing, understanding what Felix planned to do. "I'll get her out of here."

The fire had reached the hall, nearly trapping the two soldiers. Beating out the flames on their clothing and hair, they pushed passed Felix without fully realizing he was there. Their only concern was to stay alive so they could enjoy the money they had found.

Felix struggled down the corridor until he saw that

it was dangerous to go any farther. He heaved the body forward and waited only long enough to see the edges of the the meal-sack start to curl and flames shoot up it.

Teresa had regained consciousness by the time he emerged, carrying an end table from the *sala.* She was surrounded by worried peasant women, and he was afraid of approaching her directly. He went to the wagon and busied himself by keeping the frightened horses under control.

And it was over as quickly as it began. Once the fire had consumed everything burnable in the north wing, the soldiers were able to keep it from spreading. They were dirty and tired, there was smoke in their throats and hunger in their bellies. They collapsed in small groups in the courtyard, and accepted with gratitude cups of fresh water from the peasant women.

Teresa began to feel a faint twinge of hope. She didn't dare leave until Colonel Fazio returned, but she could help prepare an unusual welcome for him.

"There is no meal until the wagon load is ground," she told some of the women loud enough so the nearest soldiers could hear. "Open the smoke-house and feed them whatever you can find. We'll worry if there is enough for supper later on."

By the time her words had reached the last of the soldiers, a rumor was already spreading that there wasn't enough food to go around at that very moment. Like jungle beasts they devoured everything that the women brought forth, fearful that the next meal might be a long time coming. Even before Fazio's return, they began to grumble that the corn wagon was not yet on its way to the mill. Their stomachs were not used to the rich meats they had gorged upon. They wanted the simple fare of *tortillas* and beans.

Colonel Fazio's face was mottled and his beady eyes

fierce as he rode into the yard with Sergeant Perez's men. They had seen no one even attempting to escape.

He was nearly up to the spot where they had given Teresa a chair to sit upon when the worried wife of Manuel came to her.

"Senora," she whimpered, "I do not wish to put more on your shoulders, but my husband is nowhere to be found."

Teresa's heart sank. She prayed the woman did not look around and spot Felix in her husband's clothing. Sergeant Perez came to Teresa's rescue.

"He was here earlier," he said confidently. "I saw him on the second floor when I went to rescue Senora de Santa Anna."

"Perhaps he was the one," a nearby soldier said laconically.

"The one what?" Teresa demanded.

The soldier blushed. "Didn't they tell you, senora? There was a body that came down when the second floor collapsed."

Manuel's wife began to wail, and Teresa motioned for some of the other women to come and take her away.

"Murder," Fazio scowled. "Now the boy adds murder to his treason and arson."

Fazio nearly swallowed his last words, his mouth remaining agape, as the whole courtyard was frozen by a single shrill cry that multiplied a hundred times as it came nearer. A young Mexican woman, her battered face swollen and bloody, came stumbling among them.

"Juanita!" Teresa cried. "What has happened?"

Her words were mixed with groans of agony. "They killed my husband. They beat me and took all his clothes and our two mules."

"Who?" Teresa asked, bewildered.

"I think a man and a boy," she wailed. "I didn't see them."

"It was them," Fazio said. "What did they say?"

The girl was so grief-stricken that she could hardly talk. "Something . . . I don't know . . . about hiding . . ."

"Mount up!" Fazio called out imperiously. "The boy never left the grounds and knew where Escovarro was hiding. They can't get far on mules."

It didn't take Sergeant Perez long to realize exactly what the woman was saying. He, too, had seen the open safe of money and now couldn't see the two soldiers in the sea of faces.

"Colonel," he protested, "the men are tired and hungry."

"When I want your opinion, Sergeant, I'll ask for it. Mount up!"

Fazio didn't understand the colloquial phrases the men began muttering. He sat on his horse, glaring as they refused to move. "Go yourself," a voice shouted from the crowd. As Fazio turned to the voice, another shout came from behind him. "See that we get grain and we'll ride."

Murderous rage overcame Fazio. "You!" he glowered down at Teresa. "You are responsible for this mutinous revolt."

"Me?" Teresa was incredulous. "Me?" she repeated and couldn't help but laugh as she rose. "Why not blame everything on me, Colonel. The fire, the deaths, and your incompetent handling of everything. I would have been back with the grain by now if you had not been so obstinate with your groundless fear." Feeling she had put him on the defensive, in front of his troops, she marched defiantly to the wagon and climbed on to its seat. "You," she yelled at Felix, "Loose the horses' head, and come and drive me in

Manuel's place. I will not be bullied one more minute by this Italian *merda!*"

Keeping his sombrero low over his face, Felix immediately obeyed as if he were a mere peasant. But his heart thrilled at her daring, and he was prepared to do battle if Fazio balked.

"*Viva!*" a quite voice uttered uncertainly. It gave heart for another to shout a bit stronger: "*Viva, senora!*" Here and there, others took courage to let their true feelings for the Italian colonel be known.

"Shut up!" Fazio raged, his face an uncontrollable mask of hatred. He had to breathe deeply several times before he felt safe in speaking again. It gave the troops time to settle down and wait for his next words.

"Sergeant Perez," he said quietly, but with a bitter edge to his tone, "mount up with two of my men. Your head rests on the line for the safe return of the entire party." Then, still suspicious, he swung his horse about until he came abreast of the wagon and met Teresa's steady gaze. "Senora, what will the wagon load cost to mill?"

Teresa held his gaze as though facing her last challenge: "Between four and five hundred *pesos*, señor."

"Your purse," he demanded, as though it were a simple request.

With light-hearted unconcern, she extracted the leather pouch from her waist band and tossed it upward.

Fazio caught it in mid-air, jingled its weight and knew at once he was defeated. She had no more gold on her than what would be required to mill the corn. He could delay her no longer, or he would face the wrath and revolt of his troops.

"*Arrivederci!*" he said, with a snappy salute.

Teresa prayed that she never saw him again.

It was a typical Saturday afternoon in Saltillo. The

town center was crowded. Horses and wagons flip-flapped continually; people gossiped around the market
stalls and in the dusty plaza, swapping rumors about
the war that wasn't yet a war. Farm women in their
'come to town' clothes swarmed in and out of the dry
goods store and the other marts, doing their weekly
shopping.

Sergeant Perez stayed at the mill, chatting with Señora de Santa Anna and the wagon driver, then casually suggested to Fazio's soldiers that it was going to be
a long wait.

"How long?" one of them asked.

Perez replied with cheerful camaraderie: "As long as
it takes the four wagon loads ahead of us."

"That won't please the colonel," one of them said
with a sly grin.

"Then let him come and wait in line," Perez said
bluntly, adding cheerfully: "Let's go to the cantina
and see if the waiting there might be more enjoyable."

As soon as the trio's horses were out of sight, Teresa
called over a young boy who had been standing idly
nearby.

"*Muchacho,* I have here two *pesos* for you if you'll
look out for my wagon while this old man and I go to
the market. If its turn comes before we return, you tell
the miller that it's from Santa Anna's *Casa de la Sol.*"

The boy would have readily agreed for one *peso,*
but he wasn't going to argue against his good fortune.

The road was crowded with farmers and peasants
coming to and from market. They were all preoccupied with their own concerns and paid little attention
to the straw-hatted woman in the grey wool dress, or
the tall man who kept his face hidden under the wide
brimmed *sombrero.*

The cantina was busy even that early. Perez looked
around, but saw no one in the bar crowd nor at the

tables whom he knew—except Anna-Maria. She was coming from a rear room into the barroom and she looked relieved when she saw him, but then she noticed he wasn't alone. She eyed the two soldiers making for the bar and decided she didn't know them. As they ordered whiskey and drank, she went back into the rear room, with a cautious signal to Perez to wait.

A moment later she came back out with two young prostitutes. She walked her old way, with the insolent laziness of a stretching jaguar, a black cigarette between her full red lips, a brilliantly embroidered shawl flung around her slim shoulders. And the soldiers couldn't help but note her entrance.

Smiling, and dismissing the admirer of old who approached her, Anna-Maria strolled over to where Perez stood.

"*Hola, amigo mio!*" she greeted him. "And once again we meet, not so?"

"So," replied Perez and he grinned at her. "Will you join me in a drink, *senorita?*"

"But yes." She glanced along the crowded bar. "Not here though, *senor mio*. There are tables in the back room where one can talk and play in privacy."

Her long-lashed eyes lifted lazily to meet his. "Is not that much better?"

"For me, yes," he said offhandedly, "but I have friends."

Anna-Maria studied the soldiers, using her dark eyes in her old sensual way. "I, too, have friends," she said suggestively, snapping her fingers. The two young prostitutes moved to her side with silent grace—and inviting smiles at the soldiers.

"Of course," she whispered throatily, "you will each have to wait your turn for the back room. Shall we go, *querido mio?*"

And that was the last they saw of Anna-Maria and

her man. It was also the last they saw of their horses.

"Why all of the horses?" Anna-Maria asked. "And why this direction?"

"It is the plan of Senor Escovarro," Perez said with a grin. "And it is a wise one. We are to let people see that we head toward Veracruz with two extra horses. Colonel Fazio will think the horses are for Dona Teresa and Captain Felix. He will ride hard to take us all prisoner before we reach Santa Anna."

She smiled enigmatically. "And what will we be doing in the meantime?"

He laughed. "The same as they—walking back to the Esparza ranch. The horses we will give their head for a merry chase by Fazio. Oh, I am so happy."

Anna-Maria sighed. "I wish we all were."

Perez was puzzled. "Are you not happy, *querida mio?*"

"For us, yes. My heart is sad for Dona Teresa."

"You should be happy for her. She is getting away from a husband who pays her no attention while he dallies with your cousin."

"Oh," she scowled, "you men never see anything. I am sad because she is so much in love with the priest."

"What priest?"

The question exasperated her. "What other priest has been around? Father Felix, that's who."

Pere laughed so hard that he nearly fell off his horse. It also helped to bring them extra attention as they rode through the streets of Saltillo.

"Oh my," Perez said, "he must have played his role well. Everyone knows that was only a disguise. He is a captain and no ordained priest."

"But that isn't so," she protested. "He was the priest who married Dona Teresa and Senor de Santa Anna."

A long, low whistle escaped between Perez' teeth. "*Madre mio,* I see it all now. It puzzled me why Santa

Anna was so opposed to his wife and the captain. He would rather they were dead than this truth be known to the country. My wife, this journey is going to be more dangerous than I thought. We had better get rid of these horses quickly."

Anna-Maria wished she had never learned the truth. Her respect for Felix Escovarro vanished and her sympathy for Teresa increased. She prayed that Teresa never learned the truth.

Carlos Juarez went against orders. He refused to leave the Esparza ranch until he had some definite news of Captain Escovarro. Toward sundown, he was almost ready to ride back to Saltillo when he saw two dusty figures trudging up the road. He would have known the walk of Felix anywhere, and he said a quick prayer of thanks for his safety—for their safety.

It was quite late when Pedro and Anna-Maria joined them at the dark ranch. Look-outs had been waiting for them ever since the first of Fazio's search patrols had gone thundering down the road north, and as soon as they appeared, they were rushed into hiding in the fruit cellar, where they soon fell into an exhausted sleep with their friends.

There was no sleep however, for Colonel Luigi Fazio that night. He had had only one success, and his eyes kept returning to it all night—to two squat bodies hanging on the crooked, gnarled oak tree at the rear of the *hacienda*. He could not tolerate thieves and deserters in his ranks, although he personally pocketed the coins they had stolen.

Their capture and hanging were a frightening example to the other soldiers, who began to obey orders much faster. The drunken soldiers in the cantina were soon found. So, too, was the deserted corn wagon. And after a long chase, the four riderless horses were rounded up and brought back.

Slowly, Fazio came to see how he had been duped. He hadn't suspected Sergeant Perez until he learned Perez was married to the beautiful Anna-Maria. Her shopping companion, he reasoned, must have been the boy, Carlos. And Felix Excovarro? By sundown everyone on the *hacienda* was made to see Teresa's treachery and desertion of them. Many quickly admitted they didn't know the man who had driven her wagon away.

The peasants were not the only ones who feared Fazio. The five soldiers under Sergeant Perez quaked at the thought they might be held accountable for his desertion, and Fazio knew how to make use of that.

"Quitaque!" he screamed, and the youngest of the five soldiers came running. "How long have you been under Perez's command?"

"Three years, sir," he stammered. "Since I was fifteen."

"You are now the sergeant of the patrol."

"I—," he gulped, already scared of the resentment of the older soldiers.

"You," Fazio said coldly. "And your first duty will be to ride north and find the traitors."

Fazio knew that the boy could have spent his entire life in the army and never risen to the rank of sergeant. He was young enough to fight to keep the rank, whereas the older men would not have been as greedy—nor as loyal. What the soldiers didn't realize was that Fazio was scared himself—he was scared of Santa Anna's long ears hearing what had happened.

"I've seen it coming for some time," Senor Esparza said the next morning at breakfast. "I told your father the same, Don Felix, when I took my children north and out of danger."

"And now the danger seems to be in the north."

The old patrician smiled. "Only for the moment, my friend. Not a day passes that my wife and I don't take pity on some poor soldier walking his way back home. General Cos is losing so many men as deserters that he soon won't have enough to control San Antonio."

Felix was skeptical. "Santa Anna will march to his rescue."

"Possibly," Esparza said. "But only as far north as the Rio Grande."

Felix knew differently, but didn't want to scare the ladies.

"If only as far as that," Teresa said, "then why are you leaving this beautiful ranch?"

Senor Esparza allowed his wife to answer. Senora Espara reminded Teresa so much of her grandmother that it almost hurt to look at her.

"My dear child," she said, "when you have children, you will understand my fears. This land has been invaded six times in my life by greedy armies. The land we have in Tejas, where my children are now, will be their future. We have already divided up this land and signed the deeds over to the *peons* who work it."

"And we pray," her husband said, "that they don't get burned out if Santa Anna does march north." He sighed. "I'm not sure why I came back for this last harvest."

Senora Esparza leaned over and patted her husband's hand. "Yes, you do, my dear. We are here at the right time to help protect our friends as we travel north." She smiled around the table. "And I think we should begin to prepare. Dona Teresa, Dona Anna-Maria, if you will come with me, I will help you select travelling attire from my daughters' wardrobes. Don Felipe, show the *caballeros* to our sons' rooms. The Esparza family must look the part when they leave."

"We appreciate this, senor and senora," Perez said. "But I fear we are putting you in too much danger."

"Nonsense," she replied. "You are the right number and nearly all just about the right age." She looked at Carlos. "And how old are you, son?"

"I am eighteen, senora."

"Exactly right." She smiled sweetly. "And as you are already a Carlos, like my son, you won't have to remember a new name. Oh, please, don't worry," she told them all. "Our people here are loyal and will stick to this story before we depart and afterwards, too."

Don Felipe Esparza kept quiet. He didn't want to worry them, but he knew his people had already been put to the test during the night and the early morning hours. Soldiers had questioned them and had gone away each time convinced that no strangers had come to the ranch, and only the senor and senora and their three sons and two daughters were in the handsome ranch house. When Felix learned about it, he marvelled at their calmness. He was impatient to start.

It seemed to him they were wasting too much time in loading the carriage and the many wagons the Esparzas were taking with them. He was particularly worried about Teresa. He feared Santa Anna might hunt her down at the ranch. Teresa kept looking at him, but he couldn't tell what she was thinking. He hoped she would be friendly.

Teresa was grateful that she hadn't been introduced as Senora de Santa Anna. That was a chapter in her life she would have to discuss quite calmly and coolly with her mother and the Bishop. She respected the Esparzas and was thankful for what they were doing, and yearned only for peace between herself and Father Felix for the journey.

"I," he said slowly, "haven't had a chance to talk with you alone."

"It doesn't matter," she said indifferently, then hated herself for using such a cold tone.

"It matters to me. I was cold to you because I have never before—"

"Don't," she said. "We were both aware of the obligation of the other. We, neither one, have the right to keep something alive that could never be."

"Why? I am still a man and you are still a woman."

"We are not. We each belong to someone and something else."

"No. I don't have to be and you don't have to be."

Teresa was stunned. "You would give up the church for me?"

Felix couldn't answer, he could only stare at her lovely face with its faint blush of hope. He again decided that silence was far better than the truth.

All that needed to be said between them had been said. Only their eyes carried on the conversation, communicating what they felt. There was no doubt or distrust between them now, and Teresa took heart. If the army could take him away from the church to be a soldier, then her love for him could take him away from the church *and* the army, and she would no longer feel so guilty. She could hardly wait to get to San Antonio to learn how best she could rid herself of her unfortunate marriage to Santa Anna.

Six Mexican families had decided to go north with the Esparzas rather than stay on the land. The men would drive the carriage and the five wagons loaded with their families and the Esparza possessions. The men in Felix's party would help Senor Esparza herd the horses and cattle he had selected to take along to his new ranch.

It was just before dawn, and Teresa shivered as Senora Esparza and Anna-Maria climbed into the carriage before her. The night before soldiers had again come to the ranch and Perez had recognized his own men. It had given her a nightmare, recalling her experiences and her fears.

"It's alright, Dona Teresa," Anna-Maria whispered. "The sun is coming up now."

Teresa looked toward the growing light in the pale sky. Against the skyline, a horseman was silhouetted, a Spanish *caballero* with a straight brimmed hat, waisted jacket and skin tight trousers. Here is where he belongs, she thought proudly. Not with the church or army, but the progenitor of a new Spanish blood line in a new land. As she walked to him, she knew she could never love another.

Felix felt a light touch on his leg and looked down. Teresa's face was turned up to his. His heart ached at her fresh beauty, the magic of those lips parted in a smile. All his life he had dreamed of just this, a vision of joy and beauty and peace which he could share. A dream now in reach of his arms, a beacon shining through the grim time they were living through.

With a fierce, possessive gesture, he leaned down and swept her body up into the saddle, and crushed her lips to his.

Teresa murmured: "I—I . . . *We* are really going home."

"Yes," he whispered. "Home."

He drew a deep breath, reached around her waist and placed his hand over her breasts as if laying claim to her.

"It's not over yet," he muttered, "but we'll work out the problems as we come to them. I—I've loved you ever since I first laid eyes on you, back there in the Martins' *sala*. I knew I could never be happy without you. But—but I reckon, too, that I am the cause of most of our problems . . . letting Santa Anna make me do things I didn't want to do . . . like your—"

Teresa placed her hand over his mouth, leaning against his chest.

"Don't bother to say it," she whispered.

"It's got to be said, Teresa. It's got to."

Teresa laughed. "I am not capable of hearing your confession."

"It cannot be made to anyone but you."

Perez came riding up. "Senor Esparza is ready to leave, *brother*."

Teresa laughed again. She felt very happy. "And so it begins." She looked at Felix. "Your great confession will just have to wait, but I don't fear it, no matter what it is."

Felix, his heart pounding, spurred his horse to move alongside the carriage, kissed her full on the lips, and lowered her gently down to the seat. His whole body was excited.

"I hope no one was watching," Senora Esparza said, grinning at Anna-Maria. "They will think that I condone incest in my family."

At another time the jest would have made Anna-Maria laugh. But she could sense that Felix was not being truthful with Teresa, and it angered her.

Neither Felix, nor Teresa, nor Perez riding ahead, nor none of the others, was aware their departure was being watched by the man sent to get them. Young Sergeant Quitaque had been watching them from a secluded spot for a long while he looked down at his old comrade, Perez, and his wife with a curiously satisfied expression on his youthful features.

Promotion and fear of Colonel Fazio had not made

the young soldier forget that Perez was his friend. Quitaque was both courageous and shrewd, and he intended both to help Perez and outwit Fazio. While he sent his men on every kind of mission he could dream up, he kept watch at the Esparza ranch to make sure his friends were not in danger. But he had to take Fazio something—or somebody—back or he risked his own life. He retrieved Perez's old uniform where it had been discarded, and luck stayed him when he came across a soldier and his girl fleeing from San Antonio. At first they had feared him, until he reassured them that he would not turn them in as deserters. But he was quite willing to sacrifice them to save Perez and his wife. Their unrecognizable bodies now lay in sacks waiting down the road, one of them in Perez's old uniform.

Quitaque, a dead cigarette limp between his thin lips, watched until the cavalcade rounded the elbow on the trail and disappeared from sight. Then he raised a hand in lazy salute.

"May you find a new life!" he muttered. "Your old life and bodies I take back to Colonel Fazio. *Amigo,* you will not believe the story I will tell of your struggle for life . . . but you failed, is not so? Oh, *amigo,* my many thanks for the permanent promotion your death has made possible."

The loyal but ruthless Quitaque not only succeeded in fooling Colonel Fazio; he didn't remain a sergeant long, but was soon promoted again. Some thirty years later, when Maximilian was Emperor of Mexico, General Enrique Quitaque was to meet his death at Sisal at the hands of another commanding officer, who was once again trying to regain control of the country—the exiled Antonio Lopez de Santa Anna.

23

EIGHT HUNDRED MILES to the south, the daily dispatches turned the President's country estate into a beehive of frantic activity.

"Caro!" Santa Anna thundered, stomping from room to room. "Where in the hell is that little bastard?"

Ramon Caro, his weasel-faced secretary, sat at a portable *escritoire* taking dictation from Luisa.

"Doesn't anyone heed my call?" Santa Anna demanded, at last finding them.

The hapless secretary looked to Luisa to save him from the President's wrath.

"Of course we heard you," Luisa said with a sweet smile. "Even General Cos probably heard you all the way to San Antonio."

"He'd better start hearing me, the idiot. What are you two doing? I have a great deal of work for Ramon."

"A few minor matters," Luisa answered smoothly, "that I felt were being overlooked."

Caro flinched. "I told her that His Excellency himself attends to all matters whether important or most trivial."

"Trivial?" Santa Anna glowed. "Nothing is trivial when I personally am forced to assume the authority of major general . . . of quartermaster, of commissary, of brigadier generals, of colonels, of captains and even of corporals, purveyors, *arrieros* and *carreteros*! But I am damned if I am going to be forced to be my own secretary as well!"

Luisa had grown quite used to his temper tantrums. The workers on the estate considered her a bland chameleon who could be counted on to smooth his ruffled feathers.

"I am quite finished with Ramon, Your Excellency. But I think you will be quite pleased with the orders I have given."

Santa Anna softened. He still admired Luisa's ability to stand up to him, although it was never far from his mind that she was a threat to him. "And when am I to be pleased? Is it a surprise?"

Luisa laughed, dismissing Caro so they could be alone. "As much as I know how you love surprises, I'll tell you. When we go north—"

"Wait! I have not said that I would go north."

Luisa tapped her fan on her wrist impatiently. "Words don't have to be spoken for me to know what is in your heart. It is not General Cos who worries you, it is this other thing."

Santa Anna scowled. "That ass-wipe Fazio! How could he let them get away?"

"Still no news?"

He had been holding back the latest report from her and now saw no reason not to share it. "A little. Two of them were caught. Your cousin Anna-Maria and her sergeant husband. They are both dead."

Luisa's face remained emotionless. The news didn't disturb her. She no longer had any family but Santa Anna. Anna-Maria and her husband had been tratiors to him in her eyes, and that was all that mattered.

"And nothing of Escovarro and your wife?"

He shrugged. "Vanished. Of course I have spies watching the Escovarro ranch and the de Alarcon home in San Antonio."

Luisa pondered a moment. "If General Cos doesn't keep control of San Antonio, it will be a great embarrassment having your wife in the camp of the enemy. If Spain should hear of it, they might be so delighted they would supply Tejas with arms and money for its revolution."

Santa Anna laughed. "You have become quite the little diplomat, my dear. Don't worry. Most everyone looks on you as the Senora de Santa Anna."

Luisa scowled. "Most is a dangerous word, Antonio. You stand the graft and intrigue that swirls around this headquarters. Ramon is too much a *maricon* to tell you all the truth, and there are those who are far too jealous and suspicious of me to share all their knowledge. The problem is, there are many here who know that I am only a mistress and that you have a real wife hidden away."

Although Santa Anna felt that those in the know were probably thinking of his *real* wife in Veracruz, Teresa was a constant worry to him. It had stunned him to learn of Felix Escovarro's defection. At first he passed it off as a young man's loyalty to his home state. Hadn't he shown the same loyalty to Veracruz? Then a gnawing doubt began to upset him. Had he provided his enemies with an embarrassing situation they could use against him? As far as he knew, Teresa still believed she was his wife, and that would be to the advantage of Felix and Stephen Austin. It might even help Austin to bring the Americans into the war.

"And so," he said slowly, "you think I should go to the aid of General Cos?"

"I'd make it look as though you were preparing to do so," she said.

"And then what, my artful strategist?"

Luisa rose and twirled about. "Do you like this frock, Antonio? I'm wearing it tonight for the dinner we're giving the American Ambassador. You've probably noticed he has quite a roving eye and loves to pinch and feel. He's also a horrible gossip."

Santa Anna eyed her narrowly. "You're leading up to something."

She laughed. "I think it's time we let him have a good pinch, a good feel, and an earful of gossip. Like: how irritated you are over the kidnapping of your wife and you may just do something about it."

"Kidnapping! That possibility never crossed my mind." He warmed to the idea. "And no matter what she might say or do, I can always claim she was tortured into saying it to make me look bad. I like it!"

"Then you will like my surprise, just as well. You can't go marching about as you did years ago. You have to look like the President of Mexico and General-in-Chief of the Army. Those silver spoons that you hate, I've ordered them melted down to make new epaulets and frogging to match your sword."

"That will please Caro," he said, chuckling. "He's still aghast that the sword cost me $7,000 American dollars."

"He'll be even more aghast," she said with a snicker. "Among the *equipage* I want packed for travel are your monogrammed china, the crystal decanters and your silver chamber pot."

"You make it sound as though I am going to be entertaining all along the way."

"We," she amended. "If Napoleon can go to war in such a fashion, so shall we. I'm even having Madame Viola look up the manner of striped marquee that he used in front of his tent."

Santa Anna wasn't too thrilled that she was including herself in the plan, but the rest of it pleased him. He could handle what others might think of his fake marriage, but he suddenly began wondering what Luisa's feeling about it was now—and what she intended to do about it. She could be a dangerous woman . . .

24

EVEN AFTER FELIX announced "I'm home!" and they took leave of the Esparza wagon train, they still faced a two-day horseback ride along the Frio River.

It was a heady experience for Felix to be on family soil again. It was a world unto itself. The Spanish cowmen greeted him enthusiastically as the quintet came upon the grazing herds that darkened the land to the horizon. Come spring, the drovers would take the cattle as far south as Mexico City and as far east as St. Louis. But cattle was only a single arm of the Escovarro octopus: the river valleys were dotted with orchards and vineyards and vast fields lying dormant until their next plowing. Each area had an ancient history that Felix gleefully shared with them.

The little farm hamlet of Escovarro was only a quarter-day ride from the main ranch house, but Felix could see the weary strain on the faces of Teresa and Anna-Maria.

"We will stay here the night," he announced to their relief. Merely being on Escovarro land had lessened their fear of being followed by Mexican troops.

The town had no need of an inn, for visitors to the *Ranchero de Oro* planned their journey to make it to the sprawling Spanish-style *villa* by nightfall. But it was, in a sense, a 'company' town and Felix was accorded the full rights of a prodigal son back home. Bedrooms in the best house in town were prepared for them, and the two hundred inhabitants saw it as a worthwhile excuse to turn the evening into a *fiesta*. Lanterns were strung, tables brought to the plaza and ladden with food; kegs of wine were cracked, and rival *mariachi* brands took turns in trying to outdo the other with flashy, noisy music.

Pedro Perez and Anna-Maria were celebrating their escape by getting gloriously drunk and dancing until they collapsed. Several *senoritas* slipped away from the watchful eyes of their *dueñas* and followed the shy and blushing Carlos wherever he went. Felix, duty bound to accept each cup of wine offered, saw Carlos' dilemma and laughed uproariously. He decided he would have a man-to-man talk with Carlos and give him some advice about women.

Teresa stayed mainly on the fringe of the *fiesta*, nursing a single cup of wine until it was hot and undrinkable. After a torrid Spanish dance number, in which Pedro Perez and Anna-Maria stole the show with their suggestive body movements, Anna-Maria collasped in the chair next to Teresa.

"I used to be able to do that all night long," she gasped. "And look at my husband, the fool. He'll dance until his legs are nubs."

"Anna-Maria—," Teresa said.

"Yes, Dona Teresa?"

"You—you're awfully—in love, aren't you?"

"Completely!"

"The—the past. Does he—does it—matter?"

Anna-Maria smiled at her then, a little sadly.

"That is how I met him, of course. But now—he is all mine and I am all his."

Teresa blushed. "I wish I knew more about life. Next week I will be twenty-two and know nothing."

Anna-Maria was drunk enough to talk back to her. "You only learn from experience. No one can tell you or teach you or force you, I was always cold when I was a professional. With Pedro, I am warm and giving and love every inch of him, as he loves every inch of me. That's love, when you are no longer embarrassed to give of yourself freely."

Her Pedro stumbled up and made a mock bow. "Hey, beautiful, where you been hiding all night? Why don't you come and make love to me, before my wife finds me?"

Anna-Maria rose, giggling. "All right, handsome, but we'll have to hurry. My husband is twelve feet tall, jealous and very fierce."

A jolly laugh turned Teresa's head in the other direction as they left to dance again.

"They are having a fine time," Felix said, looking at her. "And you?"

"I'm getting very tired. I think I'll go to bed."

He grinned at her, his head light from the wine, and he bent over and kissed her.

"Alone?"

But her hands came up, resisting him.

"No," she said, "don't. Just see me back to the house. I've forgotten which one it is."

She wanted him to kiss her, but not in public. She had wanted him to dance with her, but he had been too busy to ask. She was afraid that he would just leave her at the house and return to the *fiesta*, and tried to check her surging thrill when he walked her as far as the bedroom door.

She opened the door and walked in without turning to say goodnight or closing it. Felix's wine-clouded mind accepted it as an open invitation. He followed her and sprawled backwards across the bed, putting out his arms to her.

But she just stood there.

"Felix—," she whispered, "this—this may be our *last* night together. Have you thought of that?"

"No," he said. "And I don't see why it has to be."

"Tomorrow," she murmured, "You'll be home. Then—then I've got to go on to San Antonio. I've—a feeling—he will have men there to take me back."

"Don't say such a thing. Don't even think it!"

"I do say it and I do think it! We're—going to be—separated again, Felix. If it is not Santa Anna, then it will be your parents or my mother who will try to keep us apart and sinless."

"Teresa—" But he couldn't disagree with her commonsense. His joy at being home had kept him from considering how his staunch Catholic mother and stiff patrician father would look upon the strange cavalcade he had brought with him.

"So—*you* do see it. Make me happy before we are parted. Love every inch of me tonight."

"Teresa!" he cried. "You're making me wild!"

She laughed then. But her brown eyes were full of tears. Her eyes went huge. Fiery. Demanding. Forceful.

"Take off my clothes," she whispered. "Make me naked before you."

She came to him quickly. Stood between his knees as though to trap him. He did as commanded, but very slowly. His hands trembled and his heart quaked. Haste seemed to him an enemy—he had a curious feeling that once her clothing was removed, she would dissolve and be nothing but air in his hands. That he would wake and find that it was just another of the many dreams he had had about her.

Teresa tenderly put a hand behind his head and slowly brought his face to meet the touch of her creamy, firm breasts.

"They are yours," she whispered.

He kissed her there. A long dormant memory stirred in his mind. His hand cupped a single breast as his lips and tongue caressed the nipple. The memory lasted a long time. Until she began to breathe heavily, unevenly.

"Get undressed," she whispered, peering down at him, smiling at him through the tears she could no longer control.

"All right," he said, "anything you want."

"Anything?" She laughed then freely, gaily, and watched his clothing fall helter skelter to the planked floor.

They nestled together on the bed, and he attempted to roll onto her and kiss her.

"Not yet," she whispered. "Let me get to know your body. I may never have another chance."

When he didn't budge, she rolled him on his back and put her head down upon his chest. Her soft lips touched one of his nipples. It was a scalding sensation that tickled and made him thrash and laugh. She stopped that at once, and began to kiss his ribs and nuzzle her nose onto the soft fur of his belly.

Felix froze, stunned by a curious sort of terror, as she moved, inch by tender inch, to his aching sex. Her cheek touched the turgid flesh and his skin crawled. He thought of it as only a sinful act that sometimes transpired between soldiers in the field. He would not let her debase herself. And he was too Catholic to let his body suffer such degradation.

"Stop!" he all but wailed. "This is too much!"

Teresa stopped unwillingly, her cheek marked by the fiery warmth of his manhood. She saw what she was doing as yet another mark of her love for Felix. The mere touch of him, by mouth, lips, hand or cheek transported her in a way she had never experienced before. She had instinctively known that what she intended to do next would satisfy him more than herself, and then suddenly he had brought her crashing back from her euphoric netherland.

"I—," she started, but he cut her short.

"Well, you were wrong!" He roughly pulled her up off his belly and tried to cradle her in his arms. "There is only one proper function for my . . . ah . . . manhood to perform."

Her dream world exploded. She rolled off the bed and stood up. Her womanhood on a level with his eyes, she glowered down at him.

"Teresa!" he said, shocked to the bottom of his soul. "What has come over you?"

"Nothing more than a desire to give you love—love in every manner, way, shape and form I could think of."

"But not that way," he shouted. "Never!" He jumped from the bed, grasped her about the waist and flung her back down on the pillow. He swung himself up and over her, knelt astride her waist. Put down his right hand and encircled his sex with his fingers, aiming it, positioning it carefully. Lowered himself to her ever so slowly. Fell forward onto her breasts, fully impaled. Moaned at her: "This is the only way!"

She had aroused him to his fullest, and he became savage with desire.

Being thrown on the bed had taken Teresa's breath away, and his crushing attack had kept her off balance. Her mind took up the prayer, before she realized she was whispering the words:

"Hail Mary, full of Grace, The Lord is with Thee . . ." (But not with me.) "Blessed art thou among women" (As I have become the most cursed.) "Blessed is the fruit of Thy Womb, Jesus" (Who, as the first priest, would not have acted in this wanton manner.) "Holy Mary, Mother of God, pray for us, now and at the hour of our death, Amen" (And let me die at this moment. Let me die and accept my sin and responsibility for bringing it about.)

It was a long time before she realized that she was alone. She wasn't even aware that it had been her mumbled prayer that had driven Felix from the bed. She was glad to be alone. She felt she had been a reckless, passionate woman—a woman of many sins, but not the final mortal sin. She had not given herself up to the craven, animalistic lust of a man who had wanted everything his way. She vowed, into her tear-drenched pillow, never to love again, be it man—or priest.

The half-day ride to the *Ranchero de Oro* was solemn and quiet. Pedro Perez and Anna-Maria were nursing aching heads and upset stomachs. Carlos was suffering from a frustrated heart: he had come close to possessing his first girl when the mother had snatched her away. Felix was suffering from a bad blow to his male vanity: Teresa had rejected him! Teresa suffered as much as he did. She counted off the miles until she could retrieve her gold from Carlos and hire any form of transportation available to take her to San Antonio.

The Escovarro *villa* looked impressive, but that was all. The pink adobe structure was far grander in scope than Santa Anna's estate, but the welcome there proved to be even colder than what she had experienced from Luisa.

Whether by design or oversight, Felix's introduction of his travelling companions left much to be desired.

"This," he said proudly, "is my bat-boy who has served me so faithfully all these years—Carlos Juarez, my parents. And may I present the man and woman who helped on this journey—Sergeant Pedro Perez, who saw fit to desert the Mexican army, and his

wife, Anna-Maria, who showed us last night at the
fiesta in Escovarro that she has lost none of her talent
for dancing." Then he paused, and Teresa paled.
"Mama, Papa, I last present Senora Antonio Lopez de
Santa Anna, formerly Dona Teresa de Alarcon of San
Antonio."

Senora Escovarro had been upset from the beginning of the introductions, but she now came near to
needing a whiff of smelling salts. She had not been
prepared for such a shock, although lookouts had reported that Felix was arriving with guests.

As hostess, it was up to her, and not her husband, to
welcome them and make them comfortable. A cold
and efficient woman, she reserved the questions she
would put to her son until later, and smiled weakly.

"Welcome," she said through her thin, tight lips,
addressing only Felix. "Your bat-boy will find plenty
of available space in the tack-room. Ask Fernando to
move some of his people around so that this couple
may have an apartment in the *married couples'* quarters. And—and tell the housekeeper to prepare a room
for—for the Senora."

A far off banshee wail interrupted her and diverted
everybody's attention to the distant road. A sleek,
open-topped landau of bright red and gold raced toward the villa, and the shouts were coming from a tall
young man standing on the back seat and vigorously
waving his hat.

"Miguel!" Felix shouted. "Mama, you didn't tell me
Miguel was coming home."

Senora Escovarro was near apoplexy over this uncouth display. "I am just learning of it myself," she
said coldly.

The matched greys turned in so sharply at the gate
that the carriage rolled around the corner on two

wheels. But the black driver didn't lessen his speed, nor Miguel his noise.

It was like the arrival of a circus act. The black driver sat high on his perch, resplendent in top hat, white gloves and livery to match the landau's colors. Miguel Escovarro, although splendidly dressed, attracted far less attention than the second passenger. Senora Escovarro had a vague suspicion who the second passenger—a woman—might be, and it was making her blood pressure rise at a rapid rate.

Like the driver, the woman wore a top hat, but of feminine cut and as scarlet as the painted landau, with three golden ostrich plumes bobbing rakishly from its side, and a short veil of golden lace cascading down over the back brim. Her jacket was gold silk with red velvet lapels and cuffs. Real gold coins had been fashioned for its buttons. Her shirt was mannish, high collared and decorated only by a red velvet string tie. But what held everyone's interest the longest, as she slowly rose and allowed the driver to help her down, were her silk and velvet trousers.

"My God," Senora Escovarro whispered to her husband, "has she no decency? How dare she present herself to us in . . . *pants!*"

"Hush, my dear," he warned. "We'll handle all these matters a step at a time."

No one heard this exchange, for Felix was too busy slapping his brother's back and introducing him to his travelling companions.

"Mama, Papa," Miguel enthused, running to grab his fellow passenger by the hand and bringing her forward, "May I present the angel who saved me from General Cos in San Antonio—Senorita Emilia Rosa Hoffman Morillo."

"Senor, Senora," Emilia said huskily, dipping her head in a respectful bow, "my pleasure."

"Welcome," Don Ramando said stonily, coming to realize what his wife had been suspecting.

Senora Escovarro was too incensed to speak. *Mestiza,* she thought grimly. It was unthinkable that a member of the Escovarro family would take up with a *half-breed* and expect her to play hostess to the woman.

"It's all your fault," Miguel was telling Felix. "The town is going wild looking for you. I thought I'd best make myself scarce after the soldiers came to Aunt Elena's for the third time. It really has the old gal in quite a dither."

"I should think it would," Don Ramando said sourly. "Have you no decency, Miguel? It would seem you didn't learn your lesson with my sister-in-law when you tried to push a prostitute off on her a few years ago. We'll hear from her on this, you can be sure."

The noisy scene suddenly grew quiet. Teresa remembered the gossip her mother had passed on, and she looked at Emilia in amazement. It was inconceivable to her that this gorgeous, majestic creature could be a whore. But instinct, and the look on Miguel's face, told her this had to be the same woman Senor Escovarro had referred to.

Not a single muscle in Emilia's face showed her feelings. She had been expecting something like this and had warned Miguel. But he was still highly impetuous in a boyish way, and he had imagined that it would be a trip similar to their highly sensual one from Nacogdoches that time. As she had done for the past two years, Emilia kept him at arms' length for the fifty-mile trek.

Miguel was forced to break the embarrassing silence. "It's been a dusty journey," he said lightly, "especially after we learned in Escovarro that Felix was here. You've never seen horses fly like those did, little

brother." His words were not having the right effect.
"We could certainly use something to wash the dust
from our throats and a room for the Senorita to
freshen herself."

Dona Margaretta steeled herself to deal with the situation. From the back of the landau, the black driver
was unloading several travelling cases, and she realized
they planned a lengthy stay.

"Oh, Miguel," she cried, "I wish you'd had the sense
to warn us of your arrival. What with Felix's friends
being here, we'll have to study the room situation carefully. Why don't you take the senorita to the patio for
a cool drink while I settle the others?"

Her manner and tone infuriated Teresa. It was the
same arrogant snobbery the woman had shown toward
them, as if they were travelling gypsies. Teresa realized
she was the only one of the group who was being given
a "guest" accomodation inside the villa, although its
size suggested it must have at least twenty bedrooms.

"If there is a problem," she said evenly, "Senorita
Hoffman may share my accomodation."

"That sounds fair," Miguel said quickly before his
mother could open her mouth. For the moment, he
wished only to get his parents alone and inform them
how much they really owed to Emilia. "How does it
strike you, Emilia?"

She gave Teresa a warm, friendly smile. "You are
most kind, thank you. I'll try not to impose upon your
privacy. I will only be here for the night."

"But Emilia!" Miguel cried.

"The night!" she said firmly, turning her eyes to
stare at Senora Escovarro like a poker player who has
just declared her hand.

Dona Margaretta could not meet the stare and
looked away, feeling like a winner and loser all at the
same time.

"Felix," she said weakly, "see to your other friends. Miguel will show the ladies upstairs to the . . . ah . . . rose bedroom. Your father and I will await the two of you in his study."

Everyone departed as though dismissed by a schoolmarm. Miguel didn't speak until he ushered them into the bedroom and then he realized the trick his mother had played in selecting this one.

"Wow!" he exclaimed. "I haven't been in here in years. It was my mother's maid's sister's room. God, she was a character."

Emilia laughed. "And prone to like roses, it would seem from the walls. They are everywhere." She began to giggle as she waltzed around the room, touching the walls and every object that was painted or overlaid or embroidered with roses. "Not even a *puta* could dream up such a hideous room." Then she gasped at what she'd said and Miguel howled with laughter.

"Shut up," she snapped. "I'm terribly sorry, senorita. I apologize for what I said."

Teresa smiled good-naturedly. "You needn't apologize when your words are the truth. I feel like I'm in a crazy rose garden." She pointed upwards with a giggle. "Look! They're even entwined around the ceiling border."

"Oh!" Miguel shouted joyously, "I just remembered the real prize." He stopped and pulled something from beneath the four-poster bed. "Roses on the bottom of the chamber pot."

"Miguel, *really!*" Emilia gasped in mock shock. Then she frowned. "Which reminds me, my dashing desperado, you left me in the lurch. I was presented to your parents and no one else." She gave a slight tilt of her head toward Teresa to remind him of his duty. "The senorita was gracious enough to remember my name from the introduction, however."

"I'm sorry," he said, "and it's senora. Senora de Santa Anna."

"So formal," she chided him playfully. "I am Emilia, if it pleases the senora."

After so many cold people, it relaxed Teresa to be with such a warm spirit.

"Dona Emilia, it pleases me and I am Teresa."

Emilia laughed, this time low and husky and devilish. "Do not let Miguel's mother hear you address me with such an honored title, Dona Teresa. The old crow would have a stroke on the spot."

Miguel flushed. He didn't want to fight with his mother over Emilia, or with Emilia over his mother. "And I had better go see her before she does have that stroke." At the door he turned back with a look of puzzlement. "Santa Anna? My God, then the rumors are true! I thought it was just a hoax that the soldiers were looking for Santa Anna's wife as well as my brother."

Emilia eyed Teresa in startled surprise. "Is this true?"

Teresa stilled her sudden anger so that what she said wouldn't sound offensive.

"I don't wish to appear rude," she said quietly, "but it is a subject I'd rather not discuss at this time."

"But of course," Emilia replied sympathetically, and glared at Miguel. "Goodbye, Miguel."

"Oh, bye, I'll send up something cool for you two to drink."

As he left, he almost collided with the black driver, who had panted up under the weight of three travelling cases.

"Oh, John, I'm sorry," Emilia said. "I should have let you know my change of plans. Leave me just that small case, and load the others back on the carriage. We'll only be here for the night."

Teresa walked to the window and saw Pedro Perez, Anna-Maria and Carlos talking together. She wondered if they, too, were making plans to stay just the night. She felt responsible for them.

"Excuse me," she told Emilia. "I'll leave you to freshen up alone. I'd like to know what my friends are planning to do."

At the far end of the hall, she saw the doorway to the back stairs and decided that was her quickest way to the backyard. Opening the door at the bottom landing she stepped out into a sun-drenched vestibule. To her left was a closed door, to the right an archway and in the distance the foyer and front entrance. The sun was streaming in from French windows that opened onto a garden, and, not wishing to be caught snooping around, she chose that way as the fastest exit from the house.

The garden was enclosed on three sides, with similar French windows opening into various rooms. To her dismay, the remaining side of the garden had an eight-foot high brick wall, with no gate or exit of any kind. After walking along its forty-foot length, she was uncertain which of the French windows was the one she had used. She realized how tired she was after the journey and the upsetting reception. Even the prospect of talking to her friends and comforting them seemed too much of an effort. When one of the French windows was suddenly opened, she ducked into a vine-covered arbor and sat down on a stone bench to avoid having to make a polite converstaion, and to rest. But it was only a Mexican girl who began to shake throw-rugs in the air. Teresa felt foolish, but decided to remain hidden until the girl was finished and gone.

At first she didn't pay any attention to the voices coming from the open doors on the other side of the arbor, but when a voice was raised in anger, and she heard her own name mentioned, she began to listen carefully. She was astonished to discover that the whole Escovarro family seemed to be arguing and over her!

"Where is she now?"

"In the rose room."

"Alone?"

"With Emilia."

"I thought I heard someone in the garden."

No reply. Then she heard footsteps on the flag-stones of the garden. She sat still, afraid she might be seen. Then a male grunt.

"It is only Elena shaking carpets."

She recognized the voice of Don Ramando.

"Then it's all right," shrilled Senora Escovarro, "the girl is deaf. But I have something to say before we get back to the subject of Felix. Miguel, how dare you insult this family by bringing *that* woman here?"

Miguel's voice replied forcefully, "Mother, you don't understand the facts. They arrested me, thinking I was Felix. If Emilia hadn't used her influence with some of General Cos's officers, I'd be coming home in a pine box."

Dona Margaretta sniffed so loudly that Teresa could picture the look on her face. "I would rather not hear of her *influence*, Miguel. It's embarrassing enough that you know the creature, let alone to have to feel indebted to her."

"But I am indebted, and so are you." He added quietly, "I want to marry her."

"No!" Don Ramando shouted, and his wife began to weep. "I will not hear of such a disgrace. If that is your intention, then get her and yourself out of this house at once!"

"Father's right," Felix cried. "Miguel, you can't be serious."

"Now don't you start on me, too," Miguel said. "You were the fool who put me in danger by bringing Santa Anna's wife up from Saltillo. What were you trying to do?"

"Protect her."

"That is a strange statement coming from you after what you've already told us. If your concern for Dona Teresa was so great, why did you go ahead with that marriage thing?"

"You were not there at the time, you can't understand the circumstances."

"Circumstances!" Miguel shouted. "You owe me an explanation since I was arrested as you."

"I was in no position to show Santa Anna my true colors," Felix snapped. "I had to do as he commanded. He had the papers and I was trapped."

"Jesus," Miguel wheezed, "you really went the limit to be a successful spy. I gather she knows nothing of this."

There was no reply from Felix, but Teresa could almost see him nodding his curly head.

"You're a bastard," Miguel cried. "You parade around as a fake priest, marry her off illegally to Santa Anna, live as her guardian for several months, then later smuggle her north. I don't get it. Why? Why?"

"Personal reasons," Felix said softly.

"Then we are no different, brother. Except you're a hypocrite! It embarrasses you because I desire Emilia. Why is that so different from your desire? Oh, I don't blame you. Senora de Santa Anna—who really isn't a senora at all—is an exceptionally attractive woman. If you want to make love to her so bad, why don't you let her know she's free?"

Teresa heard a resounding slap, and she felt so troubled that it might have struck her as well as Miguel.

"Enough!". Don Ramando shouted, as he prepared to smack Miguel again if he dared to say any more. "Your brother's personal feelings have nothing to do with it at the moment. It was my decision."

"On what grounds?" Miguel asked sullenly. "What is best for her or for Felix?"

"Neither!" the old patrician snapped. "What is best is to bring Santa Anna to bay."

"That's not being fair to her, as I see it."

Dona Margaretta shushed them all to silence. "It *is* the fairest thing for her. She is, after all, a de Alarcon, as Felix informs us." There was a pause, as though she raised her hand to silence someone. "No, Miguel, I do not condone what your brother has done. I will be ashamed to look the poor girl in the face, but your father is right. Let the de Alarcon family do battle with Senor Santa Anna over the matter and not the Escovarro family."

"That was hardly Father's point," Miguel said gloomily. "He wants to use her ignorance as bait to lure the Mexicans into a full-scale war against Texas. The divorce paper had to be a fake, or why else would Santa Anna be so keen to have Felix arrested and silenced?"

"That's my problem," Felix said indifferently. "You have a problem of your own."

"Which you all seem to be trying to solve for me," Miguel said indignantly. "But tell me, Felix, man-to-man, what is your involvement with Dona Teresa?"

"None," Felix said quickly. "Absolutely none!"

He might be able to lie to his parents and himself, but not to his brother. Miguel read Felix's eyes, and for the first time in his life, he hated his younger brother for being such a coward in front of their parents. Miguel decided to return with Emilia to San Antonio the next day. He had to get away even if he risked being arrested again.

Teresa sat in the arbor, stunned by the realization of how much she had been lied to and how much of the suffering had been unnecessary. But what she heard then was the final insult from the Escovarro family.

"Well," Dona Margaretta said with a sigh that Teresa could hear clearly, "let us drop the entire matter for the moment. I've given orders that we would have our lunch *en familia*. Trays are already on the way to the rose room for . . . them . . . and the others can dine with the servants, as is proper. Shall we go to the dining room?"

Teresa stood up, hoping someone would speak up for her. No one did. If Felix had been an ally and lover before, he was now lost to her. Senor Escovarro had made it plain that the de Alcarcon family would have to do battle with Santa Anna. The thought made Teresa smile bitterly, for she and her mother were the last of the de Alarcon family, and she knew what kind of a battle her weak, snobbish mother was capable of fighting against the President. Instant surrender!

She hurried inside, not caring if anyone saw her, but she missed the door to the back stairs and found herself in the front foyer. Just as she put her hand on the carved oak banisters to go upstairs the front door opened and Carlos peeked in.

"Oh," he whispered, a tremble in his voice, "I'm glad I don't have to go in search of you, senora."

"What is it, Carlos?" she asked dully.

"We want you to know what is in our minds, senora. When we were shown to our various quarters, our futures were discussed with us."

She didn't have to be told who had done the discussing and what was probably said; she remained silent.

."As you know," Carlos continued in a whisper, "my service has been with Captain Escovarro and I can remain in the same position here. He has also assured Pedro and Anna-Maria of full employment on the *ranchero* as well."

"That is nice for all of you."

There was a pause, and then Carlos whispered, "We do not wish to think of ourselves only, senora. We wish to know first if we can be of service to you in helping you to reach your home in San Antonio."

Carlos once more touched her heart with his gentle consideration for her before himself.

She smiled. "You may all make your own plans."

"And you?"

She evaded answering. "It will be seen to, Carlos."

His gulp of relief was audible. "I will tell the others."

He turned to leave her, but something told her to press the boy for information while she still had the chance.

"Carlos?"

"Yes, senora?"

"When you first started to serve Felix Escovarro, was he a priest?"

Carlos blanched. "Please, senora." His voice was husky, and he said in a despairing whisper, "it is not for me to question the orders I am given."

"It is all right, Carlos," she said gently. "I know everything now."

He whistled with relief. "Oh, senora, I am so happy. Too long my heart has been in misery over this confusion. You are too kind to be hurt in such a way, and now your heart will be free to love as it wishes."

"As it wishes?"

"Carlos has seen it in your eyes many times. He is a fine man, the captain." Then he laughed gleefully.

"Now that you know, you will not have to go. You will be staying with us all, yes?"

"We will just have to see."

He said quickly, "Carlos thinks it is best, even if the captain did say that it was wiser for Santa Anna to learn that you were home, rather than here at the Escovarro villa."

Somehow she was able to say goodbye to Carlos and get him to go outside again. His last statement had told her more about the Escovarro family than she wished to know. They had apparently decided it was better for Santa Anna to capture two defenseless women, she and her mother, in San Antonio, than to risk his storming down there and perhaps destroying the Escovarro kingdom. As long as the Escovarros weren't bothered, nothing else mattered.

Teresa stood trying to master her anger and her sudden urge to leave immediately. She wanted to be among decent people again, people with honest hearts who didn't lie every time they opened their mouths.

"My dear, what is the matter? You're as pale as a ghost."

Teresa whirled round. It was Emilia—but a different Emilia. The mannish costume was gone; her raven black hair cascaded over her shoulders and accentuated the simplicity of her white gown.

"It is nothing," Teresa said, starting to pass her on the stairs.

Emila stopped her.

"I'm not that easily fooled, Dona Teresa. Something has upset you. Is it the old crow again? Can I be of any help?"

"I wish you could," Teresa said. "However, we both seem to be in the same boat. We are not wanted here."

Emilia laughed. "I sensed that the minute the carriage stopped and I saw the look on Miguel's mother's face."

"It is probably worse since he told her that he wished to marry you."

"What? You heard him tell her that?"

"I'm afraid I've been doing a bit of unwitting eavesdropping."

"*Mia caramba!* For my sake, I'm glad you have the big ears." Emilia frowned thoughtfully. "So, senora, I think you wish to leave, yes?"

Teresa said impulsively. "Don't call me that! I'm no longer a senora!"

"Aaaha! Emilia think this is not the time for such interesting details, which might take too long. Is the time for only the *vamoose*, eh?"

Teresa blinked. "What? When? How?"

"Now!"

"You're not even dressed."

"Come, renewed senorita. Emilia will show how fast that can be changed."

In the upstairs hall, they met two serving girls with trays of steaming food. Emilia ushered them into the room with a grand sweep of her hand and supervised the arrangement of the food as if she planned a long, leisurely lunch and siesta without interruption. She took coins from her purse, and when the girls tried to bow out gracefully, she stopped them.

"This is not for the service you've just performed for the Escovarros," Emilia said grandly, "but for a great service you can do for me. Be kind enough to tell my driver to keep the horses and carriage ready. I've had a sudden urge to take a drive through the countryside after my siesta. *Por favor?*"

The extended coins were more than the two serving girls would make in a month in wages and were eagerly snatched up. They looked bewildered at being asked to do so little for so much.

"And now, Dona Teresa, we will eat, because it is a long way before we find the next place to get a proper meal." Emilia smiled. "Besides, do we not want to be like the mad Englishmen as the only ones going out in the noonday sun?"

Teresa had felt too worried to eat much, but she grew less tense as the carriage rolled slowly across the Escovarro land. Emilia had instructed her driver not to let the horses stir up too great a dust cloud, and their smooth pace eventually lulled Teresa into a heavy sleep.

It was near dusk when she woke up. She noticed how much warmer and quieter it was because, while she had been asleep, the canvas and glass cover had been raised over the back of the landau.

"Where are we?" she asked.

"Hello there," Emilia said cheerfully. "Well, we are beyond Escovarro and starting to make good time. It will be well after dark before we get to Natalia, but by then we will be a great distance from the Escovarro *ranchero*. We will be safe—at least for the time being."

"Thank you," Teresa murmured, not knowing what to say.

Emilia laughed. "Perhaps I should be thanking you. Oh God, can you imagine what might have happened to me, if I'd walked in on that harridan without knowing Miguel had told her he wished to marry. It would have been too rich."

"Then you don't love him?"

Emilia looked coy. "Not in the way I should for marriage. Oh, it might have happened long ago if it had not been for his family."

"Do you mean his aunt?" Teresa asked innocently, remembering what she had heard long ago.

Emilia turned sideways and gave her a quizzical glance. Teresa laughed.

"Don't be shocked to learn that that little piece of gossip reached me all the way down in Saltillo."

Emilia was enchanted. "That little tid-bit, my dear, was like money in the bank. It brought the suckers swarming to see what manner of woman could capture an Escovarro *caballero*. They stacked their coins high to see who would be next in line. But, believe me, Emilia had learned her lesson. They had to stack them mountain high before she would pick them up." She saw Teresa flush and chided herself, "I'm sorry. I didn't mean to sound vulgar."

Teresa smiled apologetically. "It wasn't your words that were distressing me, but my own thoughts. Here I've been doing near the same thing, and I have nothing to show for it but this dress and a few bags of gold that belonged to—Oh, my God! In my rush to get away, I even forgot to get the gold from Felix's bat-boy."

"Well, for the moment forget the gold. But, to help your peace of mind, do you want to discuss what is distressing you?"

Teresa shook her head. "No—not really—and yet—yes, I do. Oh, I don't know what I want—I'm still so confused and dumbfounded."

"Then say nothing," Emilia advised kindly. "I'll just keep jabbering away about my life, and if you want to break in with a story of your own, feel free."

If the two women had been of the same class and breeding, they would have never discussed such delicate matters, but their differences—and the shared danger—made them free of custom and convention, and drew them together. They were amazed to learn that they had been born just a few miles apart—though not the same year—when San Antonio was still the Villa de Bexar. While Emilia knew a lot about the aristocratic Castillian background of the de Alarcon family and the section of town in which they lived, Teresa was astounded to learn that Mexican brothels existed less than a mile from her old home.

"When I was a child," Emilia said, her voice soft and dreamy, "I would sneak away from all the noise, the brawls, the crudeness, the filth and the disease. The farther I walked away, the less I became the daughter of a whore. To close it out completely, I'd stand for a long time just staring at the white contours of the mission San Antonio de Valero, and I'd feel a sense of peace." She laughed. "You might say that was the nearest I came to religion of the formal kind. My religion was of the future. As I walked the plazas in my bare feet, the soft grey dust became the Persian carpets, and at every villa I passed, I would debate on whether the people who lived there were worthy enough to have me join their party or not. Oh, that was the most fun! I would peek into the shaded patios where guitars played romantic music and senoritas in flashing garments played with their fans. Oh, I wanted to be each and every one of them."

This time when she laughed, it was as though she had just discovered a joke against herself. "You know, I can still see every one of the young ladies and their houses, and can't remember the men at all. *Now* it is just the opposite, except for the houses. *That* dream, I made it come true by myself. I now have one of the loveliest villas in all of San Antonio."

"I would love to see it sometime," Teresa said with real interest.

"You?" Emilia cried with a chuckle. Then she grew more serious. "It's not that you wouldn't be welcome, anytime. But, Dona Teresa, when we get back to San Antonio and if we happen to meet, you don't have to let on that you know me. You have your reputation to think of."

"Reputation?" Teresa said, amused. "How can you say such a thing after all I've told you *about everything*?"

"Now you listen to me, young lady," Emilia replied, suddenly very serious "and you listen good. Santa Anna should be castrated for all he put you through, and I dare say Felix Escovarro should stand right in line for his dues as well. You went through enough hell just thinking you were in love with a priest. It's time you started living life over again, with your head held high."

"That's easier said than done, Emilia. I don't want to spend my life like Miguel's old lady and end up painting roses to ease my frustrations."

"And you don't want to end up a *puta*, either," Emilia said firmly. "Each day it makes you put your foot down harder on the necks of men and squeeze them worse. One day you wake up and your love for them has turned to a hatred, and a desire to steal away their power. Sex isn't love, it's a weapon."

"But Miguel seems to love you enough to want to marry you."

"That's his dream," she said grimly. "He's living in the memory of a few nights on the trail when we didn't have to conform to any society but the one we created for ourselves. He can't see how miserable he would become, but I can. He would be blacklisted by his family and the social life he thrives on in San Antonio. We would start by loving and end by hating. Best that we just stay friends."

"Aha! Then you do love him."

Emilia sighed. "There is no use loving somebody you would only ruin in the having."

BOOK IV
The Two Roses

25

IT WAS NOT the San Antonio Teresa remembered. This San Antonio was afraid of its future, grimly awaiting an invasion that could bring death and destruction. The only people Teresa saw on the streets were soldiers: soldiers building barricades; soldiers working the forge and melting pots at the blacksmith's shop; sharpshooters stationed on the house tops; soldiers looting the houses that had already been deserted for even more barricade material.

Soon after Teresa's return, the city was ringed by Texans and the siege begun. As much as possible, everyone stayed inside, and visiting between the villas ceased. That pleased Teresa's mother, who was afraid her daughter's return—leaving her powerful husband—might cause a scandal. Dona Helena couldn't understand what Teresa was doing with her life, and Teresa couldn't bring herself to tell her mother the real truth behind her return. Her mother would be too shocked.

When Dona Helena's close friends inquired about Teresa, she would turn teary eyed and whimper: "An unfortunate trip, at an unfortunate time, for her to come and visit her mother."

The situation in San Antonio became increasingly desperate. More and more people were jailed to keep down the looting, and every day there were more men deserting and going over to the Texan side. Servants at the rich villas melted into the shadows and weren't seen again. At the de Alarcon villa, there were soon only the two women and a sixty-year old male retainer—who was ill—to take care of all the echoing rooms. Her servants' desertion made Dona Helena realize at last the seriousness of the situation, and she became frightened. She would have been even more frightened if she'd known the villa was being watched. Both sides were keeping an eye on Teresa.

One night, without warning, they were invaded. Neither of them heard any sounds of breaking in, but suddenly two Mexicans came in the room where they were sitting, and glowered at them. Dona Helena started to scream, and one of the Mexicans, a lean man with an ugly knife scar across his face, rushed to her and hit her viciously in the face. Dona Helena sank back in the *sala* chair, her head like a leaden weight, all the strength and willpower drained from her.

Teresa watched them carefully, but said nothing, her face pale as she stood up in horror at what had happened to her mother.

The other one apparently was their spokesman. He called himself Sanchez. He made a vague apology to Dona Helena, gesturing with pudgy fingers. Short, stout and oily, he was less frightening than the other one and he spoke to Teresa as if he were trying to be polite.

"Is unforgiveable," he told her suavely, "but the senora was ready to scream. We wish to have words with you, Senora de Santa Anna."

"If it's robbery," Teresa said nervously, "we have little in the house."

Sanchez laughed throatily, reaching for his pack of *lobo negro* cigarettes. "We are not bandits, senora. We are here for your help."

"I fail to see how I can be of help to you."

Sanchez, caressing his black mustache, leered at her, then slowly lit a cigarette. "Many of my friends," he said slowly, letting the smoke curl from his mouth with each word, "and many of your friends, are in jail. If you saw it in your heart to return to your husband, under certain conditions, all those good people could be set free."

"It wouldn't work," she told him calmly. "He wouldn't accept me in exchange for a single one of them."

"You lie!" he bellowed.

"Then send General Cos a message and see how fast your friends are released. You'll wait until doomsday."

Teresa sounded much more confident than she was. Each day she was afraid of hearing Cos's soldiers hammering on the door, and each day it didn't happen strengthened her hope that Santa Anna and Cos had decided to take no action as long as she remained silent.

Sanchez's evil grin widened as he hitched up his gunbelt, moving around behind her.

"Perhaps you should send the message," he drawled, "before my friend takes an interest in your mother."

"Try to believe me that it would do no good," Teresa said, trying to hide her terror. He cursed behind her, and the butt of the gun suddenly crashed against the side of her ear and jaw. She was momentarily stunned and she didn't hear the scuffle of feet, the gruff exchange of voices, and the suddenly choked-off scream—her mother's scream. Teresa had staggered, but, supporting herself against the back of the sofa, she didn't fall. Her head cleared slowly and she opened her eyes.

Dona Helena, breathing unevenly, lay on the floor.

Sanchez was holding her arms over her head and the
lean Mexican was sitting on her chest.

"Sit down, senora," Sanchez told Teresa, "before
you fall down. We now begin to negotiate."

Somehow Teresa found her way around the sofa and
collapsed. Her ears were still ringing so that she barely
recognized her own voice. "There is nothing to negotiate," she gasped.

"Take your thing out, Torres," Sanchez grunted.
"Perhaps the old woman can make her daughter see
reason."

As the man pulled down his pants, Dona Helena
opened her mouth to scream again, but Sanchez
caught her jaw in his steely fingers and kept her silent.

"Oh, God," Teresa cried, " leave her alone. She has
nothing to do with this."

Sanchez and Torres ignored her. The lean man
moved forward until his butt was crushing Dona Helena's breasts, and he could use her cheeks and nose to
excite himself.

Teresa sat there as if she were hypnotized, understanding everything now, yet utterly helpless to do anything about it. She and her mother were the victims
of a cunning, vicious plot.

"You both still have a chance to stop Torres, you
know." Sanchez's glance down at Dona Helena was
humbly apologetic. "Do you wish to say something to
your daughter?" Dona Helena indicated that she did,
grunting something and rolling her eyes.

He immediately released her jaw and she flexed it
until she had it under control again and could use her
tongue.

"Teresa," she gasped, "do what they want, please, I
beg of you. I am so frightened."

"Mama," Teresa mumbled, her own tongue hardly

obeying her will, "you don't understand . . . they don't understand. I *can't* help them."

"Okay, *amigo!*" Sanchez shouted.

"Wait!" Teresa shouted. "Will you please just listen to reason? I am not Senora de Santa Anna. Oh, I'm supposed to be, yes, but it was all a great deception. Even the priest who said the vows was a fraud. Don't you see? He's not going to ransom me back if it was all a big lie."

His black eyes were gimlet points behind half-closed lids, Sanchez reflected on what she had said. He nodded once, jerkily.

"Sounds a little far-fetched," he said, as if speaking to himself. "Why'd a man take you as a false bride when he's powerful enough to take you any way he wants. Torres!"

"For God's sake," Teresa burst out, "you've *got* to believe me."

"We will," he agreed in a dead voice, "as soon as Torres and your Mama make you start telling the truth."

Again he clamped his fist on Dona Helena's jaw and forced it wide open. Torres sat waiting, as the fear in her heavy lidded eyes widened to uncontrollable terror, and then he forced himself between her parted lips and finally enduced her to swallow by rubbing her throat with his thumb.

Every detail of what was happening was clear to Teresa, and she wished she could faint or go mad—anything to avoid seeing it. Her eyes functioned, but her vocal cords seemed to be paralyzed—she couldn't say a coherent word, she couldn't even raise a hand. It was the more maddening because the scene gave her a sudden vicarious thrill. Her mother, so pious and unforgiving of the faults of others, was being demoralized

and debased, being put through the same kind of hell
that she had once suffered at the hands of Santa Anna.
Perhaps, Teresa thought dully, we will now be able to
understand each other as equals.

"Stop!" Sanchez shouted, knocking Torres aside.
"The old girl's fainted."

An evil grin came to Torres' face as he glanced at
Teresa. "I ain't finished yet."

Sanchez laughed, tossed away the butt of his cigarette, and reached for a fresh one, lighting it with de-
liberate casualness.

"She's really something," he observed, getting to his
feet and looking at Teresa with wonderment. "I'd get
sick watching that happen to my *mamacita*. But this
one . . ."

He came closer to the silent, white-lipped Teresa.
His fingers touched the dark red weal on her cheek-
bone. "But this one," he repeated, " has to be the wife
of Santa Anna. Yes, he would pick someone as cold as
his own heart to share his bed. A man would freeze up
inside of her before he was able to thaw her out. Do
you wish to try, Torres?"

"Don't either of you try," ordered a harsh voice
from the doorway. "The house is surrounded by soldiers."

It was Sanchez's turn to gasp with fear. Wide-eyed,
slack-jawed, his face the color of dirty alkali, he stared
at General Martin Cos, who stood in the doorway, gun
in hand, his face bleak and his eyes icy-cold.

In that tense second, Sanchez knew beyond a doubt
that his plot had miscarried; he had failed in his attempt to use Teresa. He knew, too, that death was the
only reward for such failure.

For perhaps the count of three, the tableau lasted,
then with a whimpering curse Torres grabbed for his
six-shooter, tilted the slit-bottomed holster, and fired.

But its crash came too late, beaten by the shattering roar of General Cos's pistol.

Torres reeled against the wall with a scream—the cry of a coward afraid to die. Sanchez quickly raised his arms.

Teresa asked General Cos if she could put her mother to bed, and he nodded. The two women didn't speak—Dona Helena seemed to be still terrified, and Teresa dreaded the forthcoming confrontation with the general and could only think of that.

He had helped himself to a glass of wine by the time she returned and he stood impassively in the *sala,* as though there had been no trouble that evening, and this was little more than a social call.

"Dona Teresa," he said affably, "may I get you a glass?"

"Thank you," she said weakly. "For once in my life, I think I could use it."

He laughed. "It would seem to me that you must have had cause for many more glasses than just this one."

"Oh?" she said, taking the glass he held out.

"I am not here tonight by accident, you know," he said expansively, preening himself. "You have friends, who have paid a dear price for your safety."

"Friends?" She had not liked the man in Saltillo and was wary of him now. "Do you mean General Santa Anna?"

Cos laughed, his voice high and girlish. "Hardly, my dear woman, hardly, although he is panting to know your whereabouts."

She was puzzled. "He doesn't know?"

"Well," Cos said, "not exactly. I have certain personal reasons for keeping the true nature of your whereabouts garbled in our communications."

She didn't understand. "My friends again?"

He eyed her with great caution. "They told me much about you, and I had my doubts. It was at their insistence that I've had soldiers secretly guarding you day and night. That's how we got here so quickly."

"Not quickly enough," she said bitterly, "considering what happened to my mother."

She knew she wasn't being fair the moment she spoke. She had done nothing to try and save her mother, and she was only beginning to realize it and feel guilty. She should have been grateful to General Cos for saving her from the same humiliation, but she feared he would humiliate her even more by returning her to Santa Anna.

"How can I apologize for that?" Cos said sincerely. "The soldiers are only human, and they're frightened by this siege as well. It took time for the news to reach me, as I was with your friend, Emilia Hoffman."

Teresa showed her surprise, and Cos said quickly, "Oh, it's quite all right. I was grateful for Emilia's candor in this matter. Your arrival, and the demands you might make, had me greatly concerned for awhile. Emilia brought me quickly into the entire picture. I was happy to stay out of your way and leave you in peace . . . until this unfortunate affair."

Teresa was irritated that Emilia had shared with Cos their private conversation on the journey, and she said sharply to Cos, "I suppose I should thank you, but I fail to see why you are taking such a personal interest in my affairs."

"Oh!" He was astonished. "Really!" Then he understood and laughed. "Of course, you don't know. Poor child! You see, I am Santa Anna's brother-in-law. My sister is the real Senora de Santa Anna."

"But," she protested, "the papers from the bishop stated he was no longer married."

Cos shrugged. "He is very clever at making things look real that are really quite false."

"And people as well."

Cos chuckled. "You mean the priest who was not a priest?"

Teresa ignored that. She was sorry Felix Escovarro had come into the conversation. She didn't want to talk about him to anybody.

Cos saw that it was a sensitive point with her. He rose and bowed gallantly. "Dona Teresa, may I say I admire you greatly? Most other women would be screaming and ranting and making great financial claims for such a wrongdoing. Only a lady knows when to keep her silence. You can rest assured that you and your mother will be more closely guarded in the future."

He bowed again and was almost to the door when he turned. "Oh, one more thing. Emilia did not want you to learn that she has taken up your battle for you. She is also proud and a lady."

Teresa sat until the fireplace logs had turned to embers, and the embers to white ash. And in all those hours, one thought obessed her. "*More* of a lady than I! *More* of a lady than I! She at least thought of my safety, and that is more than I did for my own mother. Oh, dear God, what am I becoming? What is all this turning me into? Am I doomed to hate everything and everybody who touches me, and never again to know love? I am so tired of nothing but turmoil. Please, I pray to you, let it stop. Let it stop!"

26

DONA HELENA RECOVERED slowly, often relapsing into periods of numb silence. Living conditions in the house were also growing worse as the siege dragged on. The larder was empty, cash was running low, the last barrel of flour was half gone. If they were not to starve, there was but one thing to do. For days Dona Helena had been mulling it over, but had kept it to herself.

Manuel, the old man servant, had been bedridden with a touch of fever, and it was hopeless to expect any help from him; he'd only wheeze and cough, and wonder what Dona Clara would have done in like circumstances.

Dona Helena had not wanted to worry Teresa until she had to. A wall of silence had grown up between them. It was hard enough for her to look at Teresa, let alone share a civil word. They talked only when it was essential.

Teresa sensed trouble when she opened the brick oven at the side of the fireplace. "You forgot the salt pork in the bean pot," she told her mother.

"I didn't forget," Dona Helena snapped. "There isn't any. That's the end of the molasses, too."

"I'll be glad when they fight and settle this siege, one way or the other."

"I'd expect a statement like that from you. You give me no consideration whatsoever."

Teresa sat down weakly. "Please, Mama, not today. I don't feel well."

"*You* don't feel well," Dona Helena wailed. "How do you think I feel? I'm *ruined.*"

Teresa felt her familiar guilt. "I told you that night that you had nothing to fear. General Cos is a gentleman and will keep the whole affair quiet."

"Don't be an idiot, Teresa Maria," her mother replied icily. "He has a far better reason for keeping mum—the protection of the President's good name. Oh, why didn't you just stay in Saltillo?"

"And live a lie?"

Dona Helena scowled. "You didn't know it was a lie at the time. It was your damn foolishness in leaving with Felix Escovarro that is causing my ruination."

Teresa forced herself to look at her mother. "Your ruination?" she said dully. "What of my own?"

Dona Helena shook her head. Time for plain speaking. Lord knows she'd been patient.

"That's what we must now consider. After your marriage, I was again quite socially prominent in San Antonio. You can imagine then my chagrin when it became common gossip that you had deserted your husband." Teresa tried to speak, but her mother wouldn't let her. "I was able to live with that, because difficulties do come up from time to time between husband and wife. I should know, because I went through enough of them with your ill-tempered father. However, young lady, we stayed married to protect the family name."

"Because you were legally married in the first place!"

Dona Helena ignored her. She would not be sidetracked now that she was ready to outline her plan.

"I believe, as your mother, that I possess the power to make this marriage just as legal. And that is my full intention. I've made arrangements for Manuel to be taken care of while we are gone."

"Gone? Gone where?"

"To Saltillo. We will face up to Santa Anna and make him do right by you."

She waited for her daughter's reaction, but Teresa remained silent, suppressing a sudden wave of nausea.

"Well?" Dona Helena said impatiently. "You do want to regain your good name, don't you?"

Teresa raised her head. "You don't know the man," she said. "He doesn't bluff easily. Besides, how in the world do you expect to leave town when it is under siege?"

"You leave that to me, I've made all the arrangements. You just be ready to leave in the next couple of nights."

"Mama, I told you I don't feel well, and certainly not well enough to make that long trip again."

"Look, young woman—you've never had a sick day in your life, so don't start thinking up excuses. We are going and that is that! And I'll give you a *besides*: *You owe me this!* You don't have to let those two cut-throats know the truth. To protect me, you could have gone with them and been taken safely back to Santa Anna. Well, I'm going to see that you pay me for that foolish stunt."

Teresa shut her eyes. More failure, more humiliation. She knew that Santa Anna would not take her back, no matter how much her mother screamed and ranted. Her stomach started churning again. She felt miserable. Why can't I just go away? She thought. Far away from San Antonio and Saltillo. Far away from Santa Anna and Dona Helena. Run away—there must be somewhere she could run to and never return.

"Your silence tells me that you are finally seeing sense," said Dona Helena. "You never were too good at handling your own affairs. I blame Dona Clara for that, to be sure. Any idiot can let another run their life for them."

Teresa's face flushed geranium-red, and Dona Helena saw that her choice of words had not been tactful. "Although she did the same with each of us," she began, and then stopped. "Well, enough of that. I'm due right now at the Flores villa. You be ready, just in case Senor Flores has prepared the escape for tonight."

Teresa nodded to her mother, without saying anything more, and walked back to the *sala* and let her fevered head rest on the cool window pane. The street doors to the patio were open, and she could see a sentry making his lazy march back and forth. Again, the nausea struck, and this time she fainted.

Teresa opened her eyes, blinking, her first sensation one of stinging pain in her abdomen. Her eyes burned from it, her tongue was coated with an acid residue. She pulled herself to a sitting position and rested her back against the wall. Her whole body felt strangely numb. She heard the street gate close and assumed it was her mother's departure.

Knowing that she really didn't want her mother's help, she forced herself to stand and go into the hall to take a shawl from the pegged rack. She had to do what she had known for a week must be done.

She moved cautiously into the patio, and the wind tugged at her skirts and ankles, blowing up the snow in dry, powery gusts that stung her face. She pushed open the gate and went out into the street.

"Halt!" cried the sentry. "You are not to leave! Where do you think you are going?"

Teresa looked pale and weak, leaning against the

gate, opening her mouth and then closing it without a sound.

"Are you all right, senorita? You don't look well."

"Doctor," she rasped. "Two streets over. Dr. Morales."

"I can't leave my post," he said with a worried frown. "Can you make it there on your own?"

She nodded and went down the street. It was colder now, and the snow came down so fast that she could not see five yards before her. She walked northward, moving without conscious thought toward the doctor's house.

He was not there now . . . he had deserted the city weeks ago, getting out while the trees were still bright in the fall. He had left a note on his door directing people to another doctor several blocks away.

She heard the muffled voices of the soldiers swearing at the weather, and the stamp of their feet on the hard, frosty ground. But she walked on, looking neither to the right nor the left, while the snow clung to her shawl and whitened her brows and hair. She walked very slowly, and as she walked, her lips moved, saying a strange prayer:

"Don't let it be that—Oh, God—don't let there be a life in me."

Teresa missed her visitor by no more than five minutes.

"Who are you and what do you want?" the sentry demanded of the ragged Mexican boy, whose straw hat was so wet from the snow that it was beginning to droop.

"I am Carlos," he said truthfully, and then took a chance on telling a small lie. "I have been sent to this house to work."

"No one is here," the sentry said gruffly, "except a sick servant."

Carlos' surprise was genuine. "Have they gone? Even Senorita Teresa?"

"She is only to the doctor, and who knows about the old one? She is in and out so many times a day I am near hoarse 'halting' her."

Carlos was relieved. At least they were still in San Antonio. "The doctor, you say. Is she ill?"

"Didn't look good to me."

Carlos smiled knowingly. "That might be good for for Carlos, senor soldier. Would it not be good to go help her home from the doctor and make the job easier to get?"

"You are a smart lad, I think." The sentry winked. "She said Doctor Morales, two streets over. She turned north at the corner."

"Thank you, *amigo mio!* The favor will be repaid."

"Just bring me something hot to drink now and then when you come to work here."

Teresa bent her head and walked faster, the snow stinging and freezing upon her cheeks. She did not see the streets she passed. She was unaware of people. She plunged on through the driving snow, her head bent, the pain becoming unbearable.

The second doctor, as well, had left San Antonio. He had not been kind enough to leave a note. She had no recourse, but to turn and start for home.

The cold was creeping upward now through her limbs. They were stiffening, but the pain was going away. The snow covered the unevenness of the street, and she tripped quite suddenly into a drift. Lying there, she felt strangely warm and comfortable and at peace. She was more than a little sleepy; she burrowed even deeper into the drift and lay there, calmly watching her life go out on the ebb of the storm.

Then, suddenly, annoyingly, her sleep was disturbed, and strong arms were lifting her, and she could see Carlos's brown face, sick with fear, looking into hers, and beside him, the kindly eyes of Emilia Hoffman, filled with tears.

"Don't cry, Dona Emilia," she said clearly. "It will cause your make-up to run."

"Let it," Emilia whispered. "You gave us quite a fright when we spotted you in the drift. Into the carriage with her, Carlos."

"Carlos," Teresa murmured when they had her seated and wrapped tightly in a lap robe. "What are you doing here?"

"Enough time for that later," Emilia scolded, rapping on the roof for her driver to go on.

"It's all right," Teresa said softly. "The pain is gone and I feel warm."

"Warm near to freezing," Emilia said, holding her icy hands in her own. "We're going to get you home before you catch your death."

Teresa grasped her hands so tightly that Emilia flinched. "No, not home! Mother wants to take me back to Santa Anna!"

"Fat chance she'll have of doing that," Carlos sneered. "It took me all last night to sneak into town, a little bit at a time."

Emilia had been studying Teresa curiously. "Carlos says that you were going to a doctor."

Teresa smiled. "They all seem to have made their escape."

"Not all," Emilia told her. "But the one I have in mind, I wouldn't be able to take you to him. He's on Gereral Cos's staff. I could get him to make a house visit."

Teresa shook her head. "I feel fine now," she insisted. Just as she didn't want her mother knowing about her fears, so she certainly didn't want General Cos learning anything from one of his officers.

"I can make sure that he can be trusted," Emilia said.

"Don't worry," Teresa murmured. "It's only a little stomach ache."

"Had it long?"

"Off and on for a few weeks. I'm sure that, with the food we've been getting, I'm not the only person in San Antonio with stomach trouble."

Emilia was too wise a woman not to guess Teresa's problem at once. She debated for only a moment before she made up her mind. "If it wouldn't embarrass you, Dona Teresa, I can smuggle you into my villa without being seen. Major Hernandos usually drops by each evening and wouldn't raise suspicion in making a house call."

Teresa nodded her agreement and felt relieved Emilia had taken over. *Run away*, she had thought earlier. Well, what a marvellous spot to run to—no one in their wildest imaginings would think to look for her in a brothel. But then she had a sudden doubt.

"Carlos," she said, "how ever did you think to go to Senorita Hoffman to help look for me?"

"He didn't," Emilia said. "I found him on the streets and was astonished to see him here. He told me all he knew and we set out to look for you."

"Well, I'm still astonished to see him, but pleased, too."

"Oh," Carlos gasped, quickly reaching under his poncho and loosening a string, "before we are separated again, senorita, you must take this burden from me. I have been near having a fit, hiding it and carrying it about." With an audible sigh of relief, he handed Teresa back the pouch of gold.

"Oh, Carlos," she cried. "Did you risk your life just to get this stupid gold back to me?"

He hung his head. "I wish I could say that was the

full truth, but it isn't. I have been with Captain Escovarro and the Texans surrounding the city. They need certain information and I have been sent for it. I also figured it was a good time to return what was not mine."

"Did *he* tell you to return it?" Teresa asked.

"He never learned that I had it, Dona Teresa," Carlos replied, ashamed that, for the first time, he had kept something from his captain. "It was our secret."

"Thank you, Carlos," she said, moved to tears. "It could not have come back to me at a better time."

The boy, Emilia and the returned gold all seemed like omens of changing fortune for her.

Major Hernandos was an ill omen, but Teresa never learned it.

He was short and fat and jolly and a favorite of Emilia's. A happily married man from Monterrey, he had passed into service against his wishes, and sorely missed his equally short, fat and jolly wife and twelve children. He had first come to the villa of *Amarillo Rosa* when General Cos, in a drunken stupor, had fallen down the main staircase and sprained an ankle and a knee. He had paid daily calls while the general was confined to one of Emilia's bedrooms.

His first visit had been exciting. In his forty-five years he had never visited a brothel, and anticipated a place that would be a bit seamy, mysterious and exotic.

He found Emilia Hoffman to be a gracious hostess, and her home was warm and expensively furnished, with no other available women there. In time, he came to learn that Emilia was a 'loner', a one-woman show—and her hospitality, more often than not, had nothing to do with her bedroom. The man had to be invited by her to make it past the second floor, and very few

made it. Most were just content to be included in her
social evening in the grand *sala* or the more intimate
gathering amid the French decor of the music room,
where Emilia might be persuaded to sing and dance
for them.

Emilia had been 'taken' with Dr. Hernandos because he was the first man, of any age, who had spent
a lot of time in her company and had not tried to
make a pass at her. The evenings he began to spend
there with her, especially after the start of the siege,
were taken up with anecdotes about his wife and children. She admired him for being such a devoted Catholic husband and father, and trusted him completely
as a doctor and as a man.

"So," Hernandos said, warming his glass of brandy
with his hands, as though stalling for time after examining Teresa, "that is the one they talk so much
about." He gave a deep chuckle.

Emilia eyed him curiously. "Is there something
amusing in what they say bout her?"

"Yes and no," he said, sipping at the brandy to test
its temperature. "They are saying that she is the
blanco rosa of his life—the white rose that he never
sullied after marriage. The superstitious, among the
soldiers, feel that is why he seems to be afraid of her
and stalls in his march to rescue her. She is said to
have a power that kept him from possessing her, un-
like every other woman he thought worthy of bed-
ding."

"What a bunch of drivel!" Emilia said.

"Exactly. Her condition tells us that she is hardly a
blanco rosa."

Emilia sighed. "That's what I thought it was going
to be, Doctor."

He frowned. "She's a very sick girl for so early in a

pregnancy, though. I have seen this in women in their fifth or sixth month, but never after only a month to six weeks."

Emilia paled. "But it seems she is still *blanco rosa* as far as Santa Anna is concerned."

"I thought as much, but did not want to press her for information. Her nervous condition is extreme— she is as taut as a guitar string. Do you know the man, and would it be wise to get in touch with him?"

"I'm fairly sure that I do know, and no, I don't think it would be wise to communicate with him. He, more than Santa Anna, is responsible for her nervous condition. Besides, the less you know of the situation, the less harm can befall you."

His eyes twinkled. "Who can question what has become almost the good doctor's nightly tradition of having a nightcap at the *Calle de los Pantalones*?"

Emilia's lighthearted laugh rang out. "I think you are the only one who has seen the wry joke in that name. This was not the most beautiful villa I looked at to buy, but I could not turn it down once I had seen the street it was on. The neighbors had never given a thought to it being the 'Street of the Trousers' until I moved in and then it gave them fits."

"They should really call it *Calle de los angles*—the street of the angels."

Emilia frowned. "We said we would never discuss that, Doctor."

"Ah, dear woman, why are you so fearful of praise? Many in this town, and this street alone, would have long since starved if it had not been for your unselfish generosity." He chuckled. "Of course, your gifts come primarily from the Mexican army officers to begin with. And now you take another burden unto yourself."

"She is not a burden, Doctor. She stood up for me once, when a man wouldn't. That shows her true character."

He sighed. "It is not character that worries me, Emilia, about this burden. Her will to live is ebbing and the child, fighting for its own life, is sapping her strength. We must be honest with each other, you and I. The chances are that we are going to lose one or the other, or both."

"No!" she declared, as though the final choice was hers. "I will not let her give up on herself that easily."

"At least she has one fighter on her side."

"I had been counting on two."

He chuckled. "You may count on it. We are in this together."

27

NOVEMBER CAME AND went, and Teresa didn't improve much. Carlos often came to try to cheer her up. He was careful not to discuss any bad news around her, but he shared everything with Emilia. The Texans, disgusted that Cos would not come out and fight and that Santa Anna stayed south of the Rio Grande training his troops, grew weary of the stalemated siege and began departing for their homes to be there in time for Christmas. Even Felix and Miguel Escovarro had returned to the *Ranchero de Oro*. But that news was not told to Teresa.

"How is she really?" Carlos asked, as he came out of her room.

"Your visits always seem to help her, Carlos."

"Senorita," he said sternly, pulling himself up to his full height, which was now nearing six feet, "I am almost a man. The truth will not hurt me where she is concerned."

Emilia had never realized it before, but he *was* nearly a man. It was a shame, she thought, that love was often only one-sided. The love she saw in his face for Teresa, whether just platonic or passionate, was such a waste. She knew that had that same love been expressed by Felix Escovarro, Teresa would have been out of her bed in twenty-four hours.

"All right," Emilia said, matching his stern tone, "come on to the *sala* and we'll be quite candid with each other."

Carlos's eyes widened. "The two of us alone, together?"

Emilia couldn't help but laugh. "Your male virginity, which I have long sensed you still possess, is quite safe with me, Carlos. I have never had the privilege of raping a male virgin in my life." She gave him a mischievous wink. "But you certainly are a prime subject, if I ever decide to change my mind."

He felt relieved and yet elated. No woman, certainly not one so beautiful had ever made him feel so masculine and important. He was almost crushed when the conversation came right back to Teresa.

"Not doing well at all," she told him frankly, after fixing him a weak whiskey and water. The weakness was not due to his age, but to her short supplies. "One day she gives me hope, and the next it shatters into a million pieces."

"We have caught several messengers trying to sneak through to learn if she has gone to rejoin Santa Anna."

"From her mother, no doubt. For weeks the woman drove the army frantic searching the entire city."

"But not here?"

"No one knows of our connection, unless something was said to the Escovarro family."

Carlos nearly choked on his drink and turned beet-red. "I—I may have said something, Dona Emilia."

Her heart froze. "May or did!"

"Did," he stammered. "But, please, it has been my main reason for coming back each time."

"I think you'd best explain yourself, Carlos," she said stonily.

"I thought I was doing right," he muttered. He

looked into Emilia's face and added: "After all, he is
the father of her child, even if they seem to hate each
other so much."

"Well," she said with a long sigh, "you've figured
quite a few things out for yourself, haven't you?"

Carlos was miserable. "Perhaps too much, senorita. I
have come to know and love each of these people, and
when they hurt each other, well, it's like they were
hurting me too. The captain will not tell me what
went wrong between them, and he grew furious with
Carlos when I told him of her condition."

Emilia scoffed. "And, I assume, hotly declared that
the child was not his?"

He nodded. "And forbade me from ever mentioning
the subject again."

Dirty stinking bastard, she thought to herself. In for
the fun, but out for the consequences. Several times in
her life, she had wished that she could be a man for a
few hours and bull-whip some sense into those men
who thought exactly as Felix Escovarro was now
thinking. They thought themselves *macho*—virile, masculine males. To her way of thinking, they didn't have
a right to possess what was dangling between their
legs. They were too pious to pay for their lust in a
brothel, and too weak to face up to the fruits of their
deeds. Given the power, she would have wiped the
world free of all such men, and started the population
anew with men of the caliber of Doctor Hernandos
and Carlos Juarez. Then, with a wry smile, she added
the name Miguel Escovarro to her list.

She caught Carlos staring at her and realized how
long she had been silent.

"I'm sorry. My mind wandered. You probably did
right in telling him, Carlos. I assume that you were
also told to stay away from here when you came to
town."

He blushed. "I was, senorita. But Don Miguel then gave me different orders. Oh, not to seek information about Dona Teresa. He does not even know she is here or her condition. His worry is for you and he wants a report each time on your safety and condition."

She was touched, but tried to show indifference in front of the boy.

"That was very kind of him."

"I don't think it was just kindness, senorita. I have heard the two of them fighting about you. He says he is in love with you, and the captain says it isn't possible. Is that really true, senorita?"

Emilia was puzzled. "Is what really true?"

Inexperienced and simple, Carlos dared to put a question to her that strong men would never have dared to ask.

"That women like you are incapable of love."

"No," she whispered, "it isn't true. I—I guess we are even more capable of love than the majority. But we see the true love that we are longing for given to wives and girl friends and sweethearts, because they are to be kept pure and from becoming mere objects of sensual desire. I—I think I'd better go look in on her now. Thank you for coming to see us." Then she turned very slowly and went back to the third floor. To her relief, Teresa was sleeping quietly.

She sat down beside her in the darkness, thinking:

It was so easy to be honest with him. Why can't I be just as honest with my own heart? That I cannot do.

She bent her head and gave way to a storm of weeping. Then it passed, and she straightened up, thinking:

You know what's happening to you, Emilia Rosa, and you're afraid of it. Once again you feel love, and you are fighting it. But this time, I think you are wise to fight it; this time . . . this time . . .

23

On December 2, Carlos Juarez made his last surreptitious trip out of San Antonio. During the last few
weeks, he had been in every quarter of the city and had
come to be regarded as a ragged local boy. His face
and manner he kept simple, while he watched and
listened for every changing breeze of rumor. He would
memorize facts and figures, and transfer them to maps
only when he was back safely in the Texan camp.

His reports were never questioned when Stephen
Austin was in command and Captain Escovarro was by
his side. But Austin was gone on a trip to the United
States to rally support for the cause, and the Escovarro
brothers were at home with their parents. Carlos had
no choice but to report to General Edward Burleson.

"Sir, another hundred Mexican soldiers have fled
this week. The rest are starving, dispirited and low in
ammunition."

General Burleson yawned. "Another couple of weeks
and they'll be lower in ammunition."

Ben Milam, a leathery plainsman, drawled, "Or is it
yah jest ain't got no heart for fightin', Ed?"

Burleson ignored the insult; he had been hearing it
for weeks. "Now, Ben, this is just the boy's opinion on
matters in the city."

"Not jest 'pinion, Ed. These 'ere maps he's drawed

tells all. Gawd damn, they show the weakest points fer attack. I say go now, before Cos changes his defenses."

"I'll send a rider to San Felipe to see what the Provisional Government has to say."

"Sheet!" Milam exploded. "Them damfools don't know how ta do anything but fart!"

A rider was dispatched to San Felipe, but Ben Milam continued to storm and rant and rave at the general. Burleson hesitated, but still was unwilling to fight.

"You may want to put your life on the line," Burleson shouted right back at Milam, "but I don't. After all, the boy *is* a Mexican, and how do I know he's telling the truth?"

Milam soundly cursed the man in mule-driver language, and stormed from the tent.

"Boys," he shouted, "who will come with old Ben Milam into San Antonio? The drinks will be on me!"

His words at first met with a stunned silence and then a fierce roar of approval. Within an hour, two hundred and forty men had volunteered to go with him, including Carlos Juarez. The night was spent in laying their plans, using Carlos's maps, and shortly before dawn on December 5, they advanced quietly on the sleeping city.

The first, distant musket shots woke Emilia instantly. Her bedroom faced north, and she could see nothing but blue-black sky from her window. She raced on bare feet to the bay window of the second-floor landing. By then, the grey line of dawn was a backdrop for a fire-works' display. Flashes of gunpowder made orange puffs that were beautiful to watch at that distance. The volunteers were fighting house to house, hand to hand, and leaving a new fire-works' display in their wake: the firing of the houses

that the Mexicans refused to surrender. The sun was
not needed to see the eastern skyline, it was backed in
a fiery glow already. The fierce bark of hundreds of
muskets, long-rifles and pistols competed with the
basso rumble of Cos's cannons. Only the deaf in San
Antonio could still be sleeping.

A clatter and metallic thumping on the stairs from
the third floor distracted Emilia from the window.

"Child!" she cried, amazed at seeing Teresa supporting herself on the bannister and dragging something
heavy behind her. "What are you doing out of bed?
And what have you got with you?"

Teresa, ashen, her eyes wild with fright, stared past
Emilia out of the bay window.

"It's come at last?" she whispered.

"It's still a long way off, and I don't think there will
ever be fighting on this street."

Teresa, too weak to hold herself up any longer, sank
feebly down on the stairs, and something made of
metal clattered on down to the landing.

Emilia couldn't help but laugh, as she went to pick
up the firepoker. "Who were you going to bash with
this?" she asked. "You barely have the strength to drag
it, let alone lift it in self defense."

Teresa smiled weakly. "Stupid, wasn't it? I want the
siege to end, so I don't know who I was going to bash
with it. None of our people, of course."

Emilia wanted the siege to end as well, but she was
no longer sure she wanted 'their people' to win. She
wasn't thinking so much of the effect it would have on
her business—not a single San Antonio gentleman had
crossed her threshold since the day General Cos arrived—but the effect it would have on Teresa. Defeat
for the Mexicans would mean that there would be no
Doctor Hernandos to look out for Teresa.

Teresa gave a cry of pain.

"What is it?" Emilia raced to her in alarm.

"My legs," Teresa gasped. "They're cramping. Oh . . . God! What pain!"

"Don't move!" Emilia warned. "It'll hurt, but keep your legs out straight."

Emilia squatted down between the quivering legs, pushed the nightgown up Teresa's expanding belly and quickly felt her thighs and calves to locate the knotted muscles. She began to massage them as Teresa moaned and thrashed her head back and forth on the stair.

"I know it's an uncomfortable position," Emilia said, working as fast, but as gently, as she could "but you know what Doctor Hernandos said. We mustn't let these cramps travel up to your belly. You're not strong enough to have attacks there again."

"Oh . . . I'm sorry . . . to be such a baby."

"Fiddle! I've seen grown men cry over a leg cramp. I'd like to see how they'd hold up carrying a baby for nine months." Emilia concentrated on the right leg, kneading it from ankle to groin.

Teresa let out a weak little laugh. "I'm sorry you had to remind me that I've got another six months of this hell to live through." Then she cringed.

"What is it? Where's the cramp?"

Teresa sighed. "No cramp. The stair edge is beginning to deaden my back."

Emilia frowned. "I don't want to move you too far, until we're sure this cramp isn't going to travel. Give me your hands. I'll help you slide down the steps to the hall carpet."

Emilia took her hands and gently raised her to a sitting position. Carefully, a step at a time, with Emilia pulling on her legs to keep them straight, Teresa bumped on her behind to the level surface of the hall.

She gulped as Emilia straightened up. "Emilia, you're naked!"

Emilia looked down at herself, and her laugh seemed to ripple right up from her toes. "Now look who's the stupid one. I got out of my bed so fast that I didn't even think of it."

Teresa started at her in wonderment. "You sleep without anything on?"

"Not really," she said. "I have a silk sheet under me and silk sheet over me. I love the feel of silk next to my skin."

"So do I," Teresa blurted and then flushed. "I meant a dress or something like that."

Emilia continued to laugh as she lowered herself to her knees and went back to inspecting Teresa's legs for knotted muscles. But there was something in the tone of her laugh that even she didn't like. It had a nervous sound, and she was hardly ever nervous. Her fingers now trembled as they kneaded the soft flesh. She prayed that Teresa would lie down flat and quit gaping at her nakedness. She was beginning to feel self-conscious, and it was an emotion entirely new to her. Hundreds of men had seen her naked and she had never felt this peculiar. Teresa's eyes were devouring her in such open appraisal that Emilia felt a rosy flush crawl up her cheeks.

"I—I—," Teresa stammered, "didn't mean to stare." She saw Emilia's blush and had grown embarrassed knowing she had caused it. "I've never seen another woman's body before."

"They're all the same." Emilia had tried to sound casual, but her voice had trembled slightly. Once before, when she was fifteen, she had had this kind of experience. It was like skating on thin ice, and that time she had fallen through to the chilling realm of a totally different existence. It was that existence, that different world, she had been fearing, the more she became involved with Teresa. That first love of her life had been devastating to her senses when it was abruptly ended. The *puta* left her mother's brothel one night without a word of farewell and was never heard from again. It was the last woman Emilia had allowed herself to get close to, emotionally or physically, and she was determined not to fall through the ice again.

Teresa's worried little laugh brought her back from her memories. "How can you say that we are all the same? Look at your . . . well . . . ah . . . Oh, I'm being coarse."

Emilia sat back abruptly on the hall floor and couldn't help but laugh. Teresa had nearly echoed her own words of twelve years before. She had only begun to ripen and develop at fifteen and had been enchanted at the largeness of the *puta's* breasts.

"You're far from being coarse, Teresa," she said softly. "I am of a substantial figure and never fully realized it until I was in Paris last year."

"Paris? You've never mentioned that you have been to Paris."

Emilia gave a short laugh. "I've mentioned very little of my life to you, *amiga mia.* You have heard but a sentence, and there are paragraphs, chapters and books yet untold, but, yes, I went to Paris to buy the wardrobe I now possess. While being fitted, the seamstress asked if she could introduce me to an artist friend of hers. What did I know of art, so I said yes. He was a funny little old man, whose eyes bulged when he saw my body. Of course I thought it was a sensual look, but it was really artistic appreciation of the female form at its finest. At least, those were his words. Being a well trained *puta*, I was skeptical. But he was a gentleman and took me to this gallery to see not only some of his work, but the work of men who have been dead for hundreds of years. Every work was of a nude, male and female, in paintings and smooth marble statues. There was nothing gross or coarse in what I saw; it was beauty. This may surprise you, but it took a great deal of time and courage on my part to consent to model for him in the nude."

"I don't think I could ever do it."

"Nor did I at the time. His studio was dank and cold and evil smelling, but his finished work was thrilling. It seemed so strange, to stand there and see a blue-white marble figure and know that your own body inspired it. I was really quite proud."

"That's beautiful," Teresa said, tears welling in her eyes. "A beautiful story."

Emilia, who had been working on Teresa's legs throughout, sensed that the story, perhaps more than her massaging, had eased Teresa's tensions.

"Are we all better now?" she asked.

"I think so," Teresa said. "I've still a little pain deep in my stomach, but it's fading fast. Thank you."

"Do you want me to help you back to bed now?"

"In a minute. Just let me sit here for a second. Oh, but you must be getting cold without anything on. Do you want to get a robe or something?"

"Actually, I'm as warm as a fresh *tortilla*, but I'll go get something if I am embarr—"

"You're not!" Teresa cut her short. "I may never get to Paris to see the work of art, so why should the original embarrass me?" She was silent for a moment. Then she said softly: "There's another reason I don't want to be alone, quite yet. Emilia, is it this hard on all women?"

"Child," Emilia said, shrugging expansively, "I'm the last female in the world capable of answering that question. I only know what I have heard, and I don't think so. I've seen women go the whole period as rosy and happy and delighted as they could be."

"Perhaps," Teresa said sulkily, "it's just my punishment for the way it came about."

"Nonsense! You just didn't have anyone around to tell you how to prevent it."

Teresa's eyes flashed with understanding. "Is that why you aren't . . . have never been . . . How?"

"Oh," Emilia said, "you are one of a kind. When the time comes, I'll tell you how to keep this from happening when you are with a man again."

"Again?" Teresa suddenly flared. "I never shall be again. For the little pleasure it brought, I don't want this suffering again."

"The pleasure can be there without the pain, Teresa."

"Not for me," Teresa insisted. "I shall never have another man as long as I live . . . Oh! . . . Em . . . ilia!" She was beginning to gasp in pain again. "It's— It's not better . . . Ohhh! It's worse."

The pain increased until she slipped to the floor in a semi-faint. In a dream state, she felt her body being lifted and carried and lowered onto cool, refreshing silk. She seemed to drift lower and lower into the softness of the feather-down mattress. Somehow she helped to get the nightgown off her body, but she wasn't sure how. Her only sensation was of the gentle massaging of her stomach muscles to keep them from shriveling and strangling the child's life supply.

For a moment, she prayed desperately for that to happen; but then she was totally Catholic again and prayed for the child's survival.

Emilia worked frantically to release the tension before it could harm either child or mother. She put her cheek down on the swollen belly and listened to internal sounds she did not understand.

"I can't tell if that's the child I'm hearing or not," Emilia said.

"Probably just the beans we had for supper. Your cheeks feels so cool. Am I feverish?"

"A mite. Shall I go down and get some cold water to sponge you off?"

Teresa grabbed Emilia's hand, lying just above her belly, and held it firmly. "No! Don't leave me. I feel so safe when you are close. Your hands and cheek have been cooling me more than the sponge ever would."

And even more than that, Teresa thought. When Emilia had placed her cheek to Teresa's abdomen, Teresa had felt the touch of Emilia's expansive breast on her side and thigh. They had brushed her skin softly, like a simple caress. It had sent an emotional charge surging through her body, and she knew that it had caused the nervous rumbling in her stomach, not the baby. It had not been like the rough derma of Santa Anna's body, nor the soft furry touch of Felix's chest hair. This had been mammary softness, as delicate as gossamer.

Later, Teresa wasn't sure what persuaded her to be so impulsive, except perhaps that she wanted the coolness to ease all her body. She pulled Emilia's hand up onto her feverish breast and sighed.

Emilia did not take it as a sensual invitation and began to smooth her hands over the firm globes. They were hard and firm and already beginning to produce milk for the day it would be needed. Emilia used only the merest touch of her fingertips to caress them over and over again.

Teresa gave a slight shudder of appreciation and jutted them higher. Time went backwards for Emilia and twelve years dropped away. There wasn't even a thought in her mind as she let her burning lips fall upon the conical tips, one at a time, until they were alive and swollen with the feelings aroused. Teresa pushed her head far back into the pillow and writhed with pleasure. Ironically, the sensation made her think of Anna-Maria and Pedro Perez. Was this a part of loving *all* the other person? She could not recall Santa Anna or Felix having touched her breasts with their hands, let alone their lips. She wondered what would happen next.

Emilia, encouraged that there had been no show of apprehension or disgust, let her dream state carry her lightly kissing lips down between the firm white mounds, pass over the protruding belly, and rest on the soft mass of golden fur below.

Instinctively, Teresa let her legs fall apart and was soon aware of nothing more than the faint little moans that escaped from her throat like air bubbles rising and breaking on the water surface. Denied a true fulfillment of her sexual emotions for so long, she allowed herself to swirl up to a passionate height that was dizzying. And once at the pinnacle, there was no sudden, shattering fall. She floated, feather-light and carefree, drifting gently downward like a snowflake from the clouds of bliss.

Her reviving senses brought to her the squeak of the bed at the very moment her nostrils detected the fragrance of the warm body and its touch along her entire length. Gentle arms cuddled her to an expansive bosom. Tingles rushed up and down her spine of the sort she had experienced only as a child on Christmas morning. She had been in love with life then, and knew that was the love that had slowly drained out of her in the past few years. Here was an opportunity to recapture its gentleness, its sparkling thrill, its unending mystery.

Her eyes still misty, she raised her head and brushed her lips against the cheek that tasted slightly of powder. She snuggled then into the embrace of Emilia's bosom and was soon asleep. It was the deepest, most restful sleep that her body had experienced in months.

Emilia lay awake, gently stroking Teresa's hair. It's only a way station, she thought dully. A respite from the storm, but hardly a very safe harbor. She prayed that when Teresa returned to the world of men, and she did have to return to that world, that she would always think kindly of *Amarillo Rosa*.

Doctor Hernandos did not come that day, or the next or the next. When he was finally able to find a safe way to the villa, he arrived very weary, ashen and dirty from too many hours in the infirmary.

"What is this?" he asked, smiling. "Six-thirty in the morning and my little patient has roses in her cheeks already." He felt her pulse and smiled again. "Ah, that also pleases me. How about the pains?"

Teresa caught Emilia's eye and smiled. They had not discussed what had transpired between them, only their eyes had been communicating.

"Pains?" Teresa said playfully, as though there never had been any. "I haven't had a single cramp or stomach pain since the first morning of the fighting."

"That is quite obvious," he chortled, examining her abdomen with his fingertips. "You look like a new person. Been sleeping well?"

"She can't seem to get enough," Emilia answered for her. "Yesterday she almost slept round the clock."

Hernandos boomed out his approval. "And I dare say she's the only one in San Antonio who has been able to sleep through this constant din. Well, as you seem to be doing so well, I'll get myself back to where I am really needed. Emilia, will you see me out?"

All of his jolliness faded as soon as they were back downstairs. "I didn't want to say good-bye to her," he said gloomily. "It might only frighten her to know that she will not have a doctor soon."

"How soon?"

"Cos is throwing in the towel even at this hour. We can't hold out. The Navarro house has fallen, the Zambrano row went yesterday and the priest's house the day before that. What is left of us are bottled up at the Alamo mission, and it is not defensible. All is lost but honor."

Emilia felt afraid for this man she so much admired.

"What will happen, Doctor?"

He understood and patted her cheek. "Do not worry for me, dear lady. The Texans have already made it plain that they want Cos to take his army back across the Rio Grande under parole. Mexico has lost this eastern land. We are not in any way to oppose the re-establishment of the Federal Constitution of 1824."

Emilia was skeptical. "Cos might buy those terms to save his own neck, but will Santa Anna?"

His jolly nature returned. "That's the whole point, senorita," he said. "Santa Anna has no choice. He is standing still. He is still in San Luis Potosi trying to raise a full army. He has one officer and one non-com for every two privates. He is unprepared to fight and this crushing defeat will make half of his privates disappear and return to their homes."

"And you can return to your home."

"That is a pleasant thought, a very pleasant thought." He reached out quickly, took her hand and pressed it gently to his lips. "You take good care of yourself and our patient. When I think of you, and I will often think of you, I will think that there is no lovelier bloom in God's great garden than the Yellow Rose that I found in Texas. *Adios,* my sweet and gentle creature."

The Mexican soldiers were not the only ones to leave San Antonio. The danger was over and General Burleson went home to his family. The scene was repeated everywhere as the colonists left the army to rejoin their families, celebrate Christmas and begin farming again.

Of those left to guard San Antonio, many wanted to carry the war into Mexico. They coveted the booty that would be theirs for the taking in the port city of Matamoros. They also coveted what they could take away from San Antonio, and appropriated practically everything in sight—money, clothing, saddles, arms, food, blankets, medical supplies. Behind them, they left only picked-over junk that nobody wanted—and picked over soldiers that nobody wanted. By and large, except for a few sober officers, San Antonio was left for a time in the hands of rough-swearing, knife-fighting dangerous drunkards who had tacked GTT signs on their cabin doors from Tennessee to Louisiana. The majority who had Gone To Texas were worthless, shiftless scavengers who had farmed out their land, turned for awhile to lawlessness and robbery, and now wanted new land to farm—until they tired of that as well.

Most were single, by chance or choice. The latter never said much about the various families they had often started up and deserted along the line. They were arrogant, uncouth, dirty of mind and body, and lived mainly for their next drink, their next woman, their next fight or the next bit of devilment they could stir up.

They had come to Texas with a single hatred in their souls against anyone who got in their way. The Spanish-speaking people of San Antonio, to their way of thinking, were in their way. To them, there was no difference between a Spaniard who had lived in Tejas for several generations and the Mexican peasant who had arrived during the last few years. They were all the enemy and were squatting on land they felt they had captured by breaking the siege.

The nights of the peace became noisier, rowdier and bloodier than the nights of the brief war. The more they drank, the more they saw traitors lurking in every shadow. They began to fire at anything that moved, killing nearly as many of their own drunken rogue friends as innocent San Antonio citizens.

The citizens, more fearful of this heinous tribe than they ever had been of Cos's troops, imposed a curfew on themselves. They closed their shutters, bolted their doors and stayed within from sundown to sunup. The streets and cantinas were left to the marauders.

A few days before Christmas, Carlos Juarez came to the villa to say good-bye before going to spend the holidays with the Escovarro family. A few blocks away from the villa, he was accosted by two drunken soldiers, dragged protesting to the *calaboose* and locked away. No one would listen to his protest, because the jail officials did not wish to cross swords with the Americans. They had enough troubles of their own, Carlos learned. General Cos had feared traitors in the Mexican and Spanish sections of town, and so the majority of the population of the *calaboose* was from there. And after the siege, because they were Mexican and Spanish, the Texan army overlooked them and left them to rot. They were forgotten men and the jailers wouldn't help them. Carlos couldn't even bribe them to get a message to Emilia or Teresa.

"It may sound strange," Teresa said on the afternoon of Christmas Eve, "but I feel suddenly miserable."

Emilia arched an eyebrow. "Oh, is the baby giving the mother trouble?"

"No," Teresa answered forlornly, "the mother is giving the daughter trouble. My mother. I feel guilty, Emilia. She is only a few blocks away and I don't know if she is well, or ill, or worried. When I was so sick, I didn't even give her any mind. Now . . ."

"Christmas, eh?" Emilia smiled with understanding. "The spirit of peace on earth and good will toward men. A time to forgive and forget."

Teresa flushed. "I suppose that's it. Am I wrong?"

"Good heavens, no. The woman, as far as you've told me, was only trying to do what she thought was best for you."

"And herself."

Emilia laughed, rose to warm her hands at the small fire they were allowing themselves in the fireplace, and slowly turned.

"I guess that is the way with mothers, always thinking they know what is best for their children. My mother was always the same, right or wrong."

"That's funny," Teresa said. "Isn't this the first you have ever mentioned her? I don't mean to pry, but is she dead?"

Emilia rocked the room with her laughter. "My mother, dead! She'll be on earth forever because they wouldn't know what to do with her in either heaven or hell!"

"Where is she? Still here is San Antonio?"

"Has never left it since the day she was born. She's still the biggest hellion on the south side, as far as I know. I only hear from her when she is in need of a handout, which isn't very often."

"Emilia," Teresa cried excitedly, "let's do something totally wild. Let's invite them both for Christmas dinner tomorrow."

"Both!" Emilia shrieked. "Oh, that would be rare, an ancestor of the founder of the town sitting down with an ancestor of the first madam of the town." Then she sobered. "Do what you wish," she said petulantly. "After all, it is your gold we've been living on."

"Emilia!" Teresa said firmly. "We agreed that that would not become a thorn between us. Just thank God that Carlos returned it to me when he did. I owe you my life. No amount of gold could account for that."

Emilia nodded and turned back to the fireplace. "Make out the invitations, and I'll go and deliver them."

She had been so happy in helping Teresa return to health. She could not help but feel that bringing Dona Helena back into their lives would make her lose part of Teresa, no matter how small a part it was.

To their surprise, both women agreed to come and arrived at the villa about the same time.

Ophelia Morillo had accepted the invitation because she was convinced her daughter had made millions of *pesos* while General Cos and his officers were quartered in the city. She and her "girls" had also done handsomely with Cos's soldiers, but times had been rough since their departure, and she prayed that her daughter had been more thrifty than she had.

Teresa was astonished at her apparent youth. Her rainbow dress was a sea of sequin sparkles on the figure of a mere girl. Make-up kept her fortyish face looking half that age, and her vitality reduced that again by five. She was cheerful, vivacious and quite open in admitting that she had conceived Emilia when she was only thirteen. Her only puzzlement was over the seemingly warm relationship between the patrician Teresa and her daughter. If the senorita had not been so obviously pregnant, she would have felt compelled to step in once again and drive a *lesbian* away from her daughter, as she had been forced to do twelve years before.

Helena de Alarcon had swallowed her pride and accepted the invitation because she was starving. There was no elation in her heart in learning that her daughter was safe and still in the city. She was bitter that Teresa had not heeded her sage advice because they would have been safe at that moment in the protection of Santa Anna, but the aroma of food in the house made her swallow her bitterness for another time.

Where Teresa had been astounded at Ophelia Morillo's apparent youth, she was aghast at her own mother's aging. The two mothers were contemporaries, but Dona Helena looked at least ten years past her forties. Her "widow's weeds" hung loosely on a body that had lost thirty pounds since the start of the siege. Her mouth was curved in a permanent sulk, and her eyes were hard and cold and unfriendly. She wondered why her daughter was keeping her pregnancy such a secret. She assumed that it was Santa Anna's child and she was resentful that her daughter was not making the best of a good thing—especially with times being as hard as they were.

The four women from such diverse backgrounds somehow managed to get through their Christmas meal. Each daughter kept a careful and fearful eye on her mother; and each mother grew more and more puzzled by the change in her daughter. Emilia had never before been so warm and open and affectionate toward her mother. But Teresa had been irritated by her mother no more than five minutes after her arrival, and their coolness had turned to ice after that. Teresa was saddened to hear of Manuel's passing, but Dona Helena went on and on about the lurid details of the old man's death. She began to spoil the party, and so Teresa finally interrupted her and changed the subject. It took all Emilia's tact and good humor to revive the Christmas mood after that.

Both mothers left the villa in a good humor, clutching a basket of leftover food in one hand, and a Christmas gift handkerchief of gold coins in the other. Both were human enough, when out of the sight of the other, to drop the basket onto the street and frantically claw at the knots in the handkerchief. Both women stared at the gold coins in disbelief.

"*Pu—ta!*" Ophelia spat. "She makes more in fifteen minutes than I make in a week. May her loveplace shrivel to the size of one of these miserable coins!"

A block away, Dona Helena counted them and then counted them again. Her face grew dark with rage. "She owes me a thousand times this amount for giving her life!"

Christmas gave the firebrand soldiers an excuse to begin drinking early in the day and celebrate until their minds were boggled. What wag first came up with the scheme, no one was sure, but it was a great idea in their minds from the first.

In drunken confusion, they marched from the cantinas to the *calaboos,* their off-key voices making a parody of the carols they sang and what they hoped to accomplish.

"Pardons! Pardons!" they began to shout as the jail officials came out to see what the ruckus was all about.

"*Que tal?*" a jailer asked, puzzled.

"Bullshit!" a toothless renegade spat. "Don't give us none of that Mex crap!" The jailer had not understood him and, in gun-shot fire sentences, he barked orders until he was joined on the jail steps by five comrades with rifles in their hands.

A cooler head, if not any more sober, pushed the toothless man aside and stepped forward.

"Hold them rifles down," he drawled, "or thirty pistols will rip your guts out." He, too, had not been understood, but the jailers remained frozen in place at the mere sound of his voice.

"Hey!" he bellowed. "Don't any of you polecats speak English?"

"*Si*, senor," the senior jailer said timidly. "We speak little."

"Little," he laughed mockingly. "Do you know Christmas?"

The jailer beamed. "*Si*, senor, Christmas!"

"Pardon?"

The jailer looked puzzled at the word and then grinned. "*Indulto, si!*"

"Yah got it, pardner! At Christmas we *indulto* all the prisoners, see!"

"*Si*," the jailer said slowly, and then realization dawned. "*Si*," he said more enthusiastically. His Christmas prayer was being answered by a strange messenger from God. He had no more funds with which to feed the prisoners after that day, and they were being taken off his hands. He shouted the orders jubilantly to open each and every cell. His orders were met with boisterous shouts from the Texan soldiers.

Dazed, confused, bewildered men began to emerge onto the street. The line of soldiers on the street first froze their hearts with panic, but when they were only bombarded by Christmas wishes, they fled into the shadows like the spirit of Christmas past.

"No," the jailer said sternly, and signaled for one prisoner to be taken back inside.

"What's this?" a Texan growled.

"Senor," the jailer said with a shrug of his shoulders,

"this one is different. The others are political, but he is a criminal."

The Texan, late of Tennessee, Kentucky and New Orleans, didn't regard anything as criminal unless he had committed it first.

"Wha'd he do?" he barked.

"He's accused of raping our President's mother-in-law."

The soldier's mind reeled drunkenly. "Jackson's got one 'of them down here?"

The jailer blushed. "Our *before* President, senor. The mother-in-law of Senora de Santa Anna."

Senor Sanchez, wily as ever, saw a chance for freedom and yelled for it. "Hey, *meester* . . . eee's wrong. Set me free, and Sanchez tells you something that makes you *beeg* general."

The burly Texan was amused by the Mexican. The other men were getting bored, and this was supposed to have been a lively Christmas idea. He motioned Sanchez forward and cocked his ear in a comical way.

"In the house where they caught me," Sanchez whispered, "is the real wife of Santa Anna. The troops marched passed the *calaboose* window as they left, and Sanchez saw no carriage of females. She must still be here."

The Texan's warped sense of adventure was aroused. He marched away, his arm about Sanchez's shoulder, leaving a shrugging jailer behind. He was not about to lose his life protesting over the release of his last prisoner.

Dona Helena hadn't even been in her house long enough to remove her shawl when she heard the light knock at the door. Anticipating yet another invitation to dinner, she rushed and flung the door wide open.

"Where is she?" the Texan barked, before she even had time to react. She was just about to protest, when she spotted the face of Sanchez. She froze in terror. Emilia's address came out in a stammer even as she found the strength to slam and bolt the door. She collapsed in a quivering heap.

29

HARVEY FULLER LET Sanchez go. The whore on the *Calle de la Pantalones* had been a topic of great discussion during the month that they had encircled the city. The house was always dark at night, so everyone had automatically assumed that *Amarillo Rosa* had fled with the other Mexicans.

He felt that the old woman had been lying. What would the wife of Santa Anna be doing in a whorehouse? That no longer interested him, except as an excuse to get into the villa. His mind was too drunk to even wonder why the old woman had claimed that she had just come from the villa. All it meant to him was that he would find someone at home there. But if he was going to get a belated Christmas present, he didn't want to share it with all the other soldiers.

"Boys," he drawled, "all these greasers know how to do is lie through their teeth." He prayed that none of them was aware of the address the old woman had given. Gripes and snarls reassured him.

He smacked his bulbous lips. "I'm shor'nuff gettin' dry. Let's go back to Rosa's place and raid the bar."

The suggestion was applauded and they left the de Alarcon patio singing.

On the street Fuller gave three of his friends the

high sign and they fell back from the pack and then drifted into the shadows.

"Knew ya had somethin' cookin'," a mountain of a man roared. "Ya think the old hag was right?"

"Maybe and maybe not," he said evilly. "Ya'll feel like doin' some stompin'?"

"Rather be doin' some slit stickin', but what yah got in mind, Harve?"

"That address is the house of a Mex lover. Don't seem fair ta me it ain't been hurt none by the war. Ya'all got yore stompin' boots on?"

To encourage them further, as they headed toward the villa, he pulled a jug of corn liquor from his pack and passed it around.

The day had exhausted Teresa, and she had already gone to the third floor bedroom. She had sprawled out on the bed fully clothed, thinking she would rest for only a few minutes, but had fallen asleep almost at once.

Emilia had taken away the dishes from the dining room and was considering washing them when she heard the heavy, insistent pounding on the front door panels.

"Who is it?" she demanded firmly.

"Militia!" Fuller barked with authority. "There's been a jail-break."

"There's no one here."

"Orders, ma'am. We're searchin' every house."

Emilia hesitated. She didn't like the sound of the man's drunken slur, but the last thing she wanted was trouble with the militia.

"Oh, all right," she said, unbolting the door. She sensed she had made a grave error the moment the door was open. The quartet were in filthy buckskins and molting coonskin caps. They were unshaven, and their beards were matted with food and spilled drink.

The fire in their red-rimmed eyes was caused by more than too much to drink, she realized.

"I tell you there is no one here," she said evenly.

This was the lady, Harvey Fuller thought, gaping at her. No whore he had ever seen could afford to dress in such finery; and no whore had ever looked like this. There was no doubt in his mind that he had stumbled onto the wife of the Mexican President.

"Well," he drawled, pushing in past her. "We gotta see that for ourselves. Come on in, boys."

Emilia had handled many drunken men in her life and knew that clamness was her best ally.

"If you're coming in, do it quickly. It's hard enough keeping this house warm without having the door stand wide open."

They shuffled in and look about in open-mouthed amazement.

"Lawdy, me!" the mountain man gasped. "Ain't dis sumpin' fit fur a king!"

"Damnation to hell! Harve, yore ole eyes ever seen the likes of dis?"

Fuller hadn't taken his eyes from Emilia. "Ya'all alone?"

Emilia knew she didn't dare hesitate. There was danger in saying that she was and danger for Teresa if she said she wasn't.

"I told you there was no one here," she said taking the middle ground.

Fuller eyed her from the neck down and then slowly back up again. He shrugged his shoulders as though he didn't believe her. "Do yah always dress like that when no one's here?" he mocked.

"Naturally not," she said icily. "I entertained guests for Christmas dinner earlier."

"Sumbitch," the mountain man roared. "The old hag didn't lie 'bout eatin' 'ere then."

Emilia was puzzled. "What? What is this all about? There hasn't been a jail-break, has there?"

"Hot damn!" Fuller chortled. "If ya'all ain't the coolest-headed bitch I've ever come 'cross. See that, boys? Didn't flinch a muscle when ole tubby-belly 'ere gave it all away. Hell, yes, "he snapped, "there were a jail-break." Then he came right up and laughed in her face. His foul breath nauseated her. "Course we caused it. We let all yore little Mex friends go free. That's how we learned 'bout you, 'n yore ma let us know where yah were."

Emilia's mind raced. Her own mother would have no reason to let them know where she was; these were hardly her type of clientele. She could only conclude that they were looking for Teresa.

Fuller's eyes narrowed to slits. "Now, where's the other one?"

"The other one what?"

"Lady," he said softly, "yore a nice piece of goods. I'd hate ta let my boys change that. *Where is the whore?*"

It suddenly made sense to Emilia. They thought she was Teresa. She decided to gamble. "Well, it must be obvious that you are not looking at her, and for the last time I'll tell you that I am quite alone."

Fuller walked away from her. "Well, ain't this purty," he simpered, picking up a delicate vase from the hall table and immediately let it slip right through his fingers and crash into a million pieces on the tile floor. "Awh, ain't that a shame." Then he barked, "Where?"

"Nowhere!" she barked right back.

He picked up the table and hurled it across the foyer at a full length mirror. Table and mirror shattered on impact.

"One last time, Senora de Santa Anna," he warned, "and then we tear this place apart."

Emilia, seething with fury inside, froze her face in a cold glare. "And one last time I will declare that I am alone."

"Barker!" he screamed. "Feldman! Hold the fuckin' bitch while Tubby and I have a little fun in this 'ere room over 'ere."

Even as they grasped her arms and pinned them behind her, Emilia knew it was pointless to scream. It would only cause them to grow fiercer and might arouse Teresa. Oh God, she prayed, don't let Teresa hear the commotion and come down the stairs.

The sounds from the *sala* were sickening. The breaking and crashing were intensified by the guttural shouts and laughs of ignorant men, who would rather destroy what they would never be able to possess rather than leave it for others to enjoy.

Their noise was so horrendous that the trio in the foyer did not hear the outside door open cautiously. Carlos Juarez stood for a moment confused at the scene and then he recongnized the two men holding Emilia. With a mighty heave, he slammed the front door shut and shouted:

"Let her go, Barker! Back away, Feldman! What in the hell do you think you are doing?"

They blinked at him foolishly. He had their names correct, but their sodden brains couldn't recall having ever seen him before. And he presented no threat. He was weaponless.

His shout had brought Fuller and the tubby mountain man on the run.

Emilia caught Carlos' eye and warned him not to say too much too soon.

"Fuller," Carlos exclaimed. "What is going on here?"

Harvey Fuller also had to get the boy's face in focus

and try to recall why it was familiar. His hesitation gave Emilia time to act.

"Carlos," she said quickly, "I'm glad you came. They are looking for Emilia Hoffman and think she is in the house. They will not believe that I am alone."

Carlos listened carefully as she spoke and reacted accordingly. He eyed Fuller as coldly as General Burleson might have eyed him. "How did you learn that the *senora* was here? It has been a closely guarded military secret."

The huge mountain man eyed Fuller through blurry pupils. "Harve, who is this geezet?"

Fuller's memory was coming back. "I think he's the Mex kid who drew the maps that got us into San Antonio."

"What's he got to do with her?"

Fuller didn't know and turned a weaving head to Carlos.

"That is of no interest to any of you," Carlos said sternly. "Pack up and get out."

"Bullshit!" Barker fumed. "Harve, you gonna let a little Mex give us orders?"

"It wasn't an order," Carlos declared, before Fuller could speak. "It was a suggestion before Colonel Niel learns of this. You are on private property, you know."

Carlos had touched the wrong chord in Harvey Fuller. His hatred seethed in him. "Ain't no private property no more," he snarled. "We won it all from you fuckin' spicks. It's our'n now."

Carlos tried to reason with the drunken man. "No, it isn't. Most of the people of San Antonio are Spanish, not Mexican. Their families have been here for hundreds of years. They fought this battle the same as you and me."

Fuller looked from Barker to Feldman to the tubby mountain man. "Boys," he said slowly, "he just made me realize sumpin' important. We done the fightin' and the greasers still got the land. Funny, ain't it? We hear all this talk 'bout ole Santa Anna gonna march back on San 'Tone. Wha'da make him do that? Wha'da made a Mex kid 'elp us and still protect her? Get 'em" he snarled. "Let's make sure that ole Mex president don't find her the same way he left her."

Carlos fought them until Barker hit him on the back of the head and knocked him out. Emilia remained impassive, although they were now causing her great pain in the manner they were holding her arms behind her.

"He's out!" Barker chuckled. "Time for her, huh?"

Tubby swept her onto his hip without effort. "Back off, Barker! She's only yor'n when Fuller and I get finished. Ya'd better bring 'im 'round if'n ya'all want some hole ta plug till then."

"No," Emilia cried, breaking for the first time. "Leave him alone."

Fuller came to where she was dangling from Tubby's hip. Sadistically, he slapped her face back and forth with his open palm. "Don't fret, bitch. Ya'll get it from all us, whether he does or not."

Almost too late, she began to claw and fight and scratch. Her sudden spirit delighted the man of the mountain as he ran with her into the *sala* and infuriated Fuller, as he tried to run alongside and grasp and rip her clothing to shreds.

Left with the dregs, Barker and Feldman pulled Carlos's face to bring him round, Feldman took out his hunting knife and slit the boy's trousers away from his body.

The male scream entered Teresa's happy dream on waves of contradiction. It was like the cry just before a bayonet penetrates an enemy, to be followed by fearful, hysterical pleadings for life.

She sat up in total silence, not fully awake yet. Her eyes refused to focus, her mind to lock onto a single thought for more than a split second. She crawled off the bed and crashed in a heap on the floor. The cramps in her legs and stomach were the worst she had experienced in weeks. She sat there, waiting for them to pass, until she became so terribly nauseated that she had to crawl over to the chamber pot, where she was violently ill.

Slowly she rose and moved toward the stairs, wanting to find Emilia. Wild, soul-tearing sobs came from deep in the well of the house, and for a moment, she thought she must still be asleep and dreaming. But the absence of Emilia from her bedroom was no dream; and it was no dream that the front door was standing wide open and allowing a cold draught to course up the stairs.

The shattered glass and mirror on the foyer tile were not a part of any dream. They were real and suggested that the night was going to be the beginning of endless horror.

The nightmare was centered in the *sala*, and the sight of it threw her into total panic. Emilia, her face stained by blood and contorted almost beyond recognition by terror, stood with her hands lashed together by the drapery chord and secured over her head to a wall scone. One breast was bared, and five fingernail gouges down its entire length were turning purple. Her skirt hung in shreds, and she was bleeding profusely at the groin.

She did not respond to Teresa's cries. As Teresa stumbled over the debris, her attention was caught by something that lay behind the sofa. Or somebody.

Teresa's heart froze. "Carlos?" she whimpered, almost doubting that the oddly twisted figure could be his. The youth stared back at her, with eyes that no longer saw, his jaw broken and hanging crazily to one side. He lay in twin pools of his own blood; one that had gushed from his rectum and the other from a gaping wound where his manhood had once been.

"What is this? What has been going on here?" a voice demanded from the foyer.

Tears of grief overcame Teresa. She was weak from the terrible vomiting and terrified of what she had just seen. Beyond that, she was so numb that she didn't even see the two figures standing in the foyer. Even when she did see that one of the two was a priest, she was too exhausted even to gasp or scream.

"My heavens," Father Montclava cried, "it's Teresa de Alarcon."

"We have to help Emilia," Teresa sobbed, starting to lose control. "We have to—"

"Hush child! Senora, please help me by taking her out of this horrible room. I'll find something sharp to cut down Senorita Hoffman."

Stupidly, Teresa was not listening to him or paying attention to the little old woman who came and took her gently by the arm. She was seeing only the big black figure who had come running breathless into the foyer.

"They all ran in different directions, Senora Escovarro. I didn't rightly get to see any of their faces."

"John?" Teresa asked dreamily. "Where have you been?"

Emilia's big black driver had not seen the horror in the *sala* as yet and gave her a warm grin. "No further than next door, little miss. Big John still keep an eye out over here."

It was hardly the time for the social chit-chat, but the little old woman, Senora Patricia Escovarro, saw this as a way to keep Teresa's mind off the *sala*. "Senorita Hoffman was kind enough to let me have John when all of my servants ran away during the siege. Now come along with me into the little parlor. John, will you help Father Montclava?"

It was like moving in a dream. Teresa followed her, clutching her arm as though fearful of being deserted. She was not even thinking.

Patricia Escovarro was thinking, and rapidly. She was aware of Teresa's condition, which surprised her; and she was thinking of how close-mouthed John had been in not informing her that Teresa was right next door, which amazed her. She had just got Teresa into a chair and wrapped a comforter about her when an ashen-faced John returned.

"Ma'am," he said, his voice choking. "Father say she bad off from shock. He say he don't like keepin' her in dis house case they—"

"He's right," she cut him short. She was still not aware of how much Teresa had seen and didn't want her put into shock as well. "Carry her next door and put her in the front bedroom. I'll have Father Montclava help me bring Dona Teresa along."

John hung his head and shook it slowly. "Wish we'd come an hour sooner. Big John might have heard something and stopped it before it got started."

"We can't change it now," she said smoothly, "only do what we can for them. After you have her home, John, you'd best take the carriage and inform Colonel Niel of . . . ah . . . what else is in the *sala*. Then stop by and inform Senora de Alarcon that Teresa is here and bring her back."

"Mother knows I'm here," Teresa said dully. "She was here for dinner today."

"Bring her," she repeated, noting the odd way Teresa had begun to hold her stomach.

Patricia Escovarro was hardly a weak or timid person. As an Irish lass of sixteen, she had come to Texas alone fifty years before. She had startled the Spanish community when she married Ramando Escovarro's younger brother Eduardo a month after arrival. Eduardo was immediately cut off by his family and the young couple lived a solitary, near-poverty existence for years. It was Patricia's backbone and Irish tongue that finally stirred Eduardo from the lethargy of being a worthless patrician and turned him into a successful merchant.

She was wealthy, respected and finally accepted by the Escovarro family when Eduardo died. Because she had vowed never to lose what she fought so hard to gain, she had turned on Miguel and made him a laughing stock when he introduced Emilia as a lady and wanted to make her one of the family.

The siege and Emilia's kindness toward her had began to change her mind. Oh, she was still miffed that Emilia had her ounce of revenge by buying the house right next door to her, but she began to wonder if she might not have done the very self-same thing herself if the situation had been reversed.

Childless, she had become almost a bitter woman without her husband. It was her hard-rock Irish-Catholic faith which helped her survive thirty years of Escovarro insults. She would put that faith to the test again when San Antonio learned that she had taken *Amarillo Rosa* into her home.

"Good," she said, after they had Emilia bathed, night-gowned and resting comfortably, "at least we know now that Teresa did not see the attack."

"How is she?" Father Montclava asked, as they closed the bedroom door and went down to Patricia's parlor.

"I'm more concerned over her than I am over that one."

Father Montclava laughed. It was an old and brittle sound. "That one," he mocked, "is quite a woman. Did you hear how precisely she was able to describe each of her assailants? Colonel Niel should have no trouble capturing them."

"Vultures! How does God let such things happen?"

"God, my dear woman, has no room in the heart of such men. Such as they have always been with us, the after-birth of war and destruction."

John came in quietly. "Excuse me, ma'am, but that colonel fellow is next door. He'd like to speak with Dona Emilia."

Father Montclava rose tiredly. He was seventy and longed for retirement. "I'll see to it, Dona Patricia. I don't think she should be made to tell the story again tonight."

"I quite agree. Thank you. Will you stay the night here, Father, or shall I have John take you home?"

He shrugged. "Let us see how long this will take me and then how our patient is doing."

She nodded her agreement and then a thought crossed her mind. "Oh, John, what happened to Senora de Alarcon? Did you forget?"

"Oh, no, ma'am. She was already bedded and would only talk to me through the door. I told her all, and she said she'd come when she was dressed and all."

Senora Escovarro frowned. "That's been some little time. Oh, it's just like her. She probably didn't realize what she was saying and is now afraid to come out into the night. Not that I don't blame her. John, would you mind going back for her? I really am that concerned about Dona Teresa."

Her concern, when she peeked in on Teresa a few minutes later, turned to active alarm. She was thrashing about on the bed, moaning and holding her belly as though she wanted to tear it away from her body.

"Child, what is it?" She rushed over and grasped Teresa by the shoulders, trying to still her.

"The—pain!" she gasped. "So . . . much!"

"When are you due?"

"Long time," she panted.

"Take your hands away," she commanded. "Let me look."

Teresa's dress and the bed were soaked. Her water had broken and she was in a stage of miscarriage. Patricia knew that she had no time to go for help, even if there was help to be found. Teresa would die if she didn't act immediately.

"Pull your knees up," she hissed, so that the tremor in her voice would not be detected. "Put your hands up over your head and grasp the bed rail."

"Ohhhh!" Teresa wailed. "That makes the pain worse."

"Do as I say," the old woman said sternly. "Everything I say! The pain has got to get a lot worse before it can get better."

Teresa obeyed, although the pain contorted her face and made her gasp.

"That's it," Dona Patricia said softly. Breathe deeply like that, but don't push. *Don't push!*" her voice suddenly shrilled.

"I can't help it," Teresa wailed.

"You must help it! Just breathe deep! Deep! Again! Now again!"

"Ohhhh, God!"

"Steady."

"I'm being torn apart."

"Quiet!"

"God is punishing me with this child."

"Put your knees higher, and stop talking such nonsense. If punishment is due, it should fall on Santa Anna for giving you the seed."

Teresa nearly fainted. "It isn't his," she whispered.

"Don't talk," the woman warned, feeling her stomach. It had to be done right then, or Teresa would hemorrhage. She put her frail hands atop Teresa's knees and shouted:

"Now! Push now! Grab the rail and push and scream!"

"I—I can't!"

"Don't you dare tell me can't! Push!"

"Aaaah! I'm tryinnnng!"

Big John burst into the room and stopped short. Meekly averting his eyes, he mumbled. "Senora de Alarcon ain't goin'na be able to come."

"Not now!" Dona Patricia scolded. "Go down to the kitchen and get me hot water and some more bed sheets. I'll need Father Montclava, too. She's starting to lose too much blood."

Teresa pierced the air with a wail that sent him fleeing in terror. Dona Patricia was left with a terror of her own. Teresa had collapsed and was no longer able to help. Lapsing into a semi-coma, she could only mumble and cry.

Dona Patricia had never given birth, and had never witnessed a child birth. She went on blind instinct of what she had vaguely heard, or thought she might have heard. Hands other than hers guided her and calmed her frantic heart.

By the time Father Montclava came panting into the room, she was bathed from head to foot in blood, perspiration and her own salty tears. The dead fetus had been removed and with it, the blood flow had begun to dwindle and stop. Teresa was deathly pale and her breathing abnormally shallow.

"Rest," she said gently, "I'll clean her up. John is just behind me with water and towels."

She shook her old gray head sadly. "I'll not rest until I know she is safe."

"It is in God's hands now, my daughter."

Dona Patricia knew differently. Blind anger had kept her at her task since Teresa collapsed and started to mumble. The more she heard, the blacker became her rage. Felix, the nephew she so dearly loved, had been the cause of this misery. Teresa had not had to say much to make the old woman realize that fact; and the fact that Felix had all but taken away Teresa's will to live. Because it was family, Dona Patricia felt as morally responsible for Teresa's life, as if she had been the father herself.

With the help of the two men, the bed clothes were changed, Teresa bathed and made comfortable. Only then did Dona Patricia take time to wash herself.

"I put that kettle of soup back on the fire, Senora," John said proudly. "Ya'all like a cup of it?"

"That would please us both, John," she said with a smile, drying her hands. "And keep it hot. Both of our patients are going to need it when they wake."

Father Montclava had no fear Emilia wouldn't recover; she had survived so much already that he had great faith in her ability to come through this appalling experience without permanent harm. He was less sure of Teresa, especially as she had more bad news to face when she came round. It was almost as though Dona Patricia could tell what was on his mind, for she suddenly asked, "Did John tell you why Senora de Alarcon refused to come?"

Father Montclava sat down wearily. He didn't want to talk about it, but now he had to. "Thank God Teresa can't hear," he said. "There has been another tragedy. The neighbors were in quite a state when John got back to the house. They had heard the senora scream and they broke in. She had hanged herself from the kitchen rafters."

Dona Patricia put her head in her hands. "Dear God, why?"

"A group of soldiers had been there earlier in the evening, threatening and demanding from her the whereabouts of her daughter. The neighbors heard and claim she gave the address of Senorita Hoffman. Who can say if they were the same soldiers? But John blames himself for having told Senora de Alarcon of the violence next door and she must have concluded it was her fault."

"We are all to blame, Father. Had we been strong years ago, this scum would not be on our soil today. Weak men thought we needed them to fight our battles for us. They are strong and will grow stronger. The day will come when they will be strong enough to call *us* the scum and push us completely out of Texas."

He smiled. "You're being very Spanish, senora."

"No, I'm being very sensible Irish. I haven't felt that way in years."

30

As FATHER MONTCLAVA had predicted, Emilia recovered rapidly and began to repair the damage to her home before the New Year was in. He was also right unfortunately about Teresa. She showed none of Emilia's vitality, but sank deeper into a coma, and her magnificent body began to waste away.

The four killers were soon identified and tracked down, and although they denied all knowledge of their acts, they were court-martialed and hanged before their fellow soldiers. That night, with the bodies still hanging from the nooses, fifty-six of the garrison soldiers left San Antonio and headed back north. The next morning Colonel Niel left on "twenty days leave." The explanation for the soldiers' absence were various, ranging from sickness in the family to a special mission to raise defense funds. Twenty-six year old Colonel Travis, left in charge, thought of them all as deserters, even Colonel Niel. He was sure the colonel wouldn't come back. The four men had been with him for a long time, and it had sickened Colonel Niel to order their hanging. No, he was gone for good like the rest of them.

Only Emilia came to mourn and bury Carlos. And no one came to mourn or help Father Montclava to bury Senora de Alarcon who, as a suicide, had to have her grave in unconsecrated ground.

Three hundred and fifty-six miles to the south, Santa Anna at last began to march north. The news brought more troops to San Antonio and the Alamo. Reluctantly, Colonel Travis was forced to share his command with the man who had brought in the fresh soldiers—Jim Bowie.

The sandy-haired giant from Georgia presented his men to Travis with an engaging smile. "Hundred fifty, by my count, Bill. Scouts say Santa Anna's got himself 4,600."

Lieutenant-Colonel William Barret Travis resented being addressed so informally by a backwoodsman. "Moving so big an army will make it all the more difficult for him, Mr. Bowie. Even with luck, he can't get here before the 15th of March. General Houston will have the entire Texas army here by then."

Bowie pulled his lanky frame up from his chair and stared out across the Alamo compound. "Ole Don Samuel's army is mostly on paper, boy. He sent me here to blow this place to smithereens. It's just not defensible."

"Then why haven't you done it?" Travis asked coldly.

"Don't rightly know," Bowie answered honestly. "Guess I'm just too drunk at night to do it, too hung over in the morning to hear such a bang, and by afternoon I'm too busy thinking 'bout getting drunk again."

So Bowie went against Houston's orders to blow up the Alamo and Travis stuck with his invasion date theory.

Like a ship in a storm that suddenly clears, Teresa's four-week coma ended abruptly one morning when she opened her eyes. Fully conscious, and looked around as if she were just waking up from a long night's sleep.

Dona Patricia was overjoyed and began forcing her weak system to accept rich chicken broth, quarts of egg custard and gallons of fresh milk that John brought back each day from the countryside.

Emilia was a daily visitor, as she had been during each day of Teresa's coma. There was a new understanding between the two women that went beyond words. They had been to the very gates of hell together and returned, a deep experience they had shared and that could never be taken away from them. It gave them a new intimacy and enjoyment of their friendship.

"I had a most unusual visitor yesterday," Emilia said cheerfully.

"Oh?"

"Miguel. Didn't he come over here?"

"Senora Escovarro didn't mention it if he did."

"The question is what to do with him now," Emilia said.

Teresa's head came up slowly, and her eyes, looking at Emilia, were clear.

"What do you want to do with him?" she said quietly.

"Nothing."

"Nothing!" Teresa was shocked.

"Yes; nothing. What can I do, Teresa?"

"Have you been together?"

"Yes."

"Then stop! It will be the same thing again, Emilia. It'll bring you nothing but shame and sorrow."

"I can't stop," Emilia said. "I tried. But it's no good—no good at all."

"But he still can't marry you," Teresa protested.

"His family is brutal and cruel and treacherous and . . ." She stopped, seeing Emilia's face.

"You don't have to list the family attributes," Emilia said. "I know them all—including the ones you taught me about Felix Escovarro. You failed to add that Dona Patricia is also of that family. It wouldn't matter, though. As a neighbor, I'm passable now, and that's about it." Her great dark eyes, starry with tears, stared unhappily at Teresa. "Now let me tell you what future plans I've made."

Teresa nodded grimly. "I'm waiting," she said.

"I'm going to sell out. I—I was even afraid of the touch of Miguel until we were together. He was very gentle, even tender. Our love wasn't just lust—although there was that in it, too, to be truthful. But it frightened me. It could make me start all over again, and I can't be hurt again like the Escovarros hurt me. I'll go to my grave haunted by the look in Carlos's eyes. They may not have done that to him, but the men who did had the same view of me. They thought I was evil and therefore they could do evil in front of me."

"You're the least evil person I've ever known," Teresa said.

"I wish I could believe that."

"Where is Miguel now?"

"He left this morning. He's to join Sam Houston's army in San Felipe."

"The same Sam Houston you told me about?"

"Yes," she said sourly. "Isn't it ironic? The man who loves me that I'm spurning is going to join the man I thought I loved who spurned me."

"I'm beginning to think I don't know you, Emilia."

"What?"

"You're being greedy, selfish and cowardly. Can you say that you don't love him?"

"No!" Emilia gasped. "That is for you—love!"

"Yes—for me."

Emilia stood up, shaking her head. "You want me to admit it to myself, don't you?"

"If you are truthful," Teresa said gently. "Miguel doesn't know how important your love can be—I do. He doesn't know the kind, gentle, wonderful person you are—I do. Don't deprive him, or yourself, of that love. It may be what you have been waiting for your entire life. Don't be so quick to throw it away."

"Are you echoing your own heart?"

"What heart I have you gave back to me. What will you really do?"

"Wait," Emilia said with a sigh. Then she laughed. "But my house will be nothing more than a home until he gets back from San Felipe. No business!"

It was a couple of weeks before Teresa had to face her own feelings. Felix Escovarro arrived to help with the defense of San Antonio, and his aunt gave him a tongue lashing. Big John, who told Teresa about it, recalled with a chuckle, "that little Irish runt stood right up to his Spanish arrogance and spat, 'See to your own defenses, nephew, for they are weak-livered. You'll have no quarter in this house.'"

Felix, unaware of the recent events, balked. "Aren't you confusing me with my brother, Auntie?"

She had eyed him angrily then. "Don't try to accuse me of being senile," she snapped. "I am no blind Adam who is easily fooled by a cunning Cain and Abel trick. Go to your Alamo and perish in it for all I'm concerned."

She had slammed the door so forcefully in Felix's face that the whole house rattled, and when Teresa asked what the noise was all about, Big John told her what had happened.

Big John was a born gossip, but not at all malicious. He delighted in sharing with Teresa all the news he

gathered in the market on the street and from soldiers
he talked with. He probably knew more about the
bloody advance of Santa Anna on San Antonio than
most of the soldiers in the Alamo.

He had also been the one, in casual conversation,
who had first broken the news to Teresa of the two
deaths—her mother's and Carlos's. The one she had not
been aware of came as no great shock—she and her
mother had grown too distant—but the one she was
vaguely aware of devastated her for several days. Carlos had been like a brother, and slowly the memory of
finding his castrated body came back. The look in his
dead eyes kept her awake at night.

Not knowing of her connection with Santa Anna,
Big John colored the stories of the general's advance
and did not notice the effect on her—her growing fear.

When the Alamo's 18-pounder cannon thundered
with a roar that shook the entire town, Teresa was
sure Santa Anna had arrived.

"Is this it?" Teresa gasped, as an ashen Dona Patricia came rushing into her room. "Is he here?"

"I've tried to keep it from you."

"John kept me informed."

"I'll skin him," Dona Patricia snarled.

"Don't blame him," Teresa said. "I'm the one who
let him rattle on. What's that?" she cried as more
sounds came from the far distance.

Dona Patricia listened carefully, and then her eyes
looked suddenly puzzled. "It's band music, coming this
way from the Main plaza."

They both rushed to the bedroom window to look
out.

A triumphant military procession was approaching.
It was 1813 all over again, except this was Texas and
the lead rider was not Napoleon.

His Excellency sat his white stallion stiffly, his face

a mask of arrogant disdain. The polished dragoons at his rear were not even dusty or ruffled. Those who had been drawn into the street by the music watched the procession silently.

Teresa's heart thumped fearfully. "What is he doing? Oh my God! He's coming directly here! How could he have learned I was in this house?"

Dona Patricia put her slim arm about Teresa's waist and held her close. "He'll take you away from here only over my dead body."

And it did appear as though that was Santa Anna's intention. His white stallion stopped directly in front of the house. An officer rode up, whispered in his ear, and Santa Anna nodded his agreement. The officer slipped from his horse and went to knock on Emilia's door.

That puzzled Teresa—what did he want with Emilia?—and she kept her eyes on Santa Anna directly below her. Santa Anna stiffened in his saddle and prepared to review his own parade.

Following the dragoons and the dusty ranks of the white-clad infantry came the band and the standard-bearers carrying the massed battle flags of Mexico.

But the flag that caught the eyes of those who now packed the street was no national emblem or battle flag. A lone rider brought up the rear of the procession, and a great red banner flapped and snapped in the afternoon breeze as he waved it back and forth. The blood-red symbol turned the silent crowd into a motionless, breathless mass.

The rider stopped in front of Santa Anna and saluted.

Without any kind of greeting, Santa Anna shouted at the crowd: "The city is mine! The flag will be placed for all to see. Your defenders are surrounded,

and among them is a traitor. Give me that traitor and
the flag comes down. Ride!"

The lone rider then galloped away with the flag
while the crowd watched in bewilderment. Who was
the traitor Santa Anna referred to? There were so
many. The weak show of force by the defending soldiers made them all traitors in the eyes of the San An-
tonians. Suddenly there was a great shout from the
Mexican soldiers in the Main Plaza. From the tower of
the San Fernando Church, the great red banner had
fluttered out, and eight hundred yards away, across
the San Antonio River, it was easily visible to the men
in the Alamo. The Americans and Texans were not
familiar with the traditional Mexican symbol of no
quarter—no surrender, no mercy. But the watching Felix Escovarro knew it well, and he also realized Santa
Anna was conveying a message to him with it.

As the crowd was still preoccupied with the flag, a
highly decorated carriage drawn by six fine horses was
hardly noticed as it rattled down the street and
stopped in front of Santa Anna. The carriage door
opened and a slight figure, a woman, stepped down.
Her gown of silk, spun gold and silver was so heavy
that three soldiers had to help her down and steady
her on her feet.

"Who is she?" Dona Patricia asked in open-mouthed
amazement.

"Another pretender to the Santa Anna marital bed,"
Teresa answered indifferently. She had thought she
might hate the sight of Luisa Morales, but instead she
pitied her. She guessed that Luisa was being hood-
winked and used the same as she had been.

"Such a funny little face!" Dona Patricia exclaimed.
"It's almost like a boy's."

"Don't let that fool you," Teresa said, smiling. "She
can claw and bite with the cunning of a cat." Then

she sighed. "Well, the next few minutes will be quite interesting. You know, I'm suddenly no longer afraid of the man."

"That's curious," Dona Patricia said, staring out of the window again. "Look at Emilia."

Emilia stood in her doorway, shaking her head and arguing with the dragoon officer. The she looked totally confused and nodded a weak agreement.

A moment later, Santa Anna approached with Luisa on his arm. Teresa was too far away to hear what was said, but the stance of the officer and the movement of his lips suggested introductions were being made.

Emilia put one foot behind the other and dipped into a low curtsy. Before she had even begun to rise, Santa Anna dropped Luisa's arm and took Emilia's hand to help her up.

His lips were on her hand before she was upright, and then he gave her a warm and gracious smile.

"For once," he told her, beaming, "General Cos has understated the facts. You are not just beautiful, senorita. You are the most divine creature in the land."

Emilia heard his flattery without any show of emotion, then she told him, "You are far too generous, senor."

"The dragoon officer cleared his throat, apparently to remind her of the orders he had given her. Emilia ignored him. She resented being told how she should address Santa Anna. She was also very angry about being *ordered* to invite Santa Anna to stay in her house, especially when she was informed that "Senora de Santa Anna would require a room as well as His Excellency."

Santa Anna was not offended by her coolness, because he didn't notice it. To him, she was the most divine creature he had laid eyes on in years, and his

reaction was all that mattered to him. He began to
look forward to his stay in San Antonio. Then his eyes
showed his surprise as a hulking figure filled the doorway behind Emilia.

"Senorita, do you keep slaves?" Santa Anna asked.

Emilia glanced back and laughed. "No, senor. John
is my driver and the only servant I have since the
siege."

It gave her great comfort to know that Big John had
silently come from next door and was there to protect
her.

Santa Anna gave the dragoon officer a mean look.
"Find out from her driver the servants required and
where they might be obtained." And then he added
graciously to Emilia, "We could not impose upon your
hospitality without being of assistance, Dona Emilia.
Oh, may I be so informal?"

"You might as well," Emilia replied in a sweetly
acid tone, "if this is to be your house. And as John is
to be busy securing servants, will some of your soldiers
see to Senorita Morales' luggage?"

Not "Senora de Santa Anna," but "Senorita Morales"! The dragoon officer was about to correct her,
when Santa Anna snapped his fingers at him, and he
went off to see about the luggage, glad to get away.
Santa Anna was seething, but not at Emilia. He assumed Martain Cos had been gossiping about Luisa.
He must speak to him about it! As though to show her
he wasn't annoyed with her, Santa Anna offered his
arm to Emilia to escort her indoors and away from the
gaping eyes on the street.

Luisa might have been left standing alone, wondering in dismay why Santa Anna hadn't corrected the
woman at once, but Emilia was not quite finished in
making her point.

Once in the doorway, she slid off Santa Anna's arm,

allowing him to go on into the foyer as she turned back to the fuming Luisa.

"Senorita, welcome," Emilia said smoothly, waving her in with a broad gesture, and she waited until Luisa came abreast of her. "Oh," she said, almost in a whisper, "we're to be informal, aren't we? Luisa, isn't it?"

Their eyes locked in a pitched battle of nerves. Luisa made sure Santa Anna was out of ear-shot before she hissed:

"You don't fool me, *puta!*"

Emilia smiled sweetly. "Naturally not. It was the first thing my mother taught me as well: how to tell the professional from the amateur."

31

FOR THE NEXT ten days, it was as though San Antonio was at peace—except for the various little wars taking place in the two houses on the *Calle de la Pantalones.*

Santa Anna set up his headquatrers in the Yturri house facing the Main Plaza, but spent most of his time at the home of *Amarillo Rosa.*

In the Alamo, the defenders were not allowed to forget that the Mexicans meant business. During each afternoon, the Mexican cannon would rain shells on the Alamo, but would stay out of the range of the defenders' rifle fire.

At night the darkened city was much quieter, almost gloomy. Gone were the tinkling guitars, the laughter and firelit yards. In the crumbling old mission, the only movement was the sentries keeping an eye on the sentries across the river. Here and there, people slipped in and out of the shadows of the darkened streets, quietly bent on some mysterious errand.

Many of these people were Santa Anna's personally selected henchmen and spies. They rained coins into greedy hands, but came up with little information. Their reports angered Santa Anna. Local informers always happy to accomodate either side, could offer him all the news he wished about happenings within the Alamo, but no one seemed to have any information about Teresa de Alarcon. As far as anyone knew, she had disappeared from the city during the siege. And as fate sometimes plays strange tricks, they never thought to knock on the door of Dona Patricia Escovarro once it was established that Felix Escovarro was within the walls of the Alamo.

But some people feel obligated to take fate into their own hands. Father Montclava asked for and was granted an audience with the President. Santa Anna kept him waiting at the Yturri house the entire day. Aides kept telling the old priest how busy the general was: personally supervising the distribution of shoes at nine o'clock; at eleven, riding out with a small cavalry scouting party; eating lunch with the infantry, and that afternoon watching his guns bombard the fort.

Father Montclava grew so weary of waiting that he dozed off and did not see the finely dressed young woman who brushed rudely past the guards, cast a scathing glance at the aides, and went into Santa Anna's office. Luisa Morales had been pushed aside, humiliated and forgotten for as long as she was going to endure it. In five days, she had not had as much as five minutes alone with Santa Anna. He had not come to her room at night, telling her almost comically that he did not want to embarrass their hostess. Luisa knew him well enough to know the signs: he was desperate to get into Emilia's bed, and Emilia had used every tactic in the book to keep him out. Luisa intended to keep them apart and thought she knew just how to do it.

"What's this?" Santa Anna asked when he at last returned and saw Father Montclava, who was still asleep.

"The San Fernando parish priest, Excellency. He's been waiting all day."

"Wake him and then get out. If I take him into my office, he'll want to talk all night."

It took Father Montclava a few minutes to become fully conscious. He didn't mention why he'd come immediately, but raised local parish problems and concern for the defenders who had taken their families into the besieged mission with them.

"Father," Santa Anna said grandly, "I am hardly a cruel and heartless man. I'm aware that local people slip over to the mission at night and chat with their friends in the garrison. Are they stopped or shot down? No!" He laughed. "There is even one man, Estaban Pacheco, who takes Captain Sequin his meals. It is a siege, and yet I am not letting them starve as they did with General Cos and his men." Then he made a sardonic gesture. "And tonight I have ordered my band to serenade the besieged. It will show them my terms for surrender are not as bad as they are making them out to be. Lay down their arms and give me the traitor."

Father Montclava nodded without saying anything. He could not afford to disagree openly. After a pause, he asked what he had come to put to Santa Anna, "In the meantime, would you object to me going to them and trying to bring out the women and children?"

"Everyone else is talking with them, why shouldn't you?" Santa Anna replied.

Santa Anna turned to go into his office.

"One other thing, *Senor Presidente*."

"Only if it is a short matter, *padre*," Santa Anna said impatiently. "I have much to do."

"This concerns Senorita Teresa de Alarcon."

Santa Anna walked slowly back, leaned against his aide's desk and folded his arms on his chest. "Yes?"

"Some matters I may not discuss, because they concern the confessional, you understand." Santa Anna nodded again, but his heart steadied. The priest's guarded words left little doubt in his mind that Felix

Escovarro had informed Teresa of the whole truth. With the Bishop of Tampico, he might have to haggle over the facts and open his purse to gain silence; but he didn't fear this old country priest.

"The facts may not be exactly as she might have presented them to you, Father Montclava."

"They are strange, to be sure."

"No more strange to you than to me, I can assure you. I'm sure you were acquainted with Dona Clara de Alarcon."

"To be sure," Father Montclava declared quickly. "A very great lady."

Santa Anna sighed, perhaps a little too melodramatically, because he made Luisa's blood begin to boil as she listened from the next office. "It saddened us so when she passed away in Saltillo. She had looked forward to my marriage with her granddaughter with great expectation. It was at her suggestion that we contacted her relative, the Bishop of Tampico, to set aside my first unfortunate marriage—which was never consummated."

"These facts are as I have heard them, Your Excellency."

Santa Anna scowled and began to pace up and down. "But are you aware of the treachery that followed? The blatant attempt by traitors to get me into a compromising position? I doubt you have! The papers that granted me freedom from that marriage were forged, Father. Forged by agents of Stephen Austin, even as he was coming to Mexico City to negotiate with me. Infamy, I say. But the worst, Father, was yet to come. The man I trusted as a priest, a chaplain, my personal confessor, and the man who conducted that marriage, was a liar and cheat. He was Austin's spy right in my own camp, and is now hiding like a snake behind those mission walls as surely as he hid behind monk's robes."

Santa Anna had worked himself into a temper, but he was having more of an effect on listening Luisa than on Father Montclava.

"But when you learned of this, Excellency, what did you do?"

"What did I do?" Santa Anna screamed. "What did I do? Father, what could I do? I stayed away from the woman and began working through the Bishop to put the matter in order so that I could rightfully marry her." Then he softened his tone and shrugged. "But, Father, you know how exceedingly slow the wheels of the Church do grind. Too slowly in this case, when you are dealing with desperate men. Fearing I was onto their devious plot, they kidnapped her and brought her back to Tejas to dangle in front of me like a carrot before a mule."

Santa Anna felt he had the priest at bay. In another moment, he was sure he would learn what his spies had failed to discover. He sighed deeply, pleased with the performance he was giving.

"The poor child, Father. If you have knowledge of her, then she must be safe and well. I pray so. Her mother's death must have been a great shock to her. I was amazed to hear of it, myself. However, I do not believe my agents who say she took her own life. I see it as just one more plot to embarrass me. That rabble in the Alamo probably killed her."

He had overdone it. Father Montclava had begun to distrust him. The priest's aim had been to use the power of the Church to get Santa Anna to give up any claims he thought he had on Teresa through the false marriage. Father Montclava saw he was dealing with a man who would twist all the facts to his own purpose.

"Again," Santa Anna continued. "I say, I hope she is well and safe. If she has confessed to you, Father, then you know her heart. Can you arrange a meeting between us so that I can present the same case to her as I have presented to you?"

Father Montclava hesitated, unwilling to lie. "That will be difficult."

"Difficult?" Santa Anna snapped. "Why?"

Father Montclava suddenly felt he might have gone too far. He knew that Santa Anna had it within his power to force information from him. He hedged. "There is the matter of the woman you travel with."

Santa Anna flared. "What in the hell has Luisa to do with this?"

"The Church is curious as to why your troops call her Senora de Santa Anna."

"The Church," Santa Anna snarled, "is sometimes a meddlesome old woman."

"Perhaps," Father Montclava said smoothly, "but perhaps it may be excused for being confused when it has to deal with three women who bear the title."

Santa Anna shouted, "I'll give the title to as many women as I deem deserve it. I'm the President! I don't need some puny little priest in moth-eaten robes to tell me what I can and cannot do. But if it will satisfy your stupid moral code, bring Teresa to me, and I'll send Luisa packing back to Saltillo so fast it will make the coffers of your decaying church look like the treasury in Rome."

It was threat and bribe rolled all into one. Father Montclava had never knowingly lied in his life. He prayed to God to forgive him for what he knew he must now say.

"I said before that would be difficult, Excellency," he told Santa Anna softly. "You, perhaps, did not understand."

Santa Anna unconsciously helped the old priest not to lie. "What are you saying? That she is dead?"

Montclava appeared to nod, but more to his own thought than the question. Yes, he prayed, dead to you forever.

Before Santa Anna could begin to ask how Teresa had died, his aide came bursting in and excitedly interrupted them.

"Excellency, the rebels have broken out and set fire to the La Villita district. The thatched roofs are going up like tinder."

Father Montclava was quickly left alone. Santa Anna rushed out to take charge. The old priest rose, a tall and stately man, and went out to the plaza and across to his church to say the evening vespers. Later he would accept the president's offer and go to the Alamo, but it was only Felix Escovarro that he really wanted to talk with.

Luisa sat for a long time behind the President's temporary desk. She believed that Teresa was dead, but it wasn't this that she worried about. She had come to realize that she was just as much a temporary piece of furniture to him as the chair she sat in. Even her weapon against him, her knowledge of how Dona Clara died, seemed to lose its value with Teresa dead. Teresa had been the only one to whom the information would have been important. There was no one else who could use it against Santa Anna with the necessary conviction and hatred. Teresa would have wanted her revenge, and that was the fear of Santa Anna's Luisa had played on.

The hours passed and still she didn't move. The fire was put out in *La Villita*, losing the Mexicans their cover and giving the Texans a new target area. Santa Anna, never realizing Luisa was in his office, returned to Emilia's house and prepared for dinner. The aides closed the headquarters and went about their own personal business. Father Montclava went to the Alamo garrison and had an unsatisfactory discussion with Felix Escovarro.

And Santa Anna's sardonic streak kept the bizarre events of that evening alive. His band set out to serenade the Alamo, with some foolhardy Mexican soldiers adding to the blare of trumpets and horns with the occasional blast of a gerenade.

Dinner was served at the house of *Amarillo Rosa* without Luisa. Before she left for Santa Anna's office, she had informed Big John she was retiring to her room with a headache and didn't want to be disturbed. Everyone assumed she was asleep in bed, and Santa Anna certainly wasn't worried about her.

Luisa had heard the band music and the grenades, and still she went on sitting there. She now saw Emilia as a greater threat than Teresa had ever been. She had to find a way to get her power back over him. Santa Anna didn't realize how desperately she loved him; she would do *anything* for him. Hadn't she striven to become a great lady to please him? The hours of study and struggle had not been solely for herself. She had done it to make him look greater and more powerful and more of an emperor. Would Teresa have been able to do that for him? Would Emilia be able to do that for him now?

Luisa suddenly realized how she could regain her power. One strong man, possessing the knowledge she had, could strike fear into Santa Anna's heart and preserve her position. She hurried from the headquarters building along the six blocks to the river. The festivities were over and the street was now dark, but she was unaware of it. She had to let Felix Escovarro know the truth about Dona Clara's death.

A sharp-eyed Texan spied something moving rapidly across the footbridge over the river. He raised the alarm and the sentries blasted forth with a round of rifle fire. There was no futher movement on the footbridge, and his comrades began to josh the sharp-eyed Texan for seeing ghosts in the night.

The ghost was plainly visible to both Mexicans and Texans with the coming of dawn. Luisa lay in the exact spot she had landed after falling from the bridge, with one arm raised and her clenched fist pointing in the direction of the mission. The majority of the superstitious Mexican soldiers, believing her to be Santa Anna's wife, saw it as a dire omen—no one was to be allowed to escape from those adobe walls alive.

Santa Anna mourned Luisa in the fashion he knew best. The Mexican battery, north of the Alamo, crashed into action disturbing the early morning peace. Every shot smashed the fort's north wall, showering the plaza with earth and stones. The cannon across the river then started to pound the west wall, and howitzers on the east and south side lobbed bombs into the innermost areas. The rebels began to suffer their first casualties.

Late that afternoon, two other casualties of the war found their way to the San Fernando church and secertly sought information from Father Montclava. The old priest listened to only part of their tale and then quickly hustled them off to the Escovarro house.

"Anna-Maria! Pedro!" Teresa exclaimed excitedly, coming into the *sala* after Dona Patricia's summons. "How good it is to see you!" She hugged and kissed them both, and then saw the strain in their faces. "What is it?"

"Father?" Pedro Perez said, almost pleading with Father Montclava to assume the burden of telling the news.

"It is best that *you* tell it all, my children, and from the very beginning."

Pedro Perez looked at his young wife and gulped. Anna-Maria patted his hand and turned her gaze full on Teresa. She knew she could never speak if she had to look at Senora Escovarro.

"At first," she said softly, "no one feared the reports of the coming army, although Senor Escovarro was angry even at the thought they would dare cross his land without permission. No one even thought of danger until we saw the smoke on the horizon. It kept growing bigger and bigger until the cloud was high enough to blot out the sun. Do you recall the guitarist from the band who played that night of rejoicing we had in Escovarro?" Teresa didn't, but nodded her head. "He came riding to the ranch as though the devil was on his tail. The army had ridden quietly into the town, he told Senor Escovarro, and then suddenly began to fire at anything that moved. Some escaped, but most were slaughtered, and then the whole town was set to the torch. Just because the town bore the name Escovarro, it was wiped from the face of the earth."

"The work of the devil," Father Montclava murmured.

Dona Patricia's face was ashen. "I think I know what else you must tell me, child. Save yourself the misery."

"No!" Teresa shouted, jumping from her chair. "I think it's time people began to learn what a monster that man is. I want to hear everything—to be spared nothing. One day he will have to pay for it all, and nothing must be forgotten. Nothing!"

"Perhaps you would like to be excused, Dona Patricia," the old priest said, surprised at Teresa's fierce tone.

Dona Patricia set her Irish jaw firmly. "My concern was for them, not myself. I will hear the worst, too."

Yet even she, with all her experience of life, was taken aback by the horror of what had happened. The Escovarro farmers and cowmen were no match for the soldiers who swarmed the land like a mob of hungry wild dogs. Pedro had hidden Anna-Maria in the woods and fought until he saw it was hopeless. The soldiers had already cornered the Escovarros and some house servants inside the *hacienda* when Santa Anna arrived and demanded the surrender of Felix and Teresa.

"There was no one to surrender," Anna-Maria went on dully, "but Santa Anna would not listen. The Escovarros were in a top window of the house, and Don Ramando called down: 'I am your prisoner, General. If you do not believe my word, search for yourself.' Santa Anna's face turned blood red—so red that we could even see the color change from where we were hiding. Then he screamed: 'In this war, there are to be no prisoners!' And then he had the *hacienda* set on fire. There was no way of helping them. He made the soldiers stay on guard until every roof had collapsed inward."

"We waited," Pedro said, "until the soldiers were long gone. Others, who had hidden, came then and helped us bury them. Rodriguez, the cow foreman, asked us to come to you so he could get orders from Don Miguel or Don Felix."

Dona Patricia blinked with iron self-control. She had no tears that she wished to shed in public. "That is going to be difficult, isn't it," she said, almost to herself, "with one of them off to Lord knows where, and the other in a place where the devil is breathing down his neck."

"Before," Father Montclava said slowly, "I was greatly concerned for the safety of Felix. Now I am terrified. But he is a stubborn young bull and will not try to escape from where he is."

"You've seen him?" said the old woman, suddenly coming to life. "How?"

"They have been letting me go in and out of the Alamo each evening. But after what happened last night and this morning, I doubt anyone will be able to get near it again."

"What are you talking about?" she demanded.

"The reason for all the cannon fire. That young lady of his was found shot under the footbridge this morning."

"Luisa?" Teresa and Anna-Maria gasped together. Anna-Maria began to weep softly and Pedro put his arm around her, trying to comfort her. Father Montclava stared at her, puzzled why Anna-Maria was so upset.

"You couldn't have known, *Padre*," Teresa said. "Luisa Morales was Anna-Maria's cousin."

Before he could reply, Dona Patricia took command. She gave Pedro directions to a bedroom where he and his wife could rest up before dinner. Then she discussed the situation quite calmly with the others.

"Now, more than ever, we have to get Felix out and safely away. I'll go myself, if need be."

Father Montclava strongly disagreed.

"That would be foolhardy! I've been afraid for days that Santa Anna would learn of your relationship. You must take no foolish risks. No, I will try to go again. Once he learns what has happened to his parents, he will see reason."

"No," Teresa said hotly, "you don't know him, *Padre*. That would make him stay and fight all the harder. He would never let himself look like a coward."

"She's right, at least on that point," Dona Patricia

said. "He may be a coward when it comes to facing up to his rightful obligations in certain matters, but he would do exactly as Teresa says."

"Indeed?" said the old priest, mildly astonished at Dona Patricia's vehemence. "Who then can approach him with the simple choice of life or death? Perhaps this young man—Pedro?"

Teresa shook her head. "Pedro might be recognized by one of his old soldier friends. It has to be someone who can shock him into leaving."

"Oh, no!" said Dona Patricia, suddenly realizing what Teresa was considering. "If you are spotted, Santa Anna would have you shot on the spot."

"Perhaps not—" murmured Father Montclava, suddenly embarrassed. "I—I led the man to believe that you were dead."

"Dead—?" said Teresa. "Father, stand up please."

He did so very slowly.

"Father, tell me, is there something that happens daily that no one questions?"

"Several things, but the most common is the taking of food."

"That will have to be it," Teresa said firmly. "A pregnant wife taking food to her husband."

"But," the old priest protested, "you are hardly with child."

"I will be," she said smiling, "with your help."

Father Montclava flushed scarlet.

32

WHAT HAD SEEMED like merely a fantastic idea when Teresa first mentioned it was soon planned in detail. Teresa was to replace Elia Garza, who took her husband a meal each night. Elia, nearly ready to give birth, agreed only when she learned an urgent message had to be smuggled into the mission. Elia then insisted Teresa dress in her clothes—it was too risky otherwise.

Emilia, hearing of the plan from Big John, was determined to keep Santa Anna in her house, even if it meant giving herself to him.

Teresa changed into Elia's clothes in Father Montclava's church. She padded her figure to look pregnant. Elia was to wait in the church until Teresa returned. As Father Montclava explained, "It won't arouse any suspicion because Elia always comes to the church to pray for her husband both before she takes his meal and after she returns."

"But where is the food basket?" Teresa asked impatiently.

"Elia always leaves it in the pews when she comes back for confession. You will find it and Senora Bartes in the third pew."

"Who is she?"

"She always goes with Elia to feed her husband as well, and so had to be told."

"Too many people know already," Teresa said nervously.

"I agree with you," the old priest replied, "But what can we do? We need help."

This made Teresa even more nervous. She dressed silently. She began to realize what a big risk she was taking.

Senora Bartes didn't try to talk as they left the church, and Teresa was grateful. The woman was obviously very frightened and clutched her basket of *tortillas* and beans to her breast as though each passing soldier were going to snatch it away from her.

Teresa's basket was heavy and the bulge of her stomach made it difficult to carry. She tried to hide her face with Elia's tattered shawl, and that was difficult, too, for she kept one hand pressed to the small of her back as though helping to support the extra weight of her pregnancy.

"Hey!" a male voice said sternly, when they were no more than three blocks from the church, and Teresa's heart froze. "It is you again, is it?"

A soldier stepped out of a dark doorway directly in front of the two women. The light was such that Teresa could not see him plainly, but could tell by his voice that he was quite young.

Suprisingly, his appearence seemed to calm Senora Bartes, and so Teresa relaxed, too.

"Senora," the boy said in mild reproach, "I warned you about carrying such a heavy load, and tonight I shall not let you refuse me. Here, I take it for you." With such an escort, they were not stopped or even challenged. Once over the footbridge, the young soldier was a blessing in disguise, weaving them in and out and around the embankments and trenches that Santa Anna had dug to within two-hundred yards of the mission gate.

It was only here, where the gate had been secured by a barricade of logs, that they were challenged. From the battlement high above, a stern voice rang down:

"Tie the baskets to the ropes and we'll haul 'em up."

"Hey, *cucaracha*," the young soldier called out. "What's your trouble? They want to feed their men."

"Yore damn cannon's the trouble, grease-ball. Colonel says no one inside tonight."

The young soldier laughed. "When did the likes of us listen to officers, *gringo*?"

"Waal," the Tennessean drawled down to them, "he ain't rightly my colonel, nohow. I'm one of Davey Crockett's boys. Open up fur-em," he called down.

By then they had been joined in the little cul-de-sac by several other women and Father Montclava. Teresa quickly took the basket from the soldier.

"Father," she whispered, "what are you doing here?"

"I saw the soldier approach you and so followed to make sure you were all right," said the old priest. "Don't worry, go on in. So far so good."

Teresa went through the gate tunnel and came out on the plaza, illuminated by several camp-fires. The area was much larger than she had expected as far as this—she hadn't thought about how Felix was to be found until now. She had assumed he would just be there when she went into the mission.

A squat little man came running to her and then stopped when he saw her face.

"Senor, it is all right," Teresa said breathlessly. "Here is the food from your wife with her blessing."

The man eyed her suspiciously and then grinned. "Is it the time?"

"No," Teresa whispered, drawing him close. "She is aiding me. I have a message that I must get to one of the officers."

"They will not listen," the man said sourly, "because they fight more amongst themselves than with the enemy. I sometimes wonder why we are here, Mexicans fighting Mexicans."

"It is a Mexican officer I seek."

"We have none here, Senora."

She was almost afraid to say his name. But she could not come this far and go away without seeing him. "Escovarro," she said, and it was hardly audible. "Felix Escovarro."

He acted as though he had not heard, but took her by the arm and guided her toward the northern postern and its row of wood-salt doors. He knocked but once on one of them, took the food basket and melted into the shadows. The door opened, and Felix regarded her with calm amusement. "This is a hell of a place for you to be," he said.

Teresa flushed. "You, too," she whispered. "Can we talk?"

There were several men in his room, and so he drew her outside, closed the door quietly on them and indicated a vacant bench outside along the wall.

He sat close to her and said with a rather touching shyness, "I'm really honored by this visit, Dona Teresa. You're the first touch of reality to come into my life since I arrived in this place."

"The world outside these walls is not too real these days, either."

"You still can't call me by name, can you?"

Teresa's head jerked up. "Oh, Felix—for the Lord's sake," she cried, "are you so insensitive to what is going on around you that is all you can think about?"

Felix's mouth tightened. "I've thought about little else these days," he said sulkily. "I'm responsible for what happened to you and was swayed by a sense of swollen pride. I—I just didn't want to believe what

Carlos told me about you, but I can see that he didn't lie."

It was not the time, she was wise enough to see, to tell him that the baby was gone—and Carlos, too. "And so you came here to lick your wounds."

Felix gave a grim nod. "And learn a horrible truth. My coming here was vanity, because I wanted to be on the winning side. Look at some of these other poor fools. They are men of this town, some even with relatives in Santa Anna's militia. We *are* Spanish and Mexican. This was once just a family struggle—which Mexican leader was best for Tejas; which Mexican constitution was best for Tejas; but it is no longer that. My *compadres* and I have no voice here. We are only additional bodies to make it rougher for Santa Anna and his attack. Only the *anglos* have a voice here, and I have come to fear that we won't do very well under a government dominated by them if they win."

"And yet you don't want Santa Anna to win either, do you?"

"I would rather serve the devil than that man again."

"Then I don't understand you," she said softly. "Why didn't you heed Father Montclava's advice and escape."

He eyed her coldly. "I should have known. He put you up to this, didn't he?"

"No," she answered just as coldly, "I put him up to everything."

He was skeptical. "Why? Just so you could force me to give the baby in your womb a name?"

She had felt both love and hate for him for so long that she did not immediately react to his stinging barb. She was afraid that, when she did, it would decide her attitude toward him forever. Slowly, and with care, she extracted the padding from her middle and dropped the bundle at his feet. He stared with an appalled expression at her suddenly flat stomach.

"The baby," she said, "is no more. Its threat to you is over."

A tremor shook his body. "What are you trying to do to me?" he cried.

"Felix," Teresa whispered, quickly taking his hand and pressing it to her heart. "This is what gave me the inspiration to come, to urge you to leave."

"You must really hate me to ask that of me."

Felix sounded so bitter that Teresa had to suppress an angry retort. It was within her to hurt; to prolong his torture as hers had been prolonged; to make him feel the agony of a miscarriage.

"I ask it," she said as simply as the words came into her mind, "out of love."

Without a word, he scooped up the bundle and went into the shadows of the nearest doorway. One by one, Teresa took up the garments thrown from the darkness and stuffed them under her skirt until her padding was complete again. Without looking back, she started her slow, pregnant amble back to the gate, but when Jose Garza came forward to give her back his wife's basket, she had a sudden inspiration.

"Ohhh!" she wailed, clutching Jose's arm tightly. "The time! The time!"

For a moment, Jose forgot who was clutching him and looked about desperately. "*Padre!*" he shouted. "*Padre*, quickly. She is near!"

Felix, now dressed in priest's garb, came near to panic, then he saw Teresa's sly wink. His anger at her was so fierce that he bellowed: "Not in here! My God, not in here! Open the gates!"

The mission had enough problems without being saddled with a birth, and the gates were instantly swung wide, and no questions were asked of either the priest or the other man who together were taking the expectant mother back to the other side of the river.

The church was lit only by the novena candles in the altar racks. It was so quiet that Teresa feared something bad had happened—she immediately thought of Santa Anna. But then, as the three of them were making their silent way down the side aisle to the door leading to the rectory and Father Montclava's room, they suddenly heard a sound they had never heard in a church before—the high, piercing wail of a newborn child.

"Santa Maria!" Jose Garza cried, running ahead of them.

Father Montclava, too, had been busy that night. On his simple cleric's cot, new life had been brought forth, and he was pleased with his successful midwifery effort.

"A girl," he chortled as the trio burst into the room. "A lovely, lovely little girl."

Elia, looking happy but exhausted, wept when she saw her husband. She was superstitious enough to feel that the help she had given Teresa that night had helped bring it all about—the birth and his safe return. When her husband's kisses went on and on, she nudged him to mind his manners. But no one was paying them that much attention. Father Montclava and Teresa were looking at the baby; and Felix was concentrating on getting out of his clercial clothes.

"Oh," Jose rejoiced, "I have five boys and finally I have a daughter. Senora, you have brought this about. Your name, please, for the christening of my first daughter."

Teresa was pleased, but was reluctant to give her name. Felix calmly spoke up for her and gave Jose her middle name.

"Rosa," he said proudly.

Jose beamed. "A rose. My daughter shall be a rose." His eyes glistened at Teresa. "And why not?" he cried. "Look at her namesake—a *blanca rosa.* A pure white rose, the two of them. That shall be her name forever more. And when she has children of her own, she will tell them how her papa was saved from this battle by her namesake."

Joy and sorrow are born companions. Felix, so joyful at that moment, had to catch up with a lot of bad news. It was almost too much for him at one time. The death of his parents and the way they had died was a shocking blow; that the girl he had seen lying on the river bottom was Luisa was unbelievable; and the full meaning of the loss of Teresa's—and his—baby only sank in when he witnessed the happiness of Elia and Jose over their new baby.

But it was the death of Carlos that affected him most. The day he had come to his aunt's house long ago and been lectured by her, he had been searching for the boy rather than for Teresa. Carlos had been like a younger brother. He sat for a long while, rubbing his fists into his eyes, in total disbelief.

Later that evening, still another Mexican disappeared—this time one of the women in the Alamo. Slipping through La Villita, then across the river, she made her way to the headquarters building. At first, the duty officer refused her request to be taken directly to Santa Anna. His Excellency, anticipating a quiet evening alone with the *Amarillo Rosa,* had left strict instructions he didn't want to be disturbed. But as the woman babbled on, the officer heard something that made him change his mind and hustle her quickly down the *calle* and present her to the President.

Santa Anna listened to half her story and then interrupted to send the officer back to the Yturri house to bring his secretary, Ramon Caro.

"And now, my dear woman," he said graciously, "you say that the defenses are crumbling, the men are weak, the ammunition is low, and the place can be easily be taken?"

"Yes, Excellency."

Santa Anna had assumed at first she had been sent by Colonel Travis to sound him out on the possibility of surrender. But her words against the *anglos* were so bitter that he could not help but trust her. Besides, she was quite beautiful, and his evening with Emilia had been fruitless so far.

"Why would such a lovely girl as yourself go there in the first place?" He wanted to be sure by checking her story.

The girl blushed, but did not lower her eyes from his.

"It was the wish of my father, once a soldier himself. In that place, he thought I would be safe from the soldiers, and he would be on the winning side."

"And he is still in the mission?"

"Yes, Excellency." Only then did she hang her head. "He has caught the same fever as the man Jim Bowie. They are both dying."

"And he wanted you out of there before he died?"

Again her eyes locked on his. "It has been on his mind for days, but I refused to leave him. This evening after supper, he said that if the patrician now felt he had guessed wrong and was leaving, then so must I."

Santa Anna said slowly, "Patrician? Who might that be?"

"I'm unaware of his name, Excellency. I saw him but once. He is tall and fair and most handsome."

Santa Anna felt cheated. He had let his officers talk

him out of storming the mission. Now he would have to sack the whole city to ferret out the traitor.

"One more question, senorita," he said gently. "Did your father say when this patrician left the mission?"

She frowned, trying to recall her father's feverish words after she had been summoned to his cot from the women's quarters. A pregnant woman had been sitting on a bench near the open window of the room her father shared with many other men. As she reached his cot under the window, she had seen a priest pass by and was tempted to call out and have him come comfort the sick man. But her father was already clutching at her hand and pulling her down to whisper softly in her ear so that no one would hear. His words had been so soft that she had not heard all he said.

"Excuse the delay, Excellency, but I was trying to recall his exact words. He said that the patrician was leaving and so must I."

Santa Anna was even more pleased. Leaving, not left! Not much time had been lost. With the arrival of his secretary, he ordered the officer to take the girl to her home and post a guard outside. It was not that he mistrusted her, but he wanted to keep her pure for his own purposes. He had not been with a woman since his arrival in San Antonio, and he sorely missed Luisa. Her death had puzzled him until the investigation revealed that she had been in his office during his interview with Father Montclava. Up to that moment, he had been mourning her, but then he felt relieved she had carried her knowledge to the grave and had not, as he surmised, been able to share it with the 'patrician' in the Alamo.

Ramon Caro brought with him his portable *escritoire,* dipped his quill in the little gold ink pot, and did his best to keep up as his commander poured out his instructions that had to be carried out before dawn.

Four columns would hit the Alamo at the same time.

Emilia came in at ten o'clock to say goodnight. She had known for hours that Felix was safe, but did not want to overplay her hand. The comings and goings of the siege had kept her out of Santa Anna's reach.

Santa Anna curtly dismissed Caro.

"You are most remarkable," he said, taking her hand and lightly kissing it. "Most women would be furious to be left alone during the shank of the evening."

"I am not most women," she said with a smile.

"Ah, that is true. You are a maddening creature. You allow me to kiss only your hand, when you know that I desire to kiss all of you."

She had almost run out of cat-and-mouse tricks with him. "The hour is late, and such a venture would need a full evening devoted to it."

As he kissed her hand again, she expected him to argue, but he just said, "You are always correct, my dear, always. Except—"

"You were not aware of the lateness," she interrupted, smiling.

"Too aware of it, Dona Emilia. When I most want to be nothing but a man, I must go and be the general."

"That is your lot," she said, moved to pity despite her dislike. "There are many men, but only one general."

"Have there been many men for you, senorita?"

It did not embarrass her to be truthful with him. "Enough to know that I want only a single one."

"And have you found him?"

Her answer might lead to other, more searching questions. She had to stop him now.

"Let us just say that he hasn't found me. Goodnight."

"Wait." His voice was imperious. "Will you go with me when I leave this miserable place? I will make you what you are already—a queen!"

"You're being impulsive because you miss Luisa," Emilia said calmly. "You will think differently when the siege is over, and you are on your way back to Mexico."

"I will not! Besides, the siege will be over tomorrow."

Emilia was shocked and tried to hide it. That explained why he had been so busy—he was planning an attack. The city would be in turmoil and Felix trapped again.

"Then you're not giving me much time to think over your proposal."

"Most women would have already said yes, but I will give you all the time in the world."

"You are a gentlemen," said Emilia, turning the full magic of her smile on him. "I will sleep on the suggestion. Now, before you leave, why don't you promise me to keep your cannon from making such a horrible din in the morning? You know how I love to sleep late."

She laughed gently, reducing the whole siege to an inconvenience to her rest. Santa Anna, as usual unsure of how to deal with her, decided she was just joking and laughed too. As he left the house, an oppressive silence hung over the city as if people were already preparing for more bloodshed. Santa Anna grunted a greeting to the sentry at the door and stepped off the porch. The light from Emilia's window was cast down upon the ground and, with it, a moving shadow. He paused, looking back up at the house, and frowned. Emilia was nervously pacing back and forth in her room. He had not considered his proposal that worrisome a matter, and then he cursed himself for being too open with the woman. He had all but told her of his battle plans, and he suspected that she would try to break and run. He stepped back onto the porch and whispered:

"Sentry, no one is to enter or leave this house until my return."

Midnight. The darkness is stirred by shadows. The soldiers are quietly being shaken awake and mustered into silent lines. In the Yturri house, Santa Anna is nervously gulping cups of coffee as he goes over the final details with his aid, Colonel Almonte.

Big John had gotten into the habit of supplying the night sentries with food and drink. It was not a case of friendliness, but to give him greater freedom in his movements. That night the guard was snappish with him.

"We'se either being protected or prisoned up." Big John reported to Emilia.

"The battle's tomorrow," she said anxiously, "so maybe some of both. What time was Felix going to leave town?"

"Tween now and dawn."

"He can't. The troops will be moving everywhere and he'll be shot."

"I'll stop him."

"How?"

He grinned. "You jes' leave that to Big John."

He went to the newly hired servants' rooms in the back of the *hacienda* and woke up the scrawny little scullery girl, who was always winking and making lewd suggestions in his presence. He lit a candle and began to disrobe. His blue-black muscles glistened in the flickering light, and he taunted her with a full showing of his giant physique.

"That what ya'all been hankerin' after?" he asked her with a giggle.

"*Si*," she said, patting the cot for him to join her.

"It'll cost yah."

"*Merda!* You pay, no me!"

He shrugged and picked up his pants.

"I've no money," she wailed.

He sat on the bed and took her hand so she could feel his full turgid maleness. Without invitation, she came at him with open mouth. He allowed her only a second and then roughly pulled her head away. "Payment first," he said gently and leaned down to whisper in the ear. Her eyes grew puzzled, then they crinkled with mischief, and she giggled. She was dressed and out of the room before he had put on his pants and shirt. Then he gave her fifteen minutes more.

"What is this?" he growled, coming out to the front porch with a steaming cup of coffee. "Who you got dere in de shadow with you, Garcia?"

The soldier tried to hide his open fly.

"Hump!" Big John scolded. "Such doin's in front of a respectable house." "I—I—," the soldier stammered.

"Seems ta me ya'all'd have sense 'nuff to go 'round the corner to the rose garden."

"My post," the young Mexican protested.

Big John winked. "I'm locking for the night. Who's comin' or goin'?"

Before the boy could protest further, the girl was dragging him around the corner of the house and into the darkness.

It took Big John no more than five minutes to alert the Escovarro household and return to lock up for the night. He knew he would not be bothered by the girl, she had found something to keep her interested and satisfied for the night. He chuckled to himself: *Seems dese Mexicans ain't much different than the white folk. All dey think 'bout is sex.*

Felix had been all dressed for travel when his aunt and Teresa brought him the news. The near-exhausted Dona Patricia then made her excuses and went to bed.

"Wait," Felix said as Teresa also started to leave the room. "I'd rather not be alone if you're not tired."

Teresa, still well below her full strength, slipped into a chair near the fireplace.

"If this news had come after I was gone," he said gloomily, "I might not be feeling so guilty. I really should go and warn them, shouldn't I?"

"Is that a question or a statement?" she asked indifferently.

"I don't know," he admitted. "A part of me rejoices that I won't be there. What chance have a hundred-odd men against thousands?"

"They didn't have to stay. You told your aunt that yourself."

"I know," he murmured with a sigh. He was silent for a moment and sighed again, "Poor Carlos."

The abrupt change in his thoughts startled her. She saw his eyes well again with tears.

"Felix," she said softly, "you gave me great comfort when my grandmother died in Saltillo, because we both loved her. I cannot grieve for your parents any more than you can for my mother. Luisa, I guess, is a mystery to both of us. However, we both loved Carlos."

"I don't want to talk about it," he snapped.

"What do you mean?" she snapped right back. "It's the only thing you think about. Surely it would help to discuss it. Something has been taken away from you and you sit and ask why. The word 'love' is coupled with Carlos's name and you fly into a tirade. Are you ashamed to admit that you loved him? Is it so wrong for a man to love another? Is that your fear? That in time that love might have gotten out of hand?"

He could only stare at her in dumb confusion. She knew what was troubling him—a question about his nature he had refused to face for years. Had the deep love he felt for the boy been sensual or paternal? He had sometimes felt that he wanted to express his love physically, and that was why he undressed in front of the boy, hoping for something to happen but leaving it to Carlos. He now felt guilty about the times he had posed in the nude in front of the boy. And his grief was more for himself than for Carlos.

He sat so still and forlorn that Teresa feared he was on his way to complete breakdown. She went to him and pressed his head against her breast.

"I've also known such a love. It came to me at the worst time of my life, and saved me. It fulfilled my faith in love, which was nil. I can never love that way again, just as you can never love Carlos. They are both gone, memories and no more. But how much less we would each be without those memories!"

She tilted his head and kissed him tenderly on the mouth. At first there was no response, and then he grasped her, hungrily seeking and devouring her mouth. She had entered his soul, seen the pain and extracted it. They were both free for the first time. There were still problems to solve, but they had each laid a ghost to rest.

One was not the master of the other, they were suddenly equal partners seeking to find the heart of the other. They shed their clothing and clung together as though they were the only man and woman on earth.

And this was the first time for both of them, they explored each other's body with the excitement and exhilaration of a great adventure. There was no need for embarrassment, there never is with love. Every fiber of their being merged, entwined, became inseparable.

And when Teresa whispered, "Oh, God, I love you!", the familiar words had a new meaning. They had been born in her toes and tingled up through every muscle and sinew until she muttered them with a passionate sense of revelation.

This man atop her she had never known before. All previous encounters with him were washed away. He was new, alive, daring, sensual, demanding, loving, giving, taking, exciting, enthralling and totally hers.

Deep in the house, the grandfather clock chimed once. They paid no attention to it, even if they did hear the time.

Deep in the shadows of the rose garden next door, the lonely soldier far from home didn't hear the dull tramp of marching feet in the *calle*. He knew the girl was no great beauty, but he felt sure he would be gone in a few days and would never have to see her again.

By two o'clock, both couples were growing very sleepy, and even Santa Anna far away was nervously demanding more coffee to keep himself alert. He could not be everywhere at once, but he began to mistrust everyone to carry out his orders. Finally, he could stand it no longer and stalked out into the night to take personal command.

He was not around, an hour later, to see General Cos's column shuffle into position 200 yards behind the Alamo, sink shivering into the cold, damp grass, and wait. They had been quartered well outside the

town. They had not understood why, but General Cos
had: he was being kept well away from the *Amarillo
Rosa*.

Shivering just as much, the other columns curled
their way into position and settled down just before
the appointed hour. Now all was quiet. The marching
feet had been replaced by the measured breathing of
men waiting for the signal to attack.

One hour stretched into another, and still the bu-
gler didn't receive the signal from Santa Anna. The
first streaks of dawn could already be seen in the eastern sky. Eighteen hundred men crouched in tense,
mounting, fearful excitement.

A strident shout from an overly nervous voice
knifed through the quiet calm. Others took up the cry,
and a wild burst of cheering rose behind the Alamo.

"Viva Santa Anna!"

The call to battle was given before the surprise was
totally ruined.

A cheerful sun streamed into the Escovarro *sala*.
Like every other household in San Antonio, they had
been awake since the first shots had been fired. As a
close knit group, they had remained calm during the
distant sounds of battle. It was the sudden, deathly silence that played on their nerves.

"They must have surrendered," Pedro Perez said to
no one in particular and pulled Anna-Maria a bit
closer to him.

Felix looked at the grandfather clock in disbelief.
"Six-thirty," he said dully. "Only an hour and a half. I
didn't think Travis would give up so quickly."

Dona Patricia cocked her head and turned toward
the window. "Soldiers are coming." With remarkable
agility, she was out of her chair and at the window
before anyone could speak. On the sofa, Teresa

grasped Felix's left hand so tightly that he flinched. His right hand reached between the cushions and gripped the pistol he had hidden there earlier.

"Mercy," Dona Patricia sighed, "you'd think it was just another day. It's only the changing of the guard next door, and Big John is right out there serving up mugs of steaming coffee."

Even at that distance, they could hear the excited chatter of the arriving soldiers sharing with their comrades the news of the morning. Dona Patricia could not hear their words, but the radiant glee on their faces sickened her. The two night guards, chagrined at having missed the battle, went rushing away to view its aftermath. Then Dona Patricia audibly gasped.

"Lord of mercy, the man is insane. John is coming directly over to the front of the door!"

Big John ignored her quiet scolding in the doorway and came into the *sala* like a man in a deep trance. He spoke only to Felix Escovarro in a tense, husky voice.

"All?" Felix asked, thinking of the people he'd known.

John nodded. "Except, they said, for a few women and children."

"Few? There were many there."

"They were laughing 'bout dat," he choked out. "They were slaughtered 'n when dem soldiers did'na have no one more ta shoot at, dey started shootin' at the dead bodies all ober again."

Felix didn't want to believe it. "All! There were a hundred and eighty odd men in that fort. Surely, these soldiers are mistaken."

"Ah doubts that. They say six hundred of de're own killed and wounded."

"Such futile waste," Dona Patricia sighed, sinking back into her chair.

Her voice brought John back to his senses. "I'd best get back," he said quickly. "Ah only told 'em I was checkin' to see if you was all right."

Senora Escovarro didn't think she would ever be all right again. For the first time, she began to realize how the victory would affect her and the people in that room. It wouldn't take Santa Anna long to determine that Felix Escovarro was not among the corpses. With his mind off the Alamo, he could concentrate his entire energy and intellect to searching the city. Her nephew was obviously thinking the same.

"Aunt Patricia, I've already put you in enough danger. I'd better get ready to leave as soon as possible."

Pedro Perez said quickly, "Alone? You'll never make it."

"If you're suggesting that you go along," Felix said, "you'd better remember that you have a wife to think of now."

Pedro pursed his lips. The top of his head barely came level with Felix's shoulder, and he couldn't have weighed more than one hundred and fifty pounds, but he was the kind of man who wouldn't hesitate to lead an assault on hell. When he liked people, his sharp black eyes had a warm twinkle. When his mind was made up, his eyes were apt to be like twin rapiers. They were glinting rapier-like now. They bored right through Felix. He wasted no time on formalities.

"I didn't say I would leave her behind. Where I go, she goes, and I can see no sense in staying in San Antonio."

"If Anna-Maria goes, so do I," Teresa said firmly.

Felix looked down at her. "Oh, no you don't!"

Teresa snapped back at him, "Felix, don't get stubborn with me. I am more of a danger to *Tia* Patricia than you are."

Felix drew his lips back tautly against his teeth.

"And so you think you'll put yourself in danger on the road to who knows where?"

"Look, Felix. This town will be shocked to its roots when they fully realize what happened here this morning. Somehow or other, the frightened people will try to get away. We can be just two more of the families trying to get out of the way of the war."

"Or walking right into its teeth. Santa Anna won't stop here, you know."

"Then why don't we just surrender to him right here?" The question was blurted out so suddenly that Felix had no time to think. He saw he was being forced into a corner and tried to bluster his way out.

"*Tia*, talk some sense into her. Into all of them!"

"That's what I thought I was listening to," Dona Patricia answered curtly. "If I were younger, I'd be demanding to go along as well. All this talk of sense is doing nothing more than wasting precious time. Come on, girls, let's go see what we can spare from the larder."

There was a momentary hesitation, then Felix's face broke into a smile. "Pedro, I sometimes wonder why men try to run the world; it's always the women who get the final say."

"Amen."

They left in pairs, five minutes apart, out the back door and down the alley. Love and respect kept Teresa and Dona Patricia from crying as they embraced and whispered their goodbyes. A stab of guilt pierced Teresa's heart as they shuffled past the back of Emilia's house. She knew there was no possible way of saying goodbye and felt as though she were deserting the woman who had practically given back her life.

Hasta la vista, Amarillo Rosa, she silently whispered. Until our next meeting.

It was mainly patrician Spanish and Anglo-Texans who trugged the seventy-six miles to the next outpost—Gonzales.

Santa Anna was inspecting the Alamo when the news of the exodus reached him, and he brushed the officer aside for the moment. He had just finished an interview with the survivors and was angry that they did not wish to accept his gracious offer of protection in Mexico City, but wanted to return to east Texas.

"All right," he barked. "Give the woman and her child a horse and the darky a horse. Let them go to hell for all I care." He noticed the officer who had brought him the news of the exodus, and a thought stirred his perverse mind. "They shall be the only ones to ride away. Let anyone leave who wants to leave, but let them do it on foot. Confiscate all horses, mules and wagons from those who try to leave."

"Why let them go at all, Excellency?"

"Why not? Unless they go all the way into the United States, they will still be within *my* Mexico. Their frightened voices will confuse the enemy and perhaps save us further battles."

"There should be no further battles, Excellency," the officer cried, "after they hear of this great and glorious victory."

"This?" Santa Anna shrugged. "It was but a small affair. A minor outpost manned by foolish amateurs who stood in the way of *my* Central Government. Well, they learned. We will now rid ourselves of the biggest amateur of them all, this man called Houston." He laughed sardonically. "We have learned, that two days ago, these ungrateful colonists met in convention and elected the man Commander-in-Chief of the Armies of the Republic. Pompous title, to be sure. Armies? After today, he will be lucky to talk his five closest friends into mustering arms."

That afternoon, a strong wind swept over the Texas plains and the temperature fell to thirty-two degrees. The refugees marched through the biting wind until they were exhausted and had to seek shelter. Their small fires were no match against the frosty night. By midnight the wind ceased, and their world was covered by a velvet blanket, punctuated by glistening stars.

"Now is the time to walk," Felix said, disentangling himself from his poncho and Teresa's body.

"I was just starting to get warm," she protested.

Pedro and Anna-Maria were already on their feet, flaying their arms about.

"It's an illusion," Felix told her gently. "With no wind, you think you are warm, but the temperature is dropping. We must go on to keep our blood moving."

Many others, lulled by the disappearance of the wind, never realized when the temperature dropped to zero and hovered there until sunrise. The dawn's warming rays came too late for them.

Soon after dawn, Teresa was near collapse from exhaustion. They passed a horse, which had been ridden to the same point of exhaustion, its legs frozen stiffly in the air, and she idiotically thought it was better off than she.

A moment later, two horses galloped past, snorting our great clouds of steam. Felix hailed them, but only caused the riders to spur their mounts on faster.

"Who were they?" Teresa panted, suddenly fascinated that her mouth created the same vapor as the horses' nostrils.

"I must have been mistaken. They looked like people from the fort. I was almost sure that the black boy was Colonel Travis's slave, Joe."

The other couple pulled alongside. "Might have been," Pedro said through chattering teeth. "I think they were afraid we were going to try to steal their horses."

"How did they get horses?" Anna-Maria wondered aloud. "Everyone kept complaining about the soldiers taking horses away."

It was a question that exhausted minds couldn't answer, so no one tried. Ten minutes later, they came upon another dead horse, and Teresa stopped and stared.

"Don't stop," Felix warned, taking her arm and trying to urge her on.

She was to the point of giddiness. "It's not one of theirs. It's not steaming."

"It probably belonged to someone who got out of San Antonio just before or just after the battle. Now, come on."

Pedro grasped his arm. "Captain, look! It's a farm house, with smoke coming out its chimney!"

The riderless dead horses were no mystery to Sam Houston. Still a novice in Spanish, although Anna Raguet had tutored him well, Houston had been compelled to call in Miguel Escovarro to act as his interpereter when two Mexicans had stumbled into Gonzales, and the women started shrieking over their tales of the Alamo.

"Horseshit!" Houston stormed. "Lock these men up as spies for spreading false rumors."

Miguel quietly waited until the men were taken away and he was alone with Houston. "They are simple men, senor. Their minds are not capable of concocting such a take of slaughter and massacre unless they had personally witnessed it."

"Goddamit!" Houston flared. "Don't you think I know that? But I got thirty women in this town whose husbands sent them out of the Alamo. Damn Bowie and Travis to hell for not blowing it up when I ordered it. 'Victory or death,' Travis claimed in his last message. The arrogant pup got the latter and won't be remembered for it."

"I assume Santa Anna will now march toward the Guadelupe and us."

"You're my Mexican expert," he answered sourly. "You tell me."

"It is my brother who is the expert on Santa Anna, Don Samuel, not I."

"And where in the hell is he?"

Miguel choked back his tears. "The last I heard, senor, he was at the Alamo."

That took Houston aback for only a second. "Another Spartan gone to his fate," he murmured as though mourning all the men at the Alamo in a single breath. "Rodgers," he bellowed, "get your arse in here, and, Escovarro, you stay! I'll need you here to tell me how to cut the balls off a bloody Mexican tiger!"

But as Miguel listened to the frantic orders given to the aide to write down, it seemed to him that Houston was cutting off his own, instead. Colonel Fannin, holed up in Fort Defiance at Goliad, was ordered to blow up the fort and retreat. It gave Santa Anna a clear shot at Gonzales.

"We cannot fight the enemy ten to one," Houston dictated, "and in their own country. Spring is nearly here, and the common Mexican soldier is nothing more than a displaced farmer. We will retreat to East Texas and force the enemy to divide his forces in pursuit. The first budding of the trees will reduce the butcher's forces by half. May will see the tyrant whittled down to size, and then we'll see if he can conduct himself by the rules of civilized warfare."

His dictation was hardly dry on the page when the three survivors of the Alamo rode into Gonzales.

Houston made an error in meeting them on the street in front of his headquarters. They drew a crowd of townspeople, soldiers—and women who feared they were about to learn of their widowhood.

Houston helped a woman, Mrs. A. M. Dickinson, from her horse with gentlemanly courtesy, and took her fifteen-months-old baby, Angelina, from her arms. Then he shot a scathing glance at the other rider and barked:

"Boy! Mind yourself, and get down here and take this child!"

The black body servant of Colonel Travis did as ordered.

"I have been asked," Mrs. Dickinson said hesitantly, as though she had been rehearsing her words for each of the seventy-six miles, "to express the compliments of His Excellency, General Antonio Lopez de Santa Anna, to Senor Houston."

The lack of respect in not giving Houston any military title made many gasp.

"He has let me and my daughter go free," she continued, "so that I might assure you that the story of the Alamo will be the story of all who continue to bear arms against his Mexican authority. He has no fight with his own people. He wishes only that we foreign rebels lay down our arms forthwith, or we will not be spared."

Houston laughed confidently, which kept down the first wave of panic. He intended what he said then to sound like a rallying cry, but that was his second error.

"And how many troops has he to make us Texans lay down forthwith?"

Mrs. Dickinson stood mute, but not the black boy, Joe.

"I know that, massa. I see'd 'em when they take Joe

ta get de horses. He got dis many thousand." And he
held up eight fingers for all to see.

Houston could not control the panic then. He had
to dash among the soldiery and townspeople, shouting in his booming voice, before the crowd calmed
down. But it was already too late, for twenty of the
soldiers had slipped away, and their wild tales soon
spread through the rest of Texas.

"What do you propose, sir?" Miguel asked.

"An early spring." Houston scowled. "Sink the artil-
lery in the Guadalupe River, burn what equipment
the men cannot carry on their backs, and let's get the
hell out of here!"

Were it not for certain tragic elements, the next six
weeks came near to the spirit of comic opera. Houston,
haunted by the thought of Santa Anna's pursuing
hoofbeats, pressed his retreat up to thirty exhausting
miles a day. At the Colorado River, terror-striken settlers were strung out for miles up and down the banks.
Houston showed his compassion by helping them
across and lost further favor in the eyes of his troops.
They were ready for a new leader by the time they
reached San Felipe de Austin, but the newly elected
government was no longer there to fire Houston—they
had taken flight to Harrisburg.

But to the utter dismay of all, the army continued a
northward retreat instead of going southeast to protect
the govenment. By the time they camped at Croce's on
the Brazos River, an additional five hundred soldiers
had deserted.

The only real pursuit of Sam Houston was by Felix's
small party. They arrived to find Gonzales a near
ghost town. All the *anglos* had fled, leaving a few bewildered Mexican families. There was no problem in
finding shelter and the quartet rested.

"No need to rush," Felix told them the next morning, coming back from buying provisions. "The Badillo family just rode into Gonzales on their own mounts. No one is being stopped, because Santa Anna has sent the majority of his army to capture Fort Defiance."

"Thank God," Teresa exclaimed, rubbing her swollen feet. "I don't think I could walk another mile this morning if he was right on the edge of town."

"It may not suit your style," Felix said with a grin, "but we'll ride from here."

"As long as we don't talk, I could care less."

After a day on a little mule, Teresa found she could walk faster than it would trot.

They had little trouble following Houston's retreat. Like the small boy who dropped kernels of corn to find his way back home, the army had left a well marked trail of discarded equipment. It seemed to delight Pedro to pick over every bit of it.

"Humph!" he snorted, reading a recruiting flyer he found in a soldier's knapsack. "How can one give away something they don't even own?"

"What's that?" Felix asked.

"Listen: Emigrants, who are desirous of assisting Texans at this important crisis of her affairs, may have free passage and equipment. Now is the time to ensure a fortune in Land: To all who remain in Texas during the War will be allowed 1,280 Acres. To all who remain Six Months, 640 Acres. To all who remain Three Months, 320 Acres. And as Colonists, 4,600 Acres for a family and 1,470 Acres for a Single Man."

"Very generous," Teresa said sarcastically.

"I don't understand," said Anna-Maria. "Where will they get so much land?"

Felix growled. "From the people who have owned it

for all these years. Because we speak Spanish, they will find a way to make it look as though we sided with Santa Anna and are the enemy. I heard them talk in the Alamo. We are no longer dealing with the gentlemanly likes of Mr. Austin. These are men who are used to pushing others aside to get what they want."

The emigrants were pushing all right—pushing to get out after the next bit of bad news.

San Felipe was in a panic when the quartet arrived. Fannin and his army had been captured at Goliad, marched into the woods, and the entire 400 shot. The news poured in that Santa Anna had split his army into four units and was marching to encircle Houston. And as the continuing bad news came in, the emigrants poured out.

For Santa Anna, the campaign became a holiday excursion. All of the finery that Luisa had prepared for the trip was being put to use, but for a different lady. Against her will, and under constant guard, Emilia had been forced to join his entourage. Santa Anna was in a playful mood and did not press his advantage. His vanity assured him that in time she would come to him of her own accord.

Felix found a small adobe hut on the edge of town. Miguel was just twenty miles to the north, and he wanted to get an early start the next morning to try to catch up with him.

Morning found Anna-Maria ill, a fact she had been hiding from them for days. She drew Teresa aside.

"I can't hide my illness much longer, Dona Teresa."

"Are you with child?"

Anna-Maria was radiant. "I am now most sure, but do not want it to burden our trip."

"Don't be foolish. You and the child are what is important."

She was sure that travelling had somehow hurt her own lost child. She would not let the same happen to Anna-Maria's.

Pedro was jubilant over the news and Felix oddly quiet.

"I see no reason for us women to go on," Teresa told Felix. "This little house is comfortable, and where you're heading for will be little more than an army camp. It shouldn't take the two of you more than a few days to find Miguel and come back."

"Two of us?" Pedro exploded.

Teresa glared down his protest. "If I can look after your wife, you can look out for Felix. And if you trade in the four mules for two horses, the trip will be all the faster."

"And what about Santa Anna?" Felix asked, for that was his main worry.

"Why would he come here? Even you said that, now he was across the Colorado River, he would head directly for Harrisburg to capture the government."

But before the two men could return from the Houston camp, Santa Anna had come to San Felipe and pitched his tents no more than a thousand yards from the little adobe hut. There had been no reason to capture the town, because there was nothing to capture. It was almost as though a travelling circus had arrived ready for everyone to go to see the show under the striped marquee.

Teresa and Anna-Maria stayed within the hut, fearing they might be seen and recognized. Santa Anna however, had not even been in the town. He went up and down the river bank to find a way to cross. He discovered that Houston had sunk or carried off every boat the Texans could find, and many of them had been left temptingly on the oppsite side of the wide

Brazos. But snipers kept Santa Anna's soldiers from swimming for them.

General Sesma's army arrived in San Felipe that afternoon and the cavalry were not even allowed to dismount. Santa Anna sent him directly downstream to Thompson's Ferry and let it be known that he would follow in the morning.

Houston had the news by sunset, and Felix Escovarro, who had arrived at Houston's camp, breathed a sigh of relief.

"Tell me, Don Felix," Houston said in his faltering Spanish, "who is this woman that travels with the Mexican?"

"I can't say for sure, General, but the description sounds like the woman whose house he stayed in at San Antonio."

"Emilia?" Miguel gasped. "But why would she be with him, Felix?"

"Probably not of her own choosing, brother. She was under guard in her own house."

Houston ran his tongue back and forth across his lips, as though savoring a delicious thought. "Miguel," he said in English, "are we talking about an old friend?"

Miguel flushed. "We are," he said darkly, and then quickly added: "But she has changed since that time."

Houston roared. "I don't give a damn if she declares herself a new virgin, she's been doing me a greater service than all the soldiers I've got."

"We don't know that she is sleeping with him," Miguel protested hotly.

That made Houston roar all the more. "Then she hasn't changed, our little *Amarillo Rosa.* She would only take the man she wanted and cast all others aside. Were you cast aside, Miguel?"

Miguel glared in hatred. "Sir, I could call you out for such a comment."

"Calm yourself," Felix warned, but he was just as angry himself. He had learned much about Emilia Hoffman from Teresa and so resented the insult.

Houston sobered. "You're not the only one who would like to call me out, son. And I may have just given you more excuse than the others. I was paying her a compliment, and it didn't come out sounding too gentlemanly."

Their eyes met, and each knew what the other was thinking. Had Houston not regarded her as a whore, she might have become the love of his life. Miguel loved her in spite of what she might seem to be.

"I was just wondering," Houston said slowly, "if she might be willing to do me a real service in payment for an old debt."

"Debt?" Miguel said coldly. "I am unaware of any she owes you."

"Well, she might, although I wouldn't blame her if she told me to go straight to hell. I'd have it coming to me from her."

"What service did you have in mind?" Felix asked.

Houston thought it over carefully and then shared it with the two brothers. Miguel was violently opposed to his scheme, but Felix readily agreed. The plan would take him immediately back to San Felipe and to Teresa.

Durning that afternoon, Teresa kept peeking from the hut at the distant camp. No soldiers had been in town since noon, and she could see that they were all busy striking the camp and preparing to leave. Feeling that it was now safe, she left Anna-Maria alone and went to the market square to buy them food. She had just started back, her basket full, when she rounded the corner of the main plaza and stopped short.

At first she saw only the two soldiers and Santa Anna's richly gilded carriage. Then her eyes opened wide in astonishment. Emilia was standing in the doorway of a dressmaker's shop arguing with an old crone. The soldiers were paying no attention to the spat or to anyone on the street.

Teresa kept her shawled head down and impulsively walked across the plaza and up to the two women.

"Is there a problem, senorita?" she asked softly.

Emilia nearly fainted when she recognized her friend. She looked quickly to check that the guards were still lounging and not walking, and the carriage driver was napping up on his perch.

"There seems to be," she said sweetly. "I wish the hem on this dress lowered and this woman doesn't want my business."

"I'm a decent woman," the old one wailed, trying to pull Teresa in as a referee, "as you can see, senora. No one will come to me if they see me serving the likes of her."

"There are others in town who can lower a hem without raising an eyebrow," Teresa said.

"Can you take me to one?"

"Have your carriage follow me."

"Follow," Emilia said with a laugh. "You shall ride!"

Teresa hung her head in the docile way of the peasants. "I've never ridden in anything so grand, senorita."

Trash, the old crone thought, as she slammed her shop door. That's all this war has brought. White trash down from the north and brown trash up from Mexico. Well, let that little peasant wench fix the *puta*'s dress. She'd rather starve first.

As soon as the carriage was moving fast, Teresa and Emilia collapsed into each other's arms and started to giggle. They saved all conversation until they were safely within the hut.

Anna-Maria objected to the way they talked then and thought Teresa had gone totally insane exposing them to such danger.

"I'm sure Felix will be back tonight," Teresa told Emilia confidently. "Then we will figure out a way to get you away from him."

"It really hasn't been that bad. He's like a little boy now, playing with tin soldiers. The only time he really wants me around is for dinner. We eat under the marquee so the soldiers can parade past and see the great lady their general is entertaining. Don't worry about me, I'm a big girl now."

Teresa frowned. "You don't want to escape him?"

Emilia laughed. "Of course, but not if it puts more people in danger. The only place I'd be safe from him is the other side of the Brazos, because he hasn't been able to figure out how to get there himself."

Teresa brightened. "Then it's simple. If Felix and Pedro were able to get across to Houston's camp, they'll know how to get back again."

Anna-Maria scowled. "We don't know if they made it! We don't know they are coming back tonight! What then?"

"Then nothing," Emilia said simply. The girl had irritated her since they had first seen each other at the Escovarro ranch. Instinct told each of them what the other was, or had been. Emilia resented the appearance of respectability Anna-Maria had assumed. "Nothing," she repeated. "I just ride off with his tin soldiers in the morning."

"But what if we can do it?" Teresa persisted excitedly.

Emilia thought a moment. "All right. We normally finish dinner by half past eight. Then he goes to tuck his little army into bed. Oh, that man takes care of every little detail himself. The guards change at nine and they are at least friendly—at least to the point where they think they should be getting from me what their commander isn't getting."

It delighted her that the remark seemed to shock Anna-Maria and not Teresa. She purposely shot the girl a knowing leer and shrugged.

"From there, it will have to be improvised. You keep the dress I need altered here, and I'll tell the guards that I'm expecting it to be delivered, and I'll try to ply them with drink. I swear, though, they each have hollow legs."

Only when she was at the door, and out of Anna-Maria's earshot, did she grow serious again.

"Don't do it, if it will put you in danger, Teresa. I'd rather follow the man all the way to Mexico than have that happen."

Teresa leaned forward and kissed Emilia on the cheek. "I'm sorry I didn't get to say goodbye to you in San Antonio."

"It was done for you, and graciously."

"Oh?"

Emilia's eyes twinkled. "Dona Patricia had John smuggle her over to the house while Santa Anna was gone. She didn't trust John to convey words that had to come from her heart. She's quite a crusty old piece of goods, but we had a good cry together."

"Oh, I love you!"

Tears welled in Emilia's eyes, and she gently took Teresa's chin in the palm of her hand. "I know how much you mean that," she whispered. "Not in the way we were before, but in the way that we are now. I shall always cherish you for that."

Teresa closed the door softly to find Anna-Maria behind her, and Anna-Maria whose face was ugly with rage and hatred.

"She is such a phony," she stormed. "How can you stand her?"

"She had been very good to me."

"To serve her own purpose, no doubt."

To serve both of our purposes, Teresa thought.

It was close to nine o'clock when Felix and Pedro returned to the hut. Almost before she was finished with her welcoming kiss, Teresa launched into the tale of the afternoon and how she thought Emilia could be rescued from Santa Anna.

Felix had not discussed with Pedro his conversation with Houston, and Pedro was as skeptical as his wife over such a foolhardy scheme.

"Captain Escovarro," he said in amazement, "you're not considering going into that camp, are you?"

Felix gave nothing away. "I'm thinking of it at the moment. That's all." But his thoughts were of Teresa. She never ceased to amaze him. On the twenty mile ride, he had been trying to think of a way to see Emilia alone for a few minutes. Teresa had not only shown him the way, but provided a plan already worked out with Emilia. It was all so simple, except for one minor drawback. Teresa wouldn't like what Houston wanted him to do.

Without saying anything more, to avoid any argument with Pedro and Anna-Maria, Felix picked up the dress from the back of a chair and quickly left the hut.

The guards had been expecting the delivery and joked among themselves that the *Amarillo Rosa* had selected the seamstress because she had a handsome husband to make her deliveries. Their bellies were full from the drinks Emilia had supplied, and they melted into the shadows as she accepted the dress and studied the hem.

"Teresa had told me her thoughts," Felix said softly, "but I also bring you a greeting from other friends."

"Oh?" Emilia continued to turn the dress in case anyone was watching too closely.

"Miguel, my brother, for one. He sends his best wishes." Felix was too embarrassed to repeat Miguel's actual words. He still could not understand what power this woman seemed to have over his brother and Teresa.

Emilia looked up at him through her lowered lashes and laughed softly. "Best wishes? A strange message from Miguellito."

He was annoyed that she dared to use such a familiar form of his brother's name. He felt almost as though he were in competition with the woman for the affection of Miguel and Teresa.

"The other message," he said coolly, "is from your old friend, Sam Houston."

Emilia's face turned a shade redder. She ran her tongue over her lips. "I would hardly say that we were friends."

"He seems to feel that you owe him a debt. Something about finding you on the trail."

Emilia glared, then she spat. She used every word she had ever learned in the brothel to convey her true feelings for Sam Houston.

Her bitterness took Felix by surprise. Houston had prepared him for an uncertain reception, but this was far beyond the belligerence Houston had thought was possible. His mind raced back over the looks that had passed between Houston and his brother.

Aloud, he said curtly, "All right, you loved him and

it didn't work out. That has nothing to do with what we now face."

The taunt stung like a whiplash. The muscles tightened in Emilia's high, lovely cheek bones.

"He must be desperate if he told you such a thing, senor."

"He didn't tell me. It suddenly dawned on me that I saw it in his face and in my brother's face. It wasn't hard to see which one loved you."

"And which one only wanted to use me?"

"I'm not talking of the past."

She snapped, "Neither am I, Don Felix. How does Don Samuel wish to use me *this time?*"

"He wants you to stay with Santa Anna and delay his arrival at Harrisburg."

They stood toe to toe, their eyes locked. Beads of sweat broke out on Felix's forehead, and suddenly, though there was no outward evidence of it, he sensed her surrender.

"How would that help?"

"Houston is marching tonight. It will take him a day or two longer to get to Harrisburg than Santa Anna and Sesma. He could defeat those two armies before they are joined by the others."

She laughed, and the nearby guards snickered at what they thought was a happy sound.

"He's putting a great deal of faith in a *puta's* delaying action."

"He seems to feel it will work."

"And what do you feel, senor?"

Felix wasn't sure and was openly honest. "I really don't know. Teresa seems to have all the faith in the world in you, and I'll be in her disfavor by not bringing you back. I think you know that I love her and want to marry her. Am I ruining that by asking this of you?"

It was her turn to be amazed.

"You can ask that after some of the despicable things you have done to her and she still comes back to love you? You are an idiot and a fool, and that is probably why she loves you. Tell her, if you wish, that it was my own choice to stay."

He was silent for a long time. Emilia obviously knew a lot about his affair with Teresa. It made him feel as though he were standing naked before her.

"No," he said at last, "tell me how I can get you out of the camp. I know a negro with a hidden canoe who can get you across the river."

She looked more closely at him, and it suddenly occured to her that, in another phase of her life, he would have been the type of man she would have selected to go to bed with. He was both a virile, handsome man and also a little boy, who needed a mother to soothe and care for him. He was all arrogance on the surface and completely gentle underneath. But, above all else, she sensed that he was not being honest with her.

"Senor," she said slowly, "before we decide if I cross the river here or there, tell me how this might benefit our people."

He shrugged. "I have no ready answer for that. We may rid ourselves of Santa Anna, only to learn that we have raised up some other dictator. My personal feelings are different, of course. Santa Anna is a shadow over Teresa's life, as well as a family matter that I am sure you are aware of." He shook his head like a hurt dog. "Let's face it, our people will not benefit from either."

"Strange," she mused, "the odd situation I find myself in. I wonder how many other women have been able to know personally the opposing generals in a war. And it is not really between them I must choose, but by what is really in my own heart. You could have made your request quite short, you know? Had you said do this for Miguel, I would be even now tearing the shoes from Santa Anna's horse so that it couldn't gallop."

Felix said quietly, "Then do what you heart tells you. Miguel and I will be there to get you safely away from him at Harrisburg."

Teresa had never been so furious in her life. She drew away from Felix as though he had just condemned Emilia to certain death. She didn't know words foul enough to shout at him, so she closed her ears to his explanations and sentenced him to silence. When he left near midnight to report the success of him mission to Houston, Pedro refused to go with him. This time Teresa did not raise her voice in protest, and Felix left alone. He prayed that he had done the right thing.

At dawn, Teresa in a miserable mood watched the striped marquee disappear. With it had gone the person who had helped her to heal herself and had given her a sense of belonging. They might never meet again. She sat as if mourning her friend and was snappish with Pedro and Anna-Maria. Their attitude didn't help. Anna-Maria was still hostile toward Emilia and had Pedro's mind twisted the same way. They were all soon reduced to stony silence.

Suddenly there was a sound from the riverfront. Pedro's face brightened. He exchanged quick looks with his wife. They both got up from the table and went outside. The sound came again, like a growl out of hell. Teresa came running outside this time.

Far across the field where the striped marquee had stood was a sight that left her gaping. The steamboat appeared to be crawling over the land, its tall stack vomiting clouds of smoke, its bright paddlewheels thrashing vigorously.

"Isn't that something?" Pedro enthused to his wife. "That's the *Yellowstone*. Nearly scared the hell out of me when I first saw it. Houston used it to get the troops across at Groce's Place and then sent it upstream with refugees."

"Wonder where it's going now?"

"Downriver. I talked with some of her crew."

Pedro was proud to show off his knowledge in front of her. "When she's got a full head of steam up, she'll go faster than a stagecoach. What a life! They'll go all the way down this river to the gulf and then back into the bay to dock at New Washington. Then out again and all the way to New Orleans. I'd love to travel on her someday."

"Not me," Anna-Maria said. "I'd be afraid she'd blow up."

"Don't be a mouse," he said. "She's safe and fast. Do you know that she will be at New Washington long before Houston and Santa Anna ever reach Harrisburg, and they are only five miles apart? I wonder why Houston didn't use her to get some of his troops there faster?"

"Because he's not as smart as you, my dear husband."

The steamboat disappeared behind a grove of trees and gave another blast warning that it was preparing to dock at San Felipe. Neither husband nor wife noticed that Teresa was gone when they went back inside.

It took a moment for Teresa to realize she was moving. She went to the railing and was scared. The land was slipping away from the boat. The paddlewheels groaned into life, thrashing the water. She shouted at a

husky black deck-hand that she wanted to get off, and
he had to use his full strength to keep her from jumping overboard and being swept into the paddlewheels.

Teresa bit her lip and ran a hand over her face.
This was the most foolhardy, impulsive act of her life.
She didn't even know what she could accomplish once
she reached New Washington.

The river had delayed Santa Anna more than Emilia had. Patrols roamed the bank and just after dawn
came across a black man preparing his canoe for a
morning of fishing. An hour later, just as the *Yellowstone* was arriving at San Felipe, they surprised the
Texans guarding the little, local Thompson's Ferry,
captured another canoe and, best of all, a large flatboat.

As the last of the Mexicans were crossing on the flatboat, the soldiers on the bank began to scream in terror and race for the woods. Those on the flatboat were
equally terrified as soon as they saw the *Yellowstone*
churning directly for them. The peasant soldiers had
never seen or heard of such a fire-breathing monster.
Only the fierce blast of the steamboat's whistle jarred
them back to life; they jumped from the flatboat and
tried to master the water with arms that had never
swum before.

Along the river banks, the soldiers began to fire
their muskets at the paddles to kill the beast. The captain was not about to go aground and crashed right
over the flatboat. It had never dawned on him that
the Mexicans would still be there, and he signalled
down to the engine room to give him full speed ahead.
He knew it was a dangerous move, because the river
narrowed at the crossing and the small butte would
give the Mexicans an opportunity to fire directly
down upon him.

Santa Anna was frantic with rage, issuing orders and

counter-orders one after the other. He wanted the steamboat captured and sent the only mounted soldiers he could see at a gallop to the butte.

They were not regular soldiers, but cowmen who rode the land looking for cattle to feed the army. In utter bewilderment, they took out all the weapons they possessed and tried to do as the commander had ordered—capture the smoking water dragon. Crying shrilly as they did to startle cattle, they rode back and forth on the butte edge, twirling their *riatas* in great arcs, and attempted to lasso the smokestack.

It became such sport that the other soldiers stopped firing and filled the air with *oles* and catcalls. Even the crew and passengers of the *Yellowstone* were drawn into the rodeo spirit and crowded the rail to crane their necks up toward the smokestack and watch the fun.

"Look out!" The warning from the bridge came too late. The backlash from a rope caught Teresa across her cheek, jerked her head and caused her to lose her balance. Stunned by the rope burn, she was not even aware of falling until the icy water made her gasp. Her mouth and nostrils filled as the water closed over her. Her ears did not hear the shouts from the boat or the butte.

The captain dared not stop. He knew it would be hopeless to try and save her. The *Yellowstone* rounded the bend and chugged out of sight.

The cowman whose lasso had knocked her over screamed curses after the boat, and then rode his horse at a full gallop off the butte, and man and animal hurtled down into the water.

Teresa was beginning to panic. She had luckily fallen well clear of the paddlewheel, but now it was as if a huge hand beneath the water was gripping her legs trying to pull her down to the bedrock. She tried kicking her legs against the water, but it was useless. Her skirt wound soddenly around her legs and imprisoned them. Her lungs screamed for air and her eyes stung from the icy water.

The wake of the *Yellowstone* saved her, bobbing her back to the surface like a cork. Her eyes cleared and she saw a horse's head break the surface like a snorting sea animal. A rough hand clawed at her waist, fell away, and then clawed again. This time the cowman had a firm grip on her and flung her ahead of him toward the horse. Her fingers clutched at the saddle pommel. They were swept downstream. She was jammed safely between the saddle and the man's clinging arms.

The horse, its eyes rolling wildly, struggled for the bank. Its hooves hit rock and then the sand bar. Inch by inch, it pulled them from the water.

The cowman put Teresa up across the saddle and held to the stirrup until his own footing was secure. When he felt a hard firm surface free of mud and the wet tangle of underbrush, he knew they were safe. He took a deep sobbing breath and looked at the woman he had rescued. Unconscious—and beautiful.

Teresa opened her eyes and stared at an unfamiliar ceiling. Her head ached. Every muscle in her body was stiff and sore. She tried to struggle upright and a hand restrained her gently. Somebody said, "Just rest." She turned her head. Emilia was standing by her cot.

A man's voice said, "How do you feel?"

Teresa stared, frowned, and then remembered what had happened.

She started up, thrusting Emilia's hand aside.

Santa Anna laughed. "She's quite lively for a ghost."

"A ghost?" Emilia asked in mock surprise. "Did you think she died in the river, senor?"

"No, a long time before that."

"You know this girl?"

"If you will pardon the phrase, I did in her other life."

The tension flowed out of Teresa's muscles. She sank back slowly until her head touched the pillow. She realized that Santa Anna thought she and Emilia were strangers to each other. A tremor of chill shook her.

Santa Anna felt a surge of helpless sympathy. He said quietly, "She'll be unable to ride for a few hours."

"Shall we camp here?" Emilia asked.

Santa Anna hesitated for only a second. "President Burnet and his chief officials are all in Harrisburg. It is only thirty miles away! Prompt action could capture them all and end the rebellion with one lightning stroke."

"Then what do you propose? Leave her behind?"

Santa Anna looked at Emilia as though she had lost her mind. "And lose the greatest ransom prize of the entire war? I knew something was amiss when none of the bodies in the Alamo was that of Felix Escovarro."

A tremor ran over Teresa's face, and she flung an arm across her forehead. She had put Felix and herself right back into his devilish grasp.

Santa Anna saw her reaction and was now assured that Escovarro also lived. "You will stay with her, Dona Emilia, here in the ferry cabin. When she is able to ride, the soldiers will bring you on to join me."

"Am I to be told who she is?"

"No more than that her name is Teresa." He was at the door before he turned and added: "And you should be warned that she is a compulsive liar, a traitor and will more than likely try to escape. I'll leave word that she is to be shot at the least attempt."

It was not until she heard the horsemen ride away that Teresa dared take her arm away from her forehead and open her eyes. She said emptily, "When I make a mess of things, I do a good job."

Emilia shook her head. "I'm still trying to get over the shock of seeing you come out of that river. But the look on Santa Anna's face was the real surprise. He actually did look like he had seen a ghost."

"I wish I *were* a ghost," Teresa said miserably.

Emilia sighed. "That wouldn't help. And now Santa Anna is out of my grasp, and I am no longer any help to Sam Houston or your Felix. I've never seen Santa Anna so excited. He'll drive his men to a lather to get to Harrisburg first."

"Felix led me to believe that you were doing it for Miguel."

"Because he told me to do what my heart dictated. I am no heroine, starry-eyed and daring. I did it, perhaps, for all of us."

"I only wanted to make sure that you were safe."

"How safe will we be if Santa Anna turns Harrisburg into another massacre?"

Teresa lurched dizzily to her feet, then steadied herself against the log and adobe wall.

"What do you think you're doing?" Emilia cried.

"I'll be all right in a minute."

"For what purpose?"

"To stop Santa Anna."

Emilia was startled. "And how do you propose to do that when you are supposed to be in bed?"

"If need be, by getting into his bed. That's the place where he has always wanted me."

The dragoons left with Teresa and Emilia were sick of war, longed for home, and saw this assignment as a ready excuse for missing the final battle. The women were reluctant to spur them on and arouse their suspicions.

Santa Anna was not so reluctant. All day and into

the evening, he pushed his troop of seven hundred infantry and fifty cavalry. At nine o'clock, they finally halted to make camp, so tired they didn't even notice that His Excellency had forgotten to pick a site with water. For Santa Anna, the troops were not moving fast enough. Finally, his excitement could not be controlled and he dashed ahead with some dragoons, swooping down on Harrisburg just before midnight.

"Almost no one, Excellency," a dragoon officer reported in amazement. "Nearly a ghost town. We are too late."

Santa Anna was so disappointed he could only glare.

Soldiers came down the street, pushing three *anglos* with their bayonets.

"They are printers, Excellency," said a sergeant. "We found them still cranking out issues of their newspaper. Here is a fresh copy."

Santa Anna studied it for only a second. "I have not my reading glasses with me," he said indignantly, thrusting the newspaper toward one of the dragoon officers he knew was capable of reading English.

The *Telegraph and Texas Register* supplied him with the information he sought, plus an editorial laugh.

"The Government was warned," the officer said, scanning the sheet and not reading the articles word for word, "and has fled to Galveston. This paper is indignant that Houston stayed up the Brazos so long and did not protect them. They say he is retreating again, heading for safety east of the Trinity."

"My maps!" Santa Anna demanded, and as they were in Spanish, he didn't need his reading glasses to study them. "Aha! He will have to cross the San Jacinto river at Lynch's Ferry. Get there first and we cut him off!"

"And what of these men, Excellency?"

"Throw their damn press into the bayou and them after it. Then burn this desolate little town to the ground. Let it be a signal to Houston that I am in front of him and Sesma is on his tail."

Houston's scouting party viewed the smoldering ruins near dawn and brought back one of the printers, who had survived and told what he knew.

"No," Houston said, "it don't make sense. Santa Anna wouldn't be leading such a small advance force himself. It's a trick. He'd never get there far ahead of his supply train, tent and its comforts."

Houston turned his march a little northeastward from Harrisburg.

"Where now, partner?" one Texan asked another.

"Just another little retreating march eastward," the other Texan answered bitterly.

Houston might have thought differently had his scouts kept an eye on Harrisburg for a few more hours. The slow-advancing Mexican supply train also came to view the smoldering ruins.

At first Emilia and Teresa feared the worst, but a closer inspection showed that it had not been the scene of a battle. As the dragoon colonel paused uncertainly, his own scouts brought news of Houston's movements.

Emilia, fearful of spurring him on before, now saw her chance of alarming him into action.

"Colonel, I fear the President has put himself in great danger. I know this territory, and he does not. Here he will hardly have any room for maneuvering. The enemy fight from behind trees and not out in the open. They will pull him into the bayous and swamps, and he will be trapped. If you have as much regard for him as I do, we should ride as fast as possible."

Teresa frowned, but said nothing. "I don't understand," she whispered when they were alone. "Why not let him get caught and slaughtered?"

"I haven't exactly been deaf these past weeks, Teresa. If Santa Anna and a handful of his troops are captured or die, it will end nothing. The other generals and their troops rely upon this supply column as well. With it and Santa Anna, they'll not fight on. If we get there in time, we still may be able to stall him."

Emilia was an astute student of military tactics and terrain. Santa Anna was finding that on his left ran the sluggish waters of Buffalo Bayou, ahead was the estuary of the San Jacinto River, and to his right, the marshes, swamps and inlets of Galveston Bay. And as his small force swept across Vince's Bayou, spanned by a narrow wooden bridge, there was now water behind him, too.

Scouts from the supply train reached him, and he decided to wait for its arrival before marching up the estuary toward Lynch's Ferry.

When the women arrived, he seemed completely uninterested in them or in any show of luxury. The striped marquee and tent were not raised that night, for he didn't consider the lull as anything more than a short rest stop. He even forbade his personal chuckwagon to be opened and ate the same food as the troops.

The camp was aroused just after dawn by shouts and pounding hooves.

"General! General! Stunning news! The enemy are less than eight miles ahead, and they are coming for us, not toward the ferry."

"I was right not to camp," Santa Anna cried, gloating. "Up! Up! Everyone up and march immediately!"

"Damn!" Emilia spat. "Must things always go that man's way?"

Sam Houston was thinking along the same lines. He had made his camp along the Buffalo Bayou, just where it joined the San Jacinto estuary, and let the men fall out to eat and rest.

No one had a chance to take their first mouthful before their scouts spread the word that the Mexicans were coming hard. The Texans moved into line and waited.

"Damnation!" a soldier growled after over an hour of waiting. "Where the shit are they? I'm so hungry my stomach's scrapin' my backbone."

"They's right thar, yah blind bastard," his buddy whispered. "See 'em swarming through the tall grass?"

Houston's two cannon roared, and the long line of Texan rifles cracked from the woods. The halfhearted Mexican charge quickly petered out. Firing died off.

"Bastards!" Santa Anna said through clenched teeth. "They won't come out and fight like professional soldiers, but skulk in the woods and fire from behind trees."

"That's exactly how the senorita said they would fight, Excellency."

Santa Anna looked at the dragoon colonel for a moment and blinked. "The women are with us already?"

"Since yesterday, Excellency."

"My mind has been busy," he said vaguely, then a devilish grin spread over his face. "It may be time to put them to a military use."

He ordered a pullback of a thousand yards and looked for a suitable campsite.

"Excellent," he chortled. "This hill will give me an advantageous position with water to my rear, heavy woods to my right as far as the banks of the San Jacinto, open plains to the left, and a clear front. Have my tent erected on the highest point, so that every one of those land grabbers can see who they are fighting. Tonight I'll give them a show. Have beeves brought up and slaughtered for the men to *barbeque* and make sure the fumes are wafted toward the woods."

The erection of the tent and marquee told the Texans what they had not believed before. They were not facing General Cos, but Santa Anna himself.

"Tarnation!" a bright young private bearing the highly military name Mirabeau Buonapart Kamar exclaimed, "Do y'all see and smell that? And look who's eating with the sonabitch! Ain't seen ladies dressed like that since New Orleans. Wowee!"

Felix had watched the erection of the tent through a spy-glass with the calm assurance that Emilia would give the Texans that night to prepare for battle. Then when he saw the second woman come from the tent, dressed in one of Luisa Morales' gowns, his heart froze.

"Don't ask me how," he stormed at Sam Houston and his brother, "but Teresa is in Santa Anna's camp. I've got to get her out of there tonight."

Houston put down his coffee cup, drew his shaggy brows together and stared at the young patrician. "And how do you know she didn't go to him of her own accord?"

Felix was startled. "What? How dare you say such a thing?"

Houston said gravely, "I can think it because I'm not a love sick fool. Santa Anna was not delayed on his march, was he? He had to be tipped off."

Felix colored. "And you're saying Teresa ran to tell him of the plan?"

Houston sucked his lips against his teeth thoughtfully. "She is there, isn't she? Sorry, Captain, but there will be no raids on that camp, which might ruin things—"

A sentry came into the tent and interrupted him. "Sorry, sir, but a Mexican just brought this note across the plain under a white flag."

Houston took it and opened it so no one else could see. He had expected it to be a demand for surrender.

He shook his head doggedly, so they would think the same.

"Tell the soldier," he said sternly, "that he may tell his general no."

"That is all?"

"No is quite sufficient. And now, gentlemen, I'd like to be alone for a couple of hours; and Captain Escovarro, any man leaving the camp tonight will be shot. If you don't believe me, go look at the two graves I had dug this evening for that exact purpose."

For a long time he thought about Santa Anna's note. Had he shared its real message, he would have been arguing with the Escovarro brothers for hours. In a way, it amused him that Santa Anna was so daring and cunning, demanding an exchange—his prisoner, Teresa de Alarcon, for the traitor Felix Escovarro. He dared not let the patrician fall into Santa Anna's hands or all the information he possessed would be tortured out of him before morning. Emilia—and now Teresa—were serving him well. Now he prayed that they could keep Santa Anna docile until one more event took place. He shared the knowledge of it with no one but the scout who brought the news—that General Cos and four hundred additional troops would arrive the next day. He wanted Cos in his trap as well. If I err, he thought, then the blame is all mine.

Houston's curt "No" pleased Santa Anna. He had not expected any other. He dined with the two women, as though they were all friends on the best of terms, and then amazed them by retiring early. He anticipated a raid on the camp to rescue Teresa and posted sentries accordingly. He wanted to draw them out of the woods and slowly cut down their number. He went to a nearby tent and slept like a baby.

Houston did not sleep. He took some sharp axes

from his personal stock and, at a secret meeting gave them to his chief scout, "Deaf" Smith.

"After Cos has crossed," he whispered, "chop down the bridge over Vince's Bayou."

"That'll cut you off, too, Sam. You'll both be surrounded by water."

Houston chuckled. "If it comes down to that, ole friend, I think I'll prove to be a better swimmer."

April 21, 1836, Ramon Caro wrote as Santa Anna dictated. "Cos has arrived, as ordered, and was welcomed with shouts, cheers and a special ruffle of drums to celebrate the occasion. We now greatly outnumber the enemy, who are believed to be less than 800. We await them to come out of their woods and fight like soldiers. My men have stacked their arms and are resting. If the enemy have not shown their color by noon, then we shall overwhelm them."

A rustle of silk interrupted him. "Oh, my dear Dona Emilia, forgive me. I was just dictating a few notes for my memoirs. How may I be of service to you?"

Emilia had come out of the tent for a breath of fresh air in time to hear the last sentence that was dictated. She smiled graciously.

"I was about to make a suggestion, senor, but you now have another guest. Martin, how nice to see you again," she said as General Cos approached the marquee.

"What is it?" Santa Anna snapped before his brother-in-law could acknowledge her friendly greeting.

The smile faded from Cos's pudgy face. "I wish to suggest that my cavalry be allowed to eat and water their horses."

Until he could have Emilia, Santa Anna didn't want Cos near her, for he suspected that his brother-in-law had already been favored in her bed. "Their job is to guard the camp," he shrilled.

"But all is quiet, Excellency," Cos said timidly, "and after all, the men must eat."

"All right," Santa Anna agreed acidly, "but you eat with them and keep them on the alert."

In the blink of an eyelid, his acid attitude toward Cos changed to warm friendliness as he turned to Emilia. "You were saying?"

Emilia glanced warily at Ramon Caro and the little weasel was quickly dismissed.

Emilia sat next to Santa Anna and surprised him by taking his hand.

"You are a truthful man," she said softly, "and wish others to be truthful with you. No! Don't speak or interrupt. I've had enough of that last night and this morning with Dona Teresa."

Santa Anna pursed his lips and spoke anyway. "Oh, a womanly confession time, eh?"

Emilia hadn't been quite sure what she was going to say when she sat down, but now it came to her.

"In a way," she said with a light laugh, "and I am woman enough to know when it is time for me to step aside."

"In favor of her?"

"If you were not so blind, you would see the error of your ways, senor. She does not look upon me as competition. Her competition died with Luisa Morales."

Santa Anna said quickly, "Then why didn't she come to me at once?"

"How can you be such a great general and so blind a man? How did you expect her to act upon learning that her marriage was a fraud? A woman of her station does not marry unless it is forever. But what did she do when she learned that you were free of that little trollop? She began to follow you, to seek the truth herself. And what does she find? *Merda!* You've replaced one *puta* with another *puta*."

Santa Anna was astounded by her candor. "Senorita, what are you suggesting?"

"That it is time to put an end to foolish games. I can easily step aside, for we were never really meant for each other or our juices would have flowed long before this. Take a siesta, senor, and I will prepare her for you. It will be an afternoon you shall long remember."

Santa Anna sat for along moment under the striped marquee before rising. He looked forward to big things once he had had his rest. He had waited for Teresa to come to him, and now at last it was happening. He could wait just as long for the Texans to come out of their woods, and then he would give them the same lesson he was going to give Teresa. He was never denied what he really sought in life.

Miguel Escovarro had watched the meeting through his spy-glass and was puzzled. "I don't know what her game is," he told Felix, "but he seems to have bought it. He didn't go back into the tent with her, but went and stretched out under a spacious oak tree."

"Did you see Teresa?"

"No. She must be in the tent with Emilia."

"What's he doing now?"

"Unless I'm mistaken, he's taking a siesta."

Houston accepted the report calmly and then walked among his troops. They had been ready since dawn, and fuming at Houston's inactivity. One soldier had almost attacked and killed him that morning, while he lay asleep in the sun with a coil of rope as a pillow.

He did not raise his voice, but his every word was heard or repeated down along the line. "Victory is certain! Trust in God and fear not! And remember the Alamo, remember the Alamo!"

A wild yell erupted from the ranks. Then a mad rush as 783 men surged forward—first in a column, then in a long, thin line that swept like a scythe through the tall prairie grass and into the Mexican camp.

It was all over in eighteen incredible minutes. General Cos's cavalry . . . the silver chamber pot . . . the striped marquee . . . the brightly decked dragoons . . . Caro's portable escritoire . . . the whole Mexican infantry of 1,150 men—gone forever.

The Texans had amazingly lost only nine men and counted 34 wounded—among them, Sam Houston, who had been shot in the foot.

At the first mighty cry, "remember the Alamo!," Teresa and Emilia had barricaded themselves in their tent behind cots and luggage boxes. The Escovarro brothers made straight for the tent and defended it until the last musket was fired, the last knife was flashed, the last rifle butt was used as a club.

As the slaughter, worse than anything seen at the Alamo, ended, the capture of those left alive began. The terrified Mexicans fell to their knees, imploring the Texans, "Me no Alamo."

The infuriated Texans proved that as butchers, they were the equal of Santa Anna's men, and bashed many of the simple *soldareras* to death without mercy.

Houston put a stop to it finally, not from compassion, but from fury. Santa Anna was not among the corpses or prisoners.

"Capture the rest alive," he roared, and sank down beneath the spacious oak where Santa Anna had taken his siesta.

By ones and twos, and then in small groups, the Mexicans were marched past the tree. They included

General Castrillion, who bowed to Houston and murmured: "I've never shown my back; I'm too old to do it now."

Houston stopped looking at the pitiful, nondescript little Mexicans shuffling by him. He felt he had been tricked after all and curtly sent word for the two Escovarro brothers to bring before him the two women they were guarding.

Just before their arrival, a band of soldiers came back with a solemn little Mexican in a blue cotton smock and red felt slippers. Just as they were ready to put him among the herd of other prisoners, the prisoners began to draw back and raise their hats.

"*El Presidente! El Presidente!*"

Before the soldiers could react, the man gave them a cold, hard stare and demanded to be taken to Houston.

Ironically, everyone arrived under the oak tree at nearly the same moment. Santa Anna's vanity demanded that he be first recognized, and he stepped forward and bowed gracefully.

"I am General Antonio Lopez de Santa Anna, President of Mexico, Commander-in-Chief of the Army of Operations. I place myself at the disposal of the brave General Houston."

This quick flow of Spanish was almost too great a strain on what Houston had learned as a pupil of Miss Anna Raguet. Raising himself on one elbow, he replied as words came to him:

"General Santa Anna!—Ah, indeed!—Take a seat, General. I am glad to see you, take a seat!"

Houston waved his arm toward a black box, and commanded Miguel Escovarro to come forward and interpret for him. Felix held his brother back and stepped forward. Santa Anna's face darkened with rage, then paled as he realized he was the vanquished and there was nothing he could do to Felix.

"Oh! " he said blandly. "My friend, the friend of my early life."

The young patrician bowed coldly. Santa Anna turned to General Houston.

"That man may consider himself born to no common destiny who has helped you to conquer the Napoleon of the West; but it is only you I ask to be generous to the vanquished."

"You should have remembered that at the Alamo," Houston replied.

Santa Anna was still cunning in defeat. He answered in such a bland Latin phrase that Felix had trouble giving it a proper meaning in English. Houston puzzled over the answer and asked a new question. Again Santa Anna used the same tactic and tried to end his statement with a deft and shrewd proposal for peace.

Houston grew wary and cautious. He was dealing with a strange tongue spoken by two men who once had been close comrades. He would accept only an armistice until President Burnet could arrive to negotiate peace terms. To the chagrin of the soldiers, he had the marquee reerected within a few yards of the tree where he lay, and restored the President's personal luggage to him.

A savage Texan came forward and nearly spat in Houston's face. "You retreated us right into a victory," he growled, "and now what yah up to? We want these stinkin' Mexicans off the land."

"Why, soldier," protested Houston, "these lands will be famed in history as the spots where glorious battles were fought."

"To the devil with your glorious history," the soldier replied. "Take off your stinking Mexicans." And he turned to glare at the Escovarro brothers.

Houston lowered his head. His eyes were a trife red from the fever that was starting to gnaw at his system from the wound. He said emptily, "My men are still a little hot under the collar."

"Perhaps," Felix said drily. "But will it be any different tomorrow or the next day? They've been led to believe that they are going to get many acres of land for fighting these battles. Where's all that land coming from, General?"

Houston squirmed. "Majority of them didn't want anything more than a good battle, not land."

"Then what about the few?"

Houston shook his head helplessly, but tried to avoid the issue. "My Lord, look at all of you, happy and well. I can't thank you all enough." He grimaced in pain. "What are your plans now?"

Bastard, Felix thought, I'll humiliate you into an honest answer. "Our plans are simple. I will take this woman as my wife, and my brother will take the other as his wife. We will return to the land of my family and start anew."

Houston sighed. "I was afraid you'd say that. You know the new republic's constitution makes all former land grants null and void. They all now belong to the republic."

"You don't know what you are saying. That land has been in our family for hundreds of years."

"I didn't make the law, I was only commissioned to fight the war to bring it about."

The memory of the recruiting poster flashed through Felix's mind. "We fought, too," he growled. "What about our rights? Don't we get acres for fighting the war and being colonists?"

"That's only for emigrants," Houston answered blandly.

Only a restraining hand on Felix's arm kept him

from choking Houston. Surprisingly, it was Emilia
who had come forward to hold him back and glared
down at Houston.

"Well, it's easy to see you haven't changed, Sam
Houston. Still an ex-governor licking his wounds from
a wife who left him, and too much a damn coward to
admit it. When you grow up, you may become quite a
man, but you're still a puppet on other people's string.
Come on, Felix, we've helped this man more than he
deserves."

Houston sat with his head bowed. An eternity later,
he said hoarsely, "But will any one even remember
that you helped me?"

He looked up, but they were gone.

No one challenged their departure, because the Escovarro brothers were comrades who had fought with
the army. No one even questioned whose horses they
had taken.

Emilia let her mount lag behind until Miguel had
to come back and ride at her side.

"That was a most unusual proposal," she said slyly,
"unless your brother was just blowing smoke in Houston's face."

"Would it have any more weight coming from Felix
than from me?" Miguel asked gloomily. "You've always found an excuse to turn me down before."

Emilia laughed gaily. "Why don't I just ride ahead
and see what answer he gives me when I say that 'Yes,
I will marry your brother.'"

"Wait!" Miguel shouted. "Give me the answer first.
I think they are busy enough ahead."

They were not busy, they were riding along in silence, both deep in thought. Felix could not believe
that the land could be taken away with a stroke of a
pen. That was feudalism, and this was the nineteenth

century. What did he have left to offer Teresa? Nothing! He would have been far better off if he had supported Santa Anna. Even in defeat, he could gain a land grant in Mexico or California. Now he had no property and was penniless.

"Felix," Teresa said at last, "we've got to talk. I was a blind fool for leaving San Felipe and I'm sorry."

"What?" he said, coming out of his reverie. "Oh! That hardly matters now."

"Well, it matters to me," she said hotly. "I just acted on an impulse."

"Must we always fight?" he asked with a sigh.

"I only meant that it no longer matters, because Houston has won everything."

"Oh, has he now?" she cried, sounding so much like his *Tia* Patricia that he blanched. "It's going to take months for these political idiots to even find a proper way to let Santa Anna return gracefully to Mexico. Months longer for them to decide if they want a republic or statehood under the United States. In the meantime, there are a lot of men waiting to learn what you and your brother are going to do about running the *ranchero*. To hell with these damn *anglos!* Let them come and force us off the Escovarro land. It's time you stopped being such a goody, goody priest and started being the man that . . ."

She never finished. He leaned from his saddle, his mouth on hers, crushing her to him. The breath went out of her, and she strained against him, her eyes brimming. When he released her, she clung to him fiercely, feeling his hard muscles and the throb of his manhood, while he buried his face in her hair and kissed the hollow in her neck. He wanted her then more than ever, his manhood straining under the hard cloth of his pants.

He said huskily, "I talked some with the doctor that travelled with Houston. He says there's no reason why you couldn't have another baby."

Teresa grinned mischievously at him. "Who needed a doctor to make such a profound statement? It takes only a husband, so I'm told. And with one of those, a woman might have several children. I gather," she said softly, "from the way that you've been chasing me about the land that you'd not be averse to such an effort."

The smile started at his eyes.

"I'm ready right now."

IN 1918 AMERICA FACED AN ENERGY CRISIS

UNCLE SAM NEEDS THAT EXTRA SHOVELFUL

Help Uncle Sam to Win the War
by following these Directions.

UNITED STATES FUEL ADMINISTRATION

An icy winter gripped the nation. Frozen harbors blocked the movement of coal. Businesses and factories closed. Homes went without heat. Prices skyrocketed. It was America's first energy crisis now long since forgotten, like the winter of '76-'77 and the oil embargo of '73-'74. Unfortunately, forgetting a crisis doesn't solve the problems that cause it. Today, the country is relying too heavily on foreign oil. That reliance is costing us over $40 billion dollars a year Unless we conserve, the world will soon run out of oil, if we don't run out of money first. So the crises of the past may be forgotten, but the energy problems of today and tomorrow remain to be solved. The best solution is the simplest conservation. It's something every American can do.

ENERGY CONSERVATION - IT'S YOUR CHANCE TO SAVE, AMERICA

Department of Energy, Washington, D.C